GEORGE GISSING, born in Wakefield in 1857, was the eldest of five children. His father, a pharmacist, died when he was thirteen. In 1872 Gissing won a scholarship to Owens College, Manchester. He was a brilliant student, but his prospects were blasted when in 1876 he was caught stealing from the College cloakroom. He had hoped to use the money to reclaim a young prostitute, Nell Harrison, with whom he had fallen in love. After serving one month's imprisonment, he left for America, where he stayed for a year and began to publish short stories. Back in England in 1877, he lived with Nell, whom he married in 1879. The marriage was unhappy, the couple separated and Nell died in 1888. During these years Gissing survived on the proceeds of private tuition and some journalism. His first novel, *Workers in the Dawn* (1880), initiated a series of books that dealt powerfully with the poverty and degradation of the London poor: *The Unclassed* (1884), *Demos* (1886), *Thyrza* (1887) and *The Nether World* (1889). After this series he travelled on the Continent and his fiction expanded in other directions, more often adopting a middle-class setting, though never abandoning the subject of poverty. *The Emancipated* (1890) was followed by the novels that made his reputation: *New Grub Street* (1891), *Born in Exile* (1892), *The Odd Women* (1893), *In the Year of Jubilee* (1894) and *The Whirlpool* (1897). In the 1890s he also published many short stories. In 1891 he married Edith Underwood, who bore him two sons, Walter and Alfred. This second marriage proved as disastrous as the first and Gissing left Edith in 1897. Though he now had a considerable reputation as a novelist, he never achieved financial security. He did, however, enjoy the friendship of such writers as H.G. Wells, and from 1899 till his death in 1903 he lived (mostly in France) with Gabrielle Fleury, an admirer who had offered to translate his work. Among his notable later books were his critical study of Dickens (1898), his travel book *By the Ionian Sea* (1901) and the partly autobiographical *Private Papers of Henry Ryecroft* (1903). Gissing died – of lung disease – at the age of forty-six. He had written twenty-two novels.

DAVID GRYLLS is University Lecturer in Literature (Continuing Education) at Oxford University, and a Fellow of Rewley House, Oxford. He is the author of *Guardians and Angels: Parents and Children in Nineteenth-Century Literature* (1978) and *The Paradox of Gissing* (1986).

GEORGE GISSING

Born in Exile

Edited by
David Grylls
Department for Continuing Education
University of Oxford

J.M. Dent
London
Charles E. Tuttle
Rutland, Vermont
EVERYMAN LIBRARY

Introduction, chronology and notes © J.M. Dent 1993

First published in Everyman in 1993

Printed in Great Britain by The Guernsey Press Co. Ltd,
Guernsey, C.I.
for
J. M. Dent Ltd
Orion Publishing Group
Orion House
5 Upper St Martin's Lane
London WC2H 9EA
and
Charles E. Tuttle Co., Inc.
28 South Main Street
Rutland
Vermont 05701
USA

British Library Cataloguing-in-Publication Data for
this Title is available upon request.

ISBN 0 460 87241 9

CONTENTS

INTRODUCTION

Born in Exile, Gissing declared, 'was a book I *had* to write'.[1] The eleventh novel by an author who had specialised in acrid studies of the London poor, then switched to dissections of middle-class mores, it was published in 1892. The previous year had seen the publication of Gissing's one acknowledged masterpiece, *New Grub Street*. Like that novel, *Born in Exile* combines acute psychology with mordant social analysis. It is excellent on shame, jealousy, temptation, the hopes and resentments of the socially thwarted, the nerve-frets of anxious intellectuals. It also deals with large late-Victorian issues: the conflict between science and religion; the insidious persistence of the class system; the question of the relations between the sexes; the loosening grip of conventional morality. Yet it is a novel in which almost nothing happens. In outline its plot could scarcely be simpler. Godwin Peak, a young man of humble origins, weary of exclusion from refined society, finds himself playing the hypocrite with a respectable family called the Warricombes; he pretends to be studying for Holy Orders when in fact he has published an anonymous article attacking fashionable Christian attempts to reconcile religion with evolution. Out of this situation emerges a narrative of intellectual fascination and psychological suspense. Though its action is minimal, the novel deals intensely with nuances of motive and moral judgment, with painful, perilous ambiguities of belief, identity and desire. It is in fact a highly dramatic novel – but the drama is largely internal.

The book's compulsive composition was partly an act of exorcism. 'I have the feeling', Gissing wrote in 1891, 'of being deserted by all who ought to be my companions: but then these miseries are useful in giving a peculiar originality to my work.'[2] Though part of Gissing's problem was temperamental, the material source of his unhappiness was the discrepancy between his cultural aspirations and his economic predicament. A sensitive, highly educated man, he lived for many years in squalor and poverty. Alienated by those who surrounded him, he also felt exiled from an ideal community in which wealth and comfort would be happily combined with free enquiry and a love of beauty.

At fifteen Gissing had won a scholarship to Owens College, Manchester. As a gifted and phenomenally hard-working student, he seemed set for a successful academic career. But his hopeful prospects were abruptly blasted when, having fallen in love with a young prostitute, he stole goods and money from the College cloakroom in order to reclaim her for respectable work. Caught in the act, convicted of theft, he was stripped of his honours, expelled from College, and sentenced to a month's imprisonment with hard labour.

Almost certainly the sense of exclusion in Gissing's fiction, and the constant, uneasy fear of exposure, were related to his Manchester trauma. His novels teem with guilty secrets, humiliations, plans that shrivel to ashes. The episode also left a permanent mark on his fictional treatment of sexual passion – another prominent theme in *Born in Exile*. In Gissing's life, as throughout his work, sex was constantly entangled with class. He married two women from the working class: Nell Harrison, the prostitute for whom he stole, who degenerated into alcoholism and died of syphilis; and Edith Underwood, the daughter of a London tombstone-maker, who bore him two sons before lapsing into madness. In each case he believed he could re-educate his wife but ended by abandoning her. His ostensible reason for marrying below him was that educated ladies would not bear poverty, but it seems that his deeper motivation involved a fantasy about working-class women in which the key ingredients were sexual excitement, the concept of moral reclamation and the confusion of passion with compassion. Idealised portraits of lower-class females figure in a number of his early books, most notably *The Unclassed* and *Thyrza*. At the same time he always cherished the ideal of marrying a virtuous and well-bred lady. This ambition, too, is ubiquitous in his fiction up to and including *Born in Exile*. 'I am a plebeian,' says Godwin Peak defiantly, 'and I aim at marrying a lady' (p. 113). Idealisation of the English gentlewoman is tremulously prevalent in large parts of Gissing's fiction, especially his early work. Words like 'purity', 'nobility' and 'soul' are reiterated reverentially; religious and regal imagery abounds – madonnas and haloes, queens and crowns. In *Born in Exile* these raptures recur, but what cuts them off from romantic cliché is the fierce, explicit class-consciousness now involved in their articulation.

For Gissing, as for many of his male protagonists, winning a woman of birth and breeding was desirable not only in itself but to ratify a social vision. In *Born in Exile* this is admitted and analysed. Peak realises that his falsity does not originate in conventional material ambition: 'The edifice of subtle untruth had for its foundation a mere ideal of sexual love [. . .] capable only of a social (one might say, of a political) definition. The woman throned in his imagination was no individual, but the type of an order' (p. 177). Sidwell Warricombe is initially seductive to Peak as the embodiment of the social status he covets. Only gradually do his aspirations converge on her as an individual. The whole treatment of sexual desire in the novel is closely linked to the theme of social exclusion. The shapes of both were deeply affected by Gissing's own experience.

Born in Exile is compelling not only as confession, but also as a document in social and intellectual history. In a letter of 1895 Gissing wrote: 'But what I desire to insist upon is this: that the most characteristic, the most important part of my work is that which deals with a class of young men distinctive of our time – well educated, fairly bred, *but without money*.' He cited instances from three of his novels, including Peak and Earwaker from *Born in Exile*. He might have given further examples from his fiction, including comparable female characters. What Gissing highlights here is a quite specific figure, the alienated, deracinated intellectual, produced by the extension of educational opportunities. Such characters are found in Hardy, Wells and Bennett, as well as in contemporary French and Russian fiction; they surface again, as 'angry young men', in British literature of the 1950s. Seen from this perspective, Godwin Peak's predicament is that of the meritocratic intellectual impeded by the power of class.

But to state it like this is to simplify the novel, for Peak's relationship to the established order is not wholly one of protest or revolt. He finds that the world of the English gentry both can and cannot supply what he wants. The problem arises from his discrepant aspirations in the areas of society, religion and sex. By contrast with Buckland Warricombe and Bruno Chilvers, both of whom benefit from their social origins but are nevertheless proud of their advanced opinions, Peak, disadvantaged by his humble background, is in many ways highly conservative. Sexually, his ideal is largely confected of gentility, beauty and decorative refinement: he rejects emancipated women as asexual (thus the tragedy of Marcella Moxey). Politically, he is vehemently anti-democratic, denouncing the 'vileness' of the populace and declaring that the masses are fools and brutes. But in matters of religion he is much more radical, a militant free-thinker contemptuous of Christianity, especially the evasions of current apologetics. As an outsider he suppresses his real opinions on religion – at least in the circles he wishes to join. Hence his pretence that he is about to be ordained, a ploy that 'meets every possible question that society can put' (p. 301). Or rather, perhaps, that *women* can put, for the social and religious conservatism of women, constantly emphasised by Earwaker, is a fundamental premise of the novel. It is a factor that plays havoc with Peak's tentative approaches to the genteel, sensitive Sidwell Warricombe. Socially, he finds her conservatism congenial: she listens sympathetically to his reactionary tirades. But her piety proves more of a stumbling block. Although it is partly to purchase her approval that he adopts his false posture as a clergyman-to-be, he often pines wistfully for a more enlightened woman. Yet bluestockings, he believes, aren't sexually attractive. As Peak twists around in a fever of frustration, it transpires that his peculiar permutation of ideals will simply not fit the moulds of society. Socially and sexually, he is fiercely nostalgic; intellectually, he represents modernity.

In *Born in Exile* modern intellectual trends are seen as threatening to traditional Christianity. The tension between theology and evolution is one of the most fascinating aspects of the book. Darwin's *Origin of Species* was published in 1859 and his *Descent of Man* – scarcely less controversial – in 1871. Though modern historians of religion and science repudiate a neat chronology of responses, it is generally accepted that an initial period of clerical hostility to Darwinism was succeeded by a phase of theological accommodation. *Born in Exile*, set chiefly in 1884, satirises this second period when many, as Peak says, are 'clamorous for treatises which pretend to reconcile religion and science' (p. 94). In the central sections of the book the theme is handled with a sureness of touch that owes much to Gissing's preparatory research. His own agnosticism had been strengthened in his twenties by his reading of authors such as Strauss and Gibbon and, especially, Auguste Comte, who believed that society evolved in stages, with theological and metaphysical modes of thought giving way to scientific ones. Before beginning *Born in Exile* Gissing supplemented these earlier intellectual perspectives with a survey of works concerned specifically with religious responses to evolution.

Born in Exile is partly important, then, as a novel of ideas (as such it is an atypical Victorian novel, more akin to some nineteenth-century European fiction). But the ideas are subservient to the social significance attached to them and the psychology of their proponents. Social acceptability, not religious truth, is what *Born in Exile* is concerned with. What matters is Peak's predicament and the moral acrobatics he employs to escape it. Discussion of science and theology is one tactic in his upwardly mobile campaign. As he glosses various works for Mr Warricombe, we never lose sight of the bounding ambition that underlies his enterprise. The ironies of the interloper's social position, and his queasily vertiginous states of mind, are more important than the ideas expounded.

Evolution, however, has a second significance – as a metaphor that colours the book's conception. Several characters talk about evolution; even more exemplify it. Notions of variability and heredity, competition and adaptation, are repeatedly reverted to. The question of 'instinct' emerges as vital, as too does that of 'finding a mate'; characters develop, or fail to adapt; different classes come to seem like separate species. Evolution, transcending its biological origins, is applied to ideas and social institutions. But the metaphor points in different directions. On the one hand, the key concept of 'adaptation' holds open the possibility of continuous change. It is hinted that religious apologists, being forced to adapt to the theory of evolution, are unwittingly confirming its thesis. Theology evolves, like the natural world. On the other hand, the notion of biological inheritance emphasises the forces that constrain development. Peak is born into a fierce struggle for existence, and the qualities he inherits from his father – arrogance and severity as well as integrity – curtail his powers of adaptation. Other characters have better genetic luck. Earwaker, original, vigorous and flexible, is 'naturally marked for survival among the fittest' (p. 86). Chilvers, more effortlessly sophistical than Peak, prevaricates with 'inherited aptitude' (p. 213). Near the end of the novel Sidwell tells Peak, 'You have been trying to adapt yourself to a world for which you are by nature unfitted' (p. 330). Ultimately it seems an open question whether his permanent exile is a social or biological fate.

Opening up questions rather than resolving them is characteristic of *Born in Exile*. This is especially true of its treatment of psychological and moral problems. It anticipates Freud and aligns with Nietzsche in its exploration of subconscious states and subversion of orthodox judgment. Its protagonist is a complex personality who eludes conventional appraisal. He is riddled with ambivalent attitudes, a man whose consciously formulated views conflict with his deepest instincts. Arrogant but shy, egotistical but nervous, he envies and despises the world that excludes him, a world of conservative, well-bred refinement which attracts him aesthetically, emotionally and sexually, but repels him with its mental timidity. An inveterate outsider, he wishes to belong – but to what, he can never be sure. Restless, critical, sceptical, he craves the comfort and security of a home. So pervasive is his sense of alienation that it gradually dominates his mental, and ultimately his moral, life. He cultivates a 'double consciousness' (p. 55) that allows him to conform with social requirements while critically scanning his environment. Several key moments in the novel occur when Peak is in a heightened state of mental bifurcation. His 'fatal' exegesis of the canon's sermon pours forth 'under the marvelling regard of his conscious self' (p. 128). His decisive declaration that he intends to take Orders occurs without conscious premeditation and yet, as he later recognises, is connected by forceful, hidden tendrils with anterior speculations and desires. Such episodes undermine any rigid conception of what constitutes 'voluntary' action. They also erode the notion of personal identity, for though Peak upbraids his brother's conformity with the furious question 'Have you no *self*?' (p. 60), his own sense of selfhood is frequently slippery. Pausing in the process of ventriloquial exposition, he is suddenly beset with 'a tormenting metaphysical doubt of his own identity' (p. 206).

What makes it more difficult to pass judgment on Peak is that he anticipates the reader's response by passing judgment on himself. Violently repelled by his vulgar uncle, he is ashamed of his shame and debates its justice. As a dissembler, he castigates himself for cowardice and baseness. Later he alternates between mocking self-contempt and defiant self-justification. 'Who is or can be honest?' he asks Earwaker. How does it matter what beliefs we profess, since 'truth is indeterminable'? (p. 158). Certainly, he admits, he has a bad conscience, but conscience is merely 'an inherited disease' (p. 361). Such bravado statements might well be dismissed as mere bluster – rationalisations. But the fact remains that the novel permits contradictory responses to quite crucial questions. How far is Peak's protracted deception justified? How much does he actually benefit from it? What calculations nurture and sustain it? To each of these questions the text supplies different answers in different places. There's a riskiness, a fluidity about the novel which suggests that ideas are being tested and developed – not only by Peak but perhaps by Gissing. No single discourse can claim authority: although the dominant voice is Peak's, it articulates a diversity of judgments. And it is difficult to tell where Peak's voice ends and that of the anonymous narrator takes over. This difficulty was experienced by Eduard Bertz, a friend to whom Gissing wrote in 1892:

> In judging the tendency of *Born in Exile* it is probable that you
> have been misled by the fact that the character of Godwin Peak
> is obviously, in a great degree, sympathetic to the author. But
> [. . .] it seems to me that the tone of the whole book is by no
> means identical with that of Peak's personality; certainly I did
> not mean it to be so. Peak is myself – one phase of myself. I
> described him with gusto, but surely I did not, in depicting the
> other characters, take *his* point of view?[3]

Gissing's comments are helpful but not decisive. In the early chapters of *Born in Exile* the word 'prejudiced' is frequently used of Peak, and the reiteration of similar terms (arrogance, envy, resentment, scorn) supports Gissing's clarification. Yet the narrator's voice is not always separable from Peak's (to appreciate this, one need only compare the novel's half dozen passages on the 'vilely grotesque' London accent).[4] Nor can it always take precedence over Peak's. At one point Peak declares that he recognises a true distinction of social classes: 'Social, mark. The division I instinctively support is by no means intellectual' (p. 107). Later, however, the narrator informs us that

Peak 'acknowledged no subordination save that of the hierarchy of intelligence' (p. 202). So was Peak's statement false, or insincere? Or do the passages point to a split in the protagonist – perhaps even an uncertainty in the author? The question can't be settled simply by asserting that the narrator's voice must cancel the character's. For in any case the narrator's voice is not consistent. It speaks, for example, of Peak's 'hopeful scheme' and of 'the course indicated from the first by his calm reason' (p. 261). Yet elsewhere it tells us that 'Reason had no part in the fantastic change to which his life had submitted, nor was he ever supported by a hope that would bear his cooler investigation' (p. 204).

Not long before the end of the novel, Earwaker studies a photograph of Peak and reflects that it is 'a face by which every intelligent eye must be arrested; which no two observers would interpret in the same way' (p. 397). What is true of the photograph is true of the book. Even the hero's surname is honeycombed with uncertainty, the loftiness implied by 'peak' undermined by morbid suggestions: resentment arising from wounded pride ('pique'), sickly despondence ('peak and pine'), and – from a spelling Gissing tried then rejected – a sense of furtive prying ('peek').[5]

There remains the question of the novel's structure. Gissing's fiction has sometimes been accused of lacking formal and technical finesse. Henry James, while confessing to a 'persistent taste' for Gissing's work, complained that 'The whole business of distribution and composition he strikes me as having cast to the winds'. Does the charge stick to *Born in Exile*?

Generically, the book is a *Bildungsroman* ('novel of formation') – a fiction in which a protagonist is taken from birth to maturity. Originating in the Romantic period, the genre stresses childhood experience as a crucial determinant of adult life. In its post-Darwinian versions – such as Butler's *Way of All Flesh* – it also stresses the role of heredity, adding biology to sociology as a perspective on the hero's fate. Both childhood and inherited characteristics are important in *Born in Exile*. The early *Bildungsroman* was an optimistic form; it linked emotional development to romantic and material success, suggesting that self-fulfilment could be harmonised with social integration. Spiritual crises would certainly occur but – as in *David Copperfield* – they contributed to maturation. Later in the century the genre changed, becoming ironic or tragic. An increasing number of novelists implied that maturity might not bring smiling wives and fat legacies but poverty, bitterness and alienation. One thinks, for example, of *Jude the Obscure*, published just three years after *Born in Exile*. Gissing's novel emerges from a social disillusion that was widespread in the late nineteenth century.

Born in Exile's structure was conditioned by its genre, but also, like most Victorian novels, by its publication in three volumes. At a guinea and a half the triple-decker novel was too expensive for most readers to purchase, but for a guinea they could borrow one volume at a time from the circulating libraries. It was the existence of the circulating library system that enabled so many Victorian novelists to survive. Gissing was one of these and *Born in Exile* was one of the last three-volume novels (the system collapsed in 1894). In *New Grub Street* a character famously complains that the three-volume novel is 'a triple-headed monster, sucking the blood of English novelists'. It is sometimes claimed that Gissing's fiction was a victim of this format, and it is true that his novels contain some padding (the penultimate chapter of *Born in Exile* was added in proof because the volume was too short). But he was also highly attuned to the form and conceived his novels to fit it. *Born in Exile*'s volume endings, for instance – not usually indicated in modern editions – make clear that its whole conception is tripartite. The second volume concentrates on Peak's imposture; the others are its prelude and aftermath.[6]

Across these broad blocks the novel throws a network of circumstantial irony. Events and allusions anticipate or echo the startling development at the novel's centre. One could illustrate this by tracing through the text the significant use of a single term. As a child, Peak's first recorded utterance is: 'I don't want to be a parson' (p. 24). Years later he is struck by Earwaker's remark, 'Let him be a parson, and he may aim as high as he chooses' (p. 112). Not long afterwards Buckland Warricombe stammers his amazement that Peak of all people should wish to become a – ' "Parson," supplied Peak, drily' (p. 144). The repeated noun functions as a marker, measuring Peak's movement towards deception. But it has yet another significance. Told by his mother not to use 'that word' (which had anti-clerical associations), the young Peak replies: 'Why not? It's quite a proper word. It comes from the Latin *persona*' (p. 24). The ironic implications of this retort (the Latin word means 'an actor's mask') ripple across the rest of the text, touching not only on Peak's future conduct but on that of Bruno Chilvers too.

A more sustained example of the device – prolepsis – by which a textual feature achieves its full significance only in the light of later developments is the novel's opening chapter, the account of prize-day at Whitelaw College. Several key themes are foreshadowed here: the vision of life as competition and conflict; the formative influence of social background; the pressure towards religious conformity; and the capacity of class affiliations to stultify intellect. The prizes, too, are predictive or ironic. Peak wins first prize in logic and moral philosophy and shares the geology prize with Buckland. Chilvers comes first in virtually all the arts but nowhere in philosophy or science. Earwaker, later a journalist, wins prizes for the poem and essay.

Certain figures introduced in this opening chapter are run parallel with Peak through the rest of the book. Minor characters illuminate the major plot. Not all are well depicted, but the subplots are purposeful, relieving or confirming the protagonist's fate. Bruno Chilvers, for example, consistently attains the ideals that Peak is struggling towards, but by doing so undermines their value. The stories of Malkin and Christian Moxey are burlesque versions of amorous frustration. Marcella Moxey, awkward, independent and brainy, is in many ways a female equivalent of Peak. The treatment of her gradually growing jealousy is one of the best things in *Born in Exile*, a second, almost equally subtle study of the power of subconscious impulses.

But all these narratives are strictly ancillary to the dominant predicament of Godwin Peak. And in the last resort what we think of *Born in Exile* will depend on our assessment of its central character. A 'base and deluded character' or a man of 'uncompromising intellectual honesty'?[7] The reader must decide.

Notes to the Introduction

1. *The Letters of George Gissing to Eduard Bertz, 1887–1903*, ed. Arthur C. Young (1961), p. 153.
2. *Letters of George Gissing to Members of His Family*, ed. Algernon and Ellen Gissing (1927), p. 313.
3. *Letters to Bertz*, p. 153.

4. The passages occur on pp. 16, 21, 29, 101, 108, 409.

5. Gissing first called the novel *Godwin Peak* (after thinking of calling it *Raymond Peak*). While revising the book in manuscript, he temporarily altered the protagonist's name to 'Peek'. See *London and the Life of Literature in Late Victorian England: The Diary of George Gissing, Novelist*, ed. Pierre Coustillas (1978), pp. 241, 267. Peak's divided condition – aristocratic and radical – is also implied by his first name, Godwin (see pp. 21, 23).

6. Volume One concluded at the end of Part the Second (p. 147); Volume Two, at the end of Part the Fourth (p. 282).

7. John Carey, *The Intellectuals and the Masses* (1992), p. 113; Jacob Korg, 'The Spiritual Theme of *Born in Exile*', in *Collected Articles on George Gissing*, ed. Pierre Coustillas (1968), p. 135.

A NOTE ON THE TEXT

Born in Exile was first published by Adam & Charles Black in three volumes in May 1892. In 1893 a one-volume edition was produced by the same publisher. The present text is based on that of the 1893 edition, but corrects a number of errors and misprints (most of which are also found in the first edition). In a handful of cases it also corrects orthographical errors that originate in the autograph manuscript (held in the Huntington Library, San Marino, California). All such cases are indicated in the Explanatory Notes.

ACKNOWLEDGEMENTS

I should like to thank those friends and colleagues who have responded so generously to my requests for assistance during the preparation of this edition – especially Pierre and Hélène Coustillas, Peter Kemp and John Simpson, but also Malcolm Airs, Richard Croucher, Lawrence Goldman, Angus Hawkins, Jeremy Marshall, Trevor Rowley, Paul Turner and Edmund Weiner. I should also like to thank the staff of Rewley House Library, the Bodleian Library and the Huntington Library, California.

D.G.

The publisher and editors are grateful for permission to quote from the following: Adrian Poole, *Gissing in Context*, Macmillan, 1974; John Goode, *George Gissing: Ideology and Fiction*, Vision Press, 1978; Robert L. Selig, *George Gissing*, Twayne Publishers, 1983; John Sloan, *George Gissing: the Cultural Challenge*, Macmillan, 1989; Jacob Korg, 'The Spiritual Theme of *Born in Exile*', in *Collected Essays*, ed. Pierre Coustillas, Frank Cass, 1968; Pierre Coustillas, 'Introduction', *Born in Exile* Harvester edition, Simon and Schuster, 1989; Charles Swann, 'Sincerity and Authenticity: the Problem of Identity in *Born in Exile*', *Literature and History*, 10:2 (Autumn 1984), pp. 165–86, Ohio State University, Department of English: John Carey, *The Intellectuals and the Masses*, Faber and Faber, 1992.

PART THE FIRST

I

The summer day in 1874 which closed the annual session of Whitelaw College was marked by a special ceremony, preceding the wonted distribution of academic rewards. At eleven in the morning (just as a heavy shower fell from the smoke-canopy above the roaring streets) the municipal authorities, educational dignitaries, and prominent burgesses of Kingsmill assembled on an open space before the College to unveil a statue of Sir Job Whitelaw. The honoured baronet had been six months dead. Living, he opposed the desire of his fellow-citizens to exhibit even on canvas his gnarled features and bald crown; but when his modesty ceased to have a voice in the matter, no time was lost in raising a memorial of the great manufacturer, the self-made millionaire, the borough member in three Parliaments, the enlightened and benevolent founder of an institute which had conferred humane distinction on the money-making Midland town. Beneath such a sky, orations were necessarily curtailed; but Sir Job had always been impatient of much talk. An interval of two or three hours dispersed the rain-clouds and bestowed such grace of sunshine as Kingsmill might at this season temperately desire; then, whilst the marble figure was getting dried, – with soot-stains which already foretold its nigritude of a year hence, – again streamed towards the College a varied multitude, official, parental, pupillary. The students had nothing distinctive in their garb, but here and there flitted the cap and gown of Professor or lecturer, signal for doffing of beavers along the line of its progress.

Among the more deliberate of the throng was a slender, upright, ruddy-cheeked gentleman of middle age, accompanied by his wife and a daughter of sixteen. On alighting from a carriage, they first of all directed their steps towards the statue, conversing together with pleasant animation. The father (Martin

Warricombe, Esq. of Thornhaw, a small estate some five miles from Kingsmill,) had a countenance suggestive of engaging qualities – genial humour, mildness, a turn for meditation, perhaps for study. His attire was informal, as if he disliked abandoning the freedom of the country even when summoned to urban ceremonies. He wore a grey felt hat, and a light jacket which displayed the straightness of his shoulders. Mrs Warricombe and her daughter were more fashionably equipped, with taste which proclaimed their social standing. Save her fresh yet delicate complexion the lady had no particular personal charm. Of the young girl it could only be said that she exhibited a graceful immaturity, with perchance a little more earnestness than is common at her age; her voice, even when she spoke gaily, was seldom audible save by the person addressed.

Coming to a pause before Sir Job, Mr Warricombe put on a pair of eyeglasses which had dangled against his waistcoat, and began to scrutinise carefully the sculptured lineaments. He was addressing certain critical remarks to his companions when an interruption appeared in the form of a young man whose first words announced his relation to the group.

'I say, you're very late! There'll be no getting a decent seat, if you don't mind. Leave Sir Job till afterwards.'

'The statue somehow disappoints me,' observed his father, placidly.

'Oh, it isn't bad, I think,' returned the youth, in a voice not unlike his father's, save for a note of excessive self-confidence. He looked about eighteen; his comely countenance, with its air of robust health and habitual exhilaration, told of a boyhood passed amid free and joyous circumstances. It was the face of a young English plutocrat, with more of intellect than such visages are wont to betray; the native vigour of his temperament had probably assimilated something of the modern spirit. 'I'm glad,' he continued, 'that they haven't stuck him in a toga, or any humbug of that sort. The old fellow looks baggy, but so he was. They ought to have kept his chimney-pot, though. Better than giving him those scraps of hair, when everyone knows he was as bald as a beetle.'

'Sir Job should have been granted Caesar's privilege,' said Mr Warricombe, with a pleasant twinkle in his eyes.

'What was that?' came from the son, with abrupt indifference.

'For shame, Buckland!'

'What do I care for Caesar's privileges? We can't burden our minds with that antiquated rubbish nowadays. You would despise it yourself, father, if it hadn't got packed into your head when you were young.'

The parent raised his eyebrows in a bantering smile.

'I have lived to hear classical learning called antiquated rubbish. Well, well! – Ha! there is Professor Gale.'

The Professor of Geology, a tall man, who strode over the pavement as if he were among granite hills, caught sight of the party and approached. His greeting was that of a familiar friend; he addressed young Warricombe and his sister by their Christian names, and inquired after certain younger members of the household. Mr Warricombe, regarding him with a look of repressed eagerness, laid a hand on his arm, and spoke in the subdued voice of one who has important news to communicate.

'If I am not much mistaken, I have chanced on a new species of *homalonotus*!'

'Indeed! – not in your kitchen garden, I presume?'

'Hardly. Dr Pollock sent me a box of specimens the other day'—

Buckland saw with annoyance the likelihood of prolonged discussion.

'I don't know whether you care to remain standing all the afternoon,' he said to his mother. 'At this rate we certainly shan't get seats.'

'We will walk on, Martin,' said the lady, glancing at her husband.

'We come! we come!' cried the Professor, with a wave of his arm.

The palaeontological talk continued as far as the entrance of the assembly hall. The zest with which Mr Warricombe spoke of his discovery never led him to raise his voice above the suave, mellow note, touched with humour, which expressed a modest assurance. Mr Gale was distinguished by a blunter mode of speech; he discoursed with open-air vigour, making use now and then of a racy colloquialism which the other would hardly have permitted himself.

As young Warricombe had foreseen, the seats obtainable were none too advantageous; only on one of the highest rows of the amphitheatre could they at length establish themselves.

'Buckland will enjoy the more attention when he marches down to take his prizes,' observed the father. 'He must sit at the end here, that he mayn't have a struggle to get out.'

'Don't, Martin, don't!' urged his wife, considerately.

'Oh, it doesn't affect me,' said Buckland, with a laugh.

'I feel pretty sure I have got the Logic and the Chemistry, and those are what I care most about. I dare say Peak has beaten me in Geology.'

The appearance in the lower part of the hall of a dark-robed procession, headed by the tall figure of the Principal, imposed a moment's silence, broken by outbursts of welcoming applause. The Professors of Whitelaw College were highly popular, not alone with the members of their classes, but with all the educated inhabitants of Kingsmill; and deservedly, for several of them bore names of wide recognition, and as a body they did honour to the institution which had won their services. With becoming formality they seated themselves in face of the public. On tables before them were exposed a considerable number of well-bound books, shortly to be distributed among the collegians, who gazed in that direction with speculative eyes.

Among the general concourse might have been discovered two or three representatives of the wage-earning multitude which Kingsmill depended upon for its prosperity, but their presence was due to exceptional circumstances; the College provided for proletarian education by a system of evening classes, a curriculum necessarily quite apart from that followed by the regular students. Kingsmill, to be sure, was no nurse of Toryism; the robust employers of labour who sent their sons to Whitelaw – either to complete a training deemed sufficient for an active career, or by way of transition-stage between school and university – were for the most part avowed Radicals, in theory scornful of privilege, practically supporters of that mode of freedom which regards life as a remorseless conflict. Not a few of the young men (some of these the hardest and most successful workers) came from poor, middle-class homes, whence, but for Sir Job's foundation, they must have set forth into the world with no better equipment of knowledge than was supplied by some 'academy' of the old type: a glance distinguished such students from the well-dressed and well-fed offspring of Kingsmill plutocracy. The note of the assembly was something other than refinement; rather, its high standard of health, spirits, and comfort – the characteristic of Capitalism. Decent reverence for learning, keen appreciation of scientific power, warm liberality of thought and sentiment within appreciable limits, enthusiasm for economic, civic, national ideals, – such attributes were abundantly discoverable in each serried row. From the expanse of countenances beamed a boundless self-satisfaction. To be connected in any way with Whitelaw formed a subject of pride, seeing that here was the sturdy outcome of the most modern educational endeavour, a noteworthy instance of what Englishmen can do for themselves, unaided by bureaucratic machinery. Every student who achieved distinction in to-day's class lists was felt to bestow a share of his honour upon each spectator who applauded him.

With occasional adjustment of his eye-glasses, and smiling his smile of modest tolerance, Mr Warricombe surveyed the crowded hall. His connection with the town was not intimate, and he could discover few faces that were familiar to him. A native and, till of late, an inhabitant of Devon, he had come to reside on his property near Kingsmill because it seemed to him that the education of his children would be favoured by a removal thither. Two of his oldest friends held professorships at Whitelaw; here, accordingly, his eldest son was making preparation for Cambridge, whilst his daughter attended classes at the admirable High School, of which Kingsmill was only less proud than of its College.

Seated between his father and his sister, Buckland drew their attention to such persons or personages as interested his very selective mind.

'Admire the elegant languor of Wotherspoon,' he remarked, indicating the Professor of Greek. 'Watch him for a moment, and you'll see him glance contemptuously at old Plummer. He can't help it; they hate each other.'

'But why?' whispered the girl, with timid eagerness.

'Oh, it began, they say, when Plummer once had to take one of Wotherspoon's classes; some foolery about a second aorist. Thank goodness, I don't understand the profound dispute. – Oh, do look at that fatuous idiot Chilvers!'

The young gentleman of whom he spoke, a student of Buckland's own standing, had just attracted general notice. Rising from his seat in the lower part of the amphitheatre, at the moment when all were hushed in anticipation of the Principal's address, Mr Chilvers was beckoning to someone whom his eye had descried at great distance, and for whom, as he indicated by gesture, he had preserved a place.

'See how it delights him to make an exhibition of himself!'

pursued the censorious youth. 'I'd bet a sovereign he's arranged it all. Look how he brandishes his arm to display his cuffs and gold links. Now he touches his hair, to point out how light and exquisite it is, and how beautifully he parts it!'

'What a graceful figure!' murmured Mrs Warricombe, with genuine admiration.

'There, that's just what he hopes everyone is saying,' replied her son, in a tone of laughing digust.

'But he certainly is graceful, Buckland,' persisted the lady.

'And in the meantime,' remarked Mr Warricombe, drily, 'we are all awaiting the young gentleman's pleasure.'

'Of course; he enjoys it. Almost all the people on that row belong to him – father, mother, sisters, brothers, uncles, aunts, and cousins to the fourth degree. Look at their eyes fondly fixed upon him! Now he pretends to loosen his collar at the throat, just for a change of attitude – the puppy!'

'My dear!' remonstrated his mother, with apprehensive glance at her neighbours.

'But he is really clever, isn't he, Buckland?' asked the sister, – her name was Sidwell.

'After a fashion. I shouldn't wonder if he takes a dozen or two prizes. It's all a knack, you know.'

'Where is your friend Peak?' Mr Warricombe made inquiry.

But at this moment Mr Chilvers abandoned his endeavour and became seated, allowing the Principal to rise, manuscript in hand. Buckland leaned back with an air of resignation to boredom; his father bent slightly forward, with lips close pressed and brows wrinkled; Mrs Warricombe widened her eyes, as if hearing were performed with those organs, and assumed the smile she would have worn had the speaker been addressing her in particular. Sidwell's blue eyes imitated the movement of her mother's, with a look of profound gravity which showed that she had wholly forgotten herself in reverential listening; only when five minutes' strict attention induced a sense of weariness did she allow a glance to stray first along the professorial rank, then towards the place where the golden head of young Chilvers was easily distinguishable.

Nothing could be more satisfactory than the annual report summarised by Principal Nares, whose mellifluous voice and daintily pedantic utterance fell upon expectant hearing with the impressiveness of personal compliment. So delivered, statistics partook of the grace of culture; details of academic organisation acquired something more than secular significance. In this the ninth year of its existence, Whitelaw College was flourishing in every possible way. Private beneficence had endowed it with new scholarships and exhibitions; the scheme of lectures had been extended; the number of its students steadily increased, and their successes in the field of examination had been noteworthy beyond precedent. Truly, the heart of their founder, to whom honour had this day been rendered, must have gladdened if he could but have listened to the story of dignified progress! Applause, loud and long, greeted the close of the address. Buckland Warricombe was probably the only collegian who disdained to manifest approval in any way.

'Why don't you clap?' asked his sister, who, girl-like, was excited to warmth of cheek and brightness of eye by the enthusiasm about her.

'That kind of thing is out of date,' replied the young man, thrusting his hands deep into his pockets.

As Professor of Logic and Moral Philosophy, Dr Nares began the distribution of prizes. Buckland, in spite of his resolve to exhibit no weakness, waited with unmistakable tremor for the announcement of the leading name, which might possibly be his own. A few words of comment prefaced the declaration: – never had it been the Professor's lot to review more admirable papers than those to which he had awarded the first prize. The name of the student called upon to come forward was – Godwin Peak.

'Beaten!' escaped from Buckland's lips.

Mrs Warricombe glanced at her son with smiling sympathy; Sidwell, whose cheek had paled as her nerves quivered under the stress of expectancy, murmured a syllable of disappointment; Mr Warricombe set his brows and did not venture to look aside. A moment, and all eyes were directed upon the successful student, who rose from a seat half-way down the hall and descended the middle passage towards the row of Professors. He was a young man of spare figure and unhealthy complexion, his age not easily conjectured. Embarrassment no doubt accounted for much of the awkwardness of his demeanour; but, under any circumstances, he must have appeared ungainly, for his long arms and legs had outgrown their garments, which were no fashionable specimens of tailoring. The nervous gravity of his countenance had a peculiar sternness; one might have imagined that he was fortifying his self-control with scorn of the elegantly clad people through whom he passed. Amid plaudits, he received from the hands of the Principal a couple of solid volumes, probably some standard work of philosophy, and, thus burdened, returned with hurried step to his place.

'No one expected that,' remarked Buckland to his father. 'He must have crammed furiously for the exam. It's outside his work for the First BA.'

'What a shame!' Sidwell whispered to her mother; and the reply was a look which eloquently expressed Mrs Warricombe's lack of sympathy with the victor.

But a second prize had been awarded. As soon as silence was restored, the Principal's gracious voice delivered a summons to 'Buckland Martin Warricombe.' A burst of acclamation, coming especially from that part of the amphitheatre where Whitelaw's nurslings had gathered in greatest numbers, seemed to declare the second prizeman distinctly more popular than the first. Preferences of this kind are always to be remarked on such occasions.

'Second prize be hanged!' growled the young man, as, with a flush of shame on his ruddy countenance, he set forth to receive the honour, leaving Mr Warricombe convulsed with silent laughter.

'He would far rather have had nothing at all,' murmured Sidwell, who shared her brother's pique and humiliation.

'Oh, it'll do him good,' was her father's reply. 'Buckland has got into a way of swaggering.'

Undeniable was the swagger with which the good-looking, breezy lad went and returned.

'What is the book?' inquired Mr Warricombe.

'I don't know. – Oh, Mill's *Logic*. Idiotic choice! They might have known I had it already.'

'They clap him far more than they did Mr Peak,' Sidwell whispered to her mother, with satisfaction.

Buckland kept silence for a few minutes, then muttered:

'There's nothing I care about now till Chemistry and Geology. Here comes old Wotherspoon. Now we shall know who is strongest in second aorists. I shouldn't wonder if Peak takes both Senior Greek and Latin. I heartily hope he'll beat that ass Chilvers.'

But the name so offensive to young Warricombe was the first

that issued from the Professor's lips. Beginning with the competition for a special classical prize, Professor Wotherspoon announced that the honours had fallen to 'Bruno Leathwaite Chilvers.'

'That young man is not badly supplied with brains, say what you will,' remarked Mr Warricombe.

Upon Bruno Leathwaite Chilvers keen attention was directed; every pair of female eyes studied his graces, and female hands had a great part in the applause that greeted his arising. Applause different in kind from that hitherto bestowed; less noisy, but implying, one felt, a more delicate spirit of commendation. With perfect self-command, with singular facial decorum, with a walk which betokened elegant athleticism and safely skirted the bounds of foppery, Mr Chilvers discharged the duty he was conscious of owing to a multitude of kinsfolk, friends, admirers. You would have detected something clerical in the young man's air. It became the son of a popular clergyman, and gave promise of notable aptitude for the sacred career to which Bruno Leathwaite, as was well understood, already had designed himself. In matters sartorial he presented a high ideal to his fellow-students; this seemly attention to externals, and the delicate glow of health discernible through the golden down of his cheeks, testified the compatibility of hard study and social observances. Bruno had been heard to say that the one thing it behoved Whitelaw to keep carefully in mind was the preservation of 'tone', a quality far less easy to cultivate than mere academic excellence.

'How clever he must be!' purred Mrs Warricombe. 'If he lives, he will some day be an archbishop.'

Buckland was leaning back with his eyes closed, disgusted at the spectacle. Nor did he move when Professor Wotherspoon's voice made the next announcement.

'In Senior Greek, the first prize is taken by – Bruno Leathwaite Chilvers.'

'Then I suppose Peak comes second,' muttered Buckland.

So it proved. Summoned to receive the inferior prize, Godwin Peak, his countenance harsher than before, his eyes cast down, moved ungracefully to the estrade. And during the next half-hour this twofold exhibition was several times repeated. In Senior Latin, in Modern and Ancient History, in English Language and Literature, in French, first sounded the name of Chilvers, whilst to the second award was invariably attached that of Peak. Mrs Warricombe's delight expressed itself in every permissible way:

on each occasion she exclaimed, 'How clever he is!' Sidwell cast frequent glances at her brother, in whom a shrewder eye could have divined conflict of feelings – disgust at the glorification of Chilvers and involuntary pleasure in the successive defeats of his own conqueror in Philosophy. Buckland's was by no means an ignoble face; venial malice did not ultimately prevail in him.

'It's Peak's own fault,' he declared at length, with vexation. 'Chilvers stuck to the subjects of his course. Peak has been taking up half-a-dozen extras, and they've done for him. I shouldn't wonder if he went in for the Poem and the Essay: I know he was thinking about both.'

Whether Godwin Peak had or had not endeavoured for these two prizes remained uncertain. When, presently, the results of the competition were made known, it was found that in each case the honour had fallen to a young man hitherto undistinguished. His name was John Edward Earwaker. Externally he bore a sort of generic resemblance to Peak, for his face was thin and the fashion of his clothing indicated narrow means.

'I never heard you mention him,' said Mr Warricombe, turning to his son with an air of surprise.

'I scarcely know him at all; he's only in one or two of my classes. Peak is thick with him.'

The subject of the prize poem was 'Alaric'; that of the essay, 'Trades Unionism'. So it was probable that John Edward Earwaker did not lack versatility of intellect.

On the rising of the Professor of Chemistry, Buckland had once more to subdue signs of expectancy. He knew he had done good papers, but his confidence in the result was now clouded by a dread of the second prize – which indeed fell to him, the first being taken by a student of no account save in this very special subject. Keen was his mortification; he growled, muttered, shrugged his shoulders nervously.

'If I had foreseen this, you'd never have caught me here,' was his reply, when Sidwell whispered consolation.

There still remained a chance for him, signalled by the familiar form of Professor Gale. Geology had been a lifelong study with Martin Warricombe, and his son pursued it with hereditary aptitude. Sidwell and her mother exchanged a look of courageous hope; each felt convinced that the genial Professor could not so far disregard private feeling as to place Buckland anywhere but at the head of the class.

'The results of the examination are fairly good; I'm afraid I can't say more than that,' thus rang out Mr Gale's hearty voice. 'As for the first two names on my list, I haven't felt justified in placing either before the other. I have bracketed them, and there will be two prizes. The names are – Godwin Peak and Buckland Martin Warricombe.'

'He might have mentioned Buckland first,' murmured Mrs Warricombe, resentfully.

'He of course gave them out in alphabetical order,' answered her husband.

'Still, it isn't right that Buckland should come second.'

'That's absurd,' was the good-natured reply.

The lady of course remained unconvinced, and for years she nourished a pique against Professor Gale, not so much owing to his having bracketed her son as because the letter P has alphabetical precedence of W.

In what remained of the proceedings the Warricombes had no personal interest. For a special reason, however, their attention was excited by the rising of Professor Walsh, who represented the science of Physics. Early in the present year had been published a speculative treatise which, owing to its supposed incompatibility with Christian dogmas, provoked much controversy and was largely discussed in all educated circles. The work was anonymous, but a rumour which gained general currency attributed it to Professor Walsh. In the year 1874 an imputation of religious heresy was not lightly to be incurred by a Professor – even Professor of Physics – at an English college. There were many people in Kingsmill who considered that Mr Walsh's delay in repudiating so grave a charge rendered very doubtful the propriety of his retaining the chair at Whitelaw. Significant was the dispersed applause which followed slowly upon his stepping forward to-day; on the Professor's face was perchance legible something like a hint of amused defiance. Ladies had ceased to beam; they glanced meaningly at one another, and then from under their eyelids at the supposed heretic.

'A fine fellow, Walsh!' exclaimed Buckland, clapping vigorously.

His father smiled, but with some uneasiness. Mrs Warricombe whispered to Sidwell:

'What a very disagreeable face! The only one of the Professors who doesn't seem a gentleman.'

The girl was aware of dark reports affecting Mr Walsh's reputation. She hazarded only a brief examination of his features, and looked at the applauding Buckland with alarm.

'His lectures are splendid,' said her brother, emphatically. 'If I were going to be here next session, I should take them.'

For some minutes after the Professor's return to his seat a susurration was audible throughout the hall; bonnets bent together, and beards exchanged curt comments.

The ceremony, as is usual with all ceremonies, grew wearisome before its end. Buckland was deep in one of the chapters of his geologic prize when the last speaker closed the last report and left the assembly free to disperse. Then followed the season of congratulations: Professors, students, and the friendly public mingled in a *conversazione*. A nucleus of vivacious intercourse formed at the spot where young Mr Chilvers stood amid trophies of examinational prowess. When his numerous relatives had all shaken hands with him, and laughed, smiled, or smirked their felicitations, they made way for the press of eager acquaintances. His prize library was reverently surveyed, and many were the sportive sallies elicited by the victor's obvious inability to carry away what he had won. Suavely exultant, ready with his reply to every flattering address, Bruno Chilvers exhibited a social tact in advance of his years: it was easy to imagine what he would become when Oxford terms and the seal of ordination had matured his youthful promise.

At no great distance stood his competitor, Godwin Peak — embarrassed, he also, with wealth of spoils; but about this young man was no concourse of admiring kinsfolk. No lady offered him her hand or shaped compliments for him with gracious lips. Half-a-dozen fellow-students, among them John Earwaker, talked in his vicinity of the day's results. Peak's part in the gossip was small, and when he smiled it was in a forced, anxious way, with brief raising of his eyes. For a moment only was the notice of a wider circle directed upon him when Dr Nares, moving past with a train of colloquial attendants, turned aside to repeat his praise of the young man's achievements in Philosophy: he bestowed a kindly shake of the hand, and moved on.

The Warricombe group descended, in purposeless fashion, towards the spot where Chilvers held his court. Their personal acquaintance with Bruno and his family was slight, and though Mrs Warricombe would gladly have pushed forward to claim recognition, natural diffidence restrained her. Sidwell kept in the rear, risking now and then a glance of vivid curiosity on either hand. Buckland, striving not to look petulant or sullen, allowed himself to be led on; but when he became aware of the tendency Bruno-wards, a protest broke from him.

'There's no need to swell that fellow's conceit. Here, father, come and have a word with Peak; he looks rather down in the mouth among his second prizes.'

Mr Warricombe having beckoned his companions, they reluctantly followed to the more open part of the hall.

'It's very generous of Buckland,' fell from the lady's lips, and she at length resolved to show an equal magnanimity. Peak and Earwaker were conversing together when Buckland broke in upon them with genial outburst.

'Confound it, Peak! what do you mean by getting me stuck into a bracket?'

'I had the same question to ask *you*,' returned the other, with a grim smile.

Mr Warricombe came up with extended hand.

'A species of bracket,' he remarked, smiling benevolently, 'which no algebraic process will remove. Let us hope it signifies that you and Buckland will work through life shoulder to shoulder in the field of geology. What did Professor Gale give you?'

Before he could reply, Peak had to exchange greetings with Mrs Warricombe and her daughter. Only once hitherto had he met them. Six months ago he had gone out with Buckland to the country-house and passed an afternoon there, making at the time no very favourable impression on his hostess. He was not of the young men who easily insinuate themselves into ladies' affections: his exterior was against him, and he seemed too conscious of his disadvantages in that particular. Mrs Warricombe found it difficult to shape a few civil phrases for the acceptance of the saturnine student. Sidwell, repelled and in a measure alarmed by his bilious countenance, could do no more than grant him her delicately gloved fingers. Peak, for his part, had nothing to say. He did not even affect an interest in these persons, and turned his eyes to follow the withdrawing Earwaker. Mr Warricombe, however, had found topic for discourse in the prize volume; he began to comment on the excellence of certain sections of the book.

'Do you go home?' interrupted Buckland, addressing the

question to his rival. 'Or do you stay in Kingsmill until the First BA?'

'I shall go home,' replied Peak, moving uneasily.

'Perhaps we may have the pleasure of seeing you at Thornhaw when you are up again for the examination?' said Mrs Warricombe, with faltering tongue.

'I'm afraid I shan't be able to come, thank you,' was the awkward response.

Buckland's voice came to the relief.

'I daresay I may look in upon you at your torture. Good luck, old fellow! If we don't see each other again, write to me at Trinity before the end of the year.'

As soon as she was sufficiently remote, Mrs Warricombe ejaculated in a subdued voice of irritation:

'Such a very unprepossessing young man I never met! He seems to have no breeding whatever.'

'Overweighted with brains,' replied her husband; adding to himself, 'and by no means so with money, I fear.'

Opportunity at length offering, Mrs Warricombe stepped into the circle irradiated by Bruno Chilvers; her husband and Sidwell pressed after. Buckland, with an exclamation of disgust, went off to criticise the hero among a group of his particular friends.

Godwin Peak stood alone. On the bench where he had sat were heaped the prize volumes (eleven in all, some of them massive), and his wish was to make arrangements for their removal. Gazing about him, he became aware of the College librarian, with whom he was on friendly terms.

'Mr Poppleton, who would pack and send these books away for me?'

'An *embarras de richesse!*' laughed the librarian. 'If you like to tell the porter to take care of them for the present, I shall be glad to see that they are sent wherever you like.'

Peak answered with a warmth of acknowledgment which seemed to imply that he did not often receive kindnesses. Before long he was free to leave the College, and at the exit he overtook Earwaker, who carried a brown paper parcel.

'Come and have some tea with me across the way, will you?' said the literary prizeman. 'I have a couple of hours to wait for my train.'

'All right. I envy you that five-volume Spenser.'

'I wish they had given me five authors I don't possess instead. I think I shall sell this.'

Earwaker laughed as he said it – a strange chuckle from deep down in his throat. A comparison of the young men, as they walked side by side, showed that Peak was of better physical type than his comrade. Earwaker had a slight, unshapely body and an ill-fitting head; he walked with excessive strides and swung his thin arm nervously. Probably he was the elder of the two, and he looked twenty. For Peak's disadvantages of person, his studious bashfulness and poverty of attire were mainly responsible. With improvement in general health even his features might have a tolerable comeliness, or at all events would not be disagreeable. Earwaker's visage was homely, and seemed the more so for his sprouting moustache and beard.

'Have you heard any talk about Walsh?' the latter inquired, as they walked on.

Peak shrugged his shoulders, with a laugh.

'No. Have you?'

'Some women in front of me just now were evidently discussing him. I heard "How shocking!" and "Disgraceful!"'

Peak's eyes flashed, and he exclaimed in a voice of wrath:

'Besotted idiots! How I wish I were in Walsh's position! How I should enjoy standing up before the crowd of fools and seeing their fear of me! But I couldn't keep it to myself; I should give in to the temptation to call them blockheads and jackasses.'

Earwaker was amused at his friend's vehemence. He sympathised with it, but had an unyouthful sobriety in the expression of his feelings.

'Most likely he despises them far too much to be disturbed by what they think of him. But, I say, isn't it desperately comical that one human being can hate and revile another because they think differently about the origin of the universe? Couldn't you roar with laughter when you've thought over it for a moment? "You be damned for your theory of irregular verbs!" is nothing to it.' And he uttered his croak of mirth, whilst Peak, with distorted features, laughed in rage and scorn.

They had crossed the open space in front of the College buildings, and were issuing into the highway, when a voice very unlike those that were wont to sound within the academic precincts (or indeed in the streets of Kingsmill) made sudden demand upon Peak's attention.

'Thet you, Godwin? Thoughts I, it must be 'im! 'Ow goes it, my bo-oy? You 'ardly reckonise me, I dessay, and I couldn't be sure as it was you till I'd 'ed a good squint at yer. I've jest called round at your lodgin's, and they towld me as you was at the Collige.'

He who thus accosted the student, with the most offensive purity of Cockney accent, was a man of five-and-forty, dressed in a new suit of ready-made tweeds, the folding crease strongly marked down the front of the trousers and the coat sleeves rather too long. His face bore a strong impress of vulgarity, but at the same time had a certain ingenuousness, a self-absorbed energy and simplicity, which saved it from being wholly repellent; the brow was narrow, the eyes small and bright, and the coarse lips half hid themselves under a struggling reddish growth. In these lineaments lurked a family resemblance to Godwin Peak, sufficient to support a claim of kindred which at this moment might have seemed improbable. At the summons of recognition Godwin stood transfixed; his arms fell straight, and his head drew back as if to avoid a blow. For an instant he was clay colour, then a hot flush broke upon his cheeks.

'I shan't be able to go with you,' he said, in a thick, abrupt voice, addressing Earwaker but not regarding him. 'Good-bye!'

The other offered his hand and, without speaking, walked away.

'Prize-dye at the Collige, they tell me,' pursued Godwin's relative, looking at a cluster of people that passed. 'What 'ave you took?'

'One or two class-prizes,' replied the student, his eyes on the ground. 'Shall we walk to my lodgings?'

'I thought you might like to walk me over the show. But pr'aps you're in a 'urry?'

'No, no. But there's nothing particular to see. I think the lecture-rooms are closed by now.'

'Oo's the gent as stands there? – the figger, I mean.'

'Sir Job Whitelaw, founder of the College.'

'Job, eh? And was you a-goin' 'ome to yer tea, Godwin?'

'Yes.'

'Well, then, look 'ere, 'spose we go to the little shop opposyte – nice little plyce it looks. I could do a cup o' tea myself, and we can 'ev a quite confab. It's a long time since we'ed a talk together. I come over from Twybridge this mornin'; slep' there last night, and saw yer mother an' Oliver. They couldn't give me a bed, but that didn't mike no matter; I put up at the Norfolk Harms – five-an-six for bed an' breakfast. Come along, my bo-oy; I stand treat.'

Godwin glanced about him. From the College was approaching what seemed to be a formal procession; it consisted of Bruno Chilvers, supported on either hand by ladies and followed by an admiring train.

'You had better come to my lodgings with me, uncle,' said the young man hurriedly, moving forward.

'No, no; I won't be no expense to you, Godwin, bo-oy. And I 'ave a reason for wantin' to go to the little shop opposyte.'

Already several collegians had passed, giving Peak a nod and scanning his companion; a moment's delay and Chilvers would be upon him. Without another word, Godwin moved across the broad street to the place of refreshment which his uncle had indicated, and whither Earwaker had preceded them. It was a pastry-cook's, occasionally visited by the alumni of Whitelaw. In the rear of the shop a little room offered seats and tables, and here, Godwin knew, Earwaker would be found.

'Let us go up-stairs,' he said, leading to a side entrance. 'There's a quieter room.'

'Right you are!'

The uncle – his name was Andrew Peak – paused to make a survey of the premises. When he entered, his scrutiny of the establishment was close, and he seemed to reflect with interest upon all he saw. The upper room was empty; a long table exhibited knives and forks, but there were no signs of active business. Andrew pulled a bell-rope; the summons was answered by an asthmatic woman, who received an order for tea, toast, 'watercreases', and sundry other constituents of a modest meal.

'Come 'ere often, Godwin?' inquired Andrew, as he stood by the window and mused.

'Now and then, for a bun.'

'Much custom from your show over the wye?'

'Not so much as a better place would have.'

'Young gents don't live at the Collige, they tell me?'

'No, there's no residence.'

'So naturally they want a plyce where they can 'ev a nibble, somewheres 'andy?'

'Yes. We have to go further into the town for a decent dinner.'

'Jest what I thought!' exclaimed Andrew, slapping his leg. 'With a establishment like that opposyte, there'd ought to be a medium-sized Spiers & Pond at this 'ere street corner for any man as knows 'is wye about. That's *my* idea, Godwin – see?'

Peak had as yet given but half an ear to his relative's discourse; he had answered mechanically, and only now was constrained to serious attention by a note of meaning in the last interrogative. He looked at the speaker; and Andrew, in the manner of one accustomed to regard life as a game of cunning, first winked with each eye, then extended one cheek with the pressure of his tongue. Sickened with disgust, Godwin turned suddenly away, – a movement entirely lost upon his uncle, who imagined the young man to be pondering a fruitful suggestion.

'I don't mind tellin' you, Godwin,' pursued Andrew presently, in a cautious voice, laying an open hand against his trousers-pocket, 'as I've been a-doin' pretty good business lytely. Been growin' a bit – see? I'm runnin' round an' keepin' my heyes open – understand? Thoughts I, now, if I could come acrosst a nicet little openin', somethink in the rest'rant line, *that's* what 'ud sewt me jest about down to the ground. I'm cut out for it – see? I've got the practical experience, and I've got the capital; and as soon as I got a squint of this little corner shop – understand what I mean?'

His eyes gleamed with eagerness which was too candid for the typically vulgar mind. In his self-satisfaction he exhibited a gross cordiality which might have made rather an agreeable impression on a person otherwise disinterested.

At this point the asthmatic woman reappeared, carrying a laden tray. Andrew at once entered into conversation with her, framing his remarks and queries so as to learn all he could concerning the state of the business and the disposition of its proprietors. His nephew, meanwhile, stung to the core with shame, kept apart, as if amusing himself with the prospect from the window, until summoned to partake of the meal. His uncle expressed contempt of everything laid before them.

'*This* ain't no wye of caterin' for young gents at Collige!' he exclaimed. 'If there ain't a openin' 'ere, then I never see one. Godwin, bo-oy, 'ow much longer'll it be before you're out of you're time over there?'

'It's uncertain – I can't say.'

'But ain't it understood as you stay till you've passed the top standard, or whatever it's called?'

'I really haven't made up my mind what to do.'

'But you'll be studyin' 'ere for another twelve months, I dessay?'

'Why do you ask?'

'Why? cos s'posin' I got 'old o' this 'ere little shop, or another like it close by, me an' you might come to an understandin' – see? It might be worth your while to give a 'int to the young gents as you're in with – eh?'

Godwin was endeavouring to masticate a piece of toast, but it turned to sawdust upon his palate. Of a sudden, when the bilious gloom of his countenance foretold anything but mirth, he burst into hard laughter. Andrew smote him jovially on the back.

'Tickles you, eh, bo-oy? "Peak's Refreshment an' Dinin' Rooms!" Everything tip-top, mind; respectable business, Godwin; nothing for nobody to be ashamed of – *that* wouldn't do, of course.'

The young man's laughter ended as abruptly as it had begun, but his visage was no longer clouded with bitter misery. A strange indifference seemed to have come upon him, and whilst the speculative uncle talked away with increasing excitement, he ate and drank heedlessly.

'Mother expects you to-morrow, she tells me,' said Andrew, when his companion's taciturnity had suggested a change of topic. 'Shouldn't wonder if you see me over at Twybridge again before long. I was to remember your awnt and your cousin Jowey to you. You wouldn't know Jowey? the sharpest lad of his age as ever I knowed, is Jowey. Your father 'ud a' took a delight in 'im, if 'e'd lived, that 'e would.'

For a quarter of an hour or so the dialogue was concerned with domestic history. Godwin gave brief reply to many questions, but asked none, not even such as civility required. The elder man, however, was unaffected by this reticence, and when at length his nephew pleaded an engagement as excuse for leave-taking he shook hands with much warmth. The two parted close by the shop, and Godwin, casting a glance at the now silent College, walked hastily towards his lodgings.

II

In the prosperous year of 1856, incomes of between a hundred and a hundred and fifty pounds were chargeable with a tax of elevenpence halfpenny in the pound: persons who enjoyed a revenue of a hundred and fifty or more had the honour of paying one and fourpence. Abatements there were none, and families supporting life on two pounds a week might in some cases, perchance, be reconciled to the mulct by considering how equitably its incidence was graduated.

Some, on the other hand, were less philosophical; for instance, the household consisting of Nicholas Peak, his wife, their three-year-old daughter, their newly-born son, and a blind sister of Nicholas, dependent upon him for sustenance. Mr Peak, aged thirty and now four years wedded, had a small cottage on the outskirts of Greenwich. He was employed as dispenser, at a salary of thirty-five shillings a week, by a medical man with a large practice. His income, therefore, fell considerably within the hundred pound limit; and, all things considered, it was not unreasonable that he should be allowed to expend the whole of this sum on domestic necessities. But it came to pass that Nicholas, in his greed of wealth, obtained supplementary employment, which benefited him to the extent of a yearly ten pounds. Called upon to render his statement to the surveyor of income-tax, he declared himself in possession of a hundred and one pounds per annum; consequently, he stood indebted to the Exchequer in the sum of four pounds, sixteen shillings, and ninepence. His countenance darkened, as also did that of Mrs Peak.

'This is wrong and cruel – dreadfully cruel!' cried the latter, with tears in her eyes.

'It is; but that's no new thing,' was the bitter reply.

'I think it's wrong of *you*, Nicholas. What need is there to say anything about that ten pounds? It's taking the food out of our mouths.'

Knowing only the letter of the law, Mr Peak answered sternly:

'My income is a hundred and one pounds. I can't sign my name to a lie.'

Picture the man. Tall, gaunt, with sharp intellectual features, and eyes of singular beauty, the face of an enthusiast – under given circumstances, of a hero. Poorly clad, of course, but with rigorous self-respect; his boots polished, *propria manu*, to the point of perfection; his linen washed and ironed by the indefatigable wife. Of simplest tastes, of most frugal habits, a few books the only luxury which he deemed indispensable; yet a most difficult man to live with, for to him applied precisely the description which Robert Burns gave of his own father; he was 'of stubborn, ungainly integrity and headlong irascibility'.

Ungainly, for his strong impulses towards culture were power-less to obliterate the traces of his rude origin. Born in a London alley, the son of a labourer burdened with a large family, he had made his way by sheer force of character to a position which would have seemed proud success but for the difficulty with which he kept himself alive. His parents were dead. Of his brothers, two had disappeared in the abyss, and one, Andrew, earned a hard livelihood as a journeyman baker; the elder of his sisters had married poorly, and the younger was his blind pensioner. Nicholas had found a wife of better birth than his own, a young woman with country kindred in decent circumstances, though she herself served as nursemaid in the house of the medical man who employed her future husband. He had taught himself the English language, so far as grammar went, but could not cast off the London accent; Mrs Peak was fortunate enough to speak with nothing worse than the note of the Midlands.

His bent led him to the study of history, politics, economics, and in that time of military outbreak he was frenzied by the conflict of his ideals with the state of things about him. A book frequently in his hands was Godwin's *Political Justice*, and when a son had been born to him he decided to name the child after that favourite author. In this way, at all events, he could find some expression for his hot defiance of iniquity.

He paid his income-tax, and felt a savage joy in the privation thus imposed upon his family. Mrs Peak could not forgive her husband, and in this case, though she had but dim appreciation of the point of honour involved, her censures doubtless fell on Nicholas's vulnerable spot; it was the perversity of arrogance, at least as much as honesty, that impelled him to incur taxation. His wife's perseverance in complaint drove him to stern impatience, and for a long time the peace of the household suffered.

When the boy Godwin was five years old, the death of his blind aunt came as a relief to means which were in every sense overtaxed. Twelve months later, a piece of unprecedented good fortune seemed to place the Peaks beyond fear of want, and at the same time to supply Nicholas with a fulfilment of hopeless desires. By the death of Mrs Peak's brother, they came into possession of a freehold house and about nine hundred pounds. The property was situated some twelve miles from the Midland town of Twybridge, and thither they at once removed. At Twybridge lived Mrs Peak's elder sister, Miss Cadman; but between this lady and her nearest kinsfolk there had been but slight correspondence – the deceased Cadman left her only a couple of hundred pounds. With capital at command, Nicholas Peak took a lease of certain fields near his house, and turned farmer. The study of chemistry had given a special bent to his economic speculations; he fancied himself endowed with exceptional aptitude for agriculture, and the scent of the furrow brought all his energies into feverish activity – activity which soon impoverished him: that was in the order of things. 'Ungainly integrity' and 'headlong irascibility' wrought the same results for the ex-dispenser as for the Ayrshire husbandman. His farming came to a chaotic end; and when the struggling man died, worn out at forty-three, his wife and children (there was now a younger boy, Oliver, named after the Protector) had no very bright prospects.

Things went better with them than might have been anticipated. To Mrs Peak her husband's death was not an occasion of unmingled mourning. For the last few years she had suffered severely from domestic discord, and when left at peace by bereavement she turned with a sense of liberation to the task of caring for her children's future. Godwin was just thirteen, Oliver was eleven; both had been well schooled, and with the help of friends they might soon be put in the way of self-support. The daughter, Charlotte, sixteen years of age, had accomplishments which would perhaps be profitable. The widow decided to make a home in Twybridge, where Miss Cadman kept a millinery shop. By means of this connection, Charlotte presently found employment for her skill in fine needlework. Mrs Peak was incapable of earning money, but the experiences of her early married life enabled her to make more than the most of the pittance at her disposal.

Miss Cadman was a woman of active mind, something of a busy-body – dogmatic, punctilious in her claims to respect, proud of the acknowledgment by her acquaintances that she was not as other tradespeople; her chief weakness was a fanatical ecclesiasticism, the common blight of English womanhood. Circumstances had allowed her a better education than generally falls to women of that standing, and in spite of her shop she succeeded in retaining the friendship of certain ladies long ago her schoolfellows. Among these were the Misses Lumb – middle-aged sisters, who lived at Twybridge on a small independence, their time chiefly devoted to the support of the Anglican Church. An eldest Miss Lumb had been fortunate enough to marry that growing potentate of the Midlands, Mr Job Whitelaw. Now Lady Whitelaw, she dwelt at Kingsmill, but her sisters frequently enjoyed the honour of entertaining her, and even Miss Cadman the milliner occasionally held converse with the baronet's wife. In this way it came to pass that the Widow Peak and her children were brought under the notice of persons who sooner or later might be of assistance to them.

Abounding in emphatic advice, Miss Cadman easily persuaded her sister that Godwin must go to school for at least two years longer. The boys had been at a boarding-school twenty miles away from their country home; it would be better for them now to be put under the care of some Twybridge teacher – such an one as Miss Cadman's acquaintances could recommend. For her own credit, the milliner was anxious that these nephews of hers should not be running about the town as errand-boys or the like, and with prudence there was no necessity for such degradation. An uncommon lad like Godwin (she imagined him named after the historic earl) must not be robbed of his fair chance in life; she would gladly spare a little money for his benefit; he was a boy to repay such expenditure.

Indeed it seemed probable. Godwin devoured books, and had a remarkable faculty for gaining solid information on any subject that took his fancy. What might be the special bent of his mind one could not yet discover. He read poetry with precocious gusto, but at the same time his aptitude for scientific pursuits was strongly marked. In botany, chemistry, physics, he made progress which the people about him, including his schoolmaster, were incapable of appreciating; and already the collection of books left by his father, most of them out of date, failed to satisfy his curiosity. It might be feared that tastes so discursive would be disadvantageous to a lad who must needs pursue some definite bread-study, and the strain of self-consciousness which grew strong in him was again a matter for concern. He cared nothing for boyish games and companionship; in the society of strangers – especially of females – he behaved with an excessive shyness which was easily mistaken for a surly temper. Reproof, correction, he could not endure, and it was fortunate that the decorum of his habits made remonstrance seldom needful.

Ludicrous as the project would have appeared to any unbiassed observer of character, Miss Cadman conceived a hope that Godwin might become a clergyman. From her point of view it was natural to assume that uncommon talents must be devoted to the service of the Church, and she would have gladly done her utmost for the practical furthering of such an end. Mrs Peak, though well aware that her son had imbibed the paternal prejudices, was disposed to entertain the same hope, despite solid obstacles. For several years she had nourished a secret antagonism to her husband's spirit of political, social, and religious rebellion, and in her widowhood she speedily became a pattern of the conservative female. It would have gratified her to discern any possibility of Godwin's assuming the priestly garb. And not alone on the ground of conscience. Long ago she had repented the marriage which connected her with such a family as that of the Peaks, and she ardently desired that the children, now exclusively her own, might enter life on a plane superior to their father's.

'Godwin, how would you like to go to College and be a clergyman?' she asked one Sunday afternoon, when an hour or two of congenial reading seemed to have put the boy into a gentle humour.

'To go to College' was all very well (diplomacy had prompted this preface), but the words that followed fell so alarmingly on Godwin's ear that he looked up with a resentful expression, unable to reply otherwise.

'You never thought of it, I suppose?' his mother faltered; for she often stood in awe of her son, who, though yet but fourteen, had much of his father's commanding severity.

'I don't want to be a parson,' came at length, bluntly.

'Don't use that word, Godwin.'

'Why not? It's quite a proper word. It comes from the Latin *persona*.'

The mother had enough discretion to keep silence, and Godwin, after in vain trying to settle to his book again, left the room with disturbed countenance.

He had now been attending the day-school for about a year, and was distinctly ahead of his coevals. A Christmas examination was on the point of being held, and it happened that a singular test of the lad's moral character coincided with the proof of his intellectual progress. In a neighbouring house lived an old man named Rawmarsh, kindly but rather eccentric; he had once done a good business as a printer, and now supported himself by such chance typographic work of a small kind as friends might put in his way. He conceived an affection for Godwin; often had the boy to talk with him of an evening. On one such occasion, Mr Rawmarsh opened a desk, took forth a packet of newly printed leaves, and with a mysterious air silently spread them before the boy's eyes. In an instant Godwin became aware that he was looking at the examination papers which a day or two hence would be set before him at school; he saw and recognised a passage from the book of Virgil which his class had been reading.

'That is *sub rosa*, you know,' whispered the old printer, with half averted face.

Godwin shrank away, and could not resume the conversation thus interrupted. On the following day he went about with a feeling of guilt. He avoided the sight of Mr Rawmarsh, for whom he had suddenly lost all respect, and suffered torments in the thought that he enjoyed an unfair advantage over his class-mates. The Latin passage happened to be one which he knew thoroughly well; there was no need, even had he desired, to 'look it up'; but in sitting down to the examination, he experienced a sense of shame and self-rebuke. So strong were the effects of this, that he voluntarily omitted the answer to a certain important question which he could have 'done' better than any of the other boys, thus endeavouring to adjust in his conscience the terms of competition, though in fact no such sacrifice was called for. He came out at the head of the class, but the triumph had no savour for him, and for many a year he was subject to a flush of mortification whenever this incident came back to his mind.

Mr Rawmarsh was not the only intelligent man who took an interest in Godwin. In a house which the boy sometimes visited with a school-fellow, lodged a notable couple named Gunnery – the husband about seventy, the wife five years older; they lived on a pension from a railway company. Mr Gunnery was a dabbler in many sciences, but had a special enthusiasm for geology. Two cabinets of stones and fossils gave evidence of his zealous travels about the British isles; he had even written a little hand-book of petrology which was for sale at certain booksellers' in Twybridge, and probably nowhere else. To him, about this time, Godwin began to resort, always sure of a welcome; and in the little uncarpeted room where Mr Gunnery pursued his investigations many a fateful lesson was given and received. The teacher understood the intelligence he had to deal with, and was delighted to convey, by the mode of suggested inference, sundry results of knowledge which it perhaps would not have been prudent to declare in plain, popular words.

Their intercourse was not invariably placid. The geologist had an irritable temper, and in certain states of the atmosphere his rheumatic twinges made it advisable to shun argument with him. Godwin, moreover, was distinguished by an instability of mood peculiarly trying to an old man's testy humour. Of a sudden, to Mr Gunnery's surprise and annoyance, he would lose all interest in this or that science. Thus, one day the lad declared himself unable to name two stones set before him, felspar and quartz, and when his instructor broke into angry impatience he turned sullenly away, exclaiming that he was tired of geology.

'Tired of geology?' cried Mr Gunnery, with flaming eyes. 'Then *I* am tired of *you*, Master Peak! Be off, and don't come again till I send for you!'

Godwin retired without a word. On the second day he was summoned back again, but his resentment of the dismissal rankled in him for a long time; injury to his pride was the wrong he found it hardest to forgive.

His schoolmaster, aware of the unusual pursuits which he added to the routine of lessons, gave him as a prize the English translation of a book by Figuier – *The World before the Deluge*. Strongly interested by the illustrations of the volume (fanciful scenes from the successive geologic periods), Godwin at once carried it to his scientific friend. 'Deluge?' growled Mr Gunnery. '*What* deluge? *Which* deluge?' But he restrained himself, handed the book coldly back, and began to talk of something else. All this was highly significant to Godwin, who of course began the perusal of his prize in a suspicious mood. Nor was he long before he sympathised with Mr Gunnery's distaste. Though too young to grasp the arguments at issue, his prejudices were strongly excited by the conventional Theism which pervades Figuier's work. Already it was the habit of his mind to associate popular dogma with intellectual shallowness; herein, as at every other point which fell within his scope, he had begun to scorn average people, and to pride himself intensely on views which he found generally condemned. Day by day he grew into a clearer understanding of the memories bequeathed to him by his father; he began to interpret remarks, details of behaviour, instances of wrath, which, though they had stamped themselves on his recollection, conveyed at the time no precise significance. The issue was that he hardened himself against the influence of his mother and his aunt, regarding them as in league against the free progress of his education.

As women, again, he despised these relatives. It is almost impossible for a bright-witted lad born in the lower middle class to escape this stage of development. The brutally healthy boy contemns the female sex because he sees it incapable of his own athletic sports, but Godwin was one of those upon whose awaking intellect is forced a perception of the brain-defect so general in women when they are taught few of life's graces and none of its serious concerns, – their paltry prepossessions, their vulgar sequaciousness, their invincible ignorance, their absorption in a petty self. And especially is this phase of thought to be expected in a boy whose heart blindly nourishes the seeds of poetical passion. It was Godwin's sincere belief that he held girls, as girls, in abhorrence. This meant that he dreaded their personal criticism, and that the spectacle of female beauty sometimes overcame him with a despair which he could not analyse. Matrons and elderly unmarried women were truly the objects of his disdain; in them he saw nothing but their shortcomings. Towards his mother he was conscious of no tenderness; of as little towards his sister, who often censured him with trenchant tongue; as for his aunt, whose admiration of him was modified by reticences, he could never be at ease in her company, so strong a dislike had he for her look, her voice, her ways of speech.

He would soon be fifteen years old. Mrs Peak was growing anxious, for she could no longer consent to draw upon her sister for a portion of the school fees, and no pertinent suggestion for the lad's future was made by any of the people who admired his cleverness. Miss Cadman still clung in a fitful way to the idea of making her nephew a cleric; she had often talked it over with the Misses Lumb, who of course held that 'any sacrifice' was justifiable with such a motive, and who suggested a hope that, by the instrumentality of Lady Whitelaw, a curacy might easily be obtained as soon as Godwin was old enough. But several years must pass before that Levitical stage could be reached; and then, after all, perhaps the younger boy, Oliver, placid of temper and notably pliant in mind, was better suited for the dignity of Orders. It was lamentable that Godwin should have become so intimate with that earth-burrowing Mr Gunnery, who certainly never attended either church or chapel, and who seemed to have imbued his pupil with immoral theories concerning the date of creation. Godwin held more decidedly aloof from his aunt, and had been heard by Charlotte to speak very disrespectfully of the Misses Lumb. In short, there was no choice but to discover an opening for him in some secular pursuit. Could he, perhaps, become an assistant teacher? Or must he 'go into an office'?

No common lad. A youth whose brain glowed like a furnace, whose heart throbbed with tumult of high ambitions, of inchoate desires; endowed with knowledge altogether exceptional for his years; a nature essentially militant, displaying itself in innumerable forms of callow intolerance – apt, assuredly, for some vigorous part in life, but as likely as not to rush headlong on traverse roads if no judicious mind assumed control of him. What is to be done with the boy?

All very well, if the question signified, in what way to provide for the healthy development of his manhood. Of course it meant nothing of the sort, but merely: What work can be found for him whereby he may earn his daily bread? We – his kinsfolk even, not to think of the world at large – can have no concern with his growth as an intellectual being; we are hard pressed to supply our own mouths with food; and now that we have done our recognised duty by him, it is high time that he learnt to fight for his own share of provender. Happily, he is of the robust sex; he can hit out right and left, and make standing-room. We have armed him with serviceable weapons, and now he must use them against the enemy – that is to say, against all mankind, who will quickly enough deprive him of sustenance if he fail in the conflict. We neither know, nor in great measure care, for what employment he is naturally marked. Obviously he cannot heave coals or sell dogs' meat, but with negative certainty not much else can be resolved, seeing how desperate is the competition for minimum salaries. He has been born, and he must eat. By what licensed channel may he procure the necessary viands?

Paternal relatives Godwin had as good as none. In quitting London, Nicholas Peak had ceased to hold communication with any of his own stock save the younger brother Andrew. With him he occasionally exchanged a letter, but Andrew's share in the correspondence was limited to ungrammatical and often unintelligible hints of numerous projects for money-making. Just after the removal of the bereaved family to Twybridge, they were surprised by a visit from Andrew, in answer to one of whose letters Mrs Peak had sent news of her husband's death. Though her dislike of the man amounted to loathing, the widow could not refuse him hospitality; she did her best, however, to prevent his coming in contact with anyone she knew. Andrew declared that he was at length prospering; he had started a coffee-shop at Dalston, in north-east London, and positively urged a proposal (well-meant, beyond doubt) that Godwin should be allowed to come to him and learn the business. Since then the Londoner had once again visited Twybridge, towards the end of Godwin's last school-year. This time he spoke of himself less hopefully, and declared a wish to transfer his business to some provincial town, where he thought his metropolitan experience might be of great value, in the absence of serious competition. It was not difficult to discover a family likeness between Andrew's instability and the idealism which had proved the ruin of Nicholas.

On this second occasion Godwin tried to escape a meeting with his uncle. Unable to do so, he sat mute, replying to questions monosyllabically. Mrs Peak's shame and annoyance, in face of this London-branded vulgarian, were but feeble emotions compared with those of her son. Godwin hated the man, and was in dread lest any school-fellow should come to know of such a connection. Yet delicacy prevented his uttering a word on the subject to his mother. Mrs Peak's silence after Andrew's departure made it uncertain how she regarded the obligation of kindred, and in any such matter as this the boy was far too sensitive to risk giving pain. But to his brother Oliver he spoke.

'What is the brute to us? When I'm a man, let him venture to come near me, and see what sort of a reception he'll get! I hate low, uneducated people! I hate them worse than the filthiest vermin! – don't you?'

Oliver, aged but thirteen, assented, as he habitually did to any question which seemed to await an affirmative.

'They ought to be swept off the face of the earth!' pursued

Godwin, sitting up in bed – for the dialogue took place about eleven o'clock at night. 'All the grown-up creatures, who can't speak proper English and don't know how to behave themselves, I'd transport them to the Falkland Islands,' – this geographic precision was a note of the boy's mind, – 'and let them die off as soon as possible. The children should be sent to school and purified, if possible; if not, they too should be got rid of.'

'You're an aristocrat, Godwin,' remarked Oliver, simply; for the elder brother had of late been telling him fearful stories from the French Revolution, with something of an anti-popular bias.

'I hope I am. I mean to be, that's certain. There's nothing I hate like vulgarity. That's why I can't stand Roper. When he beat me in mathematics last midsummer, I felt so ashamed I could hardly bear myself. I'm working like a nigger at algebra and Euclid this half, just because I think it would almost kill me to be beaten again by a low cad.'

This was perhaps the first time that Godwin found expression for the prejudice which affected all his thoughts and feelings. It relieved him to have spoken thus; henceforth he had become clear as to his point of view. By dubbing him aristocrat, Oliver had flattered him in the subtlest way. If indeed the title were justly his, as he instantly felt it was, the inference was plain that he must be an aristocrat of nature's own making – one of the few highly favoured beings who, in despite of circumstance, are pinnacled above mankind. In his ignorance of life, the boy visioned a triumphant career; an aristocrat *de jure* might possibly become one even in the common sense did he but pursue that end with sufficient zeal. And in his power of persistent endeavour he had no lack of faith.

The next day he walked with exalted head. Encountering the objectionable Roper, he smiled upon him contemptuously tolerant.

There being no hope of effective assistance from relatives, Mrs Peak turned for counsel to a man of business, with whom her husband had made acquaintance in his farming days, and who held a position of influence at Twybridge. This was Mr Moxey, manufacturing chemist, famous in the Midlands for his 'sheep and cattle dressings', and sundry other products of agricultural enterprise. His ill-scented, but lucrative, works were situated a mile out of the town; and within sight of the reeking chimneys stood a large, plain house, uncomfortably like an 'institution' of some kind, in which he dwelt with his five daughters. Thither, one evening, Mrs Peak betook herself, having learnt that Mr Moxey dined at five o'clock, and that he was generally to be found digging in his garden until sunset. Her reception was civil. The manufacturer – sparing of words, but with no unkindly face – requested that Godwin should be sent to see him, and promised to do his best to be of use. A talk with the boy strengthened his interest. He was surprised at Godwin's knowledge of chemistry, pleased with his general intelligence, and in the end offered to make a place for him at the works, where, though for a year or two his earnings must be small, he would gain experience likely to be of substantial use to him. Godwin did not find the proposal distasteful; it brought a change into his life, and the excitement of novelty; it flattered him with the show of release from pupilage. To Mr Moxey's he went.

The hours were not long, and it was understood that his theoretical studies should continue in the evening. Godwin's home was a very small house in a monotonous little street; a garret served as bedroom for the two boys, also as the elder one's laboratory. Servant Mrs Peak had none. She managed everything herself, as in the old Greenwich days, leaving Charlotte free to work at her embroidery. Godwin took turns with Oliver at blacking the shoes.

As a matter of course the boys accompanied their mother each Sunday morning to the parish church, and this ceremony was becoming an insufferable tax on Godwin's patience. It was not only that he hated the name of religion, and scorned with much fierceness all who came in sympathetic contact therewith; the loss of time seemed to him an oppressive injury, especially now that he began to suffer from restricted leisure. He would not refuse to obey his mother's wish, but the sullenness of his Sabbatic demeanour made the whole family uncomfortable. As often as possible he feigned illness. He tried the effect of dolorous sighs and groans; but Mrs Peak could not dream of conceding a point which would have seemed to her the condonation of deadly sin. 'When I am a man!' muttered Godwin. 'Ah! when I am a man!'

A year had gone by, and the routine to which he was bound began to have a servile flavour. His mind chafed at subjugation to commercial interests. Sick of 'sheep and cattle dressings', he grew tired of chemistry altogether, and presently of physical science in general. His evenings were given to poetry and history; he took up the classical schoolbooks again, and found a charm in Latin syntax hitherto unperceived. It was plain to him now how he had been wronged by the necessity of leaving school when his education had but just begun.

Discontent becoming ripe for utterance, he unbosomed himself to Mr Gunnery. It happened that the old man had just returned from a visit to Kingsmill, where he had spent a week in the museum, then newly enriched with geologic specimens. After listening in silence to the boy's complaints, and pondering for a long time, he began to talk of Whitelaw College.

'Does it cost much to study there?' Godwin asked, gloomily.

'No great sum, I think. There are scholarships to be had.'

Mr Gunnery threw out the suggestion carelessly. Knowing the hazards of life, he could not quite justify himself in encouraging Godwin's restiveness.

'Scholarships? For free study?'

'Yes; but that wouldn't mean free living, you know. Students don't live at the College.'

'How do you go in for a scholarship?'

The old man replied, meditatively, 'If you were to pass the Cambridge Local Examination, and to get the first place in the Kingsmill district, you would have three years of free study at Whitelaw.'

'Three years?' shouted Godwin, springing up from his chair.

'But how could you live, my boy?'

Godwin sat down again, and let his head fall forward.

How to keep oneself alive during a few years of intellectual growth? – a question often asked by men of mature age, but seldom by a lad of sixteen. No matter. He resolved that he would study for this Cambridge Local Examination, and have a try for the scholarship. His attainments were already up to the standard required for average success in such competitions. On obtaining a set of 'papers', he found that they looked easy enough. Could he not come out first in the Kingsmill district?

He worked vigorously at special subjects; aid was needless, but he wished for more leisure. Not a word to any member of his household. When his mother discovered that he was reading in the bedroom till long past midnight, she made serious objection on the score of health and on that of gas bills. Godwin quietly asserted that work he must, and that if necessary he would buy candles out of his pocket-money. He had unexpectedly become more grave, more restrained; he even ceased to grumble about going to church, having found that service time could be utilised for committing to memory lists of dates and the like, jotted down on a slip of paper. When the time for the examination drew near, he at length told his mother to what end he had been labouring, and asked her to grant him the assistance necessary for his journey and the sojourn at Kingsmill; the small sum he had been able to save, after purchase of books, would not suffice. Mrs Peak knew not whether to approve her son's ambition or to try to repress it. She would welcome an improval in his prospects, but, granting success, how was he to live whilst profiting by a scholarship? And again, what did he propose to make of himself when he had spent three years in study?

'In any case,' was Godwin's reply, 'I should be sure of a good place as a teacher. But I think I might try for something in the Civil Service; there are all sorts of positions to be got.'

It was idle to discuss the future whilst the first step was still speculative. Mrs Peak consented to favour the attempt, and what was more, to keep it a secret until the issue should be known. It was needful to obtain leave of absence from Mr Moxey, and Godwin, when making the request, stated for what purpose he was going to Kingsmill, though without explaining the hope which had encouraged his studies. The project seemed laudable, and his employer made no difficulties.

Godwin just missed the scholarship; of candidates in the prescribed district, he came out second.

Grievous was the disappointment. To come so near success exasperated his impatient temper, and for a few days his bondage at the chemical works seemed intolerable; he was ready for almost any venture that promised release and new scope for his fretting energies. But at the moment when nervous irritation was most acute, a remarkable act of kindness suddenly restored to him all the hopes he had abandoned. One Saturday afternoon he was summoned from his surly retreat in the garret, to speak with a visitor. On entering the sitting-room, he found his mother in company with Miss Cadman and the Misses Lumb, and from the last-mentioned ladies, who spoke with amiable alternation, he learnt that they were commissioned by Sir Job Whitelaw to offer for his acceptance a three-years' studentship at Whitelaw College. Affected by her son's chagrin, Mrs Peak had disclosed the story to her sister, who had repeated it to the Misses Lumb, who in turn had made it the subject of a letter to Lady Whitelaw. It was an annual practice with Sir Job to discover some promising lad whom he could benefit by the payment of his fees for a longer or shorter period of college study. The hint from Twybridge came to him just at the suitable time, and, on further inquiry, he decided to make proffer of this advantage to Godwin Peak. The only condition was that arrangements should be made by the student's relatives for his support during the proposed period.

This generosity took away Godwin's breath. The expenditure it represented was trifling, but from a stranger in Sir Job's position it had something which recalled to so fervent a mind the poetry of Medicean patronage. For the moment no faintest doubt gave warning to his self-respect; he was eager to accept nobly a benefaction nobly intended.

Miss Cadman, flattered by Sir Job's attention to her nephew, now came forward with an offer to contribute towards Godwin's livelihood. Her supplement would eke into adequacy such slender allowance as the widow's purse could afford. Details were privately discussed, resolves were taken. Mr Moxey, when it was made known to him, without explanation, that Godwin was to be sent to Whitelaw College, behaved with kindness; he at once released the lad, and added a present to the salary that was due. Proper acknowledgment of the Baronet's kindness was made by the beneficiary himself, who wrote a letter giving truer testimony of his mental calibre than would have been offered had he expressed himself by word of mouth. A genial reply summoned him to an interview as soon as he should have found an abode in Kingsmill. The lodging he had occupied during the examination was permanently secured, and a new period of Godwin's life began.

For two years, that is to say until his age drew towards nineteen, Peak pursued the Arts curriculum at Whitelaw. His mood on entering decided his choice, which was left free to him. Experience of utilitarian chemistry had for the present made his liberal tastes predominant, and neither the splendid laboratories of Whitelaw nor the repute of its scientific Professors tempted him to what had once seemed his natural direction. In the second year, however, he enlarged his course by the addition of one or two classes not included in Sir Job's design; these were paid for out of a present made to him by Mr Gunnery.

It being customary for the regular students of Whitelaw to

graduate at London University, Peak passed his matriculation, and worked on for the preliminary test then known as First BA. In the meanwhile he rose steadily, achieving distinction in the College. The more observant of his teachers remarked him even where he fell short of academic triumph, and among his fellow-students he had the name of a stern 'sweater', one not easily beaten where he had set his mind on excelling. He was not generally liked, for his mood appeared unsocial, and a repelling arrogance was sometimes felt in his talk. No doubt – said the more fortunate young men – he came from a very poor home, and suffered from the narrowness of his means. They noticed that he did not subscribe to the College Union, and that he could never join in talk regarding the diversions of the town. His two or three intimates were chosen from among those contemporaries who read hard and dressed poorly.

The details of Godwin's private life were noteworthy. Accustomed hitherto to a domestic circle, at Kingsmill he found himself isolated, and it was not easy for him to surrender all at once the comforts of home. For a time he felt as though his ambition were a delinquency which entailed the punishment of loneliness. Nor did his relations with Sir Job Whitelaw tend to mitigate this feeling. In his first interview with the Baronet, Godwin showed to little advantage. A deadly bashfulness forbade him to be natural either in attitude or speech. He felt his dependence in a way he had not foreseen; the very clothes he wore, then fresh from the tailor's, seemed to be the gift of charity, and their stiffness shamed him. A man of the world, Sir Job could make allowance for these defects. He understood that the truest kindness would be to leave a youth such as this to the forming influences of the College. So Godwin barely had a glimpse of Lady Whitelaw in her husband's study, and thereafter for many months he saw nothing of his benefactors. Subsequently he was twice invited to interviews with Sir Job, who talked with kindness and commendation. Then came the Baronet's death. Godwin received an assurance that this event would be no check upon his career, but he neither saw nor heard directly from Lady Whitelaw.

Not a house in Kingsmill opened hospitable doors to the lonely student; nor was anyone to blame for this. With no family had he friendly acquaintance. When, towards the end of his second year, he grew sufficiently intimate with Buckland Warricombe to walk out with him to Thornhaw, it could be nothing more than a scarcely welcome exception to the rule of solitude. Impossible for him to cultivate the friendship of such people as the Warricombes, with their large and joyous scheme of life. Only at a hearth where homeliness and cordiality united to unthaw his proud reserve could Godwin perchance have found the companionship he needed. Many such homes existed in Kingsmill, but no kindly fortune led the young man within the sphere of their warmth.

His lodgings were in a very ugly street in the ugliest outskirts of the town; he had to take a long walk through desolate districts (brick-yard, sordid pasture, degenerate village) before he could refresh his eyes with the rural scenery which was so great a joy to him as almost to be a necessity. The immediate vicinage offered nothing but monotone of grimy, lower middle-class dwellings, occasionally relieved by a public-house. He occupied two rooms, not unreasonably clean, and was seldom disturbed by the attentions of his landlady.

An impartial observer might have wondered at the negligence which left him to arrange his life as best he could, notwithstanding youth and utter inexperience. It looked indeed as if there were no one in the world who cared what became of him. Yet this was merely the result of his mother's circumstances, and of his own character. Mrs Peak could do no more than make her small remittances, and therewith send an occasional admonition regarding his health. She did not, in fact, conceive the state of things, imagining that the authority and supervisal of the College extended over her son's daily existence, whereas it was possible for Godwin to frequent lectures or not, to study or to waste his time, pretty much as he chose, subject only to official inquiry if his attendance became frequently irregular. His independent temper, and the seeming maturity of his mind, supplied another excuse for the imprudent confidence which left him to his own resources. Yet the perils of the situation were great indeed. A youth of less concentrated purpose, more at the mercy of casual allurement, would probably have gone to wreck amid trials so exceptional.

Trials not only of his moral nature. The sums of money with which he was furnished fell short of a reasonable total for bare necessities. In the calculation made by Mrs Peak and her sister, outlay on books had practically been lost sight of; it was presumed that ten shillings a term would cover this item. But Godwin could not consent to be at a disadvantage in his armoury for academic contest. The first mouth saw him compelled to contract his diet, that he might purchase books; thenceforth he rarely had enough to eat. His landlady supplied him with breakfast, tea, and supper – each repast of the very simplest kind; for dinner it was understood that he repaired to some public table, where meat and vegetables, with perchance a supplementary sweet when nature demanded it, might be had for about a shilling. That shilling was not often at his disposal. Dinner as it is understood by the comfortably clad, the 'regular meal' which is a part of English respectability, came to be represented by a small pork-pie, or even a couple of buns, eaten at the little shop over against the College. After a long morning of mental application this was poor refreshment; the long afternoon which followed, again spent in rigorous study, could not but reduce a growing frame to ravenous hunger. Tea and buttered bread were the means of appeasing it, until another four hours' work called for reward in the shape of bread and cheese. Even yet the day's toil was not ended. Godwin sometimes read long after midnight, with the result that, when at length he tried to sleep, exhaustion of mind and body kept him for a long time feverishly wakeful.

These hardships he concealed from the people at Twybridge. Complaint, it seemed to him, would be ungrateful, for sacrifices were already made on his behalf. His father, as he well remembered, was wont to relate, with a kind of angry satisfaction, the miseries through which he had fought his way to education and the income-tax. Old enough now to reflect with compassionate understanding upon that life of conflict, Godwin resolved that he too would bear the burdens inseparable from poverty, and in some moods was even glad to suffer as his father had done. Fortunately he had a sound basis of health, and hunger and vigils would not easily affect his constitution. If, thus hampered, he could outstrip competitors who had every advantage of circumstance, the more glorious his triumph.

Sunday was an interval of leisure. Rejoicing in deliverance from Sabbatarianism, he generally spent the morning in a long walk, and the rest of the day was devoted to non-collegiate reading. He had subscribed to a circulating library, and thus obtained new publications recommended to him in the literary paper which again taxed his stomach. Mere class-work did not satisfy him. He was possessed with throes of spiritual desire, impelling him towards that world of unfettered speculation which he had long indistinctly imagined. It was a great thing to learn what the past could teach, to set himself on the common level of intellectual men; but he understood that college learning could not be an end in itself, that the Professors to whom he listened either did not speak out all that was in their minds, or, if they did, were far from representing the advanced guard of modern thought. With eagerness he at length betook himself to the teachers of philosophy and of geology. Having paid for these lectures out of his own pocket, he felt as if he had won a privilege beyond the conventional course of study, an initiation to a higher sphere of intellect. The result was disillusion. Not even in these class-rooms could he hear the word for which he waited, the bold annunciation of newly discovered law, the science which had completely broken with tradition. He came away unsatisfied, and brooded upon the possibilities which would open for him when he was no longer dependent.

His evening work at home was subject to a disturbance which would have led him to seek other lodgings, could he have hoped to find any so cheap as these. The landlady's son, a lank youth of the clerk species, was wont to amuse himself from eight to ten with practice on a piano. By dint of perseverance he had learned to strum two or three hymnal melodies popularised by American evangelists; occasionally he even added the charm of his voice, which had a pietistic nasality not easily endured by an ear of any refinement. Not only was Godwin harassed by the recurrence of these performances; the tunes worked themselves into his brain, and sometimes throughout a whole day their burden clanged and squalled incessantly on his mental hearing. He longed to entreat forbearance from the musician, but an excess of delicacy – which always ruled his behaviour – kept him silent. Certain passages in the classics, and many an elaborate mathematical formula, long retained for him an association with the cadences of revivalist hymnody.

Like all proud natures condemned to solitude, he tried to convince himself that he had no need of society, that he despised its attractions, and could be self-sufficing. So far was this from the truth that he often regarded with bitter envy those of his fellow-students who had the social air, who conversed freely among their equals, and showed that the pursuits of the College were only a part of their existence. These young men were either preparing for the University, or would pass from Whitelaw to business, profession, official training; in any case, a track was marked out for them by the zealous care of relatives and friends, and their efforts would always be aided, applauded, by a kindly circle. Some of them Godwin could not but admire, so healthful were they, so bright of intellect, and courteous in manner, – a type distinct from any he had formerly observed. Others were antipathetic to him. Their aggressive gentility conflicted with the wariness of his self-esteem; such a one, for instance, as Bruno Chilvers, the sound of whose mincing voice, as he read in the class, so irritated him that at times he had to cover his ears. Yet, did it chance that one of these offensive youths addressed a civil word to him, on the instant his prejudice was disarmed, and his emotions flowed forth in a response to which he would gladly have given free expression. When he was invited to meet the relatives of Buckland Warricombe, shyness prepossessed him against them; but the frank kindness of his reception moved him, and on going away he was ashamed to have replied so boorishly to attentions so amiably meant. The same note of character sounded in what personal intercourse he had with the Professors. Though his spirit of criticism was at times busy with these gentlemen, he had for most of them a profound regard; and to be elected by one or other for a word of commendation, a little private assistance, a well-phrased inquiry as to his progress, always made his heart beat high with gratitude. They were his first exemplars of finished courtesy, of delicate culture; and he could never sufficiently regret that no one of them was aware how thankfully he recognised his debt.

In longing for the intimacy of refined people, he began to modify his sentiments with regard to the female sex. His first prize-day at Whitelaw was the first occasion on which he sat in an assembly where ladies (as he understood the title) could be seen and heard. The impression he received was deep and lasting. On the seat behind him were two girls whose intermittent talk held him with irresistible charm throughout the whole ceremony. He had not imagined that girls could display such intelligence, and the sweet clearness of their intonation, the purity of their accent, the grace of their habitual phrases, were things altogether beyond his experience. This was not the English he had been wont to hear on female lips. His mother and his aunt spoke with propriety; their associates were soft-tongued; but here was something quite different from inoffensiveness of tone and diction. Godwin appreciated the differentiating cause. These young ladies behind him had been trained from the cradle to speak for the delight of fastidious ears; that they should be grammatical was not enough – they must excel in the art of conversational music. Of course there existed a world where only such speech was interchanged, and how inestimably happy those men to whom the sphere was native!

When the proceedings were over, he drew aside and watched the two girls as they mingled with acquaintances; he kept them in view until they left the College. An emotion such as this he had never known; for the first time in his life he was humiliated without embitterment.

The bitterness came when he had returned to his home in the back street of Twybridge, and was endeavouring to spend the holidays in a hard 'grind'. He loathed the penurious simplicity to which his life was condemned; all familiar circumstances were become petty, coarse, vulgar, in his eyes; the contrast with the idealised world of his ambition plunged him into despair. Even Mr Gunnery seemed an ignoble figure when compared with the Professors of Whitelaw, and his authority in the sciences was now subjected to doubt. However much or little might result from the three years at College, it was clear to Godwin that his former existence had passed into infinite remoteness; he was no longer fit for Twybridge, no longer a companion for his kindred. Oliver, whose dulness as a schoolboy gave no promise of future achievements, was now learning the business of a seedsman; his brother felt ashamed when he saw him at work in the shop, and had small patience with the comrades to whom Oliver dedicated his leisure. Charlotte was estranged by religious differences. Only for his mother did the young man show increased consideration. To his aunt he endeavoured to be grateful, but his behaviour in her presence was elaborate hypocrisy. Hating the necessity for this, he laid the blame on fortune, which had decreed his birth in a social sphere where he must ever be an alien.

III

With the growth of his militant egoism, there had developed in Godwin Peak an excess of nervous sensibility which threatened to deprive his character of the initiative rightly belonging to it. Self-assertion is the practical complement of self-esteem. To be largely endowed with the latter quality, yet constrained by a coward delicacy to repress it, is to suffer martyrdom at the pleasure of every robust assailant, and in the end be driven to the refuge of a moody solitude. That encounter with his objectionable uncle after the prize distribution at Whitelaw showed how much Godwin had lost of the natural vigour which declared itself at Andrew Peak's second visit to Twybridge, when the boy certainly would not have endured his uncle's presence but for hospitable considerations and the respect due to his mother. The decision with which he then unbosomed himself to Oliver, still characterised his thoughts, but he had not courage to elude the dialogue forced upon him, still less to make known his resentment of the man's offensive vulgarity. He endured in silence, his heart afire with scornful wrath.

The affliction could not have befallen him at a time when he was less capable of supporting it resignedly. Notwithstanding his noteworthy success in two classes, it seemed to him that he had lost everything – that the day was one of signal and disgraceful defeat. In any case that sequence of second prizes must have filled him with chagrin, but to be beaten thus repeatedly by such a fellow as Bruno Chilvers was humiliation intolerable. A fopling, a mincer of effeminate English, a rote-repeater of academic catch-words – bah! The by-examinations of the year had whispered presage, but Peak always felt that he was not putting forth his strength; when the serious trial came he would show what was really in him. Too late he recognised his error, though he tried not to admit it. The extra subjects had exacted too much of him; there was a limit to his powers. Within the College this would be well enough understood, but to explain a disagreeable fact is not to change it; his name was written in pitiful subordination. And as for the public assembly – he would have sacrificed some years of his life to have stepped forward in facile supremacy, beneath the eyes of those clustered ladies. Instead of that, they had looked upon his shame; they had interchanged glances of amusement at each repetition of his defeat; had murmured comments in their melodious speech; had ended by losing all interest in him – as intuition apprised him was the wont of women.

As soon as he had escaped from his uncle, he relapsed into musing upon the position to which he was condemned when the new session came round. Again Chilvers would be in the same classes with him, and, as likely as not, with the same result. In the meantime, they were both 'going in' for the First BA; he had no fear of failure, but it might easily happen that Chilvers would achieve higher distinction. With an eye to awards that might be won – substantial cash-annuities – he was reading for Honours; but it seemed doubtful whether he could present himself, as the second examination was held only in London. Chilvers would of course be an Honours candidate. He would smile – confound him! – at an objection on the score of the necessary journey to London. Better to refrain altogether than again to see Chilvers come out ahead. General surprise would naturally be excited, questions asked on all hands. How would it sound: 'I simply couldn't afford to go up'—?

At this point of the meditation he had reached his lodgings; he admitted himself with a latch-key, turned into his murky sitting-room, and sat down.

The table was laid for tea, as usual. Though he might have gone to Twybridge this evening, he had preferred to stay overnight, for an odd reason. At a theatre in Kingsmill a London company, headed by an actress of some distinction, was to perform *Romeo and Juliet*, and he purposed granting himself this indulgence before leaving the town. The plan was made when his eye fell upon the advertisement, a few days ago. He then believed it probable that an evening at the theatre would appropriately follow upon a day of victory. His interest in the performance had collapsed, but he did not care to alter his arrangements.

The landlady came in bearing the tea-pot. He wanted nothing, yet could not exert himself to say so.

But he was losing sight of a menace more formidable than defeat by Chilvers. What was it his blackguard uncle had said? Had the fellow really threatened to start an eating-house opposite the College, and flare his name upon a placard? 'Peak's Dining and Refreshment Rooms' – merciful heavens!

Again the mood of laughter came upon him. Why, here was a solution of all difficulties, as simple as unanticipated. If indeed that awful thing came to pass, farewell to Whitelaw! What possibility of pursuing his studies when every class-companion, every Professor, – nay, the very porters, – had become aware that he was nephew to the man who supplied meals over the way? Moral philosophy had no prophylactic against an ordeal such as this. Could the most insignificant lad attending lectures afford to disregard such an occasion of ridicule and contempt?

But the scheme would not be realised; it sounded too unlikely. Andrew Peak was merely a loose-minded vagabond, who might talk of this and that project for making money, but would certainly never quit his dirty haunts in London. Godwin asked himself angrily why he had submitted to the fellow's companionship. This absurd delicacy must be corrected before it became his tyrant. The idea of scrupling to hurt the sensibilities of Andrew Peak! The man was coarse-hided enough to undergo kicking, and then take sixpence in compensation, – not a doubt of it. This detestable tie of kindred must no longer be recognised. He would speak gravely to his mother about it. If Andrew again presented himself at the house he should be given plainly to understand that his visits were something less than welcome, – if necessary, a downright blunt word must effect their liberation. Godwin felt strong enough for that, musing here alone. And, student-like, he passed on to debate the theory of the problem. Andrew was his father's brother, but what is a mere tie of blood if nature has alienated two persons by a subtler distinction? By the dead man, Andrew had never been loved or esteemed; memory supplied proof of this. The widow shrank from him. No obligation of any kind lay upon them to tolerate the London ruffian. – Enough; he should be got rid of!

Alternating his causes of misery, which – he could not quite forget – might blend for the sudden transformation of his life, Godwin let the tea grow cold upon the table, until it was time, if he still meant to visit the theatre, for setting forth. He had no mind to go, but as little to sit here and indulge harassing reflection. With an effort, he made ready and left the house.

The cost of his seat at the theatre was two shillings. So nicely had he adjusted the expenses of these last days that, after paying the landlady's bill to-morrow morning, there would remain to him but a few pence more than the money needed for his journey home. Walking into the town, he debated with himself whether it were not better to save this florin. But as he approached the pit door, the spirit of pleasure revived in him; he had seen but one of Shakespeare's plays, and he believed (naturally at his age) that to see a drama acted was necessary for its full appreciation. Sidling with affected indifference, he added himself to the crowd.

To stand thus, expectant of the opening doors, troubled him with a sense of shame. To be sure, he was in the spiritual company of Charles Lamb, and of many another man of brains who has waited under the lamp. But contact with the pittites of Kingsmill offended his instincts; he resented this appearance of inferiority to people who came at their leisure, and took seats in the better parts of the house. When a neighbour addressed him with a meaningless joke which defied grammar, he tried to grin a friendly answer, but inwardly shrank. The events of the day had increased his sensibility to such impressions. Had he triumphed over Bruno Chilvers, he could have behaved this evening with a larger humanity.

The fight for entrance – honest British stupidity, crushing ribs and rending garments in preference to seemly order of progress – enlivened him somewhat, and sent him laughing to his conquered place; but before the curtain rose he was again depressed by the sight of a familiar figure in the stalls, a fellow-student who sat there with mother and sister, black-uniformed, looking very much a gentleman. 'I, of course, am not a gentleman,' he said to himself, gloomily. Was there any chance that he might some day take his ease in that orthodox fashion? Inasmuch as it was conventionality, he scorned it; but the privileges which it represented had strong control of his imagination. That lady and her daughter would follow the play with intelligence. To exchange comments with them would be a keen delight. As for him – he had a shop-boy on one hand and a grocer's wife on the other.

By the end he had fallen into fatigue. Amid clamour of easily-won applause he made his way into the street, to find himself in a heavy downpour of rain. Having no umbrella, he looked about for a sheltered station, and the glare of a neighbouring public-house caught his eye; he was thirsty, and might as well refresh body and spirit with a glass of beer, an unwonted indulgence which had the pleasant semblance of dissipation. Arrived at the bar he came upon two acquaintances, who, to judge by their flushed cheeks and excited voices, had been celebrating jovially the close of their academic labours. They hailed him.

'Hollo, Peak! Come and help us to get sober before bedtime!'

They were not exactly studious youths, but neither did they belong to the class that Godwin despised, and he had a comrade-like feeling for them. In a few minutes his demeanour was wholly changed. A glass of hot whisky acted promptly upon his nervous system, enabled him to forget vexations, and attuned him to kindred sprightliness. He entered merrily into the talk of a time of life which is independent of morality – talk distinct from that of the blackguard, but equally so from that of the reflective man. His first glass had several successors. The trio rambled arm in arm from one place of refreshment to another, and presently sat down in hearty fellowship to a supper of such viands as recommend themselves at bibulous midnight. Peak was drawing recklessly upon the few coins that remained to him; he must leave his landlady's claim undischarged, and send the money from home. Prudence be hanged! If one cannot taste amusement once in a twelvemonth, why live at all?

He reached his lodgings, at something after one o'clock, drenched with rain, gloriously indifferent to that and all other chances of life. Pooh! his system had been radically wrong. He should have allowed himself recreation once a week or so; he would have been all the better for it, body and mind. Books and that kind of thing are all very well in their way, but one must live; he had wasted too much of his youth in solitude. *O mihi prœteritos referat si Jupiter annos!* Next session he would arrange things better. Success in examinations – what trivial fuss when one looked at it from the right point of view! And he had fretted himself into misery, because Chilvers had got more 'marks', – ha, ha, ha!

The morrow's waking was lugubrious enough. Headache and nausea weighed upon him. Worse still, a scrutiny of his pockets showed that he had only the shamefaced change of half-a-crown wherewith to transport himself and his belongings to Twybridge. Now, the railway fare alone was three shillings; the needful cab demanded eighteenpence. O idiot!

And he hated the thought of leaving his bill unpaid; the more so because it was a trifling sum, a week's settlement. To put himself under however brief an obligation to a woman such as the landlady gnawed at his pride. Not that only. He had no business to make a demand upon his mother for this additional sum. But there was no way of raising the money; no one of whom he could borrow it; nothing he could afford to sell – even if courage had supported him through such a transaction. Triple idiot!

Bread turned to bran upon his hot palate; he could only swallow cups of coffee. With trembling hands he finished the packing of his box and portmanteau, then braced himself to the dreaded interview. Of course, it involved no difficulty, the words once uttered; but, when he was left alone again, he paced the room for a few minutes in flush of mortification. It had made his headache worse.

The mode of his homeward journey he had easily arranged. His baggage having been labelled for Twybridge, he himself would book as far as his money allowed, then proceed on foot for the remaining distance. With the elevenpence now in his pocket he could purchase a ticket to a little town called Dent, and by a calculation from the railway tariff he concluded that from Dent to Twybridge was some five-and-twenty miles. Well and good. At the rate of four miles an hour it would take him from half-past eleven to about six o'clock. He could certainly reach home in time for supper.

At Dent station, ashamed to ask (like a tramp) the way to so remote a place as Twybridge, he jotted down a list of intervening railway stoppages, and thus was enabled to support the semblance of one who strolls on for his pleasure. A small hand-bag he was obliged to carry, and the clouded sky made his umbrella a requisite. On he trudged steadily, for the most part by muddy ways, now through a pleasant village, now in rural solitude. He had had the precaution, at breakfast time, to store some pieces of bread in his pocket, and after two or three hours this resource was welcome. Happily the air and exercise helped him to get rid of his headache. A burst of sunshine in the afternoon would have made him reasonably cheerful, but for the wretched meditations surviving from yesterday.

He pondered frequently on his spasmodic debauch, repeating, as well as memory permitted, all his absurdities of speech and action. Defiant self-justification was now far to seek. On the other hand, he perceived very clearly how easy it would be for him to lapse by degrees of weakened will into a ruinous dissoluteness. Anything of that kind would mean, of course, the abandonment of his ambitions. All he had to fight the world with was his brain; and only by incessant strenuousness in its exercise had he achieved the moderate prominence declared in yesterday's ceremony. By birth, by station, he was of no account; if he chose to sink, no influential voice would deplore his falling off or remind him of what he owed to himself. Chilvers, now – what a wide-spreading outcry, what calling upon gods and men, would be excited by any defection of that brilliant youth! Godwin Peak must make his own career, and that he would hardly do save by efforts greater than the ordinary man can put forth. The ordinary man? – Was he in any respect extraordinary? were his powers noteworthy? It was the first time that he had deliberately posed this question to himself, and for answer came a rush of confident blood, pulsing through all the mechanism of his being.

The train of thought which occupied him during this long trudge was to remain fixed in his memory; in any survey of the years of pupilage this recollection would stand prominently forth, associated, moreover, with one slight incident which at the time seemed a mere interruption of his musing. From a point on the high-road he observed a small quarry, so excavated as to present an interesting section; though weary, he could not but turn aside to examine these strata. He knew enough of the geology of the county to recognise the rocks and reflect with understanding upon their position; a fragment in his hand, he sat down to rest for a moment. Then a strange fit of brooding came over him. Escaping from the influences of personality, his imagination wrought back through eras of geologic time, held him in a vision of the infinitely remote, shrivelled into insignificance all but the one fact of inconceivable duration. Often as he had lost himself in such reveries, never yet had he passed so wholly under the dominion of that awe which attends a sudden triumph of the pure intellect. When at length he rose, it was with wide, blank eyes, and limbs partly numbed. These needed half-an-hour's walking before he could recover his mood of practical self-search.

Until the last moment he could not decide whether to let his mother know how he had reached Twybridge. His arrival corresponded pretty well with that of a train by which he might have come. But when the door opened to him, and the familiar faces smiled their welcome, he felt that he must have nothing to do with paltry deceit; he told of his walk, explaining it by the simple fact that this morning he had found himself short of money. How that came to pass, no one inquired. Mrs Peak, shocked at such martyrdom, tended him with all motherly care; for once, Godwin felt that it was good to have a home, however simple.

This amiable frame of mind was not likely to last beyond the first day. Matter of irritation soon enough offered itself, as was invariably the case at Twybridge. It was pleasant enough to be fêted as the hero of the family, to pull out a Kingsmill newspaper and exhibit the full report of prize-day at Whitelaw, with his own name, in very small type, demanding the world's attention, and finally to exhibit the volumes in tree-calf which his friend the librarian had forwarded to him. But domestic circumstances soon made assault upon his nerves, and trial of his brief patience.

First of all, there came an unexpected disclosure. His sister Charlotte had affianced herself to a young man of Twybridge, one Mr Cusse, whose prospects were as slender as his present means. Mrs Peak spoke of the affair in hushed privacy, with shaking of the head and frequent sighs, for to her mind Mr Cusse had few even personal recommendations. He was a draper's assistant. Charlotte had made his acquaintance on occasions of church festivity, and urged the fact of his zeal in Sunday-school tuition as sufficient reply to all doubts. As he listened, Godwin bit his lips.

'Does he come here, then?' was his inquiry.

'Once or twice a week. I haven't felt able to say anything against it, Godwin. I suppose it will be a very long engagement.'

Charlotte was just twenty-two, and it seemed probable that she knew her own mind; in any case, she was of a character which would only be driven to obstinacy by adverse criticism. Godwin learnt that his aunt Emily (Miss Cadman) regarded this connection with serious disapproval. Herself a shopkeeper, she might have been expected to show indulgence to a draper's assistant, but, so far from this, her view of Mr Cusse was severely scornful. She had nourished far other hopes for Charlotte, who surely at her age (Miss Cadman looked from the eminence of five-and-forty) should have been less precipitate. No undue harshness had been exhibited by her relatives, but Charlotte took a stand which sufficiently declared her kindred with Godwin. She held her head higher than formerly, spoke with habitual decision which bordered on snappishness, and at times displayed the absent-mindedness of one who in silence suffers wrong.

There passed but a day or two before Godwin was brought face to face with Mr Cusse, who answered too well to the idea Charlotte's brother had formed of him. He had a very smooth and shiny forehead, crowned by sleek chestnut hair; his chin was deferential; the bend of his body signified a modest hope that he did his duty in the station to which Providence had summoned him. Godwin he sought to flatter with looks of admiring interest; also, by entering upon a conversation which was meant to prove that he did not altogether lack worldly knowledge, of however little moment that might be in comparison with spiritual concerns. Examining, volume by volume and with painful minuteness, the prizes Godwin had carried off, he remarked fervently, in each instance, 'I can see how very interesting that is! So thorough, so thorough!' Even Charlotte was at length annoyed, when Mr Cusse had exclaimed upon the 'thoroughness' of Ben Jonson's works; she asked an abrupt question about some town affair, and so gave her brother an opportunity of taking the books away. There was no flagrant offence in the man. He spoke with passable accent, and manifested a high degree of amiability; but one could not dissociate him from the counter. At the thought that his sister might become Mrs Cusse, Godwin ground his teeth. Now that he came to reflect on the subject, he found in himself a sort of unreasoned supposition that Charlotte would always remain single; it seemed so unlikely that she would be sought by a man of liberal standing, and at the same time so impossible for her to accept any one less than a gentleman. Yet he remembered that to outsiders such fastidiousness must show in a ridiculous light. What claim to gentility had they, the Peaks? Was it not all a figment of his own self-conceit? Even in education Charlotte could barely assert a superiority to Mr Cusse, for her formal schooling had ended when she was twelve, and she had never cared to read beyond the strait track of clerical inspiration.

There were other circumstances which helped to depress his estimate of the family dignity. His brother Oliver, now seventeen, was developing into a type of young man as objectionable as it is easily recognised. The slow, compliant boy had grown more flesh and muscle than once seemed likely, and his wits had begun to display that kind of vivaciousness which is only compatible with a nature moulded in common clay. He saw much company, and all of low intellectual order; he had purchased a bicycle, and regarded it as a source of distinction, a means of displaying himself before shopkeepers' daughters; he believed himself a modest tenor, and sang verses of sentimental imbecility; he took in several weekly papers of unpromising title, for the chief purpose of deciphering cryptograms, in which pursuit he had singular success. Add to these characteristics a penchant for cheap jewellery, and Oliver Peak stands confessed.

It appeared to Godwin that his brother had leapt in a few months to these heights of vulgar accomplishment; each separate revelation struck unexpectedly upon his nerves and severely tried his temper. When at length Oliver, waiting for supper, began to dance grotesquely to an air which local talent had somehow caught from the London music-halls, Godwin's self-control gave way.

'Is it your ambition,' he asked, with fiery sarcasm, 'to join a troupe of nigger minstrels?'

Oliver was startled into the military posture of attention. He answered, with some embarrassment:

'I can't say it is.'

'Yet anyone would suppose so,' went on Godwin, hotly. 'Though you are employed in a shop, I should have thought you might still aim at behaving like a gentleman.'

Indisposed to quarrel, and possessed of small skill in verbal fence, Oliver drew aside with shadowed brow. As the brothers still had to share one bedroom, they were presently alone together, and their muteness, as they lay down to sleep, showed the estrangement that had at length come between them. When all had been dark and still for half-an-hour, Godwin spoke.

'Are you awake?'

'Yes.'

'There was something about Uncle Andrew. I didn't mention. He talks of opening an eating-house just opposite Whitelaw.'

'Oh.'

The tone of this signified nothing more than curiosity.

'You don't see any reason why he shouldn't?'

Oliver delayed a little before replying.

'I suppose it wouldn't be very nice for you.'

'That's rather a mild way of putting it. It would mean that I should have to leave the College, and give up all my hopes.'

'I see,' returned the other, with slow apprehension.

There followed several minutes of silence. Then Godwin sat up in bed, as had always been his wont when he talked with earnestness at night.

'If you think I lost my temper without cause at suppertime, just remember that I had that blackguard before my mind, and that it isn't very pleasant to see you taking after that branch of our family.'

'Do you mean to say I am like uncle?'

'I mean to say that, if you are not careful, you won't be the kind of man I should like to see you. Do you know what is meant by inherited tendencies? Scientific men are giving a great deal of attention to such things nowadays. Children don't always take after their parents; very often they show a much stronger likeness to a grandfather, or an uncle, or even more distant relatives. Just think over this, and make up your mind to resist any danger of that sort. I tell you plainly that the habits you are getting into, and the people you make friends of, are detestable. For heaven's sake, spend more of your time in a rational way, and learn to despise the things that shopkeepers admire. Read! Force yourself to stick hard at solid books for two or three hours every day. If you don't, it's all up with you. I am speaking for your own good. Read, read, read!'

Quietness ensued. Then Oliver began to move uneasily in his bed, and at length his protest became audible.

'I can't see what harm I do.'

'No!' burst from his brother's lips, scornfully. 'And that's just your danger. Do you suppose *I* could sing nigger songs, and run about the town with shopboys, and waste hours over idiotic puzzles?'

'We're not all alike, and it wouldn't do for us to be.'

'It would do very well for us all to have brains and to use them. The life you lead is a brainless life, brainless and vulgar.'

'Well, if I haven't got brains, I can't help it,' replied Oliver, with sullen resignation.

'You have enough to teach you to live respectably, if only you look to the right kind of example.'

There followed a vehement exhortation, now angry, now in strain of natural kindliness. To this Oliver made only a few brief and muttered replies; when it was all over, he fell asleep. But Godwin was wakeful for hours.

The next morning he attempted to work for his approaching examination, but with small result. It had begun to be very doubtful to him whether he should 'go up' at all, and this uncertainty involved so great a change in all his prospects that he could not command the mental calm necessary for study. After dinner he went out with unsettled purpose. He would gladly have conversed with Mr Gunnery, but the old people were just now on a stay with relatives in Bedfordshire, and their return might be delayed for another week. Perhaps it behoved him to go and see Mr Moxey, but he was indisposed to visit the works, and if he went to the house this evening he would encounter the five daughters, who, like all women who did not inspire him with admiration, excited his bashful dislike. At length he struck off into the country and indulged restless thoughts in places where no one could observe him.

A result of the family's removal first from London to the farm, and then into Twybridge, was that Godwin had no friends of old standing. At Greenwich, Nicholas Peak formed no intimacies, nor did a single associate remain to him from the years of his growth and struggle; his wife, until the renewal of intercourse with her sister at Twybridge, had no society whatever beyond her home. A boy reaps advantage from the half parental kindness of men and women who have watched his growth from infancy; in general it affects him as a steadying influence, keeping before his mind the social bonds to which his behaviour owes allegiance. The only person whom Godwin regarded with feeling akin to this was Mr Gunnery, but the geologist found no favour with Mrs Peak, and thus he involuntarily helped to widen the gap between the young man and his relatives. Nor had the intimacies of school time supplied Godwin with friendships for the years to come; his Twybridge class-fellows no longer interested him, nor did they care to continue his acquaintance. One was articled to a solicitor; one was learning the drug-trade in his father's shop; another had begun to deal in corn; the rest were scattered about England, as students or salary-earners. The dominion of the commonplace had absorbed them, all and sundry; they were the stuff which destiny uses for its every-day purposes, to keep the world a-rolling.

So that Godwin had no ties which bound him strongly to any district. He could not call himself a Londoner; for, though born in Westminster, he had grown to consciousness on the outskirts of Greenwich, and remembered but dimly some of the London streets, and a few places of public interest to which his father had taken him. Yet, as a matter of course, it was to London that his ambition pointed, when he forecast the future. Where else could he hope for opportunity of notable advancement? At Twybridge? Impossible to find more than means of subsistence; his soul loathed such a prospect. At Kingsmill? There was a slender hope that he might establish a connection with Whitelaw College, if he devoted himself to laboratory work; but what could come of that – at all events for many years? London, then? The only acceptable plan for supporting himself there was to succeed in a Civil Service competition. That, indeed, seemed the most hopeful direction for his efforts; a government office might afford him scope, and, he had heard, would allow him abundant leisure.

Or to go abroad? To enter for the Indian clerkships, and possibly cleave a wider way than could be hoped in England? There was allurement in the suggestion; travel had always tempted his fancy. In that case he would be safely severed from the humble origin which in his native country might long be an annoyance, or even an obstacle; no Uncle Andrew could spring up at inconvenient moments in the middle of his path. Yes; this indeed might be best of all. He must send for papers, and give attention to the matter.

Musing in this way, he had come within sight of the familiar chemical works. It was near the hour at which Mr Moxey was about to go home for his afternoon dinner; why not interrupt his walk, and have a word with him? That duty would be over.

He pushed on, and, as he approached the buildings, was aware of Mr Moxey stepping into the road, unaccompanied. Greetings speedily followed. The manufacturer, who was growing stout in his mellow years and looking more leisurely than when Godwin first knew him, beamed with smiles of approbation.

'Glad to see you; glad to see you! I have heard of your doings at College.'

'Nothing to boast of, Mr Moxey.'

'Why, what would satisfy you? A nephew of mine was there last Friday, and tells me you carried off half a hundredweight of prizes. Here he comes, I see.'

There drew near a young man of about four-and-twenty, well-dressed, sauntering with a cane in his hand. His name was Christian Moxey.

'Much pleasure in meeting you, Mr Peak,' he said, with a winning smile. 'I was at Whitelaw the other day, when you distinguished yourself, and if I had known then that you were an acquaintance of my uncle's I should have been tempted to offer a word of congratulation. Very glad indeed to meet you.'

Godwin, grateful as always for the show of kindness and flattered by such a reception, at once felt a liking for Christian Moxey. Most people would have admitted the young man's attractiveness. He had a thin and sallow face, and seemed to be of weak constitution. In talking he leant upon his cane, and his movements were languid; none the less, his person was distinguished by an air of graceful manhood. His features, separately considered, were ordinary enough; together they made a countenance of peculiar charm, vividly illumined, full of appeal to whosoever could appreciate emotional capabilities. The interest he excited in Peak appeared to be reciprocal, for his eyes dwelt as often and as long as possible on Godwin's features.

'Come along, and have something to eat with us,' said Mr Moxey, in a tone of genial invitation. 'I daresay you had dinner long enough ago to have picked up a new appetite.'

Godwin had a perturbing vision of the five Miss Moxeys and of a dinner table, such as he was not used to sit at; he wished to decline, yet knew not how to do so with civility.

'Yes, yes; come along!' added his friend, heartily. 'Tell us something about your chemistry paper. Any posers this time? My nephew won't be out of it; he belongs to the firm of Bates Brothers – the Rotherhithe people, you know.'

This information was a surprise to Godwin. He had imagined Christian Moxey either a gentleman at large, or at all events connected with some liberal profession. Glancing at the attractive face, he met a singular look, a smile which suggested vague doubts. But Christian made no remark, and Mr Moxey renewed his inquiries about the examination in chemistry.

The five daughters – all assembled in a homely sitting-room – were nothing less than formidable. Plain, soft-spoken, not ill educated, they seemed to live in perfect harmony, and to derive satisfaction from pursuits independent of external society. In the town they were seldom seen; few families called upon them; and only the most inveterate gossips found matter for small-talk in their retired lives. It had never been heard that any one of them was sought in marriage. Godwin, superfluously troubled about his attire, met them with grim endeavour at politeness; their gravity, a result of shyness, he misinterpreted, supposing them to hold aloof from a young man who had been in their father's employ. But before he could suffer much from the necessity of formal conversation the door opened to admit yet another young lady, a perfect stranger to him. Her age was about seventeen, but she had nothing of the sprightly grace proverbially connected with that time of life in girls; her pale and freckled visage expressed a haughty reserve, intensified as soon as her eye fell upon the visitor. She had a slight but well-proportioned figure, and a mass of auburn hair carelessly arranged.

'My sister,' said Christian, glancing at Godwin. 'Marcella, you recognise Mr Peak.'

'Oh yes,' the girl replied, as she came forward, and made a sudden offer of her hand.

She too had been present the other day at Whitelaw. Her 'Oh yes' sounded offensive to Godwin, yet in shaking hands with her he felt a warm pressure, and it flattered him when he became aware that Marcella regarded him from time to time with furtive interest. Presently he learnt that Christian and his sister were on a short visit at the house of their relatives; their home was in London. Marcella had seated herself stiffly by a window, and seemed to pay more attention to the view without than to the talk which went on, until dinner was announced.

Speculating on all he saw, Godwin noticed that Christian Moxey showed a marked preference for the youngest of his cousins, a girl of eighteen, whose plain features were frequently brightened with a happy and very pleasant smile. When he addressed her (by the name of Janet) his voice had a playful kindness which must have been significant to everyone who heard it. At dinner, his place was by her side, and he attended to her with more than courtesy. This astonished Peak. He deemed it incredible that any man should conceive a tender feeling for a girl so far from beautiful. Constantly occupied with thought of sexual attachments, he had never imagined anything of the kind apart from loveliness of feature in the chosen object; his instincts were, in fact, revolted by the idea of love for such a person as Janet Moxey. Christian seemed to be degraded by such a suggestion. In his endeavour to solve the mystery, Godwin grew half unconscious of the other people about him.

Such play of the imaginative and speculative faculties accounts for the common awkwardness of intelligent young men in society that is strange to them. Only the cultivation of a double consciousness puts them finally at ease. Impossible to converse with suavity, and to heed the forms of ordinary good-breeding, when the brain is absorbed in all manner of new problems: one must learn to act a part, to control the facial mechanism, to observe and anticipate, even whilst the intellect is spending its sincere energy on subjects unavowed. The perfectly graceful man will always be he who has no strong apprehension either of his own personality or of that of others, who lives on the surface of things, who can be interested without emotion, and surprised without contemplative impulse. Never yet had Godwin Peak uttered a word that was worth listening to, or made a remark that declared his mental powers, save in most familiar colloquy. He was beginning to understand the various reasons of his seeming clownishness, but this very process of self-study opposed an obstacle to improvement.

When he found himself obliged to take part in conversation about Whitelaw College, Godwin was disturbed by an uncertainty which had never left his mind at rest during the past two years; – was it, or was it not, generally known to his Twybridge acquaintances that he studied as the pensioner of Sir Job Whitelaw? To outward seeming all delicacy had been exercised in the bestowal of Sir Job's benefaction. At the beginning of each academic session Mrs Peak had privately received a cheque which represented the exact outlay in fees for the course her son was pursuing; payment was then made to the registrar as if from Peak himself. But Lady Whitelaw's sisters were in the secret, and was it likely that they maintained absolute discretion in talking with their Twybridge friends? There seemed, in the first instance, to be a tacit understanding that the whole affair should remain strictly private, and to Godwin himself, sensible enough of such refinements, it was by no means inconceivable that silence had been strictly preserved. He found no difficulty in imagining that Sir Job's right hand knew nothing of what the left performed, and it might be that the authorities of Whitelaw had no hint of his peculiar position. Still, he was perchance mistaken. The Professors perhaps regarded him as a sort of charity-boy, and Twybridge possibly saw him in the same light. The doubt flashed upon his mind while he was trying to eat and converse with becoming self-possession. He dug his heel into the carpet and silently cursed the burden of his servitude.

When the meal was over, Mr Moxey led the way out into the garden. Christian walked apart with Janet: Godwin strolled about between his host and the eldest Miss Moxey, talking of he knew not what. In a short half-hour he screwed up his courage to the point of leave-taking. Marcella and three of her cousins had disappeared, so that the awkwardness of departure was reduced. Christian, who seemed to be in a very contented mood, accompanied the guest as far as the garden gate.

'What will be your special line of work when you leave Whitelaw?' he inquired. 'Your tastes seem about equally divided between science and literature.'

'I haven't the least idea what I shall do,' was Peak's reply.

'Very much my own state of mind when I came home from Zurich a year ago. But it had been taken for granted that I was preparing for business, so into business I went.' He laughed good-humouredly. 'Perhaps you will be drawn to London?'

'Yes – I think it likely,' Godwin answered, with an absent glance this way and that.

'In any case,' pursued the other, 'you'll be there presently for First BA Honours. Try to look in at my rooms, will you? I should be delighted to see you. Most of my day is spent in the romantic locality of Rotherhithe, but I get home about five o'clock, as a rule. Let me give you a card.'

'Thank you.'

'I daresay we shall meet somewhere about here before then. Of course you are reading hard, and haven't much leisure. I'm an idle dog, unfortunately. I should like to work, but I don't quite know what at. I suppose this is a transition time with me.'

Godwin tried to discover the implication of this remark. Had it any reference to Miss Janet Moxey? Whilst he stood in embarrassed silence, Christian looked about with a peculiar smile, and seemed on the point of indulging in further self-revelation; but Godwin of a sudden held out his hand for good-bye, and with friendly smiles they parted.

Peak was older than his years, and he saw in Christian one who might prove a very congenial associate, did but circumstances favour their intercourse. That was not very likely to happen, but the meeting at all events turned his thoughts to London once more.

His attempts to 'read' were still unfruitful. For one thing, the stress and excitement of the Whitelaw examinations had wearied him; it was characteristic of the educational system in which he had become involved that studious effort should be called for immediately after that frenzy of college competition. He ought now to have been 'sweating' at his London subjects. Instead of that, he procured works of general literature from a Twybridge library, and shut himself up with them in the garret bedroom.

A letter from Mr Gunnery informed him that the writer would be home in a day or two. This return took place late one evening, and on the morrow Godwin set forth to visit his friend. On reaching the house, he learnt that Mr Gunnery had suffered an accident which threatened serious results. Walking barefoot in his bedroom the night before, he had stepped upon the point of a large nail, and was now prostrate, enduring much pain. Two days elapsed before Godwin could be admitted; he then found the old man a mere shadow of his familiar self – bloodless, hollow-eyed.

'This is the kind of practical joke that Fate likes to play upon us!' the sufferer growled in a harsh, quaking voice, his countenance divided between genial welcome and surly wrath. 'It'll be the end of me. Pooh! who doesn't know that such a thing is fatal at my age? Blood-poisoning has fairly begun. I'd a good deal rather have broken my neck among honest lumps of old red sandstone. A nail! A damned Brummagem nail! – So you collared the first prize in geology, eh? I take that as a kindness, Godwin. You've got a bit beyond Figuier and his *Deluge*, eh? His Deluge, bah!'

And he laughed discordantly. On the other side of the bed sat Mrs Gunnery, grizzled and feeble dame. Shaken into the last stage of senility by this alarm, she wiped tears from her flaccid cheeks, and moaned a few unintelligible words.

The geologist's forecast of doom was speedily justified. Another day bereft him of consciousness, and when, for a short while, he had rambled among memories of his youth, the end came. It was found that he had made a will, bequeathing his collections and scientific instruments to Godwin Peak: his books were to be sold for the benefit of the widow, who would enjoy an annuity purchased out of her husband's savings. The poor old woman, as it proved, had little need of income; on the thirteenth day after Mr Gunnery's funeral, she too was borne forth from the house, and the faithful couple slept together.

To inherit from the dead was an impressive experience to Godwin. At the present stage of his development, every circumstance affecting him started his mind upon the quest of reasons, symbolisms, principles; the 'natural supernatural' had hold upon him, and ruled his thought whenever it was free from the spur of arrogant instinct. This tendency had been strengthened by the influence of his friend Earwaker, a young man of singularly complex personality, positive and analytic in a far higher degree than Peak, yet with a vein of imaginative vigour which seemed to befit quite a different order of mind. Godwin was not distinguished by originality in thinking, but his strongly featured character converted to uses of his own the intellectual suggestions he so rapidly caught from others. Earwaker's habit of reflection had much to do with the strange feelings awakened in Godwin when he transferred to his mother's house the cabinets which had been Mr Gunnery's pride for thirty or forty years. Joy of possession was subdued in him by the conflict of metaphysical questionings.

Days went on, and nothing was heard of Uncle Andrew. Godwin tried to assure himself that he had been needlessly terrified; the eating-house project would never be carried out. Practically dismissing that anxiety, he brooded over his defeat by Chilvers, and thought with extreme reluctance of the year still to be spent at Whitelaw, probably a year of humiliation. In the meantime, should he or should he not present himself for his First BA? The five pound fee would be a most serious demand upon his mother's resources, and did the profit warrant it, was it really of importance to him to take a degree?

He lived as much as possible alone, generally avoiding the society of his relatives, save at meal times. A careless remark (not intentionally offensive) with reference to Mr Cusse had so affronted Charlotte that she never spoke to him save in reply to a question. Godwin regretted the pain he had given, but could not bring himself to express this feeling, for a discussion would inevitably have disclosed all his mind concerning the draper's assistant. Oliver seemed to have forgiven his brother's reproaches, but no longer behaved with freedom when Godwin was present. For all this, the elder's irritation was often aroused by things he saw and heard; and at length – on a memorable Saturday afternoon – debate revived between them. Oliver, as his custom was, had attired himself sprucely for a visit to acquaintances, and a silk hat of the very newest fashion lay together with his gloves upon the table.

'What is this thing?' inquired Godwin, with ominous calm, as he pointed to the piece of head-gear.

'A hat, I suppose,' replied his brother.

'You mean to say you are going to wear that in the street?'

'And why not?'

Oliver, not venturing to raise his eyes, stared at the table-cloth indignantly.

'Can't you feel,' burst from the other, 'that it's a disgrace to buy and wear such a thing?'

'Disgrace! what's the matter with the hat? It's the fashionable shape.'

Godwin mastered his wrath, and turned contemptuously away. But Oliver had been touched in a sensitive place; he was eager to defend himself.

'I can't see what you're finding fault with,' he exclaimed. 'Everybody wears this shape.'

'And isn't that quite sufficient reason why anyone who respects himself should choose something as different as possible? Everybody! That is to say, all the fools in the kingdom. It's bad enough to follow when you can't help it, but to imitate asses gratuitously is the lowest depth of degradation. Don't you know that that is the meaning of vulgarity? How you can offer such an excuse passes my comprehension. Have you no *self*? Are you made, like this hat, on a pattern with a hundred thousand others?'

'You and I are different,' said Oliver, impatiently. 'I am content to be like other people.'

'And I would poison myself with vermin-killer if I felt any risk of such contentment! Like other people? Heaven forbid and forfend! Like other people? Oh, what a noble ambition!'

The loud passionate voice summoned Mrs Peak from an adjacent room.

'Godwin! Godwin!' she remonstrated. 'Whatever is it? Why should you put yourself out so?'

She was a short and slender woman, with an air of gentility, independent of her badly made and long worn widow's dress. Self-possession marked her manner, and the even tones in which she spoke gave indication of a mild, perhaps an unemotional, temperament.

Oliver began to represent his grievance.

'What harm is there, if I choose to wear a hat that's in fashion? I pay for it out of my own'—

But he was interrupted by a loud visitor's knock at the front door, distant only a few paces. Mrs Peak turned with a startled look. Godwin, dreading contact with friends of the family, strode upstairs. When the door was opened, there appeared the smiling countenance of Andrew Peak; he wore the costume of a traveller, and by his side stood a boy of ten, too plainly his son.

'Well, Grace!' was his familiar greeting, as the widow drew back. 'I told you you'd 'ev the pleasure of seein' me again before so very long. Godwin at 'ome with you, I s'pose? Thet you, Noll?

'Ow do, my bo-oy? 'Ere's yer cousin Jowey. Shike 'ands, Jowey bo-oy! Sorry I couldn't bring my old lady over this time, Grace; she sends her respects, as usual. 'Ow's Charlotte? Bloomin', I 'ope?'

He had made his way into the front parlour, dragging the youngster after him. Having deposited his handbag and umbrella on the sofa, he seated himself in the easy-chair, and began to blow his nose with vigour.

'Set down, Jowey; set down, bo-oy! Down't be afride of your awnt.'

'Oi ain't afride!' cried the youth, in a tone which supported his assertion.

Mrs Peak trembled with annoyance and indecision. Andrew evidently meant to stay for some time, and she could not bring herself to treat him with plain discourtesy; but she saw that Oliver, after shaking hands in a very strained way, had abruptly left the room, and Godwin would be anything but willing to meet his uncle. When the name of her elder son was again mentioned she withdrew on the pretence of summoning him, and went up to his room. Godwin had heard the hateful voice, and was in profound disturbance.

'What does he say, mother?' he inquired anxiously. 'Anything about Kingsmill?'

'Not yet. Oh, I *do* so wish we could bring this connection to an end!'

It was the first time Mrs Peak had uttered her sentiments so unreservedly.

'Then, shall I see him in private,' said Godwin, 'and simply let him know the truth?'

'I dread the thought of that, Godwin. He would very likely be coarse and violent. I must try to show him by my manner. Oliver has gone out, and when Charlotte comes home I'll tell her to keep out of sight. He has brought his boy. Suppose you don't come down at all? I might say you are too busy.'

'No, no; you shan't have to do it all alone. I'll come down with you. I must hear what he has to say.'

They descended. As soon as his nephew appeared, Andrew sprang up, and shouted joyfully:

'Well, Godwin, bo-oy! It's all settled! Got the bloomin' shop from next quarter dye! "Peak's Dinin' and Refreshment Rooms!" Jowey an' me was over there all yisterday — wasn't us, Jowey? Oh, it's immense!'

Godwin felt the blood buzz in his ears, and a hot choking clutch at his throat. He took his stand by the mantelpiece, and began to turn a little glass ornament round and round. Fate had spoken. On the instant, all his College life was far behind him, all his uneasiness regarding the next session was dispelled, and he had no more connection with Kingsmill.

Mrs Peak had heard from Oliver of her brother-in-law's proposed undertaking. She had spoken of it with anxiety to Godwin, who merely shrugged his shoulders and avoided the topic, ashamed to dwell on the particulars of his shame. In hearing Andrew's announcement she had much ado to repress tears of vexation; silently she seated herself, and looked with pained countenance from uncle to nephew.

'Shall you make any changes in the place?' Godwin asked, carelessly.

'Shan't I, jest! It'll take a month to refit them eatin' rooms. I'm agoin' to do it proper – up to Dick! and I want your 'elp, my bo-oy. You an' me 'll jest write a bit of a circular – see? to send round to the big pots of the Collige, an' all the parents of the young fellers as we can get the addresses of – see?'

Even amid his pangs of mortification Godwin found himself pondering an intellectual question. Was his uncle wholly unconscious of the misery he was causing? Had it never occurred to him that the public proximity of an uneducated shopkeeping relative must be unwelcome to a lad who was distinguishing himself at Whitelaw College? Were that truly the case, then it would be unjust to regard Andrew resentfully; destiny alone was to blame. And, after all, the man might be so absorbed in his own interest, so strictly confined to the views of his own class, as never to have dreamt of the sensibilities he wounded. In fact, the shame excited by this prospect was artificial. Godwin had already felt that it was unworthy alike of a philosopher and of a high-minded man of the world. The doubt as to Andrew's state of mind, and this moral problem, had a restraining effect upon the young man's temper. A practical person justifies himself in wrath as soon as his judgment is at one with that of the multitude. Godwin, though his passions were of exceptional force, must needs refine, debate with himself points of abstract justice.

'I've been tellin' Jowey, Grace, as I 'ope he may turn out such another as Godwin 'ere. 'E'll go to Collige, will Jowey. Godwin, jest arst the bo-oy a question or two, will you? 'E ain't been doin' bad at 'is school. Jest put 'im through 'is pyces, as yer may sye. Stend up, Jowey, bo-oy.'

Godwin looked askance at his cousin, who stood with pert face, ready for any test.

'What's the date of William the Conqueror?' he asked, mechanically.

'Ow!' shouted the youth. 'Down't mike me larff! Zif I didn't know thet! Tensixsixtenightysivn, of course!'

The father turned round with an expression of such sincere pride that Godwin, for all his loathing, was obliged to smile.

'Jowey, jest sye a few verses of poitry; them as you learnt larst. 'E's good at poitry, is Jowey.'

The boy broke into fearsome recitation:

> 'The silly buckits *on* the deck
>   That 'ed so long rem'ined,
> I dreamt as they was filled with jew,
>   End when I awowk, it r'ined.'

Half-a-dozen verses were thus massacred, and the reciter stopped with the sudden jerk of a machine.

'Goes str'ight on, don't 'e, Grace?' cried the father, exultantly. 'Jowey ain't no fool. Know what he towld me the other day? Somethin' as I never knew, and shouldn't never 'ave thought of s'long as I lived. We was talkin' about jewellery, an' Jowey, 'e pops up all at wunst. "It's called jewellery," says 'e, "'cos it's mostly the Jews as sell it." Now, oo'd a thought o' that? But you see it's right as soon as you're towld, eh? Now ain't it right, Godwin?'

'No doubt,' was the dry answer.

'It never struck me,' murmured Mrs Peak, who took her son's assent seriously, and felt that it was impossible to preserve an obstinate silence.

''E ain't no fool, ain't Jowey!' cried the parent. 'Wite till 'e gits to Collige. Godwin'll put us up to all the ins and outs. Plenty o' time for that; 'e'll often run over an' 'ev a bit o' dinner, and no need to talk about p'yment.'

'Do you stay in Twybridge to-night?' inquired Godwin, who had changed in look and manner, so that he appeared all but cheerful.

'No, we're on our w'y 'ome, is Jowey an' me. Jest thought we'd break the journey 'ere. We shall ketch the six-fifty hup.'

'Then you will have a cup of tea with us,' said Mrs Peak, surprised at Godwin's transformation, but seeing that hospitality was now unavoidable.

Charlotte presently entered the house, and, after a private conversation with her mother, went to greet Andrew. If only to signify her contempt for Godwin's prejudices, Charlotte would have behaved civilly to the London uncle. In the end, Andrew took his leave in the friendliest possible way, repeating often that he would soon have the pleasure of entertaining Mrs Peak and all her family at his new dining-rooms over against Whitelaw College.

IV

Immediately upon his uncle's departure, Godwin disappeared; Mrs Peak caught only a glimpse of him as he went by the parlour window. In a short time Oliver came home, and, having learned what had happened, joined his mother and sister in a dull, intermittent conversation on the subject of Godwin's future difficulties.

'He won't go back to Whitelaw,' declared the lad. 'He said he wouldn't.'

'People must be above such false shame,' was Charlotte's opinion. 'I can't see that it will make the slightest difference in his position or his prospects.'

Whereupon her mother's patience gave way.

'Don't talk such nonsense, Charlotte! You understand perfectly well how serious it will be. I never knew anything so cruel.'

'I was never taught,' persisted the girl, with calm obstinacy, 'that one ought to be ashamed of one's relatives just because they are in a humble position.'

Oliver brought the tedious discussion to an end by clamouring for supper. The table was laid, and all were about to sit down when Godwin presented himself. To the general astonishment, he seemed in excellent spirits, and ate more heartily than usual. Not a word was spoken of Uncle Andrew, until Mrs Peak and her elder son were left alone together; then Godwin remarked in a tone of satisfied decision:

'Of course, this is the end of my work at Whitelaw. We must make new plans, mother.'

'But how can we, dear? What will Lady Whitelaw say?'

'I have to think it out yet. In a day or two I shall very likely write a letter to Lady Whitelaw. There's no need, you know, to go talking about this in Twybridge. Just leave it to me, will you?'

'It's not a subject I care to talk about, you may be sure. But I do hope you won't do anything rash, Godwin.'

'Not I. To tell you the truth, I'm not at all sorry to leave. It was a mistake that I went in for the Arts course – Greek, and Latin, and so on, you know; I ought to have stuck to science. I shall go back to it now. Don't be afraid. I'll make a position for myself before long. I'll repay all you have spent on me.'

To this conclusion had he come. The process of mind was

favoured by his defeat in all the Arts subjects; in that direction he could see only the triumphant Chilvers, a figure which disgusted him with Greeks, Romans, and all the ways of literature. As to his future efforts he was by no means clear, but it eased him greatly to have cast off a burden of doubt; his theorising intellect loved the sensation of life thrown open to new, however vague, possibilities. At present he was convinced that Andrew Peak had done him a service. In this there was an indication of moral cowardice, such as commonly connects itself with intense pride of individuality. He desired to shirk the combat with Chilvers, and welcomed as an excuse for doing so the shame which another temper would have stubbornly defied.

Now he would abandon his BA examination, – a clear saving of money. Presently it might suit him to take the BSc instead; time enough to think of that. Had he but pursued the Science course from the first, who at Whitelaw could have come out ahead of him? He had wasted a couple of years which might have been most profitably applied: by this time he might have been ready to obtain a position as demonstrator in some laboratory, on his way perhaps to a professorship. How had he thus been led astray? Not only had his boyish instincts moved strongly towards science, but was not the tendency of the age in the same direction? Buckland Warricombe, who habitually declaimed against classical study, was perfectly right; the world had learned all it could from those hoary teachers, and must now turn to Nature. On every hand, the future was with students of the laws of matter. Often, it was true, he had been tempted by the thought of a literary career; he had written in verse and prose, but with small success. An attempt to compose the Prize Poem was soon abandoned in discouragement; the essay he sent in had not been mentioned. These honours had fallen to Earwaker, with whom it was not easy to compete on such ground. No, he was not born a man of letters. But in science, granted fair opportunity, he might make a name. He might, and he would!

On the morrow, splendour of sunshine drew him forth to some distance from the town. He went along the lanes singing; now it was holiday with him, and for the first time he could enjoy the broad golden daylight, the genial warmth. In a hollow of grassy fields, where he least expected to encounter an acquaintance, it was his chance to come upon Christian Moxey, stretched at full length in the company of nibbling sheep. Since the dinner at Mr

Moxey's, he had neither seen nor heard of Christian, who, it seemed probable, was back at his work in Rotherhithe. As their looks met, both laughed.

'I won't get up,' said Christian; 'the effort would be too great. Sit down and let us have a talk.'

'I disturb your thoughts,' answered Godwin.

'A most welcome disturbance; they weren't very pleasant just then. In fact, I have come as far as this in the hope of escaping them. I'm not much of a walker, are you?'

'Well, yes, I enjoy a good walk.'

'You are of an energetic type,' said Christian, musingly. 'You will do something in life. When do you go up for Honours?'

'I have decided not to go in at all.'

'Indeed; I'm sorry to hear that.'

'I have half made up my mind not to return to Whitelaw.'

Observing his hearer's look of surprise, Godwin asked himself whether it signified a knowledge of his footing at Whitelaw. The possibility of this galled him; but it was such a great step to have declared, as it were in public, an intention of freeing himself, that he was able to talk on with something of aggressive confidence.

'I think I shall go in for some practical work of a scientific kind. It was a mistake for me to pursue the Arts course.'

Christian looked at him earnestly.

'Are you sure of that?'

'Yes, I feel sure of it.'

There was silence. Christian beat the ground with his stick.

'Your state of mind, then,' he said at length, 'is more like my own than I imagined. I, too, have wavered for a long time between literature and science, and now at last I have quite decided – quite – that scientific study is the only safe line for me. The fact is, a man must concentrate himself. Not only for the sake of practical success, but – well, for his own sake.'

He spoke lazily, dreamily, propped upon his elbow, seeming to watch the sheep which panted at a few yards from him.

'I have no right,' he pursued, with a shadow of kindly anxiety on his features, 'to offer you advice, but – well, if you will let me insist on what I have learned from my own experience. There's nothing like having a special line of work and sticking to it vigorously. I, unfortunately, shall never do anything of any account, – but I know so well the conflict between diverging tastes. It has played the deuce with me, in all sorts of ways. At

Zurich I utterly wasted my time, and I've done no better since I came back to England. Don't think me presumptuous. I only mean – well, it is so important to – to go ahead in one line.'

His air of laughing apology was very pleasant. Godwin felt his heart open to the kind fellow.

'No one needs the advice more than I,' he replied. 'I am going back to the line I took naturally when I first began to study at all.'

'But why leave Whitelaw?' asked Christian, gently.

'Because I dislike it – I can't tell you why.'

With ready tact Moxey led away from a subject which he saw was painful.

'Of course there are many other places where one can study just as well.'

'Do you know anything of the School of Mines in London?' Godwin inquired, abruptly.

'I worked there myself for a short time.'

'Then you could tell me about the – the fees, and so on?'

Christian readily gave the desired information, and the listener mused over it.

'Have you any friends in London?' Moxey asked, at length.

'No. But I don't think that matters. I shall work all the harder.'

'Perhaps so,' said the other, with some hesitation. And he added thoughtfully, 'It depends on one's temperament. Doesn't answer to be too much alone – I speak for myself at all events. I know very few people in London – very few that I care anything about. That, in fact, is one reason why I am staying here longer than I intended.' He seemed to speak rather to himself than to Godwin; the half-smile on his lips expressed a wish to disclose circumstances and motives which were yet hardly a suitable topic in a dialogue such as this. 'I like the atmosphere of a – of a comfortable home. No doubt I should get on better – with things in general – if I had a home of my own. I live in lodgings, you know; my sister lives with friends. Of course one has a sense of freedom, but then'—

His voice murmured off into silence, and again he beat the ground with his cane. Godwin was strongly interested in this broken revelation; he found it difficult to understand Moxey's yearning for domesticity, all his own impulses leading towards quite a contrary ideal. To him, life in London lodgings made rich promise; that indeed would be freedom, and full of all manner of high possibilities!

Each communed with his thoughts. Happening to glance at Christian, Godwin was struck with the graceful attitude in which the young man reclined; he himself squatted awkwardly on the grass, unable to abandon himself in natural repose, even as he found it impossible to talk with the ease of unconsciousness. The contrast, too, between his garments, his boots, and those of the Londoner was painful enough to him. Without being a dandy, Christian, it was evident, gave a good deal of thought to costume. That kind of thing had always excited Godwin's contempt, but now he confessed himself envious; doubtless, to be well dressed was a great step towards the finished ease of what is called a gentlemanly demeanour, which he knew he was very far from having attained.

'Well,' exclaimed Christian, unexpectedly, 'if I can be of ever so little use to you, pray let me. I must get back to town in a few days, but you know my address. Write to me, I beg, if you wish for any more information.'

The talk turned to less difficult topics. Godwin made inquiries about Zurich, then about Switzerland in general.

'Did you see much of the Alps?'

'Not as a climber sees them. That sort of thing isn't in my way; I haven't the energy – more's the pity. Would you like to see a lot of good photographs I brought back? I have them here; brought them to show the girls.'

In spite of the five Miss Moxeys and Christian's sister, Peak accepted the invitation to walk back with his companion, and presently they began to stroll towards Twybridge.

'I have an absurd tendency to dream – to lose myself amid ideals – I don't quite know how to express it,' Christian resumed, when both had been silent for some minutes. 'That's why I mean to go in earnestly for science – as a corrective. Fortunately, I have to work for my living; otherwise, I should moon my life away – no doubt. My sister has ten times as much energy – she knows much more than I do already. What a splendid thing it is to be of an independent character! I had rather be a self-reliant coal-heaver than a millionaire of uncertain will. My uncle – there's a man who knows his own mind. I respect those strong practical natures. Don't be misled by ideals. Make the most of your circumstances. Don't aim at – but I beg your pardon; I don't know what right I have to lecture you in this way.' And he broke off with his pleasant, kind-hearted laugh, colouring a little.

They reached Mr Moxey's house. In a garden chair on the lawn sat Miss Janet, occupied with a book. She rose to meet them, shook hands with Godwin, and said to her cousin:

'The postman has just left a letter for you – forwarded from London.'

'Indeed? I'm going to show Mr Peak my Swiss photographs. You wouldn't care to come and help me in the toil of turning them over?'

'O lazy man!'

Her laugh was joyous. Any one less prejudiced than Peak would have recognised the beauty which transformed her homely features as she met Christian's look.

On the hall table lay the letter of which Janet had spoken. Christian took it up, and Godwin, happening at that moment to observe him, caught the tremor of a sudden emotion on lip and eyelid. Instantly, prompted by he knew not what perception, he turned his gaze to Janet, and in time to see that she also was aware of her cousin's strong interest in the letter, which was at once put away in Christian's pocket.

They passed into the sitting-room, where a large portfolio stood against the back of a chair. The half-hour which ensued was to Godwin a time of uneasiness. His pleasure in the photographs suffered disturbance from a subtle stress on his nerves, due to something indeterminable in the situation, of which he formed a part. Janet's merry humour seemed to be subdued. Christian was obviously forcing himself to entertain the guest whilst his thoughts were elsewhere. As soon as possible, Godwin rose to depart. He was just saying good-bye to Janet, when Marcella entered the room. She stood still, and Christian said, hurriedly:

'It's possible, Marcella, that Mr Peak will be coming to London before long. We may have the pleasure of seeing him there.'

'You will be glad, I'm sure,' answered his sister. Then, as if forcing herself to address Peak directly, she faced to him and added, 'It isn't easy to find sympathetic companions.'

'I, at all events, haven't found very many,' Godwin replied, meaning to speak in a tone only half-serious, but conscious at once that he had made what might seem an appeal for sympathy. Thereupon his pride revolted, and in a moment drove him from the room.

Christian followed, and at the front door shook hands with him. Nervous impatience was unmistakable in the young man's look and words. Again Godwin speculated on the meaning of this, and wondered, in connection therewith, what were the characteristics which Marcella Moxey looked for in a 'sympathetic companion'.

V

In the course of the afternoon, Godwin sat down to pen the rough draft of a letter to Lady Whitelaw. When the first difficulties were surmounted, he wrote rapidly, and at considerable length. It was not easy, at his time of life, to compress into the limits of an ordinary epistle all he wished to say to the widow of his benefactor. His purpose was, with all possible respect yet as firmly as might be, to inform Lady Whitelaw that he could not spend the last of his proposed three years at the College in Kingsmill, and furthermore to request of her that she would permit his using the promised sum of money as a student at the Royal School of Mines. This had to be done without confession of the reasons for his change of plan; he could not even hint at them. Yet cause must be assigned, and the best form of words he could excogitate ran thus: 'Family circumstances render it desirable – almost necessary – that I should spend the next twelve months in London. In spite of sincere reluctance to leave Whitelaw College, I am compelled to take this step.' The lady must interpret that as best she might. Very hard indeed was the task of begging a continuance of her bounty under these changed conditions. Could he but have resigned the money, all had been well; his tone might then have been dignified without effort. But such disinterestedness he could not afford. His mother might grant him money enough barely to live upon until he discovered means of support – for his education she was unable to pay. After more than an hour's work he had moderately satisfied himself; indeed, several portions of the letter struck him as well composed, and he felt that they must heighten the reader's interest in him. With an author's pleasure (though at the same time with much uneasiness) he perused the appeal again and again.

Late in the evening, when he was alone with his mother, he told her what he had done, and read the letter for her opinion. Mrs Peak was gravely troubled.

'Lady Whitelaw will ask her sisters for an explanation,' she said.

'I have thought of that,' Godwin replied, with the confident, cheerful air he had assumed from the first. 'If the Miss Lumbs go to aunt, she must be prepared to put them off in some way. But look here, mother, when uncle has opened his shop, it's pretty certain that some one or other will hit on the true explanation of my disappearance. Let them. Then Lady Whitelaw will under-stand and forgive me.'

After much musing, the mother ventured a timid question, the result of her anxieties rather than of her judgment on the point at issue.

'Godwin, dear, are you quite sure that his shop would make so much difference?'

The young man gave a passionate start.

'What! To have the fellows going there to eat, and hearing his talk, and—? Not for a day could I bear it! Not for an hour!'

He was red with anticipated shame, and his voice shook with indignation at the suggested martyrdom. Mrs Peak dried a tear.

'You would be so alone in London, Godwin.'

'Not a bit of it. Young Mr Moxey will be a useful friend, I am convinced he will. To tell you the whole truth, I aim at getting a place at the works in Rotherhithe, where he no doubt has influence. You see, mother, I might manage it even before the end of the year. Our Mr Moxey will be disposed to help me with his recommendation.'

'But, my dear, wouldn't it come to the same thing, then, if you went back to Mr Moxey's?'

He made a gesture of impatience.

'No, no, no! I couldn't live at Twybridge. I have my way to make, mother, and the place for that is London. You know I am ambitious. Trust me for a year or two, and see the result. I depend upon your help in this whole affair. Don't refuse it me. I have done with Whitelaw, and I have done with Twybridge: now comes London. You can't regard me as a boy, you know.'

'No – but'—

'But me no buts!' he cried, laughing excitedly. 'The thing is settled. As soon as possible in the morning I post this letter. I feel it will be successful. See aunt to-morrow, and get her support. Mind that Charlotte and Oliver don't talk to people. If you all use discretion, there's no need for any curiosity to be excited.'

When Godwin had taken a resolve, there was no domestic influence strong enough to prevent his acting upon it. Mrs Peak's ignorance of the world, her mild passivity, and the faith she had in her son's intellectual resources, made her useless as a counsellor, and from no one else – now that Mr Gunnery was dead – would the young man have dreamt of seeking guidance. Whatever Lady

Whitelaw's reply, he had made up his mind to go to London.
Should his subsidy be refused, then he would live on what his
mother could allow him until – probably with the aid of Christian
Moxey – he might obtain a salaried position. The letter was
despatched, and with feverish impatience he awaited a reply.

Nine days passed, and he heard nothing. Half that delay
sufficed to bring out all the self-tormenting capacities of a nature
such as his. To his mother's conjectural explanations he could
lend no ear. Doubtless Lady Whitelaw (against whom, for subtle
reasons, he was already prejudiced) had taken offence; either she
would not reply at all, or presently there would come a few lines of
polite displeasure, intimating her disinclination to aid his project.
He silently raged against 'the woman'. Her neglect was insolence.
Had she not delicacy enough to divine the anxiety natural to one
in his dependent position? Did she take him for an every-day
writer of mendicant appeals? His pride fed upon the outrage and
became fierce.

Then arrived a small glossy envelope, containing a tiny sheet of
very thick note-paper, whereon it was written that Lady
Whitelaw regretted her tardiness in replying to him (caused by her
absence from home), and hoped he would be able to call upon her,
at ten o'clock next morning, at the house of her sisters, the Misses
Lumb, where she was stopping for a day – she remained his
sincerely.

Having duly contorted this note into all manner of painful
meanings, Godwin occupied an hour in making himself presentable (scornful that he should deem such trouble necessary), and
with furiously beating heart set out to walk through Twybridge.
Arrived at the house, he was led by a servant into the front room
on the ground floor, where Lady Whitelaw, alone, sat reading a
newspaper. Her features were of a very common order, and
nothing distinguished her from middle-aged women of average
refinement; she had chubby hands, rather broad shoulders, and
no visible waist. The scrutiny she bestowed upon her visitor was
close. To Godwin's feelings it too much resembled that with
which she would have received an applicant for the post of
footman. Yet her smile was friendly enough, and no lack of
civility appeared in the repetition of her excuses for having replied
so late.

'Let us talk about this,' she began, when Godwin was uneasily
seated. (She spoke with an excess of precision, as though it had at

one time been needful for her to premeditate polished phrases.) 'I am very sorry you should have to think of quitting the College; very sorry indeed. You are one of the students who do honour to the institution.'

This was pleasant, and Godwin felt a regret of the constraint that was upon him. In his endeavour not to display a purring smile, he looked grim, as if the compliment were beneath his notice.

'Pray don't think,' she pursued, 'that I wish you to speak more fully about the private circumstances you refer to in your letter. But do let me ask you: Is your decision final? Are you sure that when the vacations are over you will see things just as you do now?'

'I am quite sure of it,' he replied.

The emphasis was merely natural to him. He could not so govern his voice as to convey the respectful regret which at this moment he felt. A younger lady, one who had heightened the charm of her compliment with subtle harmony of tones and strongly feminine gaze, would perhaps have elicited from him a free confession. Gratitude and admiration would have made him capable of such frankness. But in the face of this newspaper-reading woman (yes, he had unaccountably felt it jar upon him that a lady should be reading a newspaper), under her matronly smile, he could do no more than plump out his 'quite sure'. To Lady Whitelaw it sounded altogether too curt; she was conscious of her position as patroness, and had in fact thought it likely that the young man would be disposed to gratify her curiosity in some measure.

'I can only say that I am sorry to hear it,' fell from her tightened lips, after a moment's pause.

Instantly Godwin's pride expelled the softer emotion. He pressed hard with his feet upon the floor, every nerve in his body tense with that distressing passion peculiar to the shyly arrogant. Regard him, and you had imagined he was submitting to rebuke for an offence he could not deny.

Lady Whitelaw waited. A minute, almost, and Peak gave no sign of opening his mouth.

'It is certainly much to be regretted,' she said at length, coolly. 'Of course, I don't know what prospects you may have in London, but, if you had remained at the College, something advantageous would no doubt have offered before long.'

There went small tact to the wording of this admonition. Impossible for Lady Whitelaw to understand the complexities of a character such as Godwin's, even had she enjoyed opportunities of studying it; but many a woman of the world would have directed herself more cautiously after reading that letter of his. Peak's impulse was to thank her for the past, and declare that henceforth he would dispense with aid; only the choking in his throat obstructed some such utterance. He resented profoundly her supposition (natural enough) that his chief aim was to establish himself in a self-supporting career. What? Am I to be grateful for a mere chance of earning my living? Have I not shown that I am capable of something more than the ordinary lot in life? From the heights of her assured independence, does she look down upon me as a young man seeking a 'place'? He was filled with wrath, and all because a good, commonplace woman could not divine that he dreamt of European fame.

'I am very sorry that I can't take that into account,' he managed to say. 'I wish to give this next year exclusively to scientific study, and after that I shall see what course is open to me.'

He was not of the men who can benefit by patronage, and be simply grateful for it. His position was a false one: to be begging with awkward show of thankfulness for a benefaction which in his heart he detested. He knew himself for an undesigning hypocrite, and felt that he might as well have been a rascal complete. Gratitude! No man capable of it in fuller measure than he; but not to such persons as Lady Whitelaw. Before old Sir Job he could more easily have bowed himself. But this woman represented the superiority of mere brute wealth, against which his soul rebelled.

There was another disagreeable silence, during which Lady Whitelaw commented on her protégé very much as Mrs Warricombe had done.

'Will you allow me to ask,' she said at length, with cold politeness, 'whether you have acquaintances in London?'

'Yes. I know some one who studied at the School of Mines.'

'Well, Mr Peak, I see that your mind is made up. And no doubt you are the best judge of your private circumstances. I must ask you to let me think over the matter for a day or two. I will write to you.'

'And I to you,' thought Godwin; a resolve which enabled him to rise with something like a conventional smile, and thus put an end to a very brief and quite unsatisfactory interview.

He strode homewards in a state of feverish excitement. His own behaviour had been wretchedly clownish; he was only too well aware of that. He ought to have put aside all the grosser aspects of his case, and have exhibited the purely intellectual motives which made such a change as he purposed seem desirable to him. That would have been to act with dignity; that would have been the very best form of gratitude for the kindness he had received. But no, his accursed lack of self-possession had ruined all. 'The woman' was now offended in good earnest; he saw it in her face at parting. The fault was admittedly on his side, but what right had she to talk about 'something advantageous'? She would write to him, to be sure; that meant, she could not yet make up her mind whether to grant the money or not. Pluto take the money! Long before sitting down to her glossy note-paper she should have received a letter from *him*.

Composed already. Now he was up in the garret bedroom, scribbling as fast as pen could fly over paper. He had been guilty of a mistake – so ran the epistle; having decided to leave Whitelaw, he ought never to have requested a continuance of the pension. He begged Lady Whitelaw would forgive this thoughtless impropriety; she had made him understand the full extent of his error. Of course he could not accept anything more from her. As for the past, it would be idle for him to attempt an expression of his indebtedness. But for Sir Job's munificence, he must now have been struggling to complete a radically imperfect education, – 'instead of going into the world to make a place for myself among the scientific investigators of our time'.

One's claims to respectful treatment must be put forward unmistakably, especially in dealing with such people as Lady Whitelaw. Now, perhaps, she would understand what his reserve concealed. The satisfaction of declining further assistance was enormous. He read his letter several times aloud. This was the great style; he could imagine this incident forming a landmark in the biography of a notable man. Now for a fair copy, and in a hand, mind you, that gave no hint of his care for caligraphic seemliness: bold, forthright.

The letter in his pocket, he went downstairs. His mother had been out all the morning; now she was just returned, and Godwin saw trouble on her forehead. Anxiously she inquired concerning the result of his interview.

Now that it was necessary to make an intelligible report of what had happened, Godwin found his tongue falter. How could he convey to another the intangible sense of wounded dignity which had impelled his pen? Instead of producing the letter with a flourish, he answered with affected carelessness:

'I am to hear in a day or two.'

'Did she seem to take it – in the right way?'

'She evidently thinks of me too much as a schoolboy.'

And he began to pace the room. Mrs Peak sat still, with an air of anxious brooding.

'You don't think she will refuse, Godwin?' fell from her presently.

His hand closed on the letter.

'Why? Well, in that case I should go to London and find some occupation as soon as possible. You could still let me have the same money as before?'

'Yes.'

It was said absently, and did not satisfy Godwin. In the course of the conversation it appeared that Mrs Peak had that morning been to see the legal friend who looked after her small concerns, and though she would not admit that she had any special cause for uneasiness, her son recalled similar occasions when an interview with Mr Dutch had been followed by several days' gloom. The truth was that Mrs Peak could not live strictly within the income at her disposal, and on being from time to time reminded of this, she was oppressed by passing worry. If Godwin and Oliver 'got on well,' things would come all right in the end, but in the meantime she could not face additional expenditure. Godwin did not like to be reminded of the razor's edge on which the affairs of the household were balanced. At present it brought about a very sudden change in his state of mind; he went upstairs again, and sat with the letter before him, sunk in misery. The reaction had given him a headache.

A fortnight, and no word from Lady Whitelaw. But neither was Godwin's letter posted.

Was he at liberty to indulge the self-respect which urged him to write? In a moment of heated confidence it was all very well to talk of 'getting some occupation' in London, but he knew that this might prove no easy matter. A year's work at the School of Mines would decidedly facilitate his endeavour; and, seeing that his mother's peace depended upon his being speedily self-supporting, was it not a form of selfishness to reject help from one who could well afford it? From a distance, he regarded Lady Whitelaw with more charity; a longer talk with her might have led to better mutual apprehension. And, after all, it was not she but her husband to whom he would stand indebted. Sir Job was a very kind-hearted old fellow; he had meant thoroughly well. Why, clearly, the bestower of this third year's allowance would not be Lady Whitelaw at all.

If it were granted. Godwin began to suffer a troublesome misgiving; perchance he had gone too far, and was now, in fact, abandoned to his own resources.

Three weeks. Then came the expected letter, and, as he opened it, his heart leaped at the sight of a cheque – talisman of unrivalled power over the emotions of the moneyless! Lady Whitelaw wrote briefly and formally. Having considered Godwin's request, she had no reason for doubting that he would make a good use of the proposed year at the School of Mines, and accordingly she sent him the sum which Sir Job had intended for his final session at Whitelaw College. She wished him all benefit from his studies, and prosperity henceforth.

Rejoicing, though shame-smitten, Godwin exhibited this remittance to his mother, from whom it drew a deep sigh of relief. And forthwith he sat down to write quite a different letter from that which still lay in his private drawer, – a letter which he strove to make the justification (to his own mind) of this descent to humility. At considerable length he dwelt upon the change of tastes of which he had been conscious lately, and did not fail to make obvious the superiority of his ambition to all thought of material advancement. He offered his thanks, and promised to give an account of himself (as in duty bound) at the close of the twelvemonths' study he was about to undertake: a letter in which the discerning would have read much sincerity, and some pathos; after all, not a letter to be ashamed of. Lady Whitelaw would not understand it; but then, how many people are capable of even faintly apprehending the phenomena of mental growth?

And now to plan seriously his mode of life in London. With Christian Moxey he was so slightly acquainted that it was impossible to seek his advice with regard to lodgings; besides, the lodgings must be of a character far too modest to come within Mr Moxey's sphere of observation. Other acquaintance he had none in the capital, so it was clear that he must enter boldly upon the unknown world, and find a home for himself as best he might.

Mrs Peak could offer suggestions as to likely localities, and this was of course useful help. In the meantime (for it would be waste of money to go up till near the end of the holiday season) he made schemes of study and completed his information concerning the School of Mines. So far from lamenting the interruption of his promising career at Whitelaw, he persuaded himself that Uncle Andrew had in truth done him a very good turn: now at length he was fixed in the right course. The only thing he regretted was losing sight of his two or three student-friends, especially Earwaker and Buckland Warricombe. They, to be sure, would soon guess the reason of his disappearance. Would they join in the laughter certain to be excited by 'Peak's Dining and Refreshment Rooms'? Probably; how could they help it? Earwaker might be superior to a prejudice of that kind; his own connections were of humble standing. But Warricombe must wince and shrug his shoulders. Perhaps even some of the Professors would have their attention directed to the ludicrous mishap: they were gentlemen, and, even though they smiled, must certainly sympathise with him.

Wait a little. Whitelaw College should yet remember the student who seemed to have vanished amid the world's obscure tumult.

Resolved that he was about to turn his back on Twybridge for ever, he found the conditions of life there quite supportable through this last month or two; the family reaped benefit from his improved temper. Even to Mr Cusse he behaved with modified contempt. Oliver was judicious enough to suppress his nigger minstrelsy and kindred demonstrations of spirit in his brother's presence, and Charlotte, though steadily resentful, did her best to avoid conflict.

Through the Misses Lumb, Godwin's change of purpose had of course become known to his aunt, who for a time took it ill that these debates had been concealed from her. When Mrs Peak, in confidence, apprised her of the disturbing cause, Miss Cadman's indignation knew no bounds. What! That low fellow had been allowed to interfere with the progress of Godwin Peak's education, and not a protest uttered? He should have been *forbidden* to establish himself in Kingsmill! Why had they not taken *her* into council? She would have faced the man, and have overawed him; he should have been made to understand the gross selfishness of his behaviour. Never had she heard of such a monstrous case—

Godwin spent much time in quiet examination of the cabinets bequeathed to him by Mr Gunnery. He used a pound or two of Lady Whitelaw's money for the purchase of scientific books, and set to work upon them with freshened zeal. The early morning and late evening were given to country walks, from which he always returned with brain excited by the forecast of great achievements.

When the time of his departure approached, he decided to pay a farewell visit to Mr Moxey. He chose an hour when the family would probably be taking their ease in the garden. Three of the ladies were, in fact, amusing themselves with croquet, while their father, pipe in mouth, bent over a bed of calceolarias.

'What's this that I hear?' exclaimed Mr Moxey, as he shook hands. 'You are not going back to Whitelaw?'

The story had of course spread among all Twybridge people who knew anything of the Peaks, and it was generally felt that some mystery was involved. Godwin had reasonably feared that his obligations to Sir Job Whitelaw must become known; impossible for such a matter to be kept secret; all who took any interest in the young man had long been privately acquainted with the facts of his position. Now that discussion was rife, it would have been prudent in the Misses Lumb to divulge as much of the truth at they knew, but (in accordance with the law of natural perversity) they maintained a provoking silence. Hence whispers and suspicious questions, all wide of the mark. No one had as yet heard of Andrew Peak, and it seemed but too likely that Lady Whitelaw, for some good reason, had declined to discharge the expenses of Godwin's last year at the College.

Mr Moxey himself felt that an explanation was desirable, but he listened with his usual friendly air to Godwin's account of the matter – which of course included no mention of Lady Whitelaw.

'Have you friends in London?' he inquired – like everyone else.

'No. Except that your nephew was so kind as to ask me to call on him, if ever I happened to be there.'

There passed over Mr Moxey's countenance a curious shadow. Godwin noticed it, and at once concluded that the manufacturer condemned Christian for undue advances to one below his own station. The result of this surmise was of course a sudden coldness on Godwin's part, increased when he found that Mr Moxey turned to another subject, without a word about his nephew.

In less than ten minutes he offered to take leave, and no one urged him to stay longer. Mr Moxey made sober expression of good wishes, and hoped he might hear that the removal to London had proved 'advantageous'. This word sufficed to convert Godwin's irritation into wrath; he said an abrupt 'good-evening', raised his hat as awkwardly as usual, and stalked away.

A few paces from the garden gate, he encountered Miss Janet Moxey, just coming home from walk or visit. Another grab at his hat, and he would have passed without a word, but the girl stopped him.

'We hear that you are going to London, Mr Peak.'

'Yes, I am, Miss Moxey.'

She examined his face, and seemed to hesitate.

'Perhaps you have just been to say good-bye to father?'

'Yes.'

Janet paused, looked away, again turned her eyes upon him.

'You have friends there, I hope?' she ventured.

'No, I have none.'

'My cousin – Christian, you remember – would, I am sure, be very glad to help you in any way.' Her voice sank, and at the same time she coloured just perceptibly under Godwin's gaze.

'So he assured me,' was the reply. 'But I must learn to be independent, Miss Moxey.'

Whereupon Godwin performed a salute, and marched forward.

His boxes were packed, and now he had but one more evening in the old home. It was made less pleasant than it might have been by a piece of information upon which he by chance alighted in a newspaper. The result of the Honours examination for the First BA at London had just been made known, and in two subjects a high place was assigned to Bruno Leathwaite Chilvers – not the first place happily, but it was disagreeable enough.

Pooh! what matter? What are academic successes? Ten years hence, which name would have wider recognition – Bruno Chilvers or Godwin Peak? He laughed with scornful superiority.

No one was to accompany him to the station; on that he insisted. He had decided for as early a train as possible, that the dolours of leave-taking might be abridged. At a quarter to eight the cab drove up to the door. Out with the trunks labelled 'London'!

'Take care of the cabinets!' were his last words to his mother. 'I may want to have them sent before long.'

He implied, what he had not ventured to say plainly, that he was leaving Twybridge for good, and henceforth would not think of it as home. In these moments of parting, he resented the natural feeling which brought moisture to his eyes. He hardened himself against the ties of blood, and kept repeating to himself a phrase in which of late he had summed his miseries: 'I was born in exile – born in exile.' Now at length had he set forth on a voyage of discovery, to end perchance in some unknown land among his spiritual kith and kin.

PART THE SECOND

I

In the spring of 1882 Mr Jarvis Runcorn, editor and co-proprietor of the London *Weekly Post*, was looking about for a young man of journalistic promise whom he might associate with himself in the conduct of that long established Radical paper. The tale of his years warned him that he could not hope to support much longer a burden which necessarily increased with the growing range and complexity of public affairs. Hitherto he had been the autocrat of the office, but competing Sunday papers exacted an alertness, a versatile vigour, such as only youth can supply; for there was felt to be a danger that the *Weekly Post* might lose its prestige in democratic journalism. Thus on the watch, Mr Runcorn – a wary man of business, who had gone through many trades before he reached that of weekly literature – took counsel one day with a fellow-campaigner, Malkin by name, who owned two or three country newspapers, and had reaped from them a considerable fortune; in consequence, his attention was directed to one John Earwaker, then editing the *Wattleborough Courier*. Mr Malkin's eldest son had recently stood as Liberal candidate for Wattleborough, and though defeated was loud in his praise of the *Courier*; with its editor he had come to be on terms of intimate friendship. Earwaker was well acquainted with journalistic life in the provinces. He sprang from a humble family living at Kingsmill, had studied at Whitelaw College, and was now but nine-and-twenty: the style of his 'leaders' seemed to mark him for a wider sphere of work. It was decided to invite him to London, and the young man readily accepted Mr Runcorn's proposals. A few months later he exchanged temporary lodgings for chambers in Staple Inn, where he surrounded himself with plain furniture and many books.

In personal appearance he had changed a good deal since that prize-day at Whitelaw when his success as versifier and essayist foretold a literary career. His figure was no longer ungainly; the big head seemed to fit better upon the narrow shoulders. He neither walked with extravagant paces, nor waved his arms like a windmill. A sufficiency of good food, and the habit of intercourse with active men, had given him an every-day aspect; perhaps the sole peculiarity he retained from student times was his hollow chuckle of mirth, a laugh which struggled vainly for enlargement. He dressed with conventional decency, even submitting to the chimney-pot hat. His features betrayed connection with a physically coarse stock; but to converse with him was to discover the man of original vigour and wide intellectual scope. With ordinary companions, it was a rare thing for him to speak of his professional interests. But for his position on *The Weekly Post* it would not have been easy to surmise how he stood with regard to politics, and he appeared to lean as often towards the conservative as to the revolutionary view of abstract questions.

The newspaper left him time for other literary work, and it was known to a few people that he wrote with some regularity for reviews, but all the products of his pen were anonymous. A fact which remained his own secret was that he provided for the subsistence of his parents, old people domiciled in a quiet corner of their native Kingsmill. The strict sobriety of life which is indispensable to success in such a career as this cost him no effort. He smoked moderately, ate and drank as little as might be, could keep his health on six hours of sleep, and for an occasional holiday liked to walk his twenty or thirty miles. Earwaker was naturally marked for survival among the fittest.

On an evening of June in the year '84, he was interrupted whilst equipping himself for dinner abroad, by a thunderous rat-tat-tat.

'You must wait, my friend, whoever you are,' he murmured placidly, as he began to struggle with the stiff button-holes of his shirt.

The knock was repeated, and more violently.

'Now there's only one man of my acquaintance who knocks like that,' he mused, elaborating the bow of his white tie. 'He, I should imagine, is in Brazil; but there's no knowing. Perhaps our office is on fire. — Anon, anon!'

He made haste to don waistcoat and swallow-tail, then crossed his sitting-room and flung open the door of the chambers.

'Ha! Then it *is* you! I was reminded of your patient habits.'

A tall man, in a light overcoat and a straw hat of spacious brim, had seized both his hands, with shouts of excited greeting.

'Confound you! Why did you keep me waiting? I thought I had missed you for the evening. How the deuce are you? And why the devil have you left me without a line from you for more than six months?'

Earwaker drew aside, and allowed his tumultuous friend to rush into the nearest room.

'Why haven't you written? – confound you!' was again vociferated, amid bursts of boyish laughter. 'Why hasn't anybody written?'

'If everybody was as well informed of your movements as I, I don't wonder,' replied the journalist. 'Since you left Buenos Ayres, I have had two letters, each containing twenty words, which gave me to understand that no answer could by possibility reach you.'

'Humbug! You could have written to half-a-dozen likely places. Did I really say that? Ha, ha, ha! – Shake hands again, confound you! How do you do? Do I look well? Have I a tropical colour? I say, what a blessed thing it was that I got beaten down at Wattleborough! All this time I should have been sitting in the fog at Westminster. What a time I've had! What a time I've had!'

It was more than twelve months since Malkin's departure from England. Though sun and sea had doubtless contributed to his robustness, he must always have been a fair example of the vigorous Briton. His broad shoulders, upright bearing, open countenance, and frank resonant voice, declared a youth passed amid the wholesome conditions which wealth alone can command. The hearty extravagance of his friendliness was only possible in a man who has never been humiliated by circumstances, never restricted in his natural needs of body and mind. Yet he had more than the heartiness of a contented Englishman. The vivacity which made a whirlwind about him probably indicated some ancestral mingling with the blood of a more ardent race. Earwaker examined him with a smile of pleasure.

'It's unfortunate,' he said, 'that I have to go out to dinner.'

'Dinner! Pooh! we can get dinner anywhere.'

'No doubt, but I am engaged.'

'The devil you are! Who is she? Why didn't you write to tell me?'

'The word has a less specific meaning, my dear fellow,' replied Earwaker, laughing. 'Only you of all men would have rushed at the wrong one. I mean to say – if your excitement can take in so common a fact – that I have promised to dine with some people at Notting Hill, and mustn't disappoint them.'

Malkin laughed at his mistake, then shouted:

'Notting Hill! Isn't that somewhere near Fulham? We'll take a cab, and I can drop you on my way.'

'It wouldn't be on the way at all.'

The journalist's quiet explanation was cut short by a petulant outcry.

'Oh, very well! Of course if you want to get rid of me! I should have thought after sixteen months'—

'Don't be idiotic,' broke in the other. 'There's a strong feminine element in you, Malkin; that's exactly the kind of talk with which women drive men to frenzy.'

'Feminine element!' shouted the traveller with hot face. 'What do you mean? I propose to take a cab with you, and you'—

Earwaker turned away laughing. 'Time and distance are nothing to you, and I shall be very glad of your company. Come by all means.'

His friend was instantly appeased.

'Don't let me make you late, Earwaker. Must we start this moment? Come along, then. Can I carry anything for you? Lord! if you could only see a tropical forest! How do you get on with old Runcorn? *Write?* What the devil was the use of my writing, when words are powerless to describe—? What a rum old place this seems, after experiences like mine; how the deuce can you live here? I say, I've brought you a ton of curiosities; will make your rooms look like a museum. Confound it! I've broken my shin against the turn in the staircase! Whew! Who are you going to dine with? – Moxey? Never heard the name.'

In Holborn a hansom was hailed, and the friends continued their dialogue as they drove westward. Having at length effervesced, Malkin began to exchange question and answer with something of the calm needful for mutual intelligibility.

'And how do you get on with old Runcorn?'

'As well as can be expected where there is not a single subject of agreement,' Earwaker replied. 'I have hopes of reducing our circulation.'

'What the deuce do you mean?'

'In other words, of improving the paper. Runcorn is strong on the side of blackguardism. We had a great fight the other day over a leader offered by Kenyon, — a true effusion of the political gutter-snipe. I refused point-blank to let it go in; Runcorn swore that, if I did not, *I* should go *out*. I offered to retire that moment. "We must write for our public," he bellowed. "True," said I, "but not necessarily for the basest among them. The standard at the best is low enough." "Do you call yourself a Radical?" "Not if this be Radicalism." "You ought to be on the *Morning* instead of the *Weekly Post*." I had my way, and probably shall end by sending Mr Kenyon back to his tinker's work shop. If not, I must look out for cleaner occupation.'

'Go it, my boy! Go it!' cried Malkin, slapping his companion's knee violently. 'Raise the tone! To the devil with mercenary considerations! Help the proletariat out of its grovelling position.'

They approached the street where Earwaker had to alight. The other declared his intention of driving on to Fulham in the hope of finding a friend who lived there.

'But I must see you again. When shall you be home to-night?'

'About half-past eleven, I dare say.'

'Right! If I am free I'll come out to Staple Inn, and we'll talk till three or four.'

The house at which the journalist presented himself was such as might be inhabited by a small family of easy means. As he was taking off his overcoat, a door opened and Christian Moxey came forward to greet him. They shook hands like men who stood on friendly, but not exactly on intimate, terms.

'Will you come up to the laboratory for a moment?' said Moxey. 'I should like to show you something I have under the microscope.'

The room he spoke of was at the top of the house; two chambers had been made into one, and the fittings were those required by a student of physical science. Various odours distressed the air. A stranger to the pursuits represented might have thought that the general disorder and encumberment indicated great activity, but the experienced eye perceived at once that no methodical work was here in progress. Mineralogy, botany, biology, physics, and probably many other sciences, were suggested by the specimens and apparatus that lay confusedly on tables, shelves, or floor.

Moxey looked very slim and elegant in his evening costume.

When he touched any object, his long, translucent fingers seemed soft and sensitive as a girl's. He stepped with peculiar lightness, and the harmonious notes of his voice were in keeping with these other characteristics. Ten years had developed in him that graceful languor which at four-and-twenty was only beginning to get mastery over the energies of a well-built frame.

'This stuff here,' he said, pointing to an open box full of mud, 'is silt from down the Thames. It's positively loaded with *diatomaceæ*, – you remember our talking about them when you were last here? I am working at the fabric of the valves. Now, just look!'

Earwaker, with attentive smile, followed the demonstration.

'Peak is busy with them as well,' said Christian, presently. 'Has he told you his theory of their locomotion? Nobody has found out yet how the little beggars move about. Peak has a bright idea.'

They spent ten minutes in the laboratory, then went downstairs. Two other guests had meanwhile arrived, and were conversing with the hostess, Miss Moxey. The shy, awkward, hard-featured girl was grown into a woman whose face made such declaration of intellect and character that, after the first moment, one became indifferent to its lack of feminine beauty. As if with the idea of compensating for personal disadvantages, she was ornately dressed; her abundant tawny hair had submitted to much manipulation, and showed the gleam of jewels; expense and finished craft were manifest in every detail of her garb. Though slightly round-shouldered, her form was well-proportioned and suggested natural vigour. Like Christian, she had delicate hands.

'Do you know a distinguished clergyman, named Chilvers?' she asked of Earwaker, with a laugh, when he had taken a place by her.

'Chilvers? – Is it Bruno Chilvers, I wonder?'

'That's the name!' exclaimed one of the guests, a young married lady of eager face and fidgety manners.

'Then I knew him at College, but I had no idea he was become distinguished.'

Miss Moxey again laughed.

'Isn't it amusing, the narrowness of a great clerical reputation? Mrs Morton was astonished that I had never heard his name.'

'Please don't think,' appealed the lady, looking anxiously at Earwaker, 'that I consider it shameful not to know him. I only happened to mention a very ridiculous sermon of his, that was forced upon me by a distressingly orthodox friend of mine. They tell me, he is one of the newest lights of the Church.'

Earwaker listened with amusement, and then related anecdotes of Bruno Chilvers. Whilst he was talking, the door opened to admit another arrival, and a servant's voice announced 'Mr Peak'. Miss Moxey rose, and moved a step or two forward; a change was visible on her countenance, which had softened and lightened.

'I am very sorry to be late,' said the new-comer, in a dull and rather husky voice, which made strong contrast with the humorous tones his entrance had interrupted.

He shook hands in silence with the rest of the company, giving merely a nod and a smile as reply to some gracious commonplace from Mrs Morton.

'Has it come to your knowledge,' Earwaker asked of him, 'that Bruno Chilvers is exciting the orthodox world by his defence of Christianity against neo-heathenism?'

'Chilvers? – No.'

'Mrs Morton tells us that all the Church newspapers ring with his name.'

'Please don't think,' cried Mrs Morton, with the same anxious look as before, 'that I read such papers. We never have such a thing in our house, Mr Peak. I have only been told about it.'

Peak smiled gravely, but made no other answer. Then he turned to Earwaker.

'Where is he?'

'I can't say. Perhaps Mrs Morton'—

'They tell me he is somewhere in Norfolk,' replied the lady. 'I forget the town.'

A summons to dinner broke off the conversation. Moxey offered his arm to the one lady present as guest, and Earwaker did the same courtesy to the hostess. Mr Morton, a meditative young man who had been listening with a smile of indifference, sauntered along in the rear with Godwin Peak.

At the dinner-table Peak was taciturn, and seemed to be musing on a disagreeable subject. To remarks, he answered briefly and absently. As Moxey, Earwaker, and Mrs Morton kept up lively general talk, this muteness was not much noticed, but when the ladies had left the room, and Peak still frowned over his wine-glass, the journalist rebuked him.

'What's the matter with you? Don't depress us.'

The other laughed impatiently, and emptied his glass.

'Malkin has come back,' pursued Earwaker. 'He burst in upon me, just as I was leaving home – as mad as a March hare. You must come and meet him some evening.'

'As you please.'

Returned to the upper room, Peak seated himself in a shadowy corner, crossed his legs, thrust his hands into his pockets, and leaned back to regard a picture on the wall opposite. This attitude gave sufficient proof of the change that had been wrought in him by the years between nineteen and nine-and-twenty; even in a drawing-room, he could take his ease unconcernedly. His face would have led one to suppose him an older man; it was set in an expression of stern, if not morose, thoughtfulness.

He had small, hard lips, indifferent teeth (seldom exhibited), a prominent chin, a long neck; his body was of firm, not ungraceful build. Society's evening uniform does not allow a man much scope in the matter of adornments; it was plain, however, that Godwin no longer scorned the tailor and haberdasher. He wore a suit which confidently challenged the criticism of experts, and the silk socks visible above his shoes might have been selected by the most fastidious of worldlings.

When he had sat there for some minutes, his eyes happened to stray towards Miss Moxey, who was just then without a companion. Her glance answered to his, and a smile of invitation left him no choice but to rise and go to a seat beside her.

'You are meditative this evening,' she said, in a voice subdued below its ordinary note.

'Not very fit for society, to tell the truth,' Godwin answered, carelessly. 'One has such moods, you know. But how would you take it if, at the last moment, I sent a telegram, "Please excuse me. Don't feel able to talk"?'

'You don't suppose I should be offended?'

'Certainly you would.'

'Then you know less of me than I thought.'

Her eyes wandered about the room, their smile betokening an uneasy self-consciousness.

'Christian tells me,' she continued, 'that you are going to take your holiday in Cornwall.'

'I thought of it. But perhaps I shan't leave town at all. It wouldn't be worth while, if I go abroad at the end of the year.'

'Abroad?' Marcella glanced at him. 'What scheme is that?'

'Haven't I mentioned it? I want to go to South America and the

Pacific islands. Earwaker has a friend, who has just come back from travel in the tropics; the talk about it has half decided me to leave England. I have been saving money for years to that end.'

'You never spoke of it – to me,' Marcella replied, turning a bracelet on her wrist. 'Should you go alone?'

'Of course. I couldn't travel in company. You know how impossible it would be for me to put up with the moods and idiosyncrasies of other men.'

There was a quiet arrogance in his tone. The listener still smiled, but her fingers worked nervously.

'You are not so unsocial as you pretend,' she remarked, without looking at him.

'Pretend! I make no pretences of any kind,' was his scornful answer.

'You are ungracious this evening.'

'Yes – and can't hide it.'

'Don't try to, I beg. But at least tell me what troubles you.'

'That's impossible,' Peak replied, drily.

'Then friendship goes for nothing,' said Marcella, with a little forced laugh.

'Yes – in all but a very few human concerns. How often could *you* tell *me* what it is that prevents your taking life cheerfully?'

He glanced at her, and Marcella's eyes fell; a moment after, there was a suspicion of colour in her cheek.

'What are you reading?' Peak asked abruptly, but in a voice of more conventional note.

'Still Hafiz.'

'I envy your power of abstraction.'

'Yet I hear that you are deeply concerned about the locomotive powers of the *diatomaceæ*?'

Their eyes met, and they laughed – not very mirthfully.

'It preserves me from worse follies,' said Peak. 'After all, there are ways more or less dignified of consuming time'—

As he spoke, his ear caught a familiar name, uttered by Christian Moxey, and he turned to listen. Moxey and Earwaker were again talking of the Rev. Bruno Chilvers. Straightway disregarding Marcella, Peak gave attention to the men's dialogue, and his forehead wrinkled into scornful amusement.

'It's very interesting,' he exclaimed, at a moment when there was silence throughout the company, 'to hear that Chilvers is really coming to the front. At Whitelaw it used to be prophesied that he would be a bishop, and now I suppose he's fairly on the way to that. Shall we write letters of congratulation to him, Earwaker?'

'A joint epistle, if you like.'

Mr Morton, who had brightened since dinner, began to speak caustically of the form of intellect necessary nowadays in a popular clergyman.

'He must write a good deal,' put in Earwaker, 'and that in a style which would have scandalised the orthodox of the last century. Rationalised dogma is vastly in demand.'

Peak's voice drew attention.

'Two kinds of books dealing with religion are now greatly popular, and will be for a long time. On the one hand there is that growing body of people who, for whatever reason, tend to agnosticism, but desire to be convinced that agnosticism is respectable; they are eager for anti-dogmatic books, written by men of mark. They couldn't endure to be classed with Bradlaugh, but they rank themselves confidently with Darwin and Huxley. Arguments matter little or nothing to them. They take their rationalism as they do a fashion in dress, anxious only that it shall be "good form". Then there's the other lot of people – a much larger class – who won't give up dogma, but have learnt that bishops, priests, and deacons no longer hold it with the old rigour, and that one must be "broad"; these are clamorous for treatises which pretend to reconcile revelation and science. It's quite pathetic to watch the enthusiasm with which they hail any man who distinguishes himself by this kind of apologetic skill, this pious jugglery. Never mind how washy the book from a scientific point of view. Only let it obtain vogue, and it will be glorified as the new evangel. The day has gone by for downright assaults on science; to be marketable, you must prove that *The Origin of Species* was approvingly foreseen in the first chapter of Genesis, and that the Apostles' Creed conflicts in no single point with the latest results of biblical criticism. Both classes seek to avoid ridicule, and to adapt themselves to a standard of respectability. If Chilvers goes in for the newest apologetics, he is bound to be enormously successful. The man has brains, and really there are so few such men who still care to go into the Church.'

There was a murmur of laughing approval. The speaker had worked himself into eloquent nervousness; he leaned forward with his hands straining together, and the muscles of his face quivering.

'And isn't it surprising,' said Marcella, 'in how short a time this apologetic attitude has become necessary?'

Peak flashed a triumphant look at her.

'I often rejoice to think of it!' he cried. 'How magnificent it is that so many of the solemn jackasses who brayed against Darwin from ten to twenty years ago should live to be regarded as beneath contempt! I say it earnestly: this thought is one of the things that make life tolerable to me!'

'You have need of charity, friend Peak,' interposed Earwaker. 'This is the spirit of the persecutor.'

'Nothing of the kind! It is the spirit of justified reason. You may say that those people were honestly mistaken; – such honesty is the brand of a brainless obstructive. *They* would have persecuted, but too gladly! There were, and are, men who would have committed Darwin to penal servitude, if they had had the power. Men like Lyell, who were able to develop a new convolution in their brains, I respect heartily. I only speak of the squalling mass, the obscene herd of idiot mockers.'

'Who assuredly,' remarked Earwaker, 'feel no shame whatever in the retrospect of their idiocy. To convert a *mind* is a subject for high rejoicing; to confute a *temper* isn't worth the doing.'

'That is philosophy,' said Marcella, 'but I suspect you of often feeling as Mr Peak does. I am sure *I* do.'

Peak, meeting an amused glance from the journalist, left his seat and took up a volume that lay on one of the tables. It was easy to see that his hands shook, and that there was perspiration on his forehead. With pleasant tact, Moxey struck into a new subject, and for the next quarter of an hour Peak sat apart in the same attitude as before his outburst of satire and invective. Then he advanced to Miss Moxey again, for the purpose of taking leave. This was the signal for Earwaker's rising, and in a few minutes both men had left the house.

'I'll go by train with you,' said Earwaker, as they walked away. 'Farringdon Street will suit me well enough.'

Peak vouchsafed no reply, but, when they had proceeded a little distance, he exclaimed harshly:

'I hate emancipated women!'

His companion stopped and laughed loudly.

'Yes, I hate emancipated women,' the other repeated, with

deliberation. 'Women ought neither to be enlightened nor dogmatic. They ought to be sexual.'

'That's unusual brutality on your part.'

'Well, you know what I mean.'

'I know what you think you mean,' said Earwaker. 'But the woman who is neither enlightened nor dogmatic is only too common in society. They are fools, and troublesome fools.'

Peak again kept silence.

'The emancipated woman,' pursued his friend, 'needn't be a Miss Moxey, nor yet a Mrs Morton.'

'Miss Moxey is intolerable,' said Peak. 'I can't quite say why I dislike her so, but she grows more antipathetic to me the better I know her. She has not a single feminine charm – not one. I often feel very sorry for her, but dislike her all the same.'

'Sorry for her,' mused Earwaker. 'Yes, so do I. I can't like her either. She is certainly an incomplete woman. But her mind is of no low order. I had rather talk with her than with one of the imbecile prettinesses. I half believe you have a sneaking sympathy with the men who can't stand education in a wife.'

'It's possible. In some moods.'

'In no mood can I conceive such a prejudice. I have no great attraction to women of any kind, but the uneducated woman I detest.'

'Well, so do I,' muttered Peak. 'Do you know what?' he added, abruptly. 'I shall be off to the Pacific. Yes, I shall go this next winter. My mind is made up.'

'I shan't try to dissuade you, old fellow, though I had rather have you in sight. Come and see Malkin. I'll drop you a note with an appointment.'

'Do.'

They soon reached the station, and exchanged but few more words before Earwaker's leaving the train at Farringdon Street. Peak pursued his journey towards the south-east of London.

On reaching home, the journalist flung aside his foolish coat of ceremony, indued a comfortable jacket, lit a pipe with long stem, and began to glance over an evening newspaper. He had not long reposed in his arm-chair when the familiar appeal thundered from without. Malkin once more shook his hand effusively.

'Had my journey to Fulham for nothing. Didn't matter; I ran over to Putney and looked up my old landlady. The rooms are occupied by a married couple, but I think we shall succeed in persuading them to make way for me. I promised to find them lodgings every bit as good in two days' time.'

'If that is so easy, why not take the new quarters yourself?'

'Why, to tell you the truth, I didn't think of it! – Oh, I had rather have the old crib; I can do as I like there, you know. Confound it! Now I shall have to spend all to-morrow lodging-hunting for other people. Couldn't I pay a man to do it? Some confidential agent – private police – you know what I mean?'

'A man of any delicacy,' replied Earwaker, with grave countenance, 'would feel bound by such a promise to personal exertion.'

'Right; quite right! I didn't mean it; of course I shall hunt conscientiously. Oh, I say; I have brought over a couple of armadilloes. Would you like one?'

'Stuffed, do you mean?'

'Pooh! Alive, man, alive! They only need a little care. I should think you might keep the creature in your kitchen; they become quite affectionate.'

The offer was unhesitatingly declined, and Malkin looked hurt. There needed a good deal of genial explanation before Earwaker could restore him to his sprightly mood.

'Where have you been dining?' cried the traveller. 'Moxey's – ah, I remember. But who *is* Moxey? A new acquaintance, eh?'

'Yes; I have known him about six months. Got to know him through Peak.'

'Peak? Peak? What, the fellow you once told me about – who disappeared from Whitelaw because of his uncle, the cat's-meat man?'

'The man's-meat man, rather.'

'Yes, yes – the eating-house; I remember. You have met him again? Why on earth didn't you tell me in your letters? What became of him? Tell me the story.'

'Certainly, if you will cease to shake down plaster from the ceiling. – We met in a restaurant (appropriate scene), happening to sit at the same table. Whilst eating, we stared at each other fitfully. "I'll be hanged if that isn't Peak," I kept saying to myself. And at the same moment we opened our lips to question each other.'

'Just the same thing happened once to a friend of mine and a friend of his. But it was on board ship, and both were devilish sea-sick. Walker – you remember my friend Walker? – tells the story

in a side-splitting way. I wonder what has become of Walker? The
last time I met him he was travelling agent for a menagerie – a
most interesting fellow, Walker. – But I beg your pardon. Go on,
old fellow!'

'Well, after that we at once saw a good deal of each other. He
has been working for years at a chemical factory down on the
river; Moxey used to be there, and got him the place.'

'Moxey? – Oh yes, the man you dined with. You must
remember that these are new names to me. I must know all these
new people, I say. You don't mind?'

'You shall be presented to the whole multitude, as soon as you
like. Peak wants to see you. He thinks of an excursion like this last
of yours.'

'He does? By Jove, we'll go together! I have always wanted a
travelling companion. We'll start as soon as ever he likes! – well,
in a month or two. I must just have time to look round. Oh, I
haven't done with the tropics yet! I must tell him of a rattling good
insect-powder I have invented; I think of patenting it. I say, how
does one get a patent? Quite a simple matter, I suppose?'

'Oh, always has been. The simplest and least worrying of all
business enterprises.'

'What? Eh? That smile of yours means mischief.'

In a quarter of an hour they had got back to the subject of
Peak's history.

'And did he really run away because of the eating-house?'
Malkin inquired.

'I shall never venture to ask, and it's not very likely he will admit
it. It was some time before he cared to talk much of Whitelaw.'

'But what is he doing? You used to think he would come out
strong, didn't you? Has he written anything?'

'A few things in *The Liberator*, five or six years ago.'

'What, the atheistic paper?'

'Yes. But he's ashamed of it now. That belongs to a bygone
stage of development.'

'Turned orthodox?'

Earwaker laughed.

'I only mean that he is ashamed of the connection with street-
corner rationalism.'

'Quite right. Devilish low, that kind of thing. But I went in for it
myself once. Did I ever tell you that I debated with a parson on
Mile-end Waste? Fact! That was in my hot-headed days. A crowd

of coster-mongers applauded me in the most flattering way. – I say, Earwaker, you haven't any whisky?'

'Forgive me; your conversation makes me forget hospitality. Shall I make hot water? I have a spirit-kettle.'

'Cold for me. I get in such a deuced perspiration when I begin to talk. – Try this tobacco; the last of half a hundred-weight I took in at Bahia.'

The traveller refreshed himself with a full tumbler, and resumed the conversation cheerily.

'Has he just been wasting his time, then, all these years?'

'He goes in for science – laboratory work, evolutionary speculations. Of course I can't judge his progress in such matters; but Moxey, a clever man in the same line, thinks very highly of him.'

'Just the fellow to travel with. I want to get hold of some solid scientific ideas, but I haven't the patience to work steadily. A confounded fault of mine, you know, Earwaker, – want of patience. You must have noticed it?'

'Oh – well, now and then, perhaps.'

'Yes, yes; but of course I know myself better. And now tell me about Moxey. A married man, of course?'

'No, lives with a sister.'

'Unmarried sister? – Brains?'

'Pretty well supplied with that commodity.'

'You must introduce me to her. I do like women with brains. – Orthodox or enlightened?'

'Bitterly enlightened.'

'Really? Magnificent! Oh, I must know her. Nothing like an emancipated woman! How any man can marry the ordinary female passes my understanding. What do *you* think?'

'My opinions are in suspense; not yet precipitated, as Peak might say.'

One o'clock sounded from neighbouring churches, but Malkin was wide awake as ever. He entered upon a detailed narrative of his travels, delightful to listen to, so oddly blended were the strains of conscious and unconscious humour which marked his personality. Two o'clock; three o'clock; – he would have talked till breakfast-time, but at last Earwaker declared that the hour had come for sleep. As Malkin had taken a room at the Inns of Court Hotel, it was easy for him to repair to his quarters. The last his friend heard of him was an unexplained laugh, echoing far down the staircase.

II

Peak's destination was Peckham Rye. On quitting the railway, he had a walk of some ten minutes along a road which smelt of new bricks and stucco heated by the summer sun; an obscure passage led him into a street partly of dwelling-houses, partly of shops, the latter closed. He paused at the side door of one over which the street lamp dimly revealed – 'Button, Herbalist'.

His latch-key admitted him to total darkness, but he moved forward with the confidence of long use. He softly ascended two flights of stairs, opened a door, struck a match, and found himself in a comfortable sitting-room, soon illumined by a reading-lamp. The atmosphere, as throughout the house, was strongly redolent of dried simples. Anyone acquainted with the characteristics of furnished lodgings must have surmised that Peak dwelt here among his own moveables, and was indebted to the occupier of the premises for bare walls alone; the tables and chairs, though plain enough, were such as civilisation permits; and though there were no pictures, sundry ornaments here and there made strong denial of lodging-house affinity. It was at once laboratory, study, and dwelling-room. Two large cabinets, something the worse for transportation, alone formed a link between this abode and the old home at Twybridge. Books were not numerous, and a good microscope seemed to be the only scientific instrument of much importance. On door-pegs hung a knapsack, a botanist's vasculum, and a geologist's wallet.

A round table was spread with the materials of supper, and here again an experienced lodger must have bestowed contemplative scrutiny, for no hand of common landlady declared itself in the arrangement. The cloth was spotless, the utensils tasteful and carefully disposed. In a bowl lay an appetising salad, ready for mingling; a fragment of Camembert cheese was relieved upon a setting of green leafage; a bottle of ale, with adjacent corkscrew, stood beside the plate; the very loaf seemed to come from no ordinary baker's, or was made to look better than its kin by the fringed white cloth in which it nestled.

The custom of four years had accustomed Peak to take these things as a matter of course, yet he would readily have admitted that they were extraordinary enough. Indeed, he even now occasionally contrasted this state of comfort with the hateful experiences of his first six years in London. The subject of lodgings was one of those on which (often intemperate of speech) he spoke least temperately. For six years he had shifted from quarter to quarter, from house to house, driven away each time by the hateful contact of vulgarity in every form, – by foulness and dishonesty, by lying, slandering, quarrelling, by drunkenness, by brutal vice, – by all abominations that distinguish the lodging-letter of the metropolis. Obliged to practise extreme economy, he could not take refuge among self-respecting people, or at all events had no luck in endeavouring to find such among the poorer working-class. To a man of Godwin's idiosyncrasy the London poor were of necessity abominable, and it anguished him to be forced to live among them.

Rescue came at last, and in a very unexpected way. Resident in the more open part of Bermondsey (winter mornings made a long journey to Rotherhithe intolerable), he happened to walk one day as far as Peckham Rye, and was there attracted by the shop window of a herbalist. He entered to make a purchase, and got into conversation with Mr Button, a middle-aged man of bright intelligence and more reading than could be expected. The herbalist led his customer to an upper room, in which were stored sundry curiosities, and happened casually to say that he was desirous of finding a lodger for two superfluous chambers. Peak's inquiries led to his seeing Mrs Button, whom he found to be a Frenchwoman of very pleasing appearance; she spoke fluent French-English, anything but disagreeable to an ear constantly tormented by the London vernacular. After short reflection he decided to take and furnish the rooms. It proved a most fortunate step, for he lived (after the outlay for furniture) at much less expense than theretofore, and in comparative luxury. Cleanliness, neatness, good taste by no means exhausted Mrs Button's virtues; her cooking seemed to the lodger of incredible perfection, and the infinite goodwill with which he was tended made strange contrast with the base usage he had commonly experienced.

In these ten years he had paid but four visits to Twybridge, each of brief duration. Naturally there were changes among his kinsfolk: Charlotte, after an engagement which prolonged itself to the fifth twelvemonth, had become Mrs Cusse, and her husband now had a draper's shop of his own, with two children already born into the world of draperdom. Oliver, twice fruit-lessly affianced, had at length (when six-and-twenty) wedded a young person whom his mother and his aunt both regarded as a most undesirable connection, the daughter (aged thirty-two) of a man who was drinking himself to death on such money as he could earn by casual reporting for a Twybridge newspaper. Mrs Peak the elder now abode with her sister at the millinery shop, and saw little of her two married children. With Oliver and Charlotte their brother had no sympathy, and affected none; he never wrote to them, nor they to him; but years had strengthened his regard for his mother, and with her he had fairly regular correspondence. Gladly he would have seen her more often, but the air of shopkeeping he was compelled to breathe when he visited Twybridge nauseated and repelled him. He recognised the suitability both of Oliver and Charlotte for the positions to which life had consigned them – they suffered from no profitless aspiration; but it seemed to him a just cause of quarrel with fate that his kindred should thus have relapsed, instead of bettering the rank their father had bequeathed to them. He would not avow to such friends as Moxey and Earwaker the social standing of his only recognised relatives.

As for the unrecognised, he had long ago heard with some satisfaction that Andrew Peak, having ultimately failed in his Kingsmill venture, returned to London. Encounter with the fatal Andrew had been spared him ever since that decisive day when Master Jowey Peak recited from Coleridge and displayed his etymological genius.

For himself, he had earned daily bread, and something more; he had studied in desultory fashion; he had seen a good deal of the British Isles and had visited Paris. The result of it all was gnawing discontent, intervals of furious revolt, periods of black despair.

He had achieved nothing, and he was alone.

Young still, to be sure; at twenty-nine it is too early to abandon ambitions which are supported by force of brain and of will. But circumstances must needs help if the desires of his soul were to be attained. On first coming to London, received with all friendliness by Christian Moxey, he had imagined that it only depended upon himself to find admission before long to congenial society – by which he then understood the companionship of intelligent and aspiring young men. Christian, however, had himself no such circle, and knew that the awkward lad from Twybridge could not associate with the one or two wealthy families to which he could have presented him. The School of Mines was only technically useful; it helped Godwin to get his place with Bates & Sons, but supplied no friendships. In the third year, Moxey inherited means and left the chemical works for continental travel.

By tormenting attraction Godwin was often led to walk in the wealthy districts of London. Why was no one of these doors open to him? There were his equals; not in the mean streets where he dwelt. There were the men of culture and capacity, the women of exquisite person and exalted mind. Was he the inferior of such people? By heaven, no!

He chanced once to be in Hyde Park on the occasion of some public ceremony, and was brought to pause at the edge of a gaping plebeian crowd, drawn up to witness the passing of aristocratic vehicles. Close in front of him an open carriage came to a stop; in it sat, or rather reclined, two ladies, old and young. Upon this picture Godwin fixed his eyes with the intensity of fascination; his memory never lost the impress of these ladies' faces. Nothing very noteworthy about them; but to Godwin they conveyed a passionate perception of all that is implied in social superiority. Here he stood, one of the multitude, of the herd; shoulder to shoulder with boors and pick-pockets; and within reach of his hand reposed those two ladies, in Olympian calm, seeming unaware even of the existence of the throng. Now they exchanged a word; now they smiled to each other. How delicate was the moving of their lips! How fine must be their enunciation! On the box sat an old coachman and a young footman; they too were splendidly impassive, scornful of the multitudinous gaze. – The block was relieved, and on the carriage rolled.

They were his equals, those ladies, merely his equals. With such as they he should by right of nature associate.

In his rebellion, he could not hate them. He hated the malodorous rabble who stared insolently at them and who envied their immeasurable remoteness. Of mere wealth he thought not; might he only be recognised by the gentle of birth and breeding for what he really was, and be rescued from the promiscuity of the vulgar!

Yet at this time he was drawn into connection with the movement of popular Radicalism which revolts against religious respectability. Inherited antipathy to all conventional forms of faith outweighed his other prejudices so far as to induce him to write savage papers for *The Liberator*. Personal contact with artisan freethinkers was disgusting to him. From the meeting of emancipated workmen he went away with scorn and detestation in his heart; but in the quiet of his lodgings he could sit down to aid their propaganda. One explanation of this inconsistency lay in the fact that no other channel was open to his literary impulses. Pure science could not serve him, for he had no original results to announce. Pure literature seemed beyond his scope, yet he was constantly endeavouring to express himself. He burned with the desire of fame, and saw no hope of achieving it save as an author. *The Liberator* would serve him as a first step. In time he might get foothold in the monthly reviews, and see his name side by side with those of the leaders of thought.

Occasions, of course, offered when he might have extended his acquaintance, but they were never of a kind that he cared to use; at best they would only have admitted him to the homes of decent, semi-educated families, and for such society he was altogether unfitted. The licence of the streets but seldom allured him. After his twenty-fourth year he was proof against the decoys of venal pleasure, and lived a life of asceticism exceedingly rare in young and lonely men. When Christian Moxey returned to London and took the house at Notting Hill, which he henceforth occupied together with his sister, a possibility of social intercourse at length appeared. Indeed it was a substantial gain to sit from time to time at a civilised table, and to converse amid graceful surroundings with people who at all events followed the intellectual current of the day. Careless hitherto of his personal appearance, he now cultivated an elegance of attire in conformity with his aristocratic instincts, and this habit became fixed. When next he visited Twybridge, the change in his appearance was generally remarked. Mrs Peak naturally understood it as a significant result of his intercourse with Miss Moxey, of whom, as it seemed to her, he spoke with singular reticence.

But Marcella had no charm for Godwin's imagination, notwithstanding that he presently suspected a warmth of interest on her side which he was far from consciously encouraging. Nor did he find among his friends any man or woman for whose acquaintance he greatly cared. The Moxeys had a very small circle, consisting chiefly of intellectual inferiors. Christian was too indolent to make a figure in society, and his sister suffered from peculiarities of mind and temperament which made it as difficult for her as for Peak himself to form intimate friendships.

When chance encounter brought him into connection with

Earwaker, the revival of bygone things was at first doubtfully pleasant. Earwaker himself, remarkably developed and become a very interesting man, was as welcome an associate as he could have found, but it cost him some effort to dismiss the thought of Andrew Peak's eating-house, and to accept the friendly tact with which the journalist avoided all hint of unpleasant memories. That Earwaker should refrain from a single question concerning that abrupt disappearance, nearly ten years ago, sufficiently declared his knowledge of the unspeakable cause, a reflection which often made Godwin writhe. However, this difficulty was overcome, and the two met very frequently. For several weeks Godwin enjoyed better spirits than he had known since the first excitement of his life in London faded away.

One result was easily foreseen. His mind grew busy with literary projects, many that he had long contemplated and some that were new. Once more he aimed at contributing to the 'advanced' reviews, and sketched out several papers of sociological tenor. None of these were written. As soon as he sat down to deliberate composition, a sense of his deficiencies embarrassed him. Godwin's self-confidence had nothing in common with the conceit which rests on imaginary strength. Power there was in him; of that he could not but be conscious: its true direction he had not yet learned. Defect of knowledge, lack of pen-practice, confusion and contradictoriness of aims, instability of conviction, – these faults he recognised in himself at every moment of inward scrutiny.

On his table this evening lay a library volume which he had of late been reading, a book which had sprung into enormous popularity. It was called *Spiritual Aspects of Evolution*, and undertook, with confidence characteristic of its kind, to reconcile the latest results of science with the dogmas of Oriental religion. This work was in his mind when he spoke so vehemently at Moxey's; already he had trembled with an impulse to write something on the subject, and during his journey home a possible essay had begun to shape itself. Late as was the hour he could not prepare for sleep. His brain throbbed with a congestion of thought; he struggled to make clear the lines on which his satire might direct itself. By two o'clock he had flung down on paper a conglomerate of burning ideas, and thus relieved he at length went to bed.

Two days later came a note from Staple Inn, inviting him to

meet Malkin the next evening. By this time he had made a beginning of his critical essay, and the exordium so far satisfied him that he was tempted to take it for Earwaker's judgment. But no; better his friend should see the thing when it was complete.

About eight o'clock he reached the journalist's chambers. Malkin had not yet arrived. Peak amused himself with examining certain tropical products which the traveller had recently cast pell-mell into his friend's sitting-room. Then sounded a knock at the door, but it was not such as would have heralded the expected man.

'A telegram,' observed Earwaker, and went to take it in.

He returned with hoarse sounds of mirth.

'Our friend excuses himself. Read this characteristic despatch.'

Peak saw with surprise that the telegram far exceeded familiar dimensions. 'Unspeakably grieved,' it began. 'Cannot possibly with you. At moment's notice undertaken escort two poor girls Rouen. Not even time look in apologise. Go via Dieppe and leave Victoria few minutes. Hope be back Thursday. Express sincerest regret Mr Peak. Lament appearance discourtesy. Will apologise personally. Common humanity constrains go Rouen. Will explain Thursday. No time add another word. Rush tickets train.'

'There you have the man!' cried Earwaker. 'How do you class such a mind as that? Ten to one this is some Quixotic obligation he has laid upon himself, and probably he has gone without even a handbag.'

'Vocally delivered,' said Peak, 'this would represent a certain stage of drunkenness. I suppose it isn't open to such an explanation?'

'Malkin never was intoxicated, save with his own vivacity.'

They discussed the singular being with good-natured mirth, then turned by degrees to other topics.

'I have just come across a passage that will delight you,' said Earwaker, taking up a book. 'Perhaps you know it.'

He read from Sir Thomas Brown's *Pscudodoxia Epidemica*. '"Men's names should not only distinguish them. A man should be something that all men are not, and individual in somewhat beside his proper name. Thus, while it exceeds not the bound of reason and modesty, we cannot condemn singularity. *Nos numerus sumus* is the motto of the multitude, and for that reason are they fools."'

Peak laughed his approval.

'It astonishes me,' he said, lighting his pipe, 'that you can go on writing for this Sunday rag, when you have just as little sympathy with its aims as I have. Do get into some less offensive connection.'

'What paper would you recommend?' asked the other, with his significant smile.

'Why need you journalise at all?'

'On the whole, I like it. And remember, to admit that the multitude are fools is not the same thing as to deny the possibility of progress.'

'Do you really believe yourself a democrat, Earwaker?'

'M–m–m! Well, yes, I believe the democratic spirit is stronger in me than any other.'

Peak mused for a minute, then suddenly looked up.

'And what am I?'

'I am glad nothing much depends on my successfully defining you.'

They laughed together.

'I suppose,' said Godwin, 'you can't call a man a democrat who recognises in his heart and soul a true distinction of social classes. Social, mark. The division I instinctively support is by no means intellectual. The well-born fool is very often more sure of my respect than the working man who struggles to a fair measure of education.'

Earwaker would have liked to comment on this with remarks personal to the speaker, but he feared to do so. His silence, however, was eloquent to Peak, who resumed brusquely.

'I am not myself well-born, – though if my parents could have come into wealth early in their lives, perhaps I might reasonably have called myself so. All sorts of arguments can be brought against my prejudice, but the prejudice is ineradicable. I respect hereditary social standing, independently of the individual's qualities. There's nothing of the flunkey in this, or I greatly deceive myself. Birth in a sphere of refinement is desirable and respectable; it saves one, absolutely, from many forms of coarseness. The masses are not only fools, but very near the brutes. Yes, they can send forth fine individuals – but remain base. I don't deny the possibility of social advance; I only say that at present the lower classes are always disagreeable, often repulsive, sometimes hateful.'

'I could apply that to the classes above them.'

'Well, I can't. But I am quite ready to admit that there are all sorts of inconsistencies in me. Now, the other day I was reading Burns, and I couldn't describe what exaltation all at once possessed me in the thought that a ploughman had so glorified a servant-girl that together they shine in the highest heaven, far above all the monarchs of earth. This came upon me with a rush – a very rare emotion. Wasn't that democratic?'

He inquired dubiously, and Earwaker for a moment had no reply but his familiar 'M–m–m!'

'No, it was not democratic,' the journalist decided at length; 'it was pride of intellect.'

'Think so? Then look here. If it happens that a whining wretch stops me in the street to beg, what do you suppose is my feeling? I am ashamed in the sense of my own prosperity. I can't look him in the face. If I yielded to my natural impulse, I should cry out, "Strike me! spit at me! show you hate me! – anything but that terrible humiliation of yourself before me!" That's how I feel. The abasement of which *he* isn't sensible affects *me* on his behalf. I give money with what delicacy I can. If I am obliged to refuse, I mutter apologies and hurry away with burning cheeks. What does that mean?'

Earwaker regarded him curiously.

'That is mere fineness of humanity.'

'Perhaps moral weakness?'

'I don't care for the scalpel of the pessimist. Let us give it the better name.'

Peak had never been so communicative. His progress in composition these last evenings seemed to have raised his spirits and spurred the activity of his mind. With a look of pleasure he pursued his self-analysis.

'Special antipathies – sometimes explicable enough – influence me very widely. Now, I by no means hate all orders of uneducated people. A hedger, a fisherman, a country mason, – people of that kind I rather like to talk with. I could live a good deal with them. But the London vulgar I abominate, root and branch. The mere sound of their voices nauseates me; their vilely grotesque accent and pronunciation – bah! I could write a paper to show that they are essentially the basest of English mortals. Unhappily, I know so much about them. If I saw the probability of my dying in a London lodging-house, I would go out into the sweet-scented fields and there kill myself.'

Earwaker understood much by this avowal, and wondered whether his friend desired him so to do.

'Well, I can't say that I have any affection for the race,' he replied. 'I certainly believe that, socially and politically, there is less hope of them than of the lower orders in any other part of England.'

'They are damned by the beastly conditions of their life!' cried Godwin, excitedly. 'I don't mean only the slum-denizens. All, all – Hammersmith as much as St George's-in-the-East. I must write about this; I must indeed.'

'Do by all means. Nothing would benefit you more than to get your soul into print.'

Peak delayed a little, then:

'Well, I am doing something at last.'

And he gave an account of his projected essay. By this time his hands trembled with nervous agitation, and occasionally a dryness of the palate half choked his voice.

'This may do very well,' opined Earwaker. 'I suppose you will try *The Critical*?'

'Yes. But have I any chance? Can a perfectly unknown man hope to get in?'

They debated this aspect of the matter. Seeing Peak had laid down his pipe, the journalist offered him tobacco.

'Thanks; I can't smoke just yet. It's my misfortune that I can't talk earnestly without throwing my body into disorder.'

'How stolid I am in comparison!' said Earwaker.

'That book of M'Naughten's,' resumed the other, going back to his subject. 'I suppose the clergy accept it?'

'Largely, I believe.'

Peak mused.

'Now, if I were a clergyman'—

But his eye met Earwaker's, and they broke into laughter.

'Why not?' pursued Godwin. 'Did I ever tell you that my people originally wished to make a parson of me? Of course I resisted tooth and nail, but it seems to me now that I was rather foolish in doing so. I wish I *had* been a parson. In many ways the position would have suited me very well.'

'M–m–m!'

'I am quite serious. Well, if I were so placed, I should preach Church dogma, pure and simple. I would have nothing to do with these reconciliations. I would stand firm as Jeremy Taylor; and in

consequence should have an immense and enthusiastic congregation.'

'I daresay.'

'Depend upon it, let the dogmas do what they still can. There's a
vast police force in them, at all events. A man may very strongly
defend himself for preaching them.'

The pursuit of this argument led Earwaker to ask:

'What proportion of the clergy can still take that standing in
stolid conscientiousness?'

'What proportion are convinced that it is untenable?' returned
Peak.

'Many wilfully shut their eyes to the truth.'

'No, they don't shut their eyes!' cried Godwin. 'They merely
lower a nictitating membrane which permits them to gaze at light
without feeling its full impact.'

'I recommend you to bring that into your paper,' said the
journalist, with his deep chuckle.

An hour later they were conversing with no less animation, but
the talk was not so critical. Christian Moxey had come up as a
topic, and Earwaker was saying that he found it difficult to divine
the man's personality.

'You won't easily do that,' replied Peak, 'until you know more
of his story. I can't see that I am bound to secrecy – at all events
with you. Poor Moxey imagines that he is in love, and the fancy
has lasted about ten years.'

'Ten years?'

'When I first knew him he was paying obvious attentions to a
rather plain cousin down at Twybridge. Why, I don't know, for he
certainly was devoted to a girl here in London. All he has
confessed to me is that he had given up hopes of her, but that a
letter of some sort or other revived them, and he hastened back to
town. He might as well have stayed away; the girl very soon
married another man. Less than a year later she had bitterly
repented this, and in some way or other she allowed Moxey to
know it. Since then they have been Platonic lovers – nothing more,
I am convinced. They see each other about once in six months,
and presumably live on a hope that the obnoxious husband may
decease. I only know the woman as "Constance"; never saw her.'

'So that's Moxey? I begin to understand better.'

'Admirable fellow, but deplorably weak. I have an affection for
him, and have had from our first meeting.'

'Women!' mused Earwaker, and shook his head.

'You despise them?'

'On the whole, I'm afraid so.'

'Yes, but *what* women?' cried the other with impatience. 'It would be just as reasonable to say that you despise men. Can't you see that?'

'I doubt it.'

'Now look here; the stock objections to women are traditional. They take no account of the vast change that is coming about. Because women were once empty-headed, it is assumed they are all still so *en masse*. The defect of the female mind? It is my belief that this is nothing more nor less than the defect of the uneducated human mind. I believe most men among the brutally ignorant exhibit the very faults which are cried out upon as exclusively feminine. A woman has hitherto been an ignorant human being; that explains everything.'

'Not everything; something, perhaps. Remember your evolutionism. The preservation of the race demands in women many kinds of irrationality, of obstinate instinct, which enrage a reasoning man. Don't suppose I speak theoretically. Four or five years ago I had really made up my mind to marry; I wasted much valuable time among women and girls, of anything but low social standing. But my passions were choked by my logical faculty. I foresaw a terrible possibility – that I might beat my wife. One thing I learned with certainty was that the woman, *qua* woman, hates abstract thought – hates it. Moreover (and of consequence) she despises every ambition that has not a material end.'

He enlarged upon the subject, followed it into all its ramifications, elaborated the inconsistencies with which it is rife. Peak's reply was deliberate.

'Admitting that some of these faults are rooted in sex, I should only find them intolerable when their expression took a vulgar form. Between irrationality and coarseness of mind there is an enormous distinction.'

'With coarse minds I have nothing to do.'

'Forgive me if I ask you a blunt question,' said Peak, after hesitating. 'Have you ever associated with women of the highest refinement?'

Earwaker laughed.

'I don't know what that phrase means. It sounds rather odd on your lips.'

'Well, women of the highest class of commoners. With peeresses we needn't concern ourselves.'

'You imagine that social precedence makes all that difference in women?'

'Yes, I do. The daughter of a county family is a finer being than any girl who can spring from the nomad orders.'

'Even supposing your nomads produce a Rachel or a Charlotte Brontë?'

'We are not talking of genius,' Peak replied.

'It was irrelevant, I know. – Well, yes, I *have* conversed now and then with what you would call well-born women. They are delightful creatures, some of them, in given circumstances. But do you think I ever dreamt of taking a wife drenched with social prejudices?'

Peak's face expressed annoyance, and he said nothing.

'A man's wife,' pursued Earwaker, 'may be his superior in whatever you like, *except* social position. That is precisely the distinction that no woman can forget or forgive. On that account they are the obstructive element in social history. If I loved a woman of rank above my own she would make me a renegade; for her sake I should deny my faith. I should write for the *St James's Gazette*, and at last poison myself in an agony of shame.'

A burst of laughter cleared the air for a moment, but for a moment only. Peak's countenance clouded over again, and at length he said in a lower tone:

'There are men whose character would defy that rule.'

'Yes – to their own disaster. But I ought to have made one exception. There *is* a case in which a woman will marry without much regard to her husband's origin. Let him be a parson, and he may aim as high as he chooses.'

Peak tried to smile. He made no answer, and fell into a fit of brooding.

'What's all this about?' asked the journalist, when he too had mused awhile. 'Whose acquaintance have you been making?'

'No one's.'

The suspicion was inevitable.

'If it were true, perhaps you would be justified in mistrusting my way of regarding these things. But it's the natural tendency of my mind. If I ever marry at all, it will be a woman of far higher birth than my own.'

'Don't malign your parents, old fellow. They gave you a brain inferior to that of few men. You will never meet a woman of higher birth.'

'That's a friendly sophism. I can't thank you for it, because it has a bitter side.'

But the compliment had excited Peak, and after a moment's delay he exclaimed:

'I have no other ambition in life – no other! Think the confession as ridiculous as you like; my one supreme desire is to marry a perfectly refined woman. Put it in the correct terms: I am a plebeian, and I aim at marrying a lady.'

The last words were flung out defiantly. He quivered as he spoke, and his face flushed.

'I can't wish you success,' returned his friend, with a grave smile.

'You couldn't help it sounding like a sneer, if you did. The desire is hopeless, of course. It's because I know that, that I have made up my mind to travel for a year or two; it'll help me on towards the age when I shall regard all women with indifference. We won't talk about it any more.'

'One question. You seriously believe that you could find satisfaction in the life to which such a marriage would condemn you?'

'What life?' asked Peak, impatiently.

'That of an average gentleman, let us say, with house in town and country, with friends whose ruling motive was social propriety.'

'I could enjoy the good and throw aside the distasteful.'

'What about the distastefulness of your wife's crass conventionalism, especially in religion?'

'It would not be *crass*, to begin with. If her religion were genuine, I could tolerate it well enough; if it were merely a form, I could train her to my own opinions. Society is growing liberal – the best of it. Please remember that I have in mind a woman of the highest type our civilisation can produce.'

'Then you mustn't look for her in society!'cried Earwaker.

'I don't care; where you will, so long as she had always lived among people of breeding and high education, and never had her thoughts soiled with the vile contact of poverty.'

Earwaker started up and reached a volume from a shelf. Quickly finding the desired page, he began to read aloud:

'Dear, had the world in its caprice
   Deigned to proclaim – I know you both,
   Have recognised your plighted troth,
  Am sponsor for you; live in peace!'—

He read to the end of the poem, and then looked up with an admiring smile.

'An ideal!' exclaimed Peak. 'An ideal akin to Murger's and Musset's grisettes, who never existed.'

'An ideal, most decidedly. But pray what is this consummate lady you have in mind? An ideal every bit as much, and of the two I prefer Browning's. For my own part, I am a polygamist; my wives live in literature, and too far asunder to be able to quarrel. Impossible women, but exquisite. They shall suffice to me.'

Peak rose, sauntered about the room for a minute or two, then said:

'I have just got a title for my paper. I shall call it "The New Sophistry."'

'Do very well, I should think,' replied the other, smiling. 'Will you let me see it when it's done?'

'Who knows if I shall finish it? Nothing I ever undertook has been finished yet – nothing won that I ever aimed at. Good night. Let me hear about Malkin.'

In a week's time Godwin received another summons to Staple Inn, with promise of Malkin's assured presence. In reply he wrote:

'Owing to a new arrangement at Bates's, I start tomorrow for my holiday in Cornwall, so cannot see you for a few weeks. Please offer Malkin my apologies; make them (I mean it) as profuse as those he telegraphed. Herewith I send you my paper, "The New Sophistry", which I have written at a few vehement sittings, and have carelessly copied. If you think it worth while, will you have the kindness to send it for me to *The Critical*? I haven't signed it, as my unmeaning name would perhaps indispose the fellow to see much good in it. I should thank you if you would write in your own person, saying that you act for a friend; you are probably well known in those quarters. If it is accepted, time enough to claim my glory. If it seems to you to have no chance, keep it till I return, as I hate the humiliation of refusals. – Don't think I made an ass of myself the other night. We will never speak on that subject again. All I said was horribly sincere, but I'm afraid you can't understand that side of my nature. I should never have spoken so frankly to Moxey, though he has made no secret with

me of his own weaknesses. If I perish before long in a South
American swamp, you will be able to reflect on my personality
with completer knowledge, so I don't regret the indiscretion.'

III

'*Pereunt et imputantur.*'

Godwin Peak read the motto beneath the clock in Exeter Cathedral, and believed it of Christian origin. Had he known that the words were found in Martial, his rebellious spirit would have enjoyed the consecration of a phrase from such an unlikely author. Even as he must have laughed had he stood in the Vatican before the figures of those two Greek dramatists who, for ages, were revered as Christian saints.

His ignorance preserved him from a clash of sentiments. This afternoon he was not disposed to cynicism; rather he welcomed the softening influence of this noble interior, and let the golden sunlight form what shapes it would – heavenly beam, mystic aureole – before his mind's eye. Architecture had no special interest for him, and the history of church or faith could seldom touch his emotions; but the glorious handiwork of men long dead, the solemn stillness of an ancient sanctuary, made that appeal to him which is independent of names.

'*Pereunt et imputantur.*'

He sat down where the soft, slow ticking of the clock could guide his thoughts. This morning he had left London by the earliest train, and after a night in Exeter would travel westward by leisurely stages, seeing as much as possible of the coast and of that inland scenery which had geological significance. His costume declared him bent on holiday, but, at the same time, distinguished him with delicate emphasis from the tourist of the season. Trustworthy sartorial skill had done its best for his person. Sitting thus, he had the air of a gentleman who enjoys no unwonted ease. He could forget himself in reverie, and be unaware of soft footfalls that drew near along the aisle.

But the sound of a young voice, subdued yet very clear, made claim upon his attention.

'Sidwell! – Sidwell!'

She who spoke was behind him; on looking up, he saw that a lady just in front had stopped and turned to the summons; smiling, she retraced her steps. He moved, so as to look discreetly in the backward direction, and observed a group of four persons, who were occupied with a tablet on the wall: a young man (not long out of boyhood), a girl who might be a year or two younger, and two ladies, of whom it could only be said that they were mature in the beauty of youth, probably of maidenhood – one of them, she who had been called back by the name of 'Sidwell'.

Surely an uncommon name. From a guide-book, with which he had amused himself in the train, he knew that one of the churches of Exeter was dedicated to St Sidwell, but only now did his recollection apprise him of a long past acquaintance with the name of the saint. Had not Buckland Warricombe a sister called Sidwell? And – did he only surmise a connection between the Warricombes and Devon? No, no; on that remote day, when he went out with Buckland to the house near Kingsmill, Mr Warricombe spoke to him of Exeter, – mentioning that the town of his birth was Axminster, where William Buckland, the geologist, also was born; whence the name of his eldest son. How suddenly it all came back!

He rose and moved apart to a spot whence he might quietly observe the strangers. 'Sidwell', once remarked, could not be confused with the companion of her own age; she was slimmer, shorter (if but slightly), more sedate in movement, and perhaps better dressed – though both were admirable in that respect. Ladies, beyond a doubt. And the young man—

At this distance it was easy to deceive oneself, but did not that face bring something back? Now, as he smiled, it seemed to recall Buckland Warricombe – with a difference. This might well be a younger brother; there used to be one or two.

They were familiar with the Cathedral, and at present appeared to take exclusive interest in certain mural monuments. For perhaps ten minutes they lingered about the aisle, then, after a glance at the west window, went forth. With quick step, Godwin pursued them; he issued in time to see them entering an open carriage, which presently drove away towards High Street.

For half an hour he walked the Cathedral Close. Not long ago, on first coming into that quiet space, with its old houses, its smooth lawns, its majestic trees, he had felt the charm peculiar to such scenes – the natural delight in a form of beauty especially English. Now, the impression was irrecoverable; he could see nothing but those four persons, and their luxurious carriage, and the two beautiful horses which had borne them – whither? As likely as not the identity he had supposed for them was quite imaginary; yet it would be easy to ascertain whether a Warricombe family dwelt at Exeter. The forename of Buckland's father –? He never had known it. Still, it was worth while consulting a directory.

He walked to his hotel.

Yes, the name Warricombe stood there, but it occurred more than once. He sought counsel of the landlord. Which of these Warricombes was a gentleman of position, with grown-up sons and daughters? To such a description answered Martin Warricombe, Esquire, well known in the city. His house was in the Old Tiverton Road, out beyond St Sidwell's, two miles away; anyone in that district would serve as guide to it.

With purpose indefinite, Godwin set forth in the direction suggested. At little more than a saunter, he passed out of High Street into its continuation, where he soon descried the Church of St Sidwell, and thence, having made inquiry, walked towards the Old Tiverton Road. He was now quite beyond the town limits, and few pedestrians came in sight; if he really wished to find the abode of Martin Warricombe, he must stop the first questionable person. But to what end this inquiry? He could not even be certain that Martin was the man he had in mind, and even were he right in all his conjectures, what had he to do with the Warricombes?

Ten years ago the family had received him courteously as Buckland's fellow-student; he had spent an hour or two at their house, and subsequently a few words had passed when they saw him on prize-day at Whitelaw. To Buckland he had never written; he had never since heard of him; that name was involved in the miserable whirl of circumstances which brought his College life to a close, and it was always his hope that Buckland thought no more of him. Even had there been no disagreeable memories, it was surely impossible to renew after this interval so very slight an acquaintance. How could they receive him, save with civilly mild astonishment?

An errand-boy came along, whistling townwards, a big basket over his head. No harm in asking where Mr Warricombe lived. The reply was prompt: second house on the right hand, rather a large one, not a quarter of a mile onward.

Here, then. The site was a good one. From this part of the climbing road one looked over the lower valley of the Exe, saw the whole estuary, and beyond that a horizon of blue sea. Fair, rich land, warm under the westering sun. The house itself seemed to be old, but after all was not very large; it stood amid laurels, and in the garden behind rose a great yew-tree. No person was visible;

but for the wave-like murmur of neighbouring pines, scarce a sound would have disturbed the air.

Godwin walked past, and found that the road descended into a deep hollow, whence between high banks, covered with gorse and bracken and many a summer flower, it led again up a hill thick planted with firs; at the lowest point was a bridge over a streamlet, offering on either hand a view of soft green meadows. A spot of exquisite retirement: happy who lived here in security from the struggle of life!

It was folly to spoil his enjoyment of country such as this by dreaming impossible opportunities. The Warricombes could be nothing to him; to meet with Buckland would only revive the shame long ago outlived. After resting for a few minutes he turned back, passed the silent house again, delighted himself with the wide view, and so into the city once more, where he began to seek the remnants of its old walls.

The next morning was Sunday, and he had planned to go by the Plymouth train to a station whence he could reach Start Point; but his mood was become so unsettled that ten o'clock, when already he should have been on his journey, found him straying about the Cathedral Close. A mere half-purpose, a vague wavering intention, which might at any moment be scattered by common sense, drew his steps to the door of the Cathedral, where people were entering for morning service; he moved idly within sight of the carriages which drew up. Several had discharged their freightage of tailoring and millinery, when two vehicles, which seemed companions, stopped at the edge of the pavement, and from the second alighted the young ladies whom Godwin had yesterday observed; their male companion, however, was different. The carriage in advance also contained four persons: a gentleman of sixty, his wife, a young girl, and the youth of yesterday. It needed but a glance to inform Godwin that the oldest of the party was Mr Warricombe, Buckland's father; ten years had made no change in his aspect. Mrs Warricombe was not less recognisable. They passed at once into the edifice, and he had scarcely time to bestow a keen look upon Sidwell.

That was a beautiful girl; he stood musing upon the picture registered by his brain. But why not follow, and from a neighbouring seat survey her and the others at his leisure? Pooh! But the impulse constrained him. After all, he could not get a place that allowed him to see Sidwell. Her companion, however, the one who seemed to be of much the same age, was well in view. Sisters they could not be; nothing of the Warricombe countenance revealed itself in those handsome but strongly-marked features. A beautiful girl, she also, yet of a type that made slight appeal to him. Sidwell was all he could imagine of sweet and dignified; more modest in bearing, more gracile, more—

Monday at noon, and he still walked the streets of Exeter. Early this morning he had been out to the Old Tiverton Road, and there, on the lawn amid the laurels, had caught brief glimpse of two female figures, in one of which he merely divined Sidwell. Why he tarried thus he did not pretend to explain to himself. Rain had just come on, and the lowering sky made him low-spirited; he mooned about the street under his umbrella.

And at this rate, might vapour away his holiday. Exeter was tedious, but he could not make up his mind to set forth for the sea-shore, where only his own thoughts awaited him. Packed away in his wallet lay geological hammer, azimuth compass, clinometer, miniature microscope, – why should he drag all that lumber about with him? What to him were the bygone millions of ages, the hoary records of unimaginable time? One touch of a girl's hand, one syllable of musical speech, – was it not that whereof his life had truly need?

As remote from him, however, as the age of the pterodactyl. How often was it necessary to repeat this? On a long voyage, such as he had all but resolved to take, one might perchance form acquaintances. He had heard of such things; not impossibly, a social circle might open to him at Buenos Ayres. But here in England his poor origin, his lack of means would for ever bar him from the intimacy of people like the Warricombes.

He loitered towards the South-Western station, dimly conscious of a purpose to look for trains. Instead of seeking the time-tables he stood before the bookstall and ran his eye along the titles of new novels; he had half a mind to buy one of Hardy's and read himself into the temper which suited summer rambles. But just as his hand was stretched forth, a full voice, speaking beside him, made demand for a London weekly paper. Instantly he turned. The tones had carried him back to Whitelaw; the face disturbed that illusion, but substituted a reality which threw him into tremor.

His involuntary gaze was met with one of equal intensity. A man of his own years, but in splendid health and with bright eyes that looked enjoyment of life, suddenly addressed him.

'Godwin Peak – surely—?'

'Buckland Warricombe, no less surely.'

They shook hands with vigour, laughing in each other's faces; then, after a moment's pause, Warricombe drew aside from the bookstall, for sake of privacy.

'Why did we lose sight of each other?' he asked, flashing a glance at Godwin's costume. 'Why didn't you write to me at Cambridge? What have you been doing this half-century?'

'I have been in London all the time.'

'I am there most of the year. Well, I rejoice to have met you. On a holiday?'

'Loitering towards Cornwall.'

'In that case, you can come and have lunch with me at my father's house. It's only a mile or two off. I was going to walk, but we'll drive, if you like.'

There was no refusing, and no possibility of reflection. Buckland's hearty manner made the invitation in itself a thoroughly pleasant one, and before Peak could sufficiently command his thoughts to picture the scene towards which he was going they were walking side by side through the town. In appearance, Warricombe showed nothing of the revolutionary which, in old days, he aimed at making himself, and his speech had a suavity which no doubt resulted from much intercourse with the polished world; Godwin was filled with envious admiration of his perfect physique, and the mettle which kept it in such excellent vigour. Even for a sturdy walker, it was no common task to keep pace with Buckland's strides; Peak soon found himself conversing rather too breathlessly for comfort.

'What is your latest record for the mile?' he inquired.

Warricombe, understanding at once the reference to his old athletic pastime and its present application, laughed merrily, and checked his progress.

'A bad habit of mine; it gets me into trouble with everyone. By-the-bye, haven't you become a stronger man than used to seem likely? I'm quite glad to see how well you look.'

The sincerity of these expressions, often repeated, put Godwin far more at his ease than the first moment's sensation had promised. He too began to feel a genuine pleasure in the meeting, and soon bade defiance to all misgivings. Delicacy perhaps withheld Warricombe from further mention of Whitelaw, but on the other hand it was not impossible that he knew nothing of the circumstances which tormented Godwin's memory. On leaving the College perchance he had lost all connection with those common friends who might have informed him of subsequent jokes and rumours. Unlikely, to be sure; for doubtless some of his Whitelaw contemporaries encountered him at Cambridge; and again, was it not probable that the younger Warricombe had become a Whitelaw student? Then Professor Gale – no matter! The Warricombes of course knew all about Andrew Peak and his dining-rooms, but they were liberal-minded, and could forgive a boy's weakness, as well as overlook an acquaintance's obscure origin. In the joy of finding himself exuberantly welcomed by a man of Buckland's world he overcame his ignoble self-consciousness.

'Did you know that we were in this part of the country?' Warricombe asked, once more speeding ahead.

'I always thought of you in connection with Kingsmill.'

'We gave up Thornhaw seven years ago. My father was never quite comfortable out of Devonshire. The house I am taking you to has been in our family for three generations. I have often tried to be proud of the fact, but, as you would guess, that kind of thing doesn't come very natural to me.'

In the effort to repudiate such sentiment, Buckland distinctly betrayed its hold upon him. He imagined he was meeting Godwin on equal ground, but the sensibility of the proletarian could not thus be deceived. There was a brief silence, during which each looked away from the other.

'Still keep up your geology?' was Warricombe's next question.

'I can just say that I haven't forgotten it all.'

'I'm afraid that's more than I can. During my Cambridge time it caused disagreeable debates with my father. You remember that his science is of the old school. I wouldn't say a word to disparage him. I believe the extent of his knowledge is magnificent; but he can't get rid of that old man of the sea, the Book of Genesis. A few years ago I wasn't too considerate in argument, and I talked as I oughtn't to have done, called names, and so on. The end of it was, I dropped science altogether, having got as much out of it as I needed. The good old pater has quite forgiven my rudeness. At present we agree to differ, and get on capitally. I'm sure he'll be delighted to see you. There are some visitors with us; a Miss Moorhouse and her brother. I think you'll like them. Couldn't you stay overnight?'

Godwin was unable to reply on the instant, and his companion proceeded with the same heartiness.

'Just as you like, you know. But do stay if you can. On Wednesday morning I must go back to town. I act as secretary to Godolphin, the member for Slacksea.'

Peak's acquaintance with current politics was slight, but Mr Ellis Godolphin, the aristocratic Radical, necessarily stood before his imagination with some clearness of outline. So this was how life had dealt with Buckland. The announcement was made with a certain satisfaction, as if it implied more than the hearer would readily appreciate. Again there was a slight shrinking on Godwin's part; it would be natural for him to avow his own position, and so leave no room for misunderstandings, but before he could shape a phrase Buckland was again questioning.

'Do you ever see any of the old fellows?'

'I have met one or two of them, by chance.'

As if his tact informed him that this inquiry had been a mistake, Warricombe resumed the subject of his family.

'My brother Louis is at home – of course you can't remember him; he was a youngster when you were at Thornhaw. The younger boy died some years ago, a pony accident; cut up my father dreadfully. Then there's my sister Sidwell, and my sister Fanny – that's all of us. I can't quite answer for Louis, but the rest are of the old school. Liberal enough, don't be afraid. But – well, the old school.'

As Godwin kept silence, the speaker shot a glance at him, keenly scrutinising. Their eyes did not meet; Peak kept his on the ground.

'Care much about politics nowadays?'

'Not very much.'

'Can't say that I do myself,' pursued Buckland. 'I rather drifted into it. Godolphin, I daresay, has as little humbug about him as most parliamentarians; we stick to the practical fairly well. I shall never go into the House on my own account. But there's a sort of pleasure in being in the thick of public movements. I'm not cut out for debate; should lose my temper, and tell disagreeable truths – which wouldn't do, you know. But behind the scenes – it isn't bad, in a way.'

A longer pause obliged Godwin to speak of himself.

'My life is less exciting. For years I have worked in a manufacturing laboratory at Rotherhithe.'

'So science has carried the day with you, after all. It used to be very doubtful.'

This was a kind and pleasant way of interpreting necessity. Godwin felt grateful, and added with a smile:

'I don't think I shall stick to it much longer. For one thing, I am sick of town. Perhaps I shall travel for a year or two; perhaps – I'm in a state of transition, to tell the truth.'

Buckland revolved this information; his face told that he found it slightly puzzling.

'You once had thoughts of literature.'

'Long given up.'

'Leisure would perhaps revive them?'

'Possibly; but I think not.'

They were now quitting the town, and Peak, unwilling to appear before strangers in a state of profuse perspiration, again moderated his friend's speed. They began to talk about the surrounding country, a theme which occupied them until the house was reached. With quick-beating heart, Godwin found himself at the gate by which he had already twice passed. Secure in the decency of his apparel, and no longer oppressed by bashfulness, he would have gone joyously forward but for the dread of a possible ridiculous association which his name might revive in the thoughts of Mr and Mrs Warricombe. Yet Buckland – who had no lack of kindly feeling – would hardly have brought him here had the reception which awaited him been at all dubious.

'If we don't come across anyone,' said Warricombe, 'we'll go straight up to my room.'

But the way was not clear. Within the beautiful old porch sat Sidwell Warricombe and her friend of the striking countenance, whom Godwin now knew as Miss Moorhouse. Buckland addressed his sister in a tone of lively pleasure.

'Whom do you think I have met and brought home with me? Here is my old friend, Godwin Peak.'

Under the two pairs of female eyes, Godwin kept a calm, if rather stern, face.

'I should have had no difficulty in recognising Mr Peak,' said Sidwell, holding out her hand. 'But was the meeting quite by chance?'

To Godwin himself the question was of course directed, with a look of smiling interest – such welcome as could not have been improved upon; she listened to his reply, then presented him to

Miss Moorhouse. A slight languor in her movements and her voice, together with the beautiful coldness of her complexion, made it probable that she did not share the exuberant health manifest in her two brothers. She conversed with mature self-possession, yet showed a slight tendency to abstractedness. On being addressed, she regarded the speaker steadily for an instant before shaping her answer, which always, however trifling the subject, seemed carefully worded. In these few moments of dialogue, Godwin reached the conclusion that Sidwell had not much sense of humour, but that the delicacy of her mind was unsurpassable.

In Miss Moorhouse there was no defect of refinement, but her conversation struck a note of sprightliness at once more energetic and more subtle than is often found in English girls. Thus, though at times she looked so young that it might be doubted whether she had long been out of her teens, at others one suspected her older than Sidwell. The friends happened to be as nearly as possible of an age, which was verging to twenty-six.

When he spoke to Miss Moorhouse, Buckland's frank tone subdued itself. He watched her face with reverent attention, smiled when she smiled, and joined in her laughter with less than his usual volume of sound. In acuteness he was obviously inferior to her, and there were moments when he betrayed some nervousness under her rejoinders. All this was matter of observation for Peak, who had learnt to exercise his discernment even whilst attending to the proprieties.

The sounding of the first luncheon-bell left the young men free to go upstairs. When at length they presented themselves in the drawing-room, Mrs Warricombe and her younger daughter sat there alone. The greeting of his hostess did not quite satisfy Godwin, though it was sufficiently courteous; he remembered that ten years ago Mrs Warricombe had appeared to receive him with some restraint, and his sensation in renewing her acquaintance was one of dislike. But in a moment the master of the house joined them, and no visitor could have had a more kindly welcome than that he offered to his son's friend. With genial tact, Mr Warricombe ignored the interval since his last conversation with Godwin, and spoke as if this visit were the most natural thing in the world.

'Do you already know the country about Exeter?'

'I have seen very little of it yet.'

'Oh, then, we must show you our points of view. Our own garden offers a glimpse of the river-mouth and a good prospect of Haldon – the ridge beyond the Exe; but there are many much better points within easy reach. You are in no hurry, I hope?'

Louis Warricombe and Miss Moorhouse's brother were away on a long walk; they did not return for lunch. Godwin was glad of this, for time had wrought the change in him that he felt more at ease in female society than under the eyes of young men whose social position inclined them to criticism. The meal proved as delightful as luncheon is wont to be in a luxurious country-house, when brilliant sunshine gleams on the foliage visible from windows, and the warmth of the season sanctions clear colours in costume. The talk was wholly of country pleasures. It afforded the visitor no little satisfaction to be able to make known his acquaintance with parts of England to which the Warricombes had not penetrated. Godwin learnt that the family were insular in their tastes; a mention by Miss Moorhouse of continental scenes led the host to avow a strong preference for his own country, under whatever aspect, and Sidwell murmured her sympathy.

No less introspective than in the old days, though he could better command his muscles, Peak, after each of his short remarks, made comparison of his tone and phraseology with those of the other speakers. Had he still any marks of the ignoble world from which he sprang? Any defect of pronunciation, any native awkwardness of utterance? Impossible to judge himself infallibly, but he was conscious of no vulgar mannerism. Though it was so long since he left Whitelaw, the accent of certain of the Professors still remained with him as an example: when endeavouring to be graceful, he was wont to hear the voice of Dr Nares, or of Professor Barber who lectured on English Literature. More recently he had been observant of Christian Moxey's speech, which had a languid elegance worth imitating in certain particulars. Buckland Warricombe was rather a careless talker, but it was the carelessness of a man who had never needed to reflect on such a matter, the refinement of whose enunciation was assured to him from the nursery. That now was a thing to be aimed at. Preciseness must be avoided, for in a young man it seemed to argue conscious effort: a loose sentence now and then, a colloqualism substituted for the more grammatical phrase.

Heaven be thanked that he was unconcerned on the point of garb! Inferiority in that respect would have been fatal to his ease.

His clothes were not too new, and in quality were such as he had the habit of wearing. The Warricombes must have immediately detected any pretentiousness, were it but in a necktie; that would impress them more unfavourably than signs of poverty. But he defied inspection. Not Sidwell herself, doubtless sensitive in the highest degree, could conceive a prejudice against him on this account.

His misgivings were overcome. If these people were acquainted with the 'dining-rooms' joke, it certainly did not affect their behaviour to him, and he could hope, by the force of his personality, to obliterate from their minds such disagreeable thoughts as they might secretly entertain. Surely he could make good his claim to be deemed a gentleman. To Buckland he had declared his position, and no shame attached to it. A man of scientific tastes, like Mr Warricombe, must consider it respectable enough. Grant him a little time, and why should he not become a recognised friend of this family?

If he were but resident in Exeter.

For the first time, he lost himself in abstraction, and only an inquiry from Sidwell recalled him.

'You have seen the Cathedral, Mr Peak?'

'Oh yes! I attended service there yesterday morning.'

Had he reflected, perhaps he would not have added this circumstance; even in speaking he suffered a confused doubtfulness. But as soon as the words were uttered, he felt strangely glad. Sidwell bestowed upon him an unmistakable look of approval; her mother gazed with colder interest; Mr Warricombe regarded him, and mused; Buckland, a smile of peculiar meaning on his close lips, glanced from him to Miss Moorhouse.

'Ah, then, you heard Canon Grayling,' remarked the father of the family, with something in his tone which answered to Sidwell's facial expression. 'How did you like his sermon?'

Godwin was trifling with a pair of nut-crackers, but the nervousness evident in his fingers did not prevent him from replying with a natural air of deliberation.

'I was especially struck with the passage about the barren fig-tree.'

The words might have expressed a truth, but in that case a tone of sarcasm must have winged them. As it was, they involved either hypocrisy or ungenerous irony at the expense of his questioner. Buckland could not but understand them in the latter sense; his

face darkened. At that moment, Peak met his eye, and encountered its steady searching gaze with a perfectly calm smile.
Half-a-dozen pulsings of his heart – violent, painful, and the fatal
hour of his life had struck.

'What had he to say about it?' Buckland asked, carelessly.

Peak's reply was one of those remarkable efforts of mind – one
might say, of character – which are sometimes called forth,
without premeditation, almost without consciousness, by a
profound moral crisis. A minute or two ago he would have
believed it impossible to recall and state in lucid terms the
arguments to which, as he sat in the Cathedral, he had barely
given ear; he remembered vaguely that the preacher (whose name
he knew not till now) had dwelt for a few moments on the topic
indicated, but at the time he was indisposed to listen seriously,
and what chance was there that the chain of thought had fixed
itself in his memory? Now, under the marvelling regard of his
conscious self, he poured forth an admirable rendering of the
Canon's views, fuller than the original – more eloquent, more
subtle. For five minutes he held his hearers in absorbed attention,
even Buckland bending forward with an air of genuine interest;
and when he stopped, rather suddenly, there followed a silence.

'Mr Peak,' said the host, after a cough of apology, 'you have
made that clearer to me than it was yesterday. I must thank you.'

Godwin felt that a slight bow of acknowledgment was perhaps
called for, but not a muscle would obey his will. He was
enervated; perspiration stood on his forehead. The most severe
physical effort could not have reduced him to a feebler state.

Sidwell was speaking:

'Mr Peak has developed what Canon Grayling only suggested.'

'A brilliant effort of exegesis,' exclaimed Buckland, with a
good-natured laugh.

Again the young men exchanged looks. Godwin smiled as one
might under a sentence of death. As for the other, his suspicion
had vanished, and he now gave way to frank amusement.
Luncheon was over, and by a general movement all went forth on
to the lawn in front of the house. Mr Warricombe, even more
cordial than hitherto, named to Godwin the features of the
extensive landscape.

'But you see that the view is in a measure spoilt by the growth of
the city. A few years ago, none of those ugly little houses stood in
the mid-distance. A few years hence, I fear, there will be much

more to complain of. I daresay you know all about the ship-canal: the story of the countess, and so forth?'

Buckland presently suggested that the afternoon might be used for a drive.

'I was about to propose it,' said his father. 'You might start by the Stoke Canon Road, so as to let Mr Peak have the famous view from the gate; then go on towards Silverton, for the sake of the reversed prospect from the Exe. Who shall be of the party?'

It was decided that four only should occupy the vehicle, Miss Moorhouse and Fanny Warricombe to be the two ladies. Godwin regretted Sidwell's omission, but the friendly informality of the arrangement delighted him. When the carriage rolled softly from the gravelled drive, Buckland holding the reins, he felt an animation such as no event had ever produced in him. No longer did he calculate phrases. A spontaneous aptness marked his dialogue with Miss Moorhouse, and the laughing words he now and then addressed to Fanny. For a short time Buckland was laconic, but at length he entered into the joyous tone of the occasion. Earwaker would have stood in amazement, could he have seen and heard the saturnine denizen of Peckham Rye.

The weather was superb. A sea-breeze mitigated the warmth of the cloudless sun, and where a dark pine-tree rose against the sky it gave the azure depths a magnificence unfamiliar to northern eyes.

'On such a day as this,' remarked Miss Moorhouse, dividing her look between Buckland and his friend, 'one feels that there's a good deal to be said for England.'

'But for the vile weather,' was Warricombe's reply, 'you wouldn't know such enjoyment.'

'Oh, I can't agree with that for a moment! My capacity for enjoyment is unlimited. That philosophy is unworthy of you; it belongs to a paltry scheme called "making the best of things".'

'In which you excel, Miss Moorhouse.'

'That she does!' agreed Fanny — a laughing, rosy-cheeked maiden.

'I deny it! No one is more copious in railing against circumstances.'

'But you turn them all to a joke,' Fanny objected.

'That's my profound pessimism. I am misunderstood. No one expects irony from a woman.'

Peak found it difficult not to gaze too persistently at the subtle countenance. He was impelled to examine it by a consciousness that he himself received a large share of Miss Moorhouse's attention, and a doubt as to the estimation in which she held him. Canon Grayling's sermon and Godwin's comment had elicited no remark from her. Did she belong to the ranks of emancipated women? With his experience of Marcella Moxey, he welcomed the possibility of this variation of the type, but at the same time, in obedience to a new spirit that had strange possession of him, recognised that such phenomena no longer aroused his personal interest. By the oddest of intellectual processes he had placed himself altogether outside the sphere of unorthodox spirits. Concerning Miss Moorhouse he cared only for the report she might make of him to the Warricombes.

Before long, the carriage was stopped that he might enjoy one of the pleasantest views in the neighbourhood of the city. A gate, interrupting a high bank with which the road was bordered, gave admission to the head of a great cultivated slope, which fell to the river Exe; hence was suddenly revealed a wide panorama. Three well-marked valleys – those of the Creedy, the Exe, and the Culm – spread their rural loveliness to remote points of the horizon; gentle undulations, with pasture and woodland, with long winding roads, and many a farm that gleamed white amid its orchard leafage, led the gaze into regions of evanescent hue and outline. Westward, a bolder swell pointed to the skirts of Dartmoor. No inappropriate detail disturbed the impression. Exeter was wholly hidden behind the hill on which the observers stood, and the line of railway leading thither could only be descried by special search. A foaming weir at the hill's foot blended its soft murmur with that of the fir branches hereabouts; else, no sound that the air could convey beyond the pulsing of a bird's note.

All had alighted, and for a minute or two there was silence. When Peak had received such geographical instruction as was needful, Warricombe pointed out to him a mansion conspicuous on the opposite slope of the Exe valley, the seat of Sir Stafford Northcote. The house had no architectural beauty, but its solitary lordship amid green pastures and tracts of thick wood declared the graces and privileges of ancestral wealth. Standing here alone, Godwin would have surveyed these possessions of an English aristocrat with more or less bitterness; envy would, for a moment at all events, have perturbed his pleasure in the natural scene.

Accompanied as he was, his emotion took a form which indeed was allied to envy, but had nothing painful. He exulted in the prerogatives of birth and opulence, felt proud of hereditary pride, gloried that his mind was capable of appreciating to the full those distinctions which, by the vulgar, are not so much as suspected. Admitted to equal converse with men and women who represented the best in English society, he could cast away the evil grudge, the fierce spirit of self-assertion, and be what nature had proposed in endowing him with large brain, generous blood, delicate tissues. What room for malignancy? He was accepted by his peers, and could regard with tolerance even those ignoble orders of mankind amid whom he had so long dwelt unrecognised.

A bee hummed past him, and this sound – of all the voices of nature that which most intenerates – filled his heart to overflowing. Moisture made his eyes dim, and at the impulse of a feeling of gratitude, such as only the subtlest care of psychology could fully have explained, he turned to Buckland, saying:

'But for my meeting with you I should have had a lonely and not very cheerful holiday. I owe you a great deal.'

Warricombe laughed, but as an Englishman does when he wishes to avoid show of emotion.

'I am very glad indeed that we did meet. Stay with us over to-morrow. I only wish I were not obliged to go to London on Wednesday. – Look, Fanny, isn't that a hawk, over Cowley Bridge?'

'Do you feel you would like to shoot it?' asked Miss Moorhouse – who a moment ago had very closely examined Peak's face.

'To shoot it – why do you ask that?'

'Confess that you felt the desire.'

'Every man does,' replied Buckland, 'until he has had a moment to recover himself. That's the human instinct.'

'The male human instinct. Thank you for your honesty.'

They drove on, and by a wide circuit, occasionally stopping for the view, returned to the Old Tiverton Road, and so home. By this time Louis Warricombe and Mr Moorhouse were back from their walk. Reposing in the company of the ladies, they had partaken of such refreshments as are lawful at five o'clock, and now welcomed with vivacity the later arrivals. Moorhouse was something older than Buckland, a sallow-cheeked man with forehead and eyes expressive of much intelligence. Till of late he had been a Cambridge tutor, but was now privately occupied in mathematical pursuits. Louis Warricombe had not yet made up his mind what profession to follow, and to aid the process of resolve had for the present devoted himself to physical exercise.

Tea-cup in hand, Godwin seated himself by Sidwell, who began by inquiring how the drive had pleased him. The fervour of his reply caused her to smile with special graciousness, and their conversation was uninterrupted for some minutes. Then Fanny came forward with a book of mosses, her own collection, which she had mentioned to Peak as they were talking together in the carriage.

'Do you make special study of any science?' Sidwell asked, when certain remarks of Godwin's had proved his familiarity with the things he was inspecting.

'It is long since I worked seriously at anything of the kind,' he answered; adding in a moment, 'except at chemistry – that only because it is my business.'

'Organic or inorganic chemistry?' inquired Fanny, with the promptness of a schoolgirl who wishes to have it known that her ideas are no longer vague.

'Organic for the most part,' Godwin replied, smiling at her. 'And of the most disagreeable kind.'

Sidwell reflected, then put another question, but with some diffidence.

'I think you were once fond of geology?'

It was the first allusion to that beginning of their acquaintance, ten years ago. Peak succeeded in meeting her look with steadiness.

'Yes, I still like it.'

'Father's collections have been much improved since you saw them at Thornhaw.'

'I hope Mr Warricombe will let me see them.'

Buckland came up and made an apology for drawing his friend aside.

'Will you let us send for your traps? You may just as well have a room here for a night or two.'

Perpetually imagining some kind chance that might associate him with civilised people, Godwin could not even pack his portmanteau for a ramble to Land's End without stowing away a dress suit. He was thus saved what would have been an embarrassment of special annoyance. Without hesitation, he accepted Buckland's offer, and named the hotel at which the luggage was deposited.

'All right; the messenger shall explain. Our name's well enough known to them. If you would like to look up my father in his study, he'll be delighted to go over his collections with you. You still care for that kind of thing?'

'Most certainly. How can you doubt it?'

Buckland smiled, and gave no other reply.

'Ask Fanny to show you the way when you care to go.' And he left the room.

IV

Sidwell had fallen into conversation with Mr Moorhouse. Miss Moorhouse, Mrs Warricombe, and Louis were grouped in animated talk. Observing that Fanny threw glances towards him from a lonely corner, Peak went over to her, and was pleased with the smile he met. Fanny had watchet eyes, much brighter than Sidwell's; her youthful vivacity blended with an odd little fashion of schoolgirl pedantry in a very piquant way. Godwin's attempts at conversation with her were rather awkward; he found it difficult to strike the suitable note, something not too formal yet not deficient in respect.

'Do you think,' he asked presently, 'that I should disturb your father if I went to him?'

'Oh, not at all! I often go and sit in the study at this time.'

'Will you show me the way?'

Fanny at once rose, and together they crossed the hall, passed through a sort of anteroom connecting with a fernery, and came to the study door. A tap was answered by cheerful summons, and Fanny looked in.

'Well, my ladybird? Ah, you are bringing Mr Peak; come in, come in!'

It was a large and beautiful room, its wide windows, in a cushioned recess, looking upon the lawn where the yew tree cast solemn shade. One wall presented an unbroken array of volumes, their livery sober but handsome; detached bookcases occupied other portions of the irregular perimeter. Cabinets, closed and open, were arranged with due regard to convenience. Above the mantelpiece hung a few small photographs, but the wall-space at disposal was chiefly occupied with objects which illustrated Mr Warricombe's scientific tastes. On a stand in the light of the window gleamed two elaborate microscopes, provocative of enthusiasm in a mind such as Godwin's.

In a few minutes, Fanny silently retired. Her father, by no means forward to speak of himself and his pursuits, was led in that direction by Peak's expressions of interest, and the two were soon busied with matters which had a charm for both. A collection of elvans formed the starting-point, and when they had entered upon the wide field of palæontology it was natural for Mr Warricombe to invite his guest's attention to the species of *homalonotus* which he had had the happiness of identifying some ten years ago – a discovery now recognised and chronicled. Though his sympathy was genuine enough, Godwin struggled against an uneasy sense of manifesting excessive appreciation. Never oblivious of himself, he could not utter the simplest phrase of admiration without criticising its justice, its tone. And at present it behoved him to bear in mind that he was conversing with no half-bred sciolist. Mr Warricombe obviously had his share of human weakness, but he was at once a gentleman and a student of well-stored mind; insincerity must be very careful if it would not jar upon his refined ear. So Godwin often checked himself in the utterance of what might sound too much like flattery. A young man talking with one much older, a poor man in dialogue with a wealthy, must under any circumstances guard his speech; for one of Godwin's aggressive idiosyncrasy the task of discretion had peculiar difficulties, and the attitude he had assumed at luncheon still further complicated the operations of his mind. Only at moments could he speak in his true voice, and silence meant for the most part a studious repression of much he would naturally have uttered.

Resurgent envy gave him no little trouble. On entering the room, he could not but exclaim to himself, 'How easy for a man to do notable work amid such surroundings! If I were but thus equipped for investigation!' And as often as his eyes left a particular object to make a general survey, the same thought burned in him. He feared lest it should be legible on his countenance.

Taking a pamphlet from the table, Mr Warricombe, with a humorous twinkle in his eyes, inquired whether Peak read German; the answer being affirmative:

'Naturally,' he rejoined, 'you could hardly have neglected so important a language. I, unfortunately, didn't learn it in my youth, and I have never had perseverance enough to struggle with it since. Something led me to take down this brochure the other day – an old attempt of mine to write about the weathering of rocks. It was printed in '76, and no sooner had it seen the light than friends of mine wanted to know what I meant by appropriating, without acknowledgement, certain facts quite recently pointed out by Professor Pfaff of Erlangen! Unhappily, Professor Pfaff's results were quite unknown to me, and I had to get them translated. The coincidences, sure enough, were very noticeable. Just before you came in, I was reviving that old discomfiture.'

Peak, in glancing over the pages, murmured with a smile:

'*Pereant qui ante nos nostra dixerunt!*'

'Even so!' exclaimed Mr Warricombe, laughing with a subdued heartiness which was one of his pleasant characteristics. And, after a pause, he inquired, 'Do you find any time to keep up your classics?'

'By fits and starts. Sometimes I return to them for a month or two.'

'Why, it's pretty much the same with me. Here on my table, for instance, lies Tacitus. I found it mentioned not long ago that the first sentence of the *Annals* is a hexameter – did you know it? – and when I had once got hold of the book I thought it a shabby thing to return it to the dust of its shelf without reading at least a few pages. So I have gone on from day to day, with no little enjoyment. Buckland, as you probably know, regards these old fellows with scorn.'

'We always differed about that.'

'I can't quite decide whether he is still sincere in all he says about them. Time, I suspect, is mellowing his judgment.'

They moved to the shelves where Greek and Latin books stood in serried order, and only the warning dinner-bell put an end to their sympathetic discussion of the place such authors should hold in modern educational systems.

'Have they shown you your room?' Mr Warricombe asked.

But, as he spoke, the face of his eldest son appeared at the door.

'Your traps have safely arrived, Peak.'

The bedroom to which Godwin was conducted had a delicious fragrance, of source indeterminable. When he had closed the door, he stood for a few moments looking about him; it was his first experience of the upper chambers of houses such as this. Merely to step upon the carpet fluttered his senses: merely to breathe the air was a purification. Luxury of the rational kind, dictated by regard for health of body and soul, appeared in every detail. On the walls were water-colours, scenery of Devon and Cornwall; a hanging book-case held about a score of volumes – poets, essayists, novelists. Elsewhere, not too prominent, lay a Bible and a Prayer-book.

He dressed, as never before, with leisurely enjoyment of the process. When the mirror declared him ready, his eyes returned frequently to an inspection of the figure he presented, and it seemed to him that he was not unworthy to take his place at the dinner-table. As for his visage, might he not console himself with the assurance that it was of no common stamp? 'If I met that man in a room, I should be curious about him; I should see at once that he didn't belong to the vulgar; I should desire to hear him speak.' And the Warricombes were not lacking in discernment. He would compare more than favourably with Mr Moorhouse, whose aspect, bright and agreeable enough, made no promise of originality. – It must be time to go down. He left the room with an air of grave self-confidence.

At dinner he was careful to attempt no repetition of the display which had done very well at luncheon; it must not be thought that he had the habit of talking for effect. Mrs Warricombe, unless he mistook, had begun to view him more favourably; her remarks made less distinction between him and the other guests. But he could not like his hostess; he thought her unworthy to be the mother of Sidwell and Fanny, of Buckland and Louis; there was a marked strain of the commonplace in her. The girls, costumed for the evening, affected him with a return of the awe he had all but overcome. Sidwell was exquisite in dark colours, her sister in white. Miss Moorhouse (addressed by her friends as 'Sylvia') looked older than in the day-time, and had lost something of her animation; possibly the country routine had begun to weary her a little.

Peak was at a vast distance from the hour which saw him alight at Exeter and begin his ramble about the city. He no longer felt himself alone in the world; impossible to revive the mood in which he deliberately planned to consume his economies in a year or two of desert wandering; far other were the anticipations which warmed his mind when the after-dinner repose attuned him to unwonted hopefulness. This family were henceforth his friends, and it depended only upon himself to make the connection lasting, with all manner of benefits easily imagined. Established in the country, the Warricombes stood to him in quite a different relation from any that could have arisen had he met with them in London. There he would have been nothing more than a casual dinner-guest, welcomed for the hour and all but forgotten when he had said good-night. For years he had understood that London offered him no prospect of social advancement. But a night passed under this roof practically raised him to a level whence he surveyed a rich field of possible conquest. With the genial geologist he felt himself on excellent terms, and much of this was ascribable to a singular chance which had masked his real being, and represented him, with scarce an effort of his own, in a light peculiarly attractive to Mr Warricombe. He was now playing the conscious hypocrite; not a pleasant thing to face and accept, but the fault was not his – fate had brought it about. At all events, he aimed at no vulgar profit; his one desire was for human fellowship; he sought nothing but that solace which every code of morals has deemed legitimate. Let the society which compelled to such an expedient bear the burden of its shame.

That must indeed have been a circle of great intellects amid which Godwin Peak felt himself subordinate. He had never known that impression, and in the Warricombe family was no one whom he could regard even as his equal. Buckland, doubtless, had some knowledge of the world, and could boast of a free mind; but he lacked subtlety: a psychological problem would easily puzzle him. Mr Warricombe's attainments were respectable, but what could be said of a man who had devoted his life to geology, and still (in the year 1884) remained an orthodox member of the Church of England? Godwin, as he sat in the drawing-room and enjoyed its atmosphere of refinement, sincerely held himself of far more account as an intellectual being than all the persons about him.

But if his brain must dwell in solitude his heart might compass worthy alliances – the thing most needful to humanity. One may find the associates of his intellect in libraries – the friend of one's emotions must walk in flesh and blood. Earwaker, Moxey – these were in many respects admirable fellows, and he had no little love for them, but the world they represented was womanless, and so of flagrant imperfection. Of Marcella Moxey he could not think emotionally; indeed she emphasised by her personality the lack which caused his suffering. Sidwell Warricombe suggested, more completely than any woman he had yet observed, that companionship without which life must to the end taste bitter. His interest in her was not strictly personal; she moved and spoke before him as a typical woman, not as the daughter of Martin Warricombe and the sister of Buckland. Here at last opened to his view that sphere of female society which he had known as remotely existing, the desperate aim of ambition.

Conventional women – but was not the phrase tautological? In the few females who have liberated their souls, was not much of the woman inevitably sacrificed, and would it not be so for long years to come? On the other hand, such a one as Sidwell might be held a perfect creature, perfect in relation to a certain stage of human development. Look at her, as she sat conversing with Moorhouse, soft candle-light upon her face; compare her on the one hand with an average emancipated girl, on the other with a daughter of the people. How unsatisfying was the former; the latter, how repulsive! Here one had the exquisite mean, the lady as England has perfected her towards the close of this nineteenth century. A being of marvellous delicacy, of purest instincts, of unsurpassable sweetness. Who could not detail her limitations, obvious and, in certain moods, irritating enough? These were nothing to the point, unless one would roam the world a hungry idealist; and Godwin was weary of the famined pilgrimage.

The murmur of amiable voices softened him to the reception of all that was good in his present surroundings, and justified in the light of sentiment his own dishonour. This English home, was it not surely the best result of civilisation in an age devoted to material progress? Here was peace, here was scope for the kindliest emotions. Upon him – the born rebel, the scorner of average mankind, the consummate egoist – this atmosphere exercised an influence more tranquillising, more beneficent, than even the mood of disinterested study. In the world to which sincerity would condemn him, only the worst elements of his character found nourishment and range; here he was humanised, made receptive of all gentle sympathies. Heroism might point him to an unending struggle with adverse conditions, but how was heroism possible without faith? Absolute faith he had none; he was essentially a negativist, guided by the mere relations of phenomena. Nothing easier than to contemn the mode of life represented by this wealthy middle class; but compare it with other existences conceivable by a thinking man, and it was emphatically good. It aimed at placidity, at benevolence, at supreme cleanliness, – things which more than compensated for the absence of higher spirituality. We can be but what we are; these people accepted themselves, and in so doing became estimable mortals. No imbecile pretensions exposed them to the rebuke of a social satirist; no vulgarity tainted their familiar intercourse. Their allegiance to a worn-out creed was felt as an added grace; thus only could their souls aspire, and the imperfect poetry of their natures be developed.

He took an opportunity of seating himself by Mrs Warricombe, with whom as yet he had held no continuous dialogue.

'Has there been anything of interest at the London theatres lately?' she asked.

'I know so little of them,' Godwin replied, truthfully. 'It must be several years since I saw a play.'

'Then in that respect you have hardly become a Londoner.'

'Nor in any other, I believe,' said Peak, with a smile. 'I have lived there ten years, but am far from regarding London as my home. I hope a few months more will release me from it altogether.'

'Indeed! – Perhaps you think of leaving England?'

'I should be very sorry to do that – for any length of time. My wish is to settle somewhere in the country, and spend a year or two in quiet study.'

Mrs Warricombe looked amiable surprise, but corrected herself to approving interest.

'I have heard some of our friends say that their minds get unstrung, if they are long away from town, but I should have thought that country quietness would be much better than London noise. My husband certainly finds it so.'

'People are very differently constituted,' said Godwin. 'And then it depends much on the nature of one's work.'

Uttering these commonplaces with an air of reflection, he observed that they did not cost him the self-contempt which was wont to be his penalty for concession to the terms of polite gossip; rather, his mind accepted with gratitude this rare repose. He tasted something of the tranquil self-content which makes life so enjoyable when one has never seen a necessity for shaping original remarks. No one in this room would despise him for a platitude, were it but recommended with a pleasant smile. With the Moxeys, with Earwaker, he durst not thus have spoken.

When the hour of separation was at hand, Buckland invited his guest to retire with him to a part of the house where they could smoke and chat comfortably.

'Moorhouse and Louis are fagged after their twenty mile stretch this morning; I have caught both of them nodding during the last few minutes. We can send them to bed without apology.'

He led the way upstairs to a region of lumber-rooms, whence a narrow flight of steps brought them into a glass-house, octangular and with pointed tops, out upon the roof. This, he explained, had been built some twenty years ago, at a time when Mr Warricombe amused himself with photography. A few indications of its original purposes were still noticeable; an easel and a box of oil-colours showed that someone – doubtless of the younger generation – had used it as a painting-room; a settee and deep cane chairs made it an inviting lounge on a warm evening like the present, when, by throwing open a hinged wall, one looked forth into the deep sky and tasted the air from the sea.

'Sidwell used to paint a little,' said Buckland, as his companion bent to examine a small canvas on which a landscape was roughed in. It lay on a side table, and was half concealed by an ordnance map, left unfolded. 'For the last year or two I think she has given it up. I'm afraid we are not strong in matters of art. Neither of the girls can play very well, though of course they both tinkle for their own amusement. Maurice – the poor lad who was killed – gave a good deal of artistic promise; father keeps some little water-colours of his, which men in that line have praised – perhaps sincerely.'

'I remember you used to speak slightingly of art,' said Godwin, as he took an offered cigar.

'Did I? And of a good many other things, I daresay. It was my habit at one time, I believe, to grow heated in scorn of Euclid's definitions. What an interesting book Euclid is! Half a year ago, I was led by a talk with Moorhouse to go through some of the old "props", and you can't imagine how they delighted me. Moorhouse was so obliging as to tell me that I had an eminently deductive mind.'

He laughed, but not without betraying some pleasure in the remark.

'Surprising,' he went on, 'how very little such a mind as Moorhouse's suggests itself in common conversation. He is really profound in mathematics, a man of original powers, but I never heard him make a remark of the slightest value on any other subject. Now his sister – she has studied nothing in particular, yet she can't express an opinion that doesn't bear the stamp of originality.'

Godwin was contented to muse, his eyes fixed on a brilliant star in the western heaven.

'There's only one inconsistency in her that annoys and puzzles me,' Buckland pursued, speaking with the cigar in his mouth. 'In religion, she seems to be orthodox. True, we have never spoken on the subject, but – well, she goes to church, and carries prayer-books. I don't know how to explain it. Hypocrisy is the last thing one could suspect her of. I'm sure she hates it in every form. And such a clear brain! – I can't understand it.'

The listener was still star-gazing. He had allowed his cigar, after the first few puffs, to smoulder untasted; his lips were drawn into an expression very unlike the laxity appropriate to pleasurable smoking. When the murmur of the pines had for a moment been audible, he said, with a forced smile:

'I notice you take for granted that a clear brain and religious orthodoxy are incompatible.'

The other gave him a keen look.

'Hardly,' was Buckland's reply, spoken with less ingenuousness of tone than usual. 'I say that Miss Moorhouse has undeniably a strong mind, and that it is impossible to suspect her of the slightest hypocrisy.'

'Whence the puzzle that keeps you occupied,' rejoined Peak, in a voice that sounded like assumption of superiority, though the accent had an agreeable softness.

Warricombe moved as if impatiently, struck a match to rekindle his weed, blew tumultuous clouds, and finally put a blunt question:

'What do you think about it yourself?'

'From my point of view, there is no puzzle at all,' Godwin replied, in a very clear voice, smiling as he met the other's look.

'How am I to understand that?' asked Buckland, good-naturedly, though with a knitting of his brows.

'Not as a doubt of Miss Moorhouse's sincerity. I can't see that a belief in the Christian religion is excluded by any degree of intellectual clearness.'

'No – your views have changed, Peak?'

'On many subjects, this among them.'

'I see.'

The words fell as if involuntarily from Warricombe's lips. He gazed at the floor awhile, then, suddenly looking up, exclaimed:

'It would be civil to accept this without surprise, but it is too much for me. How has it come about?'

'That would take me a long time to explain.'

'Then,' pursued his companion, watching him closely, 'you were quite in sympathy with that exposition you gave at lunch to-day?'

'Quite. I hope there was nothing in my way of speaking that made you think otherwise?'

'Nothing at all. I couldn't help wondering what it meant. You seemed perfectly in earnest, yet such talk had the oddest sound on your lips – to me, I mean. Of course I thought of you as I used to know you.'

'Naturally.' Peak was now in an attitude of repose, his legs crossed, thumb and forefinger stroking his chin. 'I couldn't very well turn aside to comment on my own mental history.'

Here again was the note of something like genial condescension. Buckland seemed sensible of it, and slightly raised his eyebrows.

'I am to understand that you have become strictly orthodox in matters of religious faith?'

'The proof is,' replied Godwin, 'that I hope before long to take Orders.'

Again there was silence, and again the sea-breath made its whispering in the pines. Warricombe, with a sudden gesture, pointed towards the sky.

'A shooting star – one of the brightest I ever saw!'

'I missed it,' said Peak, just glancing in that direction.

The interruption enabled Buckland to move his chair; in this new position he was somewhat further from Peak, and had a better view of his face.

'I should never have imagined you a clergyman,' he said, thoughtfully, 'but I can see that your mind has been developing powers in that direction. – Well, so be it! I can only hope you have found your true work in life.'

'But you doubt it?'

'I can't say that I doubt it, as I can't understand you. To be sure, we have been parted for many years. In some respects *I* must seem much changed'—

'Greatly changed,' Godwin put in, promptly.

'Yes,' pursued the other, correctively, 'but not in a way that would seem incredible to anyone whatever. I am conscious of growth in tolerance, but my attitude in essentials is unchanged. Thinking of you – as I have often enough done – I always kept the impression you made on me when we were both lads; you seemed most distinctly a modern mind – one of the most modern that ever came under my notice. Now, I don't find it impossible to understand my father, when he reconciles science with religion; he was born sixty years ago. But Godwin Peak as a – a –'

'Parson,' supplied Peak, drily.

'Yes, as a parson – I shall have to meditate much before I grasp the notion.'

'Perhaps you have dropped your philosophical studies?' said Godwin, with a smile of courteous interest.

'I don't know. Metaphysics have no great interest for me, but I philosophise in a way. I thought myself a student of human nature, at all events.'

'But you haven't kept up with philosophical speculation on the points involved in orthodox religion?'

'I confess my ignorance of everything of the kind – unless you include Bishop Blougram among the philosophers?'

Godwin bore the gaze which accompanied this significant inquiry. For a moment he smiled, but there followed an expression of gravity touched with pain.

'I hadn't thought of broaching this matter,' he said, with slow utterance, but still in a tone of perfect friendliness. 'Let us put it aside.'

Warricombe seemed to make an effort, and his next words had the accent of well-bred consideration which distinguished his ordinary talk.

'Pray forgive my bad joke. I merely meant that I have no right whatever to argue with anyone who has given serious attention to such things. They are altogether beyond my sphere. I was born an agnostic, and no subtlety of demonstration could incline me for a moment to theological views; my intellect refuses to admit a single preliminary of such arguments. You astonish me, and that's all I am justified in saying.'

'My dear Warricombe, you are justified in saying whatever your mind suggests. That is one of the principles which I hold unaltered – let me be quite frank with you. I should never have decided upon such a step as this, but for the fact that I have managed to put by a small sum of money which will make me independent for two or three years. Till quite lately I hadn't a thought of using my freedom in this way; it was clear to me that I must throw over the old drudgery at Rotherhithe, but this resolve which astonishes you had not yet ripened – I saw it only as one of the possibilities of my life. Well, now, it's only too true that there's something of speculation in my purpose; I look to the Church, not only as a congenial sphere of activity, but as a means of subsistence. In a man of no fortune this is inevitable; I hope there is nothing to be ashamed of. Even if the conditions of the case allowed it, I shouldn't present myself for ordination forthwith; I must study and prepare myself in quietness. How the practical details will be arranged, I can't say; I have no family influence, and I must hope to make friends who will open a way for me. I have always lived apart from society; but that isn't natural to me, and it becomes more distasteful the older I grow. The probability is that I shall settle somewhere in the country, where I can live decently on a small income. After all, it's better I should have let you know this at once. I only realised a few minutes ago that to be silent about my projects was in a way to be guilty of false pretences.'

The adroitness of this last remark, which directed itself, with such show of candour, against a suspicion precisely the opposite of that likely to be entertained by the listener, succeeded in disarming Warricombe; he looked up with a smile of reassurance, and spoke encouragingly.

'About the practical details I don't think you need have any anxiety. It isn't every day that the Church of England gets such a recruit. Let me suggest that you have a talk with my father.'

Peak reflected on the proposal, and replied to it with grave thoughtfulness:

'That's very kind of you, but I should have a difficulty in asking Mr Warricombe's advice. I'm afraid I must go on in my own way for a time. It will be a few months, I daresay, before I can release myself from my engagements in London.'

'But I am to understand that your mind is really made up?'

'Oh, quite!'

'Well, no doubt we shall have opportunities of talking. We must meet in town, if possible. You have excited my curiosity, and I can't help hoping you'll let me see a little further into your mind some day. When I first got hold of Newman's *Apologia*, I began to read it with the utmost eagerness, flattering myself that now at length I should understand how a man of brains could travel such a road. I was horribly disappointed, and not a little enraged, when I found that he began by assuming the very beliefs I thought he was going to justify. In you I shall hope for more logic.'

'Newman is incapable of understanding such an objection,' said Peak, with a look of amusement.

'But you are not.'

The dialogue grew chatty. When they exchanged good-night, Peak fancied that the pressure of Buckland's hand was less fervent than at their meeting, but his manner no longer seemed to indicate distrust. Probably the agnostic's mood was one of half-tolerant disdain.

Godwin turned the key in his bedroom door, and strayed aimlessly about. He was fatigued, but the white, fragrant bed did not yet invite him; a turbulence in his brain gave warning that it would be long before he slept. He wound up his watch; the hands pointed to twelve. Chancing to come before the mirror, he saw that he was unusually pale, and that his eyes had a swollen look.

The profound stillness was oppressive to him; he started nervously at an undefined object in a dim corner, and went nearer to examine it; he was irritable, vaguely discontented, and had even a moment of nausea, perhaps the result of tobacco stronger than he was accustomed to smoke. After leaning for five minutes at the open window, he felt a soothing effect from the air, and could think consecutively of the day's events. What had happened seemed to him incredible; it was as though he revived a mad dream, of ludicrous coherence. Since his display of rhetoric at luncheon all was downright somnambulism. What fatal power had subdued him? What extraordinary influence had guided his tongue, constrained his features? His conscious self had had no part in all this comedy; now for the first time was he taking count of the character he had played.

Had he been told this morning that— Why, what monstrous folly was all this? Into what unspeakable baseness had he fallen? Happily, he had but to take leave of the Warricombe household, and rush into some region where he was unknown. Years hence, he would relate the story to Earwaker.

For a long time he suffered the torments of this awakening. Shame buffeted him on the right cheek and the left; he looked about like one who slinks from merited chastisement. Oh, thrice ignoble varlet! To pose with unctuous hypocrisy before people who had welcomed him under their roof, unquestioned, with all the grace and kindliness of English hospitality! To lie shamelessly in the face of his old fellow-student, who had been so genuinely glad to meet him again!

Yet such possibility had not been unforeseen. At the times of his profound gloom, when solitude and desire crushed his spirit, he had wished that fate would afford him such an opportunity of knavish success. His imagination had played with the idea that a man like himself might well be driven to this expedient, and might even use it with life-long result. Of a certainty, the Church numbered such men among her priests, – not mere lukewarm sceptics who made religion a source of income, nor yet those who had honestly entered the portal and by necessity were held from withdrawing, though their convictions had changed; but deliberate schemers from the first, ambitious but hungry natures, keen-sighted, unscrupulous. And they were at no loss to defend themselves against the attack of conscience. Life is a terrific struggle for all who begin it with no endowments save their brains. A hypocrite was not necessarily a harm-doer; easy to picture the unbelieving priest whose influence was vastly for good, in word and deed.

But he, he who had ever prided himself on his truth-fronting intellect, and had freely uttered his scorn of the credulous mob! He who was his own criterion of moral right and wrong! No wonder he felt like a whipped cur. It was the ancestral vice in his blood, brought out by over-tempting circumstance. The long line of base-born predecessors, the grovelling hinds and mechanics of his genealogy, were responsible for this. Oh for a name wherewith honour was hereditary!

His eyes were blinded by a rush of hot tears. Down, down – into the depths of uttermost despondency, of self-pity and self-contempt! Had it been practicable, he would have fled from the house, leaving its occupants to think of him as they would; even as, ten years ago, he had fled from the shame impending over him at Kingsmill. A cowardly instinct, this; having once acted upon it gave to his whole life a taint of craven meanness. Mere bluster, all his talk of mental dignity and uncompromising scorn of superstitions. A weak and idle man, whose best years were already wasted!

He gazed deliberately at himself in the glass, at his red eyelids and unsightly lips. Darkness was best; perhaps he might forget his shame for an hour or two, ere the dawn renewed it. He threw off his garments heedlessly, extinguished the lamp, and crept into the ready hiding-place.

PART THE THIRD

I

'Why are you obstinately silent? [wrote Earwaker, in a letter addressed to Godwin at his Peckham lodgings]. I take it for granted that you must by this time be back from your holiday. Why haven't you replied to my letter of a fortnight ago? Nothing yet from *The Critical*. If you are really at work as usual, come and see me to-morrow evening, any time after eight. The posture of my affairs grows dubious; the shadow of Kenyon thickens about me. In all seriousness I think I shall be driven from *The Weekly Post* before long. My quarrels with Runcorn are too frequent, and his blackguardism keeps more than pace with the times. Come or write, for I want to know how things go with you.   *Tuissimus*, J.E.E.'

Peak read this at breakfast on a Saturday morning. It was early in September, and three weeks had elapsed since his return from the west of England. Upon the autumn had fallen a blight of cold and rainy weather, which did not enhance the cheerfulness of daily journeying between Peckham Rye and Rotherhithe. When it was necessary for him to set forth to the train, he muttered imprecations, for a mood of inactivity possessed him; he would gladly have stayed in his comfortable sitting-room, idling over books or only occupied with languid thought.

In the afternoon he was at liberty to follow his impulse, and this directed him to the British Museum, whither of late he had several times resorted as a reader. Among the half-dozen books for which he applied was one in German, Reusch's *Bibel und Natur*. After a little dallying, he became absorbed in this work, and two or three hours passed before its hold on his attention slackened. He seldom changed his position; the volume was propped against others, and he sat bending forward, his arms folded upon the desk. When he was thus deeply engaged, his face had a hard, stern aspect; if by chance his eye wandered for a moment, its look seemed to express resentment of interruption.

At length he threw himself back with a sudden yielding to weariness, crossed his legs, sank together in the chair, and for half-an-hour brooded darkly. A fit of yawning admonished him that it was time to quit the atmosphere of study. He betook himself to a restaurant in the Strand, and thence about eight o'clock made his way to Staple Inn, where the journalist gave him cheerful welcome.

'Day after day I have meant to write,' thus he excused himself. 'But I had really nothing to say.'

'You don't look any better for your holiday,' Earwaker remarked.

'Holiday? Oh, I had forgotten all about it. When do *you* go?'

'The situation is comical. I feel sure that if I leave town, my connection with the *Post* will come to an end. I shall have a note from Runcorn saying that we had better take this opportunity of terminating my engagement. On the whole I should be glad, yet I can't make up my mind to be ousted by Kenyon – that's what it means. They want to get me away, but I stick on, postponing holiday from week to week. Runcorn can't decide to send me about my business, yet every leader I write enrages him. But for Kenyon, I should gain my point; I feel sure of it. It's one of those cases in which homicide would be justified by public interest. If Kenyon gets my place, the paper becomes at once an organ of ruffiandom, the delight of the blackguardry.'

'How's the circulation?' inquired Peak.

'Pretty sound; that adds to the joke. This series of stories by Doubleday has helped us a good deal, and my contention is, if we can keep financially right by help of this kind, why not make a little sacrifice for the sake of raising our political tone? Runcorn won't see it; he listens eagerly to Kenyon's assurance that we might sell several thousand more by striking the true pot-house note.'

'Then pitch the thing over! Wash your hands, and go to cleaner work.'

'The work I am doing is clean enough,' replied Earwaker. 'Let me have my way, and I can make the paper a decent one and a useful one. I shan't easily find another such chance.'

'Your idealism has a strong root,' said Godwin, rather

contemptuously. 'I half envy you. There must be a distinct pleasure in believing that any intellectual influence will exalt the English democracy.'

'I'm not sure that I do believe it, but I enjoy the experiment. The chief pleasure, I suppose, is in fighting Runcorn and Kenyon.'

'They are too strong for you, Earwaker. They have the spirit of the age to back them up.'

The journalist became silent; he smiled, but the harassment of conflict marked his features.

'I hear nothing about "The New Sophistry",' he remarked, when Godwin had begun to examine some books that lay on the table. 'Dolby has the trick of keeping manuscripts a long time. Everything that seems at the first glance tolerable, he sends to the printer, then muses over it at his leisure. Probably your paper is in type.'

'I don't care a rap whether it is or not. What do you think of this book of Oldwinkle's?'

He was holding a volume of humorous stories, which had greatly taken the fancy of the public.

'It's uncommonly good,' replied the journalist, laughing. 'I had a prejudice against the fellow, but he has overcome me. It's more than good farce – something like really strong humour here and there.'

'I quite believe it,' said Peak, 'yet I couldn't read a page. Whatever the mob enjoys is at once spoilt for me, however good I should otherwise think it. I am sick of seeing and hearing the man's name.'

Earwaker shook his head in deprecation.

'Narrow, my boy. One must be able to judge and enjoy impartially.'

'I know it, but I shall never improve. This book seems to me to have a bad smell; it looks mauled with dirty fingers. I despise Oldwinkle for his popularity. To make them laugh, and to laugh *with* them – pah!'

They debated this point for some time, Peak growing more violent, though his friend preserved a smiling equanimity. A tirade of virulent contempt, in which Godwin exhibited all his powers of savage eloquence, was broken by a visitor's summons at the door.

'Here's Malkin,' said the journalist; 'you'll see each other at last.'

Peak could not at once command himself to the look and tone
desirable in meeting a stranger; leaning against the mantelpiece,
he gazed with a scowl of curiosity at the man who presented
himself, and when he shook hands, it was in silence. But Malkin
made speech from the others unnecessary for several minutes.
With animated voice and gesture, he poured forth apologies for
his failure to keep the appointment of six or seven weeks ago.

'Only the gravest call of duty could have kept me away, I do
assure you! No doubt Earwaker has informed you of the
circumstances. I telegraphed – I think I telegraphed; didn't I,
Earwaker?'

'I have some recollection of a word or two of scant excuse,'
replied the journalist.

'But I implore you to consider the haste I was in,' cried Malkin;
'not five minutes, Mr Peak, to book, to register luggage, to do
everything; not five minutes, I protest! But here we are at last. Let
us talk! Let us talk!'

He seated himself with an air of supreme enjoyment, and began
to cram the bowl of a large pipe from a bulky pouch.

'How stands the fight with Kenyon and Co.?' he cried, as soon
as the tobacco was glowing.

Earwaker briefly repeated what he had told Peak.

'Hold out! No surrender and no compromise! What's your
opinion, Mr Peak, on the abstract question? Is a popular paper
likely, or not, to be damaged in its circulation by improvement of
style and tone – within the limits of discretion?'

'I shouldn't be surprised if it were,' Peak answered, drily.

'I'm afraid you're right. There's no use in blinking truths,
however disagreeable. But, for Earwaker, that isn't the main
issue. What he has to do is to assert himself. Every man's first duty
is to assert himself. At all events, this is how I regard the matter. I
am all for individualism, for the development of one's personality
at whatever cost. No compromise on points of faith! Earwaker
has his ideal of journalistic duty, and in a fight with fellows like
Runcorn and Kenyon he must stand firm as a rock.'

'I can't see that he's called upon to fight at all,' said Peak. 'He's
in a false position; let him get out of it.'

'A false position? I can't see that. No man better fitted than
Earwaker to raise the tone of Radical journalism. Here's a big
Sunday newspaper practically in his hands; it seems to me that the
circumstances give him a grand opportunity of making his force

felt. What are we all seeking but an opportunity for striking out with effect?'

Godwin listened with a sceptical smile, and made answer in slow, careless tones.

'Earwaker happens to be employed and paid by certain capitalists to increase the sale of their paper.'

'My dear sir!' cried the other, bouncing upon his seat. 'How can you take such a view? A great newspaper surely cannot be regarded as a mere source of income. These capitalists declare that they have at heart the interests of the working classes; so has Earwaker, and he is far better able than they to promote those interests. His duty is to apply their money to the best use, morally speaking. If he were lukewarm in the matter, I should be the first to advise his retirement; but this fight is entirely congenial to him. I trust he will hold his own to the last possible moment.'

'You must remember,' put in the journalist, with a look of amusement, 'that Peak has no sympathy with Radicalism.'

'I lament it, but that does not affect my argument. If you were a high Tory, I should urge you just as strongly to assert yourself. Surely you agree with this point of mine, Mr Peak? You admit that a man must develop whatever strength is in him.'

'I'm not at all sure of that.'

Malkin fixed himself sideways in the chair, and examined his collocutor's face earnestly. He endeavoured to subdue his excitement to the tone of courteous debate, but the words that at length escaped him were humorously blunt.

'Then of what *are* you sure?'

'Of nothing.'

'Now we touch bottom!' cried Malkin. 'Philosophically speaking, I agree with you. But we have to live our lives, and I suppose we must direct ourselves by some conscious principle.'

'I don't see the necessity,' Peak replied, still in an impassive tone. 'We may very well be guided by circumstances as they arise. To be sure, there's a principle in that, but I take it you mean something different.'

'Yes I do. I hold that the will must direct circumstances, not receive its impulse from them. How, then, are we to be guided? What do you set before yourself?'

'To get through life with as much satisfaction and as little pain as possible.'

'You are a hedonist, then. Well and good! Then that is your conscious principle'—

'No, it isn't.'

'How am I to understand you?'

'By recognising that a man's intellectual and moral principles as likely as not tend to anything but his happiness.'

'I can't admit it!' exclaimed Malkin, leaping from his chair. 'What *is* happiness?'

'I don't know.'

'Earwaker, *what* is happiness? What *is* happiness?'

'I really don't know,' answered the journalist, mirthfully.

'This is trifling with a grave question. We all know perfectly well that happiness is the conscious exertion of individual powers. Why is there so much suffering under our present social system? Because the majority of men are crushed to a dead level of mechanical toil, with no opportunity of developing their special faculties. Give a man scope, and happiness is put within his reach.'

'What do you mean by scope?' inquired Godwin.

'Scope? Scope? Why, room to expand. The vice of our society is hypocrisy; it comes of over-crowding. When a man isn't allowed to be himself, he takes refuge in a mean imitation of those other men who appear to be better off. That was what sent me off to South America. I got into politics, and found that I was in danger of growing dishonest, of compromising, and toadying. In the wilderness, I found myself again. – Do you seriously believe that happiness can be obtained by ignoring one's convictions?'

He addressed the question to both, snuffing the air with head thrown back.

'What if you have no convictions?' asked Peak.

'Then you are incapable of happiness in any worthy sense! You may graze, but you will never feast.'

The listeners joined in laughter, and Malkin, after a moment's hesitation, allowed his face to relax in good-humoured sympathy.

'Now look here!' he cried. 'You – Earwaker; suppose you sent conscience to the devil, and set yourself to please Runcorn by increasing the circulation of your paper by whatever means. You would flourish, undoubtedly. In a short time you would be chief editor, and your pockets would burst with money. But what about your peace of mind? What about happiness?'

'Why, I'm disposed to agree with Peak,' answered the

journalist. 'If I *could* take that line, I should be a happier man than conscientiousness will ever make me.'

Malkin swelled with indignation.

'You don't mean it! You are turning a grave argument into jest! – Where's my hat? Where the devil is my hat? Send for me again when you are disposed to talk seriously.'

He strode towards the door, but Earwaker arrested him with a shout.

'You're leaving your pipe!'

'So I am. Where is it? – Did I tell you where I bought this pipe?'

'No. What's the wood?'

On the instant Malkin fell into a cheerful vein of reminiscence. In five minutes he was giving a rapturous description of tropical scenes, laughing joyously as he addressed now one now the other of his companions.

'I hear you have a mind to see those countries, Mr Peak,' he said at length. 'If you care for a travelling companion – rather short-tempered, but you'll pardon that – pray give me the preference. I should enjoy above all things to travel with a man of science.'

'It's very doubtful whether I shall ever get so far,' Godwin replied, musingly.

And, as he spoke, he rose to take leave. Earwaker's protest that it was not yet ten o'clock did not influence him.

'I want to reflect on the meaning of happiness,' he said, extending his hand to Malkin; and, in spite of the smile, his face had a sombre cast.

The two who were left of course discussed him.

'You won't care much for Peak,' said Earwaker. 'He and I suit each other, because there's a good deal of indifferentism in both of us. Moral earnestness always goes against the grain with him; I've noticed it frequently.'

'I'm sorry I spoke so dogmatically. It wasn't altogether good manners. Suppose I write him a short letter, just expressing my regret for having been led away'—

'Needless, needless,' laughed the journalist. 'He thinks all the better of you for your zeal. But happiness is a sore point with him; few men, I should think, have known less of it. I can't imagine any circumstances which would make him thoroughly at peace with himself and the world.'

'Poor fellow! You can see something of that in his face. Why doesn't he get married?'

'A remarkable suggestion! – By the way, why don't *you*?'

'My dear boy, there's nothing I wish more, but it's a business of such fearful precariousness. I'm one of those men whom marriage will either make or ruin. You know my characteristics; the slightest check upon my independence, and all's up with me. The woman I marry must be perfectly reasonable, perfectly good-tempered; she must have excellent education, and every delicacy of breeding. Where am I to find this paragon?'

'Society is open to you.'

'True, but I am not open to society. I don't take kindly to the people of my own class. No, I tell you what – my only chance of getting a suitable wife is to train some very young girl for the purpose. Don't misunderstand me, for heaven's sake! I mean that I must make a friendship with some schoolgirl in whose education I can have a voice, whose relatives will permit me to influence her mind and develop her character. What do you think of this idea?'

'Not bad, but it demands patience.'

'And who more patient than I? But let us talk of that poor Mrs Jacox and her girls. You feel that you know them pretty well from my letters, don't you? Nothing more monstrous can be imagined than the treatment to which this poor woman has been subjected! I couldn't have believed that such dishonesty and brutality were possible in English families of decent position. Her husband deserted her, her brother robbed her, her sister-in-law libelled her, – the whole story is nauseating!'

'You're quite sure that she tells you the truth?'

Malkin glared with sudden resentment.

'The truth? What! you also desire to calumniate her? For shame, Earwaker! A poor widow toiling to support herself in a foreign country, with two children dependent on her.'

'Yes, yes, yes; but you seem to know very little of her.'

'I know her perfectly, and all her circumstances!'

Mrs Jacox was the mother of the two girls whom Malkin had escorted to Rouen, after an hour or so of all but casual acquaintance. She and her history had come in a very slight degree under the notice of certain good-natured people with whom Malkin was on friendly terms, and hearing that the children, Bella and Lily, aged fourteen and twelve respectively, were about to undertake alone a journey to the Continent, the erratic hero felt it incumbent upon him to see them safe at their mother's side. Instead of returning forthwith, he lingered in Normandy for several weeks, striking off at length, on the summons of a friend, to Orleans, whence he was only to-day returned. Two or three letters had kept Earwaker informed of his movements. Of Mrs Jacox he wrote as he now spoke, with compassionate respect, and the girls, according to him, were exquisite models of budding maidenhood.

'You haven't told me,' said Earwaker, calmly fronting the indignant outburst, 'what her circumstances are – at present.'

'She assists an English lady in the management of a boarding-house,' Malkin replied, with an air which forbade trivial comment. 'Bella and Lily will of course continue their studies. I daresay I shall run over now and then to see them.'

'May I, without offence, inquire if either of these young ladies seems suitable for the ideal training of which you spoke?'

Malkin smiled thoughtfully. He stood with his legs apart and stroked his blond beard.

'The surmise is not unnatural. Well, I confess that Bella has inspired me with no little interest. She is rather mature, unfortunately; I wish she had been Lily's age. We shall see; we shall see.'

Musing, he refilled his pipe, and gossip was prolonged till something after one o'clock. Malkin was never known to retire willingly from an evening's congenial talk until the small hours were in progress.

Peak, on reaching home about eleven, was surprised to see a light in his sitting-room window. As he entered, his landlady informed him that Mr Moxey had been waiting upstairs for an hour or two. Christian was reading. He laid down the book and rose languidly. His face was flushed, and he spoke with a laugh which suggested that a fit of despondency (as occasionally happened) had tempted him to excess in cordials. Godwin understood these signs. He knew that his friend's intellect was rather brightened than impaired by such stimulus, and he affected not to be conscious of any peculiarity.

'As you wouldn't come to me,' Christian began, 'I had no choice but to come to you. My visit isn't unwelcome, I hope?'

'Certainly not. But how are you going to get home? You know the time?'

'Don't trouble. I shan't go to bed to-night. Let me sit here and read, will you? If I feel tired I can lie down on the sofa. What a delightful book this is! I must get it.'

It was a history of the Italian Renaissance, recently published.

'Where does this phrase come from?' he continued, pointing to a scrap of paper, used as a book-mark, on which Godwin had pencilled a note. The words were: '*Foris ut moris, intus ut libet.*'

'It's mentioned there,' Peak replied, 'as the motto of those humanists who outwardly conformed to the common faith.'

'I see. All very well when the Inquisition was flourishing, but sounds ignoble nowadays.'

'Do you think so? In a half-civilised age, whether the sixteenth or the nineteenth century, a wise man may do worse than adopt it.'

'Better be honest, surely?'

Peak stood for a moment as if in doubt, then exclaimed irritably:

'Honest? Honest? Who is or can be honest? Who truly declares himself? When a man has learnt that truth is indeterminable, how is it more moral to go about crying that you don't believe a certain dogma than to concede that the dogma may possibly be true? This new morality of the agnostics is mere paltry conceit. Why must I make solemn declaration that I don't believe in absolute knowledge? I might as well be called upon to inform all my acquaintances how I stand with regard to the theories of chemical affinity. One's philosophy has nothing to do with the business of life. If I chose to become a Church of England clergyman, what moral objection could be made?'

This illustration was so amusing to Moxey, that his surprise at what preceded gave way to laughter.

'I wonder,' he exclaimed, 'that you never seriously thought of a profession for which you are so evidently cut out.'

Godwin kept silence; his face had darkened, and he seated himself with sullen weariness.

'Tell me what you've been doing,' resumed Moxey. 'Why haven't I heard from you?'

'I should have come in a day or two. I thought you were probably out of town.'

'Her husband is ill,' said the other, by way of reply. He leaned forward with his arms upon the table, and gazed at Godwin with eyes of peculiar brightness.

'Ill, is he?' returned Godwin, with slow interest. 'In the same way as before?'

'Yes, but much worse.'

Christian paused; and when he again spoke it was hurriedly, confusedly.

'How can I help getting excited about it? How can I behave decently? You're the only man I ever speak to on the subject, and no doubt I both weary and disgust you; but I *must* speak to some one. My nerves are strung beyond endurance; it's only by speaking that I can ease myself from the intolerable strain.'

'Have you seen her lately?'

'Yesterday, for a moment, in the street. It's ten months since the last meeting.'

'Well,' remarked Godwin, abruptly, 'it's probable the man will die one of these days, then your trials will have a happy end. I see no harm in hoping that his life may be short – that's a conventional feeling. If two people can be benefited by the death of a single person, why shouldn't we be glad in the prospect of his dying? Not of his suffering – that's quite another thing. But die he must; and to curtail the life of a being who at length wholly ceases to exist is no injury. You can't injure a nonentity. Do you think I should take it ill if I knew that some persons were wishing my death? Why, look, if ever I crush a little green fly that crawls upon me in the fields, at once I am filled with envy of its fate – sincerest envy. To have passed so suddenly from being into nothingness – how blessed an extinction! To feel in that way, instinctively, in the very depths of your soul, is to be a true pessimist. If I had ever doubted my sincerity in pessimism, this experience, several times repeated, would have reassured me.'

Christian covered his face, and brooded for a long time, whilst Godwin sat with his eyes on vacancy.

'Come and see us to-morrow,' said the former, at length.

'Perhaps.'

'Why do you keep away?'

'I'm in no mood for society.'

'We'll have no one. Only Marcella and I.'

Again a long silence.

'Marcella is going in for comparative philology,' Christian resumed, with the gentle tone in which he invariably spoke of his sister. 'What a mind that girl has! I never knew any woman of half her powers.'

Godwin said nothing.

'No,' continued the other fervently, 'nor of half her goodness. I sometimes think that no mortal could come nearer to our ideal of moral justice and purity. If it were not for her, I should long ago have gone to perdition, in one way or another. It's her

strength, not my own, that has saved me. I daresay you know this?'

'There's some truth in it, I believe,' Peak answered, his eye wandering.

'See how circumstances can affect one's judgment. If, just about the time I first knew you, I had abandoned myself to a life of sottish despair, of course I should have charged Constance with the blame of it. Now that I have struggled on, I can see that she has been a blessing to me instead of a curse. If Marcella has given me strength, I have to thank Constance for the spiritual joy which otherwise I should never have known.'

Peak uttered a short laugh.

'That is only saying that she *might* have been ruinous, but in the course of circumstances has proved helpful. I envy your power of deriving comfort from such reflections.'

'Well, we view things differently. I have the habit of looking to the consolatory facts of life, you to the depressing. There's an unfortunate lack in you, Peak; you seem insensible to female influence, and I believe that is closely connected with your desperate pessimism.'

Godwin laughed again, this time with mocking length of note.

'Come now, isn't it true?' urged the other. 'Sincerely, do you care for women at all?'

'Perhaps not.'

'A grave misfortune, depend upon it! It accounts for nearly everything that is unsatisfactory in your life. If you had ever been sincerely devoted to a woman, be assured your powers would have developed in a way of which you have no conception. It's no answer to tell me that *I* am still a mere trifler, never likely to do anything of account; I haven't it in me to be anything better, and I might easily have become much worse. But you might have made yourself a great position – I mean, you *might* do so; you are still very young. If only you knew the desire of a woman's help.'

'You really think so?' said Godwin, with grave irony.

'I am sure of it! There's no harm in repeating what you have often told me – your egoism oppresses you. A woman's influence takes one out of oneself. No man can be a better authority on this than I. For more than eleven years I have worshipped one woman with absolute faithfulness'—

'Absolute?' interrupted Godwin, bluntly.

'What exception occurs to you?'

'As you challenge inquiry, forgive me for asking what your interest was in one of your cousins at Twybridge?'

Christian started, and averted his face with a look of embarrassment.

'Do you mean to say that you knew anything about that?'

'I was always an observer,' Peak replied, smiling. 'You don't remember, perhaps, that I happened to be present when a letter had just arrived for you at your uncle's house – a letter which evidently disturbed you?'

'This is astonishing! Peak, you're a terrible fellow! Heaven forbid that I should ever be at your mercy! Yes, you are quite right,' he continued, despondently. 'But that was no real unfaithfulness. I don't quite know how to explain it. I *did* make love to poor Janet, and with the result that I have never since seen any of the family. My uncle, when he found I had drawn back, was very savage – naturally enough. Marcella and I never again went to Twybridge. I liked Janet; she was a good, kind girl. I believed just then that my love for Constance was hopeless; my mood impelled me to the conviction that the best thing I could do was to marry Janet and settle down to a peaceful domestic life. Then came that letter – it was from Constance herself. It meant nothing, yet it was enough to revive all my hopes. I rushed off –! How brutally I had behaved! Poor little Janet!'

He let his face fall upon his hands.

'Allow me an indiscreet question,' said Peak, after a silence. 'Have you any founded hope of marrying Constance if she becomes a widow?'

Christian started and looked up with wide eyes.

'Hope? Every hope! I have the absolute assurance of her love.'

'I see.'

'But I mustn't mislead you,' pursued the other, hurriedly. 'Our relations are absolutely pure. I have only allowed myself to see her at very long intervals. Why shouldn't I tell you? It was less than a year after her marriage; I found her alone in a room in a friend's house; her eyes were red with weeping. I couldn't help holding my hand to her. She took it, and held it for a moment, and looked at me steadily, and whispered my name – that was all. I knew then that she repented of her marriage – who can say what led her into it? I was poor, you know; perhaps – but in spite of all, she *did* love me. There has never since been anything like a scene of emotion between us – *that* her conscience couldn't allow. She is a noble-minded woman, and has done her duty. But if she is free'—

He quivered with passionate feeling.

'And you are content,' said Godwin, drily, 'to have wasted ten years of your life for such a possibility?'

'Wasted!' Christian exclaimed. 'Come, come, Peak; why *will* you affect this wretched cynicism? Is it waste of years to have lived with the highest and purest ideal perpetually before one's mind? What can a man do better than, having found an admirable woman, to worship her thenceforth, and defy every temptation that could lead him astray? I don't like to seem boastful, but I *have* lived purely and devotedly. And if the test endured to the end of my life, I could sustain it. Is the consciousness of my love nothing to Constance? Has it not helped her?'

Such profound sincerity was astonishing to Peak. He did not admire it, for it seemed to him, in this case at all events, the fatal weakness of a character it was impossible not to love. Though he could not declare his doubts, he thought it more than probable that this Laura of the voiceless Petrarch was unworthy of such constancy, and that she had no intention whatever of rewarding it, even if the opportunity arrived. But this was the mere speculation of a pessimist; he might be altogether wrong, for he had never denied the existence of high virtue, in man or woman.

'There goes midnight!' he remarked, turning from the subject. 'You can't sleep, neither can I. Why shouldn't we walk into town?'

'By all means; on condition that you will come home with me, and spend to-morrow there.'

'Very well.'

They set forth, and with varied talk, often broken by long silences, made their way through sleeping suburbs to the dark valley of Thames.

There passed another month, during which Peak was neither seen nor heard of by his friends. One evening in October, as he sat studying at the British Museum, a friendly voice claimed his attention. He rose nervously and met the searching eye of Buckland Warricombe.

'I had it in mind to write to you,' said the latter. 'Since we parted down yonder I have been running about a good deal, with few days in town. Do you often read here?'

'Generally on Saturday afternoon.'

Buckland glanced at the open volume, and caught a heading, 'Apologetic Theology.'

'Still at the works?'

'Yes; I shall be there till Christmas – no longer.'

'Are you by chance disengaged to-morrow? Could you dine with me? I shall be alone; perhaps you don't mind that? We could exchange views on "fate, free-will, foreknowledge absolute".'

Godwin accepted the invitation, and Warricombe, unable to linger, took leave of him.

They met the next evening in Buckland's rooms, not far from the Houses of Parliament. Commonplace comfort was the note of these quarters. Peak wondered that a man who had it in his power to surround himself with evidences of taste should be content to dwell thus. His host seemed to detect this thought in the glances Godwin cast about him.

'Nothing but a *pied-à-terre*. I have been here three or four years, but I don't think of it as a home. I suppose I shall settle somewhere before long: yet, on the whole, what does it matter where one lives? There's something in the atmosphere of our time that makes one indisposed to strike roots in the old way. Who knows how long there'll be such a thing as real property? We are getting to think of ourselves as lodgers; it's as well to be indifferent about a notice to quit.'

'Many people would still make a good fight for the old homes,' replied Peak.

'Yes; I daresay I should myself, if I were a family man. A wife and children are strong persuasions to conservatism. In those who have anything, that's to say. Let the families who have nothing learn how they stand in point of numbers, and we shall see what we shall see.'

'And you are doing your best to teach them that.'

Buckland smiled.

'A few other things at the same time. One isn't necessarily an anarchist, you know.'

'What enormous faith you must have in the metaphysical powers of the multitude!'

'Trenchant! But say, rather, in the universal self-interest. That's the trait of human nature which we have in mind when we speak of enlightenment. The aim of practical Radicalism is to instruct men's selfishness. Astonishing how capable it is of being instructed! The mistake of the Socialist lies in his crediting men with far too much self-esteem, far too little perception of their own limits. The characteristic of mankind at large is humility.'

Peak began to understand his old acquaintance; he had imagined him less acute. Gratified by the smile of interest, Warricombe added:

'There are forces of madness; I have shown you that I make allowance for them. But they are only dangerous so long as privilege allies itself with hypocrisy. The task of the modern civiliser is to sweep away sham idealisms.'

'I agree with you,' Godwin replied.

With sudden change of mood, Buckland began to speak of an indifferent topic of the day, and in a few minutes they sat down to dinner.

Not till the welcome tobacco blended its aroma with that of coffee did a frankly personal note sound in their conversation.

'So at Christmas you are free,' said Warricombe. 'You still think of leaving London?'

'I have decided to go down into Devonshire.'

'The seaside?'

'I shall stay first of all in Exeter,' Godwin replied, with deliberation; 'one can get hold of books there.'

'Yes, especially of the ecclesiastical colour.'

'You are still unable to regard my position with anything but contempt?' Peak asked, looking steadily at the critical face.

'Come now; what does it all mean? Of course I quite understand how tolerant the Church is becoming: I know what latitude it permits in its servants. But what do you propose to yourself?'

'Precisely what you call the work of the civiliser – to attack sham ideals.'

'As for instance—?'

'The authority of the mob,' answered Peak, suavely.

'Your clericalism is political, then?'

'To a great extent.'

'I discern a vague sort of consistency in this. You regard the Church formulas as merely symbolical – useful for the purposes of the day?'

'Rather for the purposes of eternity.'

'In the human sense.'

'In every sense.'

Warricombe perceived that no directness of questioning would elicit literal response, and on the whole this relieved him. To hear Godwin Peak using the language of a fervent curate would have excited in him something more than disgust. It did not seem impossible that a nature like Peak's – intellectually arrogant, vehemently anti-popular – should have been attracted by the traditions, the social prestige, of the Anglican Church; nor at all unlikely that a mind so constituted should justify a seeming acceptance of dogmas, which in the strict sense it despised. But he was made uneasy by his ignorance of Peak's private life during the years since their parting at College. He did not like to think of the possible establishment of intimacy between this man of low origin, uncertain career, boundless ambition, and the household of Martin Warricombe. There could be no doubt that Peak had decided to go to Exeter because of the social prospects recently opened to him. In the vulgar phrase, he had probably 'taken stock' of Mr Warricombe's idiosyncrasy, and saw therein a valuable opportunity for a theological student, who at the same time was a devotee of natural science. To be sure, the people at Exeter could be put on their guard. On the other hand, Peak had plainly avowed his desire to form social connections of the useful kind; in his position such an aim was essential, a mere matter of course.

Godwin's voice interrupted this train of thought.

'Let me ask you a plain question. You have twice been kind enough to introduce me to your home as a friend of yours. Am I guilty of presumption in hoping that your parents will continue to regard me as an acquaintance? I trust there's no need to assure you that I know the meaning of discretion.'

An appeal to Buckland's generosity seldom failed. Yes, it was true that he had more than once encouraged the hope now frankly expressed. Indulging a correspondent frankness, he might explain that Peak's position was so distasteful to him that it disturbed the future with many kinds of uncertainty. But this would be churlish. He must treat his guest as a gentleman, so long as nothing compelled him to take the less agreeable view.

'My dear Peak, let us have none of these formalities. My parents have distinctly invited you to go and see them whenever you are in the neighbourhood. I am quite sure they will help to make your stay in Exeter a pleasant one.'

Therewith closed the hazardous dialogue. Warricombe turned at once to a safe topic – that of contemporary fiction, and they chatted pleasantly enough for the rest of the evening.

Not many days after this, Godwin received by post an envelope which contained certain proof sheets, and therewith a note in

which the editor of *The Critical Review* signified his acceptance of
a paper entitled 'The New Sophistry'. The communication was
originally addressed to Earwaker, who had scribbled at the foot,
'Correct, if you are alive, and send back to Dolby.'

The next morning he did not set out as usual for Rotherhithe.
Through the night he had not closed his eyes; he was in a state of
nervousness which bordered on fever. A dozen times he had read
over the proofs, with throbbing pulse, with exultant self-
admiration: but the printer's errors which had caught his eye, and
a few faults of phrase, were still uncorrected. What a capital piece
of writing it was! What a flagellation of M'Naughten and all his
tribe! If this did not rouse echoes in the literary world—

Through the long day he sat in languor or paced his room like
one made restless by pain. Only when the gloom of nightfall
obliged him to light his lamp did he at length sit down to the table
and carefully revise the proofs, pen in hand. When he had made
up the packet for post, he wrote to Earwaker.

'I had forgotten all about this thing. Proofs have gone to Dolby.
I have not signed; probably he would object to my doing so. As it
is, the paper can be ascribed to anyone, and attention thus excited.
We shall see paragraphs attributing it to men of mark – perhaps
scandal will fix it on a bishop. In any case, don't let out the secret. I
beg this seriously, and for a solid reason. Not a word to anyone,
however intimate. If Dolby betrays *your* name, grin and bear it. I
depend upon your friendship.'

II

In a by-way which declines from the main thoroughfare of Exeter, and bears the name of Longbrook Street, is a row of small houses placed above long strips of sloping garden. They are old and plain, with no architectural feature calling for mention, unless it be the latticed porch which gives the doors an awkward quaintness. Just beyond, the road crosses a hollow, and begins the ascent of a hill here interposed between the city and the inland-winding valley of Exe. The little terrace may be regarded as urban or rural, according to the tastes and occasions of those who dwell there. In one direction, a walk of five minutes will conduct to the middle of High Street, and in the other it takes scarcely longer to reach the open country.

On the upper floor of one of these cottages, Godwin Peak had made his abode. Sitting-room and bedchamber, furnished with homely comfort, answered to his bachelor needs, and would allow of his receiving without embarrassment any visitor whom fortune might send him. Of quietness he was assured, for a widow and her son, alike remarkable for sobriety of demeanour, were the only persons who shared the house with him. Mrs Roots could not compare in grace and skill with the little Frenchwoman who had sweetened his existence at Peckham Rye, but her zeal made amends for natural deficiency, and the timorous respect with which she waited upon him was by no means disagreeable to Godwin. Her reply to a request or suggestion was always, 'If you please, sir.' Throughout the day she went so tranquilly about her domestic duties, that Godwin seldom heard anything except the voice of the cuckoo-clock, a pleasant sound to him. Her son, employed at a nurseryman's, was a great sinewy fellow with a face of such ruddiness that it seemed to diffuse warmth; on Sunday afternoon, whatever the state of the sky, he sat behind the house in his shirt-sleeves, and smoked a pipe as he contemplated the hart's-tongue which grew there upon a rockery.

'The gentleman from London' – so Mrs Roots was wont to style her lodger in speaking with neighbours – had brought his books with him; they found place on a few shelves. His microscope had its stand by the window, and one or two other scientific implements lay about the room. The cabinets bequeathed to him by Mr Gunnery he had sent to Twybridge, to remain in his mother's care. In taking the lodgings, he described himself merely as a student, and gave his landlady to understand that he hoped to remain under her roof for at least a year. Of his extreme respectability, the widow could entertain no doubt, for he dressed with aristocratic finish, attended services at the Cathedral and elsewhere very frequently, and made the most punctual payments. Moreover, a casual remark had informed her that he was on friendly terms with Mr Martin Warricombe, whom her son knew as a gentleman of distinction. He often sat up very late at night, but, doubtless, that was the practice of Londoners. No lodger could have given less trouble, or have acknowledged with more courtesy all that was done for his convenience.

No one ever called upon Mr Peak, but he was often from home for many hours together, probably on visits to great people in city or country. It seemed rather strange, however, that the postman so seldom brought anything for him. Though he had now been more than two months in the house, he had received only three letters, and those at long intervals.

Noticeable was the improvement in his health since his arrival here. The pallor of his cheeks was giving place to a wholesome tinge; his eye was brighter; he showed more disposition to converse, and was readier with pleasant smiles. Mrs Roots even heard him singing in his bedroom – though, oddly enough, it was a secular song on Sunday morning. The weekly bills for food, which at first had been very modest, grew richer in items. Godwin had, in fact, never felt so well. He extended his walks in every direction, sometimes rambling up the valley to sleepy little towns where he could rest in the parlours of old inns, sometimes striking across country to this or that point of the sea-coast, or making his way to the nearer summits of Dartmoor, noble in their wintry desolation. He marked with delight every promise of returning spring. When he could only grant himself a walk of an hour or two in the sunny afternoon, there was many a deep lane within easy reach, where the gorse gleamed in masses of gold, and the little oak-trees in the hedges were ruddy with last year's clinging leafage, and catkins hung from the hazels, and the fresh green of sprouting ivy crept over bank and wall. Had he now been in London, the morning would have awakened him to fog and slush and misery. As it was, when he looked out upon the glow of sunrise, he felt the sweet air breathing health into his frame and vigour into his mind. There were moments when he could all but say of himself that he was at peace with the world.

As on a morning towards the end of March, when a wind from the Atlantic swept spaces of brightest blue amid the speeding clouds, and sang joyously as it rushed over hill and dale. It was the very day for an upland walk, for a putting forth of one's strength in conflict with boisterous gusts and sudden showers, that give a taste of earth's nourishment. But Godwin had something else in view. After breakfast, he sat down to finish a piece of work which had occupied him for two or three days, a translation from a German periodical. His mind wrought easily, and he often hummed an air as his pen moved over the paper. When the task was completed, he rolled his papers and the pamphlet together, put them into the pocket of his overcoat, and presently went forth.

Twenty minutes' walk brought him to the Warricombes' house. It was his second call within the present week, but such assiduity had not hitherto been his wont. Though already summoned twice or thrice by express invitation, he was sparing of voluntary visits. Having asked for Mr Warricombe, he was forthwith conducted to the study. In the welcome which greeted his appearance, he could detect no suspicion of simulated warmth, though his ear had unsurpassable discrimination.

'Have you looked through it?' Martin exclaimed, as he saw the foreign periodical in his visitor's hand.

'I have written a rough translation'—

'Oh, how could you think of taking such trouble! These things are sent to me by the dozen – I might say, by the cartload. My curiosity would have been amply satisfied if you had just told me the drift of the thing.'

'It seemed to me,' said Peak, modestly, 'that the paper was worth a little careful thought. I read it rapidly at first, but found myself drawn to it again. It states the point of view of the average scientific mind with such remarkable clearness, that I wished to think it over, and the best way was to do so pen in hand.'

'Well, if you really did it on your own account'—

Mr Warricombe took the offered sheets and glanced at the first of them.

'My only purpose,' said Godwin, 'in calling again so soon was to leave this with you.'

He made as though he would take his departure.

'You want to get home again? Wait at least till this shower is over. I enjoy that pelting of spring rain against the window. In a minute or two we shall have the laurels flashing in the sunshine, as if they were hung with diamonds.'

They stood together looking out on to the garden. Presently their talk returned to the German disquisition, which was directed against the class of quasi-scientific authors attacked by Peak himself in his *Critical* article. In the end Godwin sat down and began to read the translation he had made, Mr Warricombe listening with a thoughtful smile. From time to time the reader paused and offered a comment, endeavouring to show that the arguments were merely plausible; his air was that of placid security, and he seemed to enjoy the irony which often fell from his lips. Martin frequently scrutinised him, and always with a look of interest which betokened grave reflection.

'Here,' said Godwin at one point, 'he has a note citing a passage from Reusch's book on *The Bible and Nature*. If I am not mistaken, he misrepresents his author, though perhaps not intentionally.'

'You know the book?'

'I have studied it carefully, but I don't possess it. I thought I remembered this particular passage very well.'

'Is it a work of authority?'

'Yes; it is very important. Unfortunately, it hasn't yet been translated. Rather bulky, but I shouldn't mind doing it myself if I were sure of finding a publisher.'

'*The Bible and Nature*,' said Martin, musingly. 'What is his scheme? How does he go to work?'

Godwin gave a brief but lucid description of the book, and Mr Warricombe listened gravely. When there had been silence for some moments, the latter spoke in a tone he had never yet used when conversing with Peak. He allowed himself, for the first time, to betray a troubled doubt on the subject under discussion.

'So he makes a stand at Darwinism as it affects man?'

Peak had yet no means of knowing at what point Martin himself 'made a stand'. Modes of reconcilement between scientific discovery and religious tradition are so very numerous, and the geologist was only now beginning to touch upon these topics with his young acquaintance. That his mind was not perfectly at ease amid the conflicts of the day, Godwin soon perceived, and by this time he had clear assurance that Martin would willingly thrash out the whole debate with anyone who seemed capable of supporting orthodox tenets by reasoning not unacceptable to a man of broad views. The negativist of course assumed from the first that Martin, however respectable his knowledge, was far from possessing the scientific mind, and each conversation had supplied him with proofs of this defect; it was not at all in the modern spirit that the man of threescore years pursued his geological and kindred researches, but with the calm curiosity of a liberal intellect which has somehow taken this direction instead of devoting itself to literary study. At bottom, Godwin had no little sympathy with Mr Warricombe; he too, in spite of his militant instincts, dwelt by preference amid purely human interests. He grasped with firm intelligence the modes of thought which distinguish scientific men, but his nature did not prompt him to a consistent application of them. Personal liking enabled him to subdue the impulses of disrespect which, under other circumstances, would have made it difficult for him to act with perfection his present part. None the less, his task was one of infinite delicacy. Martin Warricombe was not the man to unbosom himself on trivial instigation. It must be a powerful influence which would persuade him to reveal whatever self-questionings lay beneath his genial good breeding and long-established acquiescence in a practical philosophy. Godwin guarded himself against his eager emotions; one false note, one syllable of indiscretion, and his aims might be hopelessly defeated.

'Yes,' was his reply to the hesitating question. 'He argues strenuously against the descent of man. If I understand him, he regards the concession of this point as impossible.'

Martin was deep in thought. He held a paper-knife bent upon his knee, and his smooth, delicate features wore an unquiet smile.

'Do you know Hebrew, Mr Peak?'

The question came unexpectedly, and Godwin could not help a momentary confusion, but he covered it with the tone of self-reproach.

'I am ashamed to say that I am only now taking it up seriously.'

'I don't think you need be ashamed,' said Martin, good-naturedly. 'Even a mind as active as yours must postpone some studies. Reusch, I suppose, is sound on that head?'

The inquiry struck Godwin as significant. So Mr Warricombe attached importance to the verbal interpretation of the Old Testament.

'Distinctly an authority,' he replied. 'He devotes whole chapters to a minute examination of the text.'

'If you had more leisure,' Martin began, deliberately, when he had again reflected, 'I should be disposed to urge you to undertake that translation.'

Peak appeared to meditate.

'Has the book been used by English writers?' the other inquired.

'A good deal. – It was published in the sixties, but I read it in a new edition dated a few years ago. Reusch has kept pace with the men of science. It would be very interesting to compare the first form of the book with the latest.'

'It would, very.'

Raising his head from the contemplative posture, Godwin exclaimed, with a laugh of zeal:

'I think I must find time to translate him. At all events, I might address a proposal to some likely publisher. Yet I don't know how I should assure him of my competency.'

'Probably a specimen would be the surest testimony.'

'Yes. I might do a few chapters.'

Mr Warricombe's lapse into silence and brevities intimated to Godwin that it was time to take leave. He always quitted this room with reluctance. Its air of luxurious culture affected his senses deliciously, and he hoped that he might some day be permitted to linger among the cabinets and the library shelves. There were so many books he would have liked to take down, some with titles familiar to him, others which kindled his curiosity when he chanced to observe them. The library abounded in such works as only a wealthy man can purchase, and Godwin, who had examined some of them at the British Museum, was filled with the humaner kind of envy on seeing them in Mr Warricombe's possession. Those publications of the Palæontological Society, one volume of which (a part of Davidson's superb work on the *Brachiopoda*) even now lay open within sight – his hand trembled with a desire to touch them! And those maps of the Geological Surveys, British and foreign, how he would have enjoyed a day's poring over them!

He rose, but Martin seemed in no haste to bring the conversation to an end.

'Have you read M'Naughten's much-discussed book?'

'Yes.'

'Did you see the savage attack in *The Critical* not long ago?'

Godwin smiled, and made quiet answer:

'I should think it was the last word of scientific bitterness and intolerance.'

'Scientific?' repeated Martin, doubtfully. 'I don't think the writer was a man of science. I saw it somewhere attributed to Huxley, but that was preposterous. To begin with, Huxley would have signed his name; and, again, his English is better. The article seemed to me to be stamped with literary rancour; it was written by some man who envies M'Naughten's success.'

Peak kept silence. Martin's censure of the anonymous author's style stung him to the quick, and he had much ado to command his countenance.

'Still,' pursued the other, 'I felt that much of his satire was only too well pointed. M'Naughten is suggestive; but one comes across books of the same purpose which can have no result but to injure their cause with all thinking people.'

'I have seen many such,' remarked Godwin.

Mr Warricombe stepped to a bookcase and took down a small volume.

'I wonder whether you know this book of Ampère's, *La Grèce, Rome, et Dante?* Delightful for odd moments! – There came into my mind a passage here at the beginning, apropos of what we were saying: "*Il faut souvent un vrai courage pour persister dans une opinion juste en dépit de ses défenseurs.*" – Isn't that capital?'

Peak received it with genuine appreciation; for once he was able to laugh unfeignedly. The aphorism had so many applications from his own point of view.

'Excellent! – I don't remember to have seen the book.'

'Take it, if you care to.'

This offer seemed a distinct advance in Mr Warricombe's friendliness. Godwin felt a thrill of encouragement.

'Then you will let me keep this translation for a day or two?' Martin added, indicating the sheets of manuscript. 'I am greatly obliged to you for enabling me to read the thing.'

They shook hands. Godwin had entertained a slight hope that he might be asked to stay to luncheon; but it could not be much past twelve o'clock, and on the whole there was every reason for feeling satisfied with the results of his visit. Before long he would probably receive another invitation to dine. So with light step he went out into the hall, where Martin again shook hands with him.

The sky had darkened over, and a shrilling of the wind sounded through the garden foliage – fir, and cypress, and laurel. Just as

Godwin reached the gate, he was met by Miss Warricombe and
Fanny, who were returning from a walk. They wore the costume
appropriate to March weather in the country, close-fitting,
defiant of gusts; and their cheeks glowed with health. As he
exchanged greetings with them, Peak received a new impression
of the sisters. He admired the physical vigour which enabled them
to take delight in such a day as this, when girls of poorer blood
and ignoble nurture would shrink from the sky's showery tumult,
and protect their surface elegance by the fireside. Impossible for
Sidwell and Fanny to be anything but graceful, for at all times they
were perfectly unaffected.

'There'll be another storm in a minute,' said the younger of
them, looking with interest to the quarter whence the wind came.
'How suddenly they burst! What a rush! And then in five minutes
the sky is clear again.'

Her eyes shone as she turned laughingly to Peak.

'You're not afraid of getting wet? Hadn't you better come
under cover?'

'Here it is!' exclaimed Sidwell, with quieter enjoyment. 'Take
shelter for a minute or two, Mr Peak.'

They led the way to the portico, where Godwin stood with
them and watched the squall. A moment's downpour of furious
rain was followed by heavy hailstones, which drove horizontally
before the shrieking wind. The prospect had wrapped itself in grey
gloom. At a hundred yards' distance, scarcely an object could be
distinguished; the storm-cloud swooped so low that its skirts
touched the branches of tall elms, a streaming, rushing ragged-
ness.

'Don't you enjoy that?' Fanny asked of Godwin.

'Indeed I do.'

'You should be on Dartmoor in such weather,' said Sidwell.
'Father and I were once caught in storms far worse than this – far
better, I ought to say, for I never knew anything so terrifically
grand.'

Already it was over. The gusts diminished in frequency and
force, the hail ceased, the core of blackness was passing over to the
eastern sky. Fanny ran out into the garden, and pointed upward.

'Look where the sunlight is coming!'

An uncloaked patch of heaven shone with colour like that of the
girl's eyes – faint, limpid blue. Reminding himself that to tarry
longer in this company would be imprudent, Godwin bade the

sisters good-morning. The frank heartiness with which Fanny pressed his hand sent him on his way exultant. Not too strong a word; for, independently of his wider ambitions, he was moved and gratified by the thought that kindly feeling towards him had sprung up in such a heart as this. Nor did conscience so much as whisper a reproach. With unreflecting ingenuousness he tasted the joy as if it were his right. Thus long he had waited, through years of hungry manhood, for the look, the tone, which were in harmony with his native sensibilities. Fanny Warricombe was but an undeveloped girl, yet he valued her friendship above the passionate attachment of any woman bred on a lower social plane. Had it been possible, he would have kissed her fingers with purest reverence.

When out of sight of the house, he paused to regard the sky again. Its noontide splendour was dazzling; masses of rosy cloud sailed swiftly from horizon to horizon, the azure deepening about them. Yet before long the west would again send forth its turbulent spirits, and so the girls might perhaps be led to think of him.

By night the weather grew more tranquil. There was a full moon, and its radiance illumined the ever-changing face of heaven with rare grandeur. Godwin could not shut himself up over his books; he wandered far away into the country, and let his thoughts have freedom.

He was learning to review with calmness the course by which he had reached his now steadfast resolve. A revulsion such as he had experienced after his first day of simulated orthodoxy, half a year ago, could not be of lasting effect, for it was opposed to the whole tenor of his mature thought. It spoilt his holiday, but had no chance of persisting after his return to the atmosphere of Rotherhithe. That he should have been capable of such emotion was, he said to himself, in the just order of things; callousness in the first stages of an undertaking which demanded gross hypocrisy would signify an ignoble nature – a nature, indeed, which could never have been submitted to trial of so strange a kind. But he had overcome himself; that phase of difficulty was outlived, and henceforth he saw only the material obstacles to be defied by his vindicated will.

What he proposed to himself was a life of deliberate baseness. Godwin Peak never tried to play the sophist with this fact. But he succeeded in justifying himself by a consideration of the circumstances which had compelled him to a vile expedient. Had his project involved conscious wrong to other persons, he would scarcely even have speculated on its possibilities. He was convinced that no mortal could suffer harm, even if he accomplished the uttermost of his desires. Whom was he in danger of wronging? The conventional moralist would cry: Everyone with whom he came in slightest contact! But a mind such as Peak's has very little to do with conventional morality. Injury to himself he foresaw and accepted; he could never be the man nature designed in him; and he must frequently submit to a self-contempt which would be very hard to bear. Those whom he consistently deceived, how would they suffer? Martin Warricombe to begin with. Martin was a man who had lived his life, and whose chief care would now be to keep his mind at rest in the faiths which had served him from youth onwards. In that very purpose, Godwin believed he could assist him. To see a young man, of strong and trained intellect, championing the old beliefs, must doubtless be a source of reassurance to one in Martin's position. Reassurance derived from a lie? – And what matter, if the outcome were genuine, if it lasted until the man himself was no more? Did not every form of content result from illusion? What was truth without the mind of the believer?

Society, then – at all events that part of it likely to be affected by his activity? Suppose him an ordained priest, performing all the functions implied in that office. Why, to think only of examples recognised by the public at large, how would he differ for the worse from this, that, and the other clergyman who taught Christianity, all but with blunt avowal, as a scheme of human ethics? No wolf in sheep's clothing he! He plotted against no man's pocket, no woman's honour; he had no sinister design of sapping the faith of congregations – a scheme, by-the-bye, which fanatic liberators might undertake with vast self-approval. If by a word he could have banished religious dogma from the minds of the multitude, he would not have cared to utter it. Wherein lay, indeed, a scruple to be surmounted. The Christian priest must be a man of humble temper; he must be willing, even eager, to sit down among the poor in spirit as well as in estate, and impart to them his unworldly solaces. Yes, but it had always been recognised that some men who could do the Church good service were personally unfitted for those meek ministrations. His place was in the hierarchy of intellect; if he were to be active at all, it must be with the brain. In his conversation with Buckland Warricombe, last October, he had spoken not altogether insincerely. Let him once be a member of the Church militant, and his heart would go with many a stroke against that democratic movement which desired, among other things, the Church's abolition. He had power of utterance. Roused to combat by the proletarian challenge, he could make his voice ring in the ears of men, even though he used a symbolism which he would not by choice have adopted.

For it was natural that he should anticipate distinction. Whatever his lot in life, he would not be able to rest among an inglorious brotherhood. If he allied himself with the Church, the Church must assign him leadership, whether titular or not was of small moment. In days to come, let people, if they would, debate his history, canvass his convictions. His scornful pride invited any degree of publicity, when once his position was secure.

But in the meantime he was leaving aside the most powerful of all his motives, and one which demanded closest scrutiny. Not ambition, in any ordinary sense; not desire of material luxury; no incentive recognised by unprincipled schemers first suggested his dishonour. This edifice of subtle untruth had for its foundation a mere ideal of sexual love. For the winning of some chosen woman, men have wrought vehemently, have ruined themselves and others, have achieved triumphs noble or degrading. But Godwin Peak had for years contemplated the possibility of baseness at the impulse of a craving for love capable only of a social (one might say, of a political) definition. The woman throned in his imagination was no individual, but the type of an order. So strangely had circumstances moulded him, that he could not brood on a desire of spiritual affinities, could not, as is natural to most cultivated men, inflame himself with the ardour of soul reaching to soul; he was pre-occupied with the contemplation of qualities which characterise a class. The sense of social distinctions was so burnt into him, that he could not be affected by any pictured charm of mind or person in a woman who had not the stamp of gentle birth and breeding. If once he were admitted to the intimacy of such women, then, indeed, the canons of selection would have weight with him; no man more capable of disinterested choice. Till then, the ideal which possessed him was merely such an assemblage of qualities as would excite the democrat to disdain or fury.

In Sidwell Warricombe this ideal found an embodiment; but

Godwin did not thereupon come to the conclusion that Sidwell was the wife he desired. Her influence had the effect of deciding his career, but he neither imagined himself in love with her, nor tried to believe that he might win her love if he set himself to the endeavour. For the first time he was admitted to familiar intercourse with a woman whom he *could* make the object of his worship. He thought much of her; day and night her figure stood before him; and this had continued now for half a year. Still he neither was, nor dreamt himself, in love with her. Before long his acquaintance would include many of her like, and at any moment Sidwell might pale in the splendour of another's loveliness.

But what reasoning could defend the winning of a wife by false pretences? This, his final aim, could hardly be achieved without grave wrong to the person whose welfare must in the nature of things be a prime motive with him. The deception he had practised must sooner or later be discovered; lifelong hypocrisy was incompatible with perfect marriage; some day he must either involve his wife in a system of dishonour, or with her consent relinquish the false career, and find his happiness in the obscurity to which he would then be relegated. Admit the wrong. Grant that some woman whom he loved supremely must, on his account, pass through a harsh trial – would it not be in his power to compensate her amply? The wife whom he imagined (his idealism in this matter was of a crudity which made the strangest contrast with his habits of thought on every other subject) would be ruled by her emotions, and that part of her nature would be wholly under his governance. Religious fanaticism could not exist in her, for in that case she would never have attracted him. Little by little she would learn to think as he did, and her devotedness must lead her to pardon his deliberate insincerities. Godwin had absolute faith in his power of dominating the woman whom he should inspire with tenderness. This was a feature of his egoism, the explanation of those manifold inconsistencies inseparable from his tortuous design. He regarded his love as something so rare, so vehement, so exalting, that its bestowal must seem an abundant recompense for any pain of which he was the cause.

Thus, with perfect sincerity of argument, did Godwin Peak face the undertaking to which he was committed. Incidents might perturb him, but his position was no longer a cause of uneasiness – save, indeed, at those moments when he feared lest any of his old acquaintances might hear of him before time was ripe. This was a source of anxiety, but inevitable; one of the risks he dared.

Had it seemed possible, he would have kept even from his mother the secret of his residence at Exeter; but this would have necessitated the establishment of some indirect means of communication with her, a troublesome and uncertain expedient. He shrank from leaving her in ignorance of his whereabouts, and from passing a year or two without knowledge of her condition. And, on the whole, there could not be much danger in this correspondence. The Moxeys, who alone of his friends had ever been connected with Twybridge, were now absolutely without interests in that quarter. From them he had stolen away, only acquainting Christian at the last moment, in a short letter, with his departure from London. 'It will be a long time before we again see each other – at least, I think so. Don't trouble your head about me. I can't promise to write, and shall be sorry not to hear how things go with you; but may all happen as you wish!' In the same way he had dealt with Earwaker, except that his letter to Staple Inn was much longer, and contained hints which the philosophic journalist might perchance truly interpret. '"He either fears his fate too much" – you know the old song. I have set out on my life's adventure. I have gone to seek that without which life is no longer worth having. Forgive my shabby treatment of you, old friend. You cannot help me, and your displeasure would be a hindrance in my path. A last piece of counsel: throw overboard the weekly rag, and write for people capable of understanding you.' Earwaker was not at all likely to institute a search; he would accept the situation, and wait with quiet curiosity for its upshot. No doubt he and Moxey would discuss the affair together, and any desire Christian might have to hunt for his vanished comrade would yield before the journalist's surmises. No one else had any serious reason for making inquiries. Probably he might dwell in Devonshire, as long as he chose, without fear of encountering anyone from his old world.

Occasionally – as to-night, under the full moon – he was able to cast off every form of trouble, and rejoice in his seeming liberty. Though every step in the life before him was an uncertainty, an appeal to fortune, his faith in himself grasped strongly at assurance of success. Once more he felt himself a young man, with unwearied energies; he had shaken off the burden of those ten frustrate years, and kept only their harvest of experience. Old in

one sense, in another youthful, he had vast advantages over such
men as would henceforth be his competitors – the complex brain,
the fiery heart, passion to desire, and skill in attempting. If with
such endowment he could not win the prize which most men
claim as a mere matter of course, a wife of social instincts
correspondent with his own, he must indeed be luckless. But he
was not doomed to defeat! Foretaste of triumph urged the current
of his blood and inflamed him with exquisite ardour. He sang
aloud in the still lanes the hymns of youth and of love; and, when
weariness brought him back to his lonely dwelling, he laid his
head on the pillow, and slept in dreamless calm.

As for the details of his advance towards the clerical state, he
had decided to resume his career at the point where it was
interrupted by Andrew Peak. Twice had his education received a
check from hostile circumstances: when domestic poverty compelled him to leave school for Mr Moxey's service, and when
shame drove him from Whitelaw College. In reflecting upon his
own character and his lot he gave much weight to these
irregularities, no doubt with justice. In both cases he was turned
aside from the way of natural development and opportunity. He
would now complete his academic course by taking the London
degree at which he had long ago aimed; the preliminary examination might without difficulty be passed this summer, and next year
he might write himself Bachelor of Arts. A return to the studies of
boyhood probably accounted in some measure for the frequent
gaiety which he attributed to improving health and revived hopes.
Everything he undertook was easy to him, and by a pleasant self-
deception he made the passing of a school task his augury of
success in greater things.

During the spring he was indebted to the Warricombes'
friendship for several new acquaintances. A clergyman named
Lilywhite, often at the Warricombes' house, made friendly
overtures to him; the connection might be a useful one, and
Godwin made the most of it. Mr Lilywhite was a man of forty –
well-read, of scientific tastes, an active pedestrian. Peak had no
difficulty in associating with him on amicable terms. With Mrs
Lilywhite, the mother of six children and possessed of many
virtues, he presently became a favourite, – she saw in him 'a great
deal of quiet moral force'. One or two families of good standing
made him welcome at their houses; society is very kind to those
who seek its benefits with recognised credentials. The more he

saw of these wealthy and tranquil middle-class people, the more fervently did he admire the gracefulness of their existence. He had not set before himself an imaginary ideal; the girls and women were sweet, gentle, perfect in manner, and, within limits, of bright intelligence. He was conscious of benefiting greatly, and not alone in things extrinsic, by the atmosphere of such homes.

Nature's progress towards summer kept him in a mood of healthful enjoyment. From the window of his sitting-room he looked over the opposite houses to Northernhay, the hill where once stood Rougemont Castle, its wooded declivities now fashioned into a public garden. He watched the rooks at their building in the great elms, and was gladdened when the naked branches began to deck themselves, day by day the fresh verdure swelling into soft, graceful outline. In his walks he pried eagerly for the first violet, welcomed the earliest blackthorn blossom; every common flower of field and hedgerow gave him a new, keen pleasure. As was to be expected he found the same impulses strong in Sidwell Warricombe and her sister. Sidwell could tell him of secret spots where the wood-sorrel made haste to flower, or where the white violet breathed its fragrance in security from common pilferers. Here was the safest and pleasantest matter for conversation. He knew that on such topics he could talk agreeably enough, revealing without stress or importunity his tastes, his powers, his attainments. And it seemed to him that Sidwell listened with growing interest. Most certainly her father encouraged his visits to the house, and Mrs Warricombe behaved to him with increase of suavity.

In the meantime he had purchased a copy of Reusch's *Bibel und Natur*, and had made a translation of some fifty pages. This experiment he submitted to a London publishing house, with proposals for the completion of the work; without much delay there came a civil letter of excuse, and with it the sample returned. Another attempt again met with rejection. This failure did not trouble him. What he really desired was to read through his version of Reusch with Martin Warricombe, and before long he had brought it to pass that Martin requested a perusal of the manuscript as it advanced, which it did but slowly. Godwin durst not endanger his success in the examination by encroaching upon hours of necessary study; his leisure was largely sacrificed to *Bibel und Natur*, and many an evening of calm golden loveliness, when he longed to be amid the fields, passed in vexatious imprisonment.

The name of Reusch grew odious to him, and he revenged himself
for the hypocrisy of other hours by fierce scorn, cast audibly at
this laborious exegetist.

III

It occasionally happens that a woman whose early life has been directed by native silliness and social bias, will submit to a tardy education at the hands of her own children. Thus was it with Mrs Warricombe.

She came of a race long established in squirearchic dignity amid heaths and woodlands. Her breeding was pure through many generations of the paternal and maternal lines, representative of a physical type, fortified in the males by much companionship with horse and hound, and by the corresponding country pursuits of dowered daughters. At the time of her marriage she had no charms of person more remarkable than rosy comeliness and the symmetry of supple limb. As for the nurture of her mind, it had been intrusted to home-governesses of respectable incapacity. Martin Warricombe married her because she was one of a little circle of girls, much alike as to birth and fortune, with whom he had grown up in familiar communication. Timidity imposed restraints upon him which made his choice almost a matter of accident. As befalls often enough, the betrothal became an accomplished fact whilst he was still doubting whether he desired it or not. When the fervour of early wedlock was outlived, he had no difficulty in accepting as a matter of course that his life's companion should be hopelessly illogical and at heart indifferent to everything but the small graces and substantial comforts of provincial existence. One of the advantages of wealth is that it allows husband and wife to keep a great deal apart without any show of mutual unkindness, a condition essential to happiness in marriage. Time fostered in them a calm attachment, independent of spiritual sympathy, satisfied with a common regard for domestic honour.

Not that Mrs Warricombe remained in complete ignorance of her husband's pursuits; social forms would scarcely have allowed this, seeing that she was in constant intercourse, as hostess or guest, with Martin's scientific friends. Of fossils she necessarily knew something. Up to a certain point they amused her; she could talk of ammonites, of brachiopods, and would point a friend's attention to the *Calceola sandalina* which Martin prized so much. The significance of palæontology she dimly apprehended, for in the early days of their union her husband had felt it desirable to explain to her what was meant by geologic time, and how he reconciled his views on that subject with the demands of religious faith. Among the books which he induced her to read were Buckland's Bridgewater Treatise and the works of Hugh Miller. The intellectual result was chaotic, and Mrs Warricombe settled at last into a comfortable private opinion, that though the record of geology might be trustworthy that of the Bible was more so. She would admit that there was no impiety in accepting the evidence of nature, but held to a secret conviction that it was safer to believe in Genesis. For anything beyond a quasi-permissible variance from biblical authority as to the age of the world she was quite unprepared, and Martin, in his discretion, imparted to her nothing of the graver doubts which were wont to trouble him.

But as her children grew up, Mrs Warricombe's mind and temper were insensibly modified by influences which operated through her maternal affections, influences no doubt aided by the progressive spirit of the time. The three boys – Buckland, Maurice, and Louis – were distinctly of a new generation. It needed some ingenuity to discover their points of kindred with paternal and maternal grandparents; nor even with father and mother had they much in common which observation could readily detect. Sidwell, up to at least her fifteenth year, seemed to present far less change of type. In her Mrs Warricombe recognised a daughter, and not without solace. But Fanny again was a problematical nature, almost from the cradle. Latest born, she appeared to revive many characteristics of the youthful Buckland, so far as a girl could resemble her brother. It was a strange brood to cluster around Mrs Warricombe. For many years the mother was kept in alternation between hopes and fears, pride and disapproval, the old hereditary habits of mind, and a new order of ideas which could only be admitted with the utmost slowness. Buckland's Radicalism deeply offended her; she marvelled how such depravity could display itself in a child of hers. Yet in the end her ancestral prejudices so far yielded as to allow of her smiling at sentiments which she once heard with horror. Maurice, whom she loved more tenderly, all but taught her to see the cogency of a syllogism – amiably set forth. And Louis, with his indolent good-nature, laughed her into a tolerance of many things which had moved her indignation. But it was to Sidwell that in the end she owed most. Beneath the surface of ordinary and rather backward girlhood, which discouraged her father's hopes, Sidwell was quietly developing a personality distinguished by the refinement of its ethical motives. Her orthodoxy seemed as unimpeachable as Mrs Warricombe could desire, yet as she grew into womanhood, a curiosity, which in no way disturbed the tenor of her quietly contented life, led her to examine various forms of religion, ancient and modern, and even systems of philosophy which professed to establish a moral code, independent of supernatural faith. She was not of studious disposition – that is to say, she had never cared as a schoolgirl to do more mental work than was required of her, and even now it was seldom that she read for more than an hour or two in the day. Her habit was to dip into books, and meditate long on the first points which arrested her thoughts. Of continuous application she seemed incapable. She could read French, but did not attempt to pursue the other languages of which her teachers had given her a smattering. It pleased her best when she could learn from conversation. In this way she obtained some insight into her father's favourite sciences, occasionally making suggestions or inquiries which revealed a subtle if not an acute intelligence.

Little by little Mrs Warricombe found herself changing places with the daughter whom she had regarded as wholly subject to her direction. Sidwell began to exercise an indeterminate control, the proofs of which were at length manifest in details of her mother's speech and demeanour. An exquisite social tact, an unfailing sincerity of moral judgment, a gentle force which operated as insensibly as the qualities of pure air: these were the points of character to which Mrs Warricombe owed the humanisation observable when one compared her in 1885 with what she was, say, in 1874, when the sight of Professor Walsh moved her to acrimony, and when she conceived a pique against Professor Gale because the letter P has alphabetical precedence of W. Her limitations were of course the same as ever, and from her sons she had only learnt to be ashamed of announcing them too vehemently. Sidwell it was who had led her to that degree of genuine humility, which is not satisfied with hiding a fault but strives to amend it.

Martin Warricombe himself was not unaffected by the growth about him of young men and maidens who looked upon the world with new eyes, whose world, indeed, was another than that in which he had spent the better part of his life. In his case contact

with the young generation tended to unsettlement, to a troublesome persistency of speculations which he would have preferred
to dismiss altogether. At the time of his marriage, and for some
years after, he was content to make a broad distinction between
those intellectual pursuits which afforded him rather a liberal
amusement than the pleasures of earnest study and the questions
of metaphysical faith which concerned his heart and conscience.
His native prejudices were almost as strong, and much the same,
as those of his wife; but with the vagueness of emotional logic
natural to his constitution, he satisfied himself that, by conceding
a few inessential points, he left himself at liberty to follow the
scientific movements of the day without damage to his religious
convictions. The tolerant smile so frequently on his countenance
was directed as often in the one quarter as in the other. Now it
signified a gentle reproof of those men of science who, like
Professor Walsh, 'went too far', whose zeal for knowledge led
them 'to forget the source of all true enlightenment'; now it
expressed a forbearing sympathy with such as erred in the
opposite direction, who were 'too literal in their interpretation of
the sacred volume'. Amiable as the smile was, it betrayed
weakness, and at moments Martin became unpleasantly
conscious of indisposition to examine his own mind on certain
points. His life, indeed, was one of debate postponed. As the
realm of science extended, as his intercourse with men who
frankly avowed their 'infidelity' grew more frequent, he ever and
again said to himself that, one of these days, he must sit down and
'have it out' in a solemn self-searching. But for the most part he
got on very well amid his inconsistencies. Religious faith has
rarely any connection with reasoning. Martin believed because he
believed, and avoided the impact of disagreeable arguments
because he wished to do so.

The bent of his mind was anything but polemical; he cared not
to spend time even over those authors whose attacks on the
outposts of science, or whose elaborate reconcilements of old and
new, might have afforded him some support. On the other hand,
he altogether lacked that breadth of intellect which seeks to
comprehend all the results of speculation, to discern their
tendency, to derive from them a consistent theory of the nature of
things. Though a man be well versed in a science such as
palæontology it does not follow that he will view it in its
philosophical relations. Martin had kept himself informed of all

the facts appertaining to his study which the age brought forth, but without developing the new modes of mental life requisite for the recognition of all that such facts involved. The theories of evolution he did not venture openly to resist, but his acceptance of them was so half-hearted that practically he made no use of their teaching. He was no man of science, but an idler among the wonders which science uses for her own purposes.

He regarded with surprise and anxiety the tendencies early manifested in his son Buckland. Could he have had his way the lad would have grown up with an impossible combination of qualities, blending the enthusiasm of modern research with a spirit of expansive teleology. Whilst Buckland was still of boyish years, the father treated with bantering good-humour such outbreaks of irreverence as came immediately under his notice, weakly abstaining from any attempt at direct argument or influence. But, at a later time, there took place serious and painful discussions, and only when the young man had rubbed off his edges in the world's highways could Martin forget that stage of most unwelcome conflict.

At the death of his younger boy, Maurice, he suffered a blow which had results more abiding than the melancholy wherewith for a year or two his genial nature was overshadowed. From that day onwards he was never wholly at ease among the pursuits which had been wont to afford him an unfailing resource against whatever troubles. He could no longer accept and disregard, in a spirit of cheerful faith, those difficulties science was perpetually throwing in his way. The old smile of kindly tolerance had still its twofold meaning, but it was more evidently a disguise of indecision, and not seldom touched with sadness. Martin's life was still one of postponed debate, but he could not regard the day when conclusions would be demanded of him as indefinitely remote. Desiring to dwell in the familiar temporary abode, his structure of incongruities and facile reconcilements, he found it no longer weather-proof. The times were shaking his position with earthquake after earthquake. His sons (for he suspected that Louis was hardly less emancipated than Buckland) stood far aloof from him, and must in private feel contemptuous of his old-fashioned beliefs. In Sidwell, however, he had a companion more and more indispensable, and he could not imagine that *her* faith would ever give way before the invading spirit of agnosticism. Happily she was no mere pietist. Though he did not quite understand her attitude towards Christianity, he felt assured that Sidwell had thought deeply and earnestly of religion in all its aspects, and it was a solace to know that she found no difficulty in recognising the large claims of science. For all this, he could not deliberately seek her confidence, or invite her to a discussion of religious subjects. Some day, no doubt, a talk of that kind would begin naturally between them, and so strong was his instinctive faith in Sidwell that he looked forward to this future communing as to a certain hope of peace.

That a figure such as Godwin Peak, a young man of vigorous intellect, preparing to devote his life to the old religion, should excite Mr Warricombe's interest was of course to be anticipated; and it seemed probable enough that Peak, exerting all the force of his character and aided by circumstances, might before long convert this advantage to a means of ascendency over the less self-reliant nature. But here was no instance of a dotard becoming the easy prey of a scientific Tartufe. Martin's intellect had suffered no decay. His hale features and dignified bearing expressed the mind which was ripened by sixty years of pleasurable activity, and which was learning to regard with steadier view the problems it had hitherto shirked. He could not change the direction nature had given to his thoughts, and prepossession would in some degree obscure his judgment where the merits and trustworthiness of a man in Peak's circumstances called for scrutiny; but self-respect guarded him against vulgar artifices, and a fine sensibility made it improbable that he would become the victim of any man in whom base motives predominated.

Left to his own impulses, he would still have proceeded with all caution in his offers of friendly services to Peak. A letter of carefully-worded admonition, which he received from his son, apprising him of Peak's resolve to transfer himself to Exeter, scarcely affected his behaviour when the young man appeared. It was but natural – he argued – that Buckland should look askance on a case of 'conversion'; for his own part, he understood that such a step might be prompted by interest, but he found it difficult to believe that to a man in Peak's position, the Church would offer temptation thus coercive. Nor could he discern in the candidate for a curacy any mark of dishonourable purpose. Faults, no doubt, were observable, among them a tendency to spiritual pride – which seemed (Martin could admit) an argument for, rather than against, his sincerity. The progress of acquaintance decidedly confirmed his favourable impressions; they were supported by the remarks of those among his friends to whom Peak presently became known.

It was not until Whitsuntide of the next year, when the student had been living nearly five months at Exeter, that Buckland again came down to visit his relatives. On the evening of his arrival, chancing to be alone with Sidwell, he asked her if Peak had been to the house lately.

'Not many days ago,' replied his sister, 'he lunched with us, and then sat with father for some time.'

'Does he come often?'

'Not very often. He is translating a German book which interests father very much.'

'Oh, what book?'

'I don't know. Father has only mentioned it in that way.'

They were in a little room sacred to the two girls, very daintily furnished and fragrant of sweet-brier, which Sidwell loved so much that, when the season allowed it, she often wore a little spray of it at her girdle. Buckland opened a book on the table, and, on seeing the title, exclaimed with a disparaging laugh:

'I can't get out of the way of this fellow M'Naughten! Wherever I go, there he lies about on the tables and chairs. I should have thought he was thoroughly smashed by an article that came out in *The Critical* last year.'

Sidwell smiled, evidently in no way offended.

'That article could "smash" nobody,' she made answer. 'It was too violent; it overshot the mark.'

'Not a bit of it! — So you read it, eh? You're beginning to read, are you?'

'In my humble way, Buckland.'

'M'Naughten, among other things. Humble enough, that, I admit.'

'I am not a great admirer of M'Naughten,' returned his sister, with a look of amusement.

'No? I congratulate you. — I wonder what Peak thinks of the book?'

'I really don't know.'

'Then let me ask another question. What do you think of Peak?'

Sidwell regarded him with quiet reflectiveness.

'I feel,' she said, 'that I don't know him very well yet. He is certainly interesting.'

'Yes, he is. Does he impress you as the kind of man likely to make a good clergyman?'

'I don't see any reason why he should not.'

Her brother mused, with wrinkles of dissatisfaction on his brow.

'Father gets to like him, you say?'

'Yes, I think father likes him.'

'Well, I suppose it's all right.'

'All right?'

'It's the most astounding thing that ever came under my observation,' exclaimed Buckland, walking away and then returning.

'That Mr Peak should be studying for the Church?'

'Yes.'

'But do reflect more modestly!' urged Sidwell, with something that was not quite archness, though as near it as her habits of tone and feature would allow. 'Why should you refuse to admit an error in your own way of looking at things? Wouldn't it be better to take this as a proof that intellect isn't necessarily at war with Christianity?'

'I never stated it so broadly as that,' returned her brother, with impatience. 'But I should certainly have maintained that *Peak's* intellect was necessarily in that position.'

'And you see how wrong you would have been,' remarked the girl, softly.

'Well – I don't know.'

'You don't know?'

'I mean that I can't acknowledge what I can't understand.'

'Then do try to understand, Buckland! – Have you ever put aside your prejudice for a moment to inquire what our religion really means? Not once, I think – at all events, not since you reached years of discretion.'

'Allow me to inform you that I studied the question thoroughly at Cambridge.'

'Yes, yes; but that was in your boyhood.'

'And when does manhood begin?'

'At different times in different persons. In your case it was late.'

Buckland laughed. He was considering a rejoinder, when they were interrupted by the appearance of Fanny, who asked at once:

'Shall you go to see Mr Peak this evening, Buckland?'

'I'm in no hurry,' was the abrupt reply.

The girl hesitated.

'Let us all have a drive together – with Mr Peak, I mean – like when you were here last.'

'We'll see about it.'

Buckland went slowly from the room.

Late the same evening he sat with his father in the study. Mr Warricombe knew not the solace of tobacco, and his son, though never quite at ease without pipe or cigar, denied himself in this room, with the result that he shifted frequently upon his chair and fell into many awkward postures.

'And how does Peak impress you?' he inquired, when the subject he most wished to converse upon had been postponed to many others. It was clear that Martin would not himself broach it.

'Not disagreeably,' was the reply, with a look of frankness, perhaps over-emphasised.

'What is he doing? I have only heard from him once since he came down, and he had very little to say about himself.'

'I understand that he proposes to take the London BA.'

'Oh, then, he never did that? Has he unbosomed himself to you about his affairs of old time?'

'No. Such confidences are hardly called for.'

'Speaking plainly, father, you don't feel any uneasiness?'

Martin deliberated, fingering the while an engraved stone which hung upon his watch-guard. He was at a disadvantage in this conversation. Aware that Buckland regarded the circumstances of Peak's sojourn in the neighbourhood with feelings allied to contempt, he could neither adopt the tone of easy confidence natural to him on other occasions of difference in opinion, nor express himself with the coldness which would have obliged his son to quit the subject.

'Perhaps you had better tell me,' he replied, 'whether *you* are really uneasy.'

It was impossible for Buckland to answer as his mind prompted. He could not without offence declare that no young man of brains now adopted a clerical career with pure intentions, yet such was his sincere belief. Made tolerant in many directions by the cultivation of his shrewdness, he was hopelessly biassed in judgment as soon as his anti-religious prejudice came into play – a point of strong resemblance between him and Peak. After fidgeting for a moment, he exclaimed:

'Yes, I am; but I can't be sure that there's any cause for it.'

'Let us come to matters of fact,' said Mr Warricombe, showing that he was not sorry to discuss this side of the affair. 'I suppose there is no doubt that Peak had a position till lately at the place he speaks of?'

'No doubt whatever. I have taken pains to ascertain that. His account of himself, so far, is strictly true.'

Martin smiled, with satisfaction he did not care to disguise.

'Have you met some acquaintance of his?'

'Well,' answered Buckland, changing his position, 'I went to work in rather an underhand way, perhaps – but the results are satisfactory. No, I haven't come across any of his friends, but I happened to hear not long ago that he was on intimate terms with some journalists.'

His father laughed.

'Anything compromising in that association, Buckland?'

'I don't say that – though the fellows I speak of are hot Radicals.'

'Though?'

'I mean,' replied the young man, with his shrewder smile, 'that they are not exactly the companions a theological student would select.'

'I understand. Possibly he has journalised a little himself?'

'That I can't say, though I should have thought it likely enough. I might, of course, find out much more about him, but it seemed to me that to have assurance of his truthfulness in that one respect was enough for the present.'

'Do you mean, Buckland,' asked his father, gravely, 'that you have been setting secret police at work?'

'Well, yes. I thought it the least objectionable way of getting information.'

Martin compressed his lips and looked disapproval.

'I really can't see that such extreme measures were demanded. Come, come; what is all this about? Do you suspect him of planning burglaries? That was an ill-judged step, Buckland; decidedly ill-judged. I said just now that Peak impressed me by no means disagreeably. Now I will add that I am convinced of his good faith – as sure of it as I am of his remarkable talents and aptitude for the profession he aims at. In spite of your extraordinary distrust, I can't feel a moment's doubt of his honour. Why, I could have told you myself that he has known Radical journalists. He mentioned it the other day, and explained how far his sympathy went with that kind of thing. No, no; that was hardly permissible, Buckland.'

The young man had no difficulty in bowing to his father's reproof when the point at issue was one of gentlemanly behaviour.

'I admit it,' he replied. 'I wish I had gone to Rotherhithe and made simple inquiries in my own name. That, all things considered, I might have allowed myself; at all events, I shouldn't have been at ease without getting that assurance. If Peak had heard, and had said to me, "What the deuce do you mean?" I should have told him plainly, what I have strongly hinted to him already, that I don't understand what he is doing in this galley.'

'And have placed yourself in a position not easy to define.'

'No doubt.'

'All this arises, my boy,' resumed Martin, in a tone of grave kindness, 'from your strange inability to grant that on certain matters you may be wholly misled.'

'It does.'

'Well, well; that is forbidden ground. But do try to be less narrow. Are you unable then to meet Peak in a friendly way?'

'Oh, by no means! It seems more than likely that I have wronged him.'

'Well said! Keep your mind open. I marvel at the dogmatism of men who are set on overthrowing dogma. Such a position is so strangely unphilosophic that I don't know how a fellow of your brains can hold it for a moment. If I were not afraid of angering you,' Martin added, in his pleasantest tone, 'I would quote the Master of Trinity.'

'A capital epigram, but it is repeated too often.'

Mr Warricombe shook his head, and with a laugh rose to say good-night.

'It's a great pity,' he remarked next day to Sidwell, who had been saying that her brother seemed less vivacious than usual, 'that Buckland is defective on the side of humour. For a man who claims to be philosophical he takes things with a rather obtuse seriousness. I know nothing better than humour as a protection against the kind of mistake he is always committing.'

The application of this was not clear to Sidwell.

'Has something happened to depress him?' she asked.

'Not that I know of. I spoke only of his general tendency to intemperate zeal. That is enough to account for intervals of reaction. And how much sounder his judgment of men would be if he could only see through a medium of humour now and then! – You know he is going over to Budleigh Salterton this afternoon?'

Sidwell smiled, and said quietly:

'I thought it likely he would.'

At Budleigh Salterton, a nook on the coast some fifteen miles away, Sylvia Moorhouse was now dwelling. Her mother, a widow of substantial means, had recently established herself there, in the proximity of friends, and the mathematical brother made his home with them. That Buckland took every opportunity of enjoying Sylvia's conversation was no secret; whether the predilection was mutual, none of his relatives could say, for in a matter such as this Buckland was by nature disposed to reticence. Sidwell's intimacy with Miss Moorhouse put her in no better position than the others for forming an opinion; she could only suspect that the irony which flavoured Sylvia's talk with and concerning the Radical, intimated a lurking kindness. Buckland's preference was easily understood, and its growth for five or six years seemed to promise stability.

Immediately after luncheon the young man set forth, and did not reappear until the evening of the next day. His spirits had not benefited by the excursion; at dinner he was noticeably silent, and instead of going to the drawing-room afterwards he betook himself to the studio up on the roof, and smoked in solitude. There, towards ten o'clock, Sidwell sought him. Heavy rain was beating upon the glass, and a high wind blended its bluster with the cheerless sound.

'Don't you find it rather cold here?' she asked, after observing her brother's countenance of gloom.

'Yes; I'm coming down. – Why don't you keep up your painting?'

'I have lost interest in it, I'm afraid.'

'That's very weak, you know. It seems to me that nothing interests you permanently.'

Sidwell thought it better to make no reply.

'The characteristic of women,' Buckland pursued, with some asperity, throwing away the stump of his cigar. 'It comes, I suppose, of their ridiculous education – their minds are never trained to fixity of purpose. They never understand themselves, and scarcely ever make an effort to understand any one else. Their life is a succession of inconsistencies.'

'This generalising is so easy,' said Sidwell, with a laugh, 'and so worthless. I wonder you should be so far behind the times.'

'What light have the times thrown on the subject?'

'There's no longer such a thing as *woman* in the abstract. We are individuals.'

'Don't imagine it! That may come to pass three or four generations hence, but as yet the best of you can only vary the type in unimportant particulars. By the way, what is Peak's address?'

'Longbrook Street; but I don't know the number. Father can give it you, I think.'

'I shall have to drop him a note. I must get back to town early in the morning.'

'Really? We hoped to have you for a week.'

'Longer next time.'

They descended together. Now that Louis no longer abode here (he had decided at length for medicine, and was at work in London), the family as a rule spent very quiet evenings. By ten o'clock Mrs Warricombe and Fanny had retired, and Sidwell was left either to talk with her father, or to pursue the calm meditations which seemed to make her independent of companionship as often as she chose.

'Are they all gone?' Buckland asked, finding a vacant room.

'Father is no doubt in the study.'

'It occurs to me—. Do you feel satisfied with this dead-alive existence?'

'Satisfied? No life could suit me better.'

'You really think of living here indefinitely?'

'As far as I am concerned, I hope nothing may ever disturb us.'

'And to the end of your life you will scent yourself with sweet-brier? Do try a bit of mint for a change.'

'Certainly, if it will please you.'

'Seriously, I think you might all come to town for next winter. You are rusting, all of you. Father was never so dull, and mother doesn't seem to know how to pass the days. It wouldn't be bad for Louis to be living with you instead of in lodgings. Do just think of it. It's ages since you heard a concert, or saw a picture.'

Sidwell mused, and her brother watched her askance.

'I don't know whether the others would care for it,' she said, 'but I am not tempted by a winter of fog.'

'Fog? Pooh! Well, there *is* an occasional fog, just now and then, but it's much exaggerated. Who ever thinks of the weather in

England? Fanny might have a time at Bedford College or some such place – she learns nothing here. Think it over. Father would be delighted to get among the societies, and so on.'

He repeated his arguments in many forms, and Sidwell listened patiently, until they were joined by Mr Warricombe, whereupon the subject dropped; to be resumed, however, in correspondence, with a persistency which Buckland seldom exhibited in anything which affected the interests of his relatives. As the summer drew on, Mrs Warricombe began to lend serious ear to this suggestion of change, and Martin was at all events moved to discuss the pros and cons of half a year in London. Sidwell preserved neutrality, seldom making an allusion to the project; but Fanny supported her brother's proposal with sprightly zeal, declaring on one occasion that she began distinctly to feel the need of 'a higher culture', such as London only could supply.

In the meantime there had been occasional interchange of visits between the family and their friends at Budleigh Salterton. One evening, when Mrs Moorhouse and Sylvia were at the Warricombes', three or four Exeter people came to dine, and among the guests was Godwin Peak – his invitation being due in this instance to Sylvia's express wish to meet him again.

'I am studying men,' she had said to Sidwell not long before, when the latter was at the seaside with her. 'In our day this is the proper study of womankind. Hitherto we have given serious attention only to one another. Mr Peak remains in my memory as a type worth observing; let me have a chance of talking to him when I come next.'

She did not neglect her opportunity, and Mrs Moorhouse, who also conversed with the theologian and found him interesting, was so good as to hope that he would call upon her if ever his steps turned towards Budleigh Salterton.

After breakfast next morning, Sidwell found her friend sitting with a book beneath one of the great trees of the garden. At that moment Sylvia was overcome with laughter, evidently occasioned by her reading.

'Oh,' she exclaimed, 'if this man isn't a great humorist! I don't think I ever read anything more irresistible.'

The book was Hugh Miller's *Testimony of the Rocks*, a richly bound copy belonging to Mrs Warricombe.

'I daresay you know it very well; it's the chapter in which he discusses, with perfect gravity, whether it would have been possible for Noah to collect examples of all living creatures in the ark. He decides that it wouldn't – that the deluge *must* have spared a portion of the earth; but the details of his argument are delicious, especially this place where he says that all the insects could have been brought together only "at enormous expense of miracle"! I suspected a secret smile; but no – that's out of the question. "At enormous expense of miracle"!'

Sylvia's eyes winked as she laughed, a peculiarity which enhanced the charm of her frank mirth. Her dark, pure complexion, strongly-marked eyebrows, subtle lips, were shadowed beneath a great garden hat, and a loose white gown, with no oppressive moulding at the waist, made her a refreshing picture in the glare of mid-summer.

'The phrase is ridiculous enough,' assented Sidwell. 'Miracle can be but miracle, however great or small its extent.'

'Isn't it strange, reading a book of this kind nowadays? What a leap we have made! I should think there's hardly a country curate who would be capable of bringing this argument into a sermon.'

'I don't know,' returned Sidwell, smiling. 'One still hears remarkable sermons.'

'What will Mr Peak's be like?'

They exchanged glances. Sylvia wore a look of reflective curiosity, and her friend answered with some hesitation, as if the thought were new to her:

'They won't deal with Noah, we may take that for granted.'

'Most likely not with miracles, however little expensive.'

'Perhaps not. I suppose he will deal chiefly with the moral teaching of Christianity.'

'Do you think him strong as a moralist?' inquired Sylvia.

'He has very decided opinions about the present state of our civilisation.'

'So I find. But is there any distinctly moral force in him?'

'Father thinks so,' Sidwell replied, 'and so do our friends the Lilywhites.'

Miss Moorhouse pondered awhile.

'He is a great problem to me,' she declared at length, knitting her brows with a hint of humorous exaggeration. 'I wonder whether he believes in the dogmas of Christianity.'

Sidwell was startled.

'Would he think of becoming a clergyman?'

'Oh, why not? Don't they recognise nowadays that the spirit is enough?'

There was silence. Sidwell let her eyes wander over the sunny grass to the red-flowering creeper on the nearest side of the house.

'That would involve a great deal of dissimulation,' she said at length. 'I can't reconcile it with what I know of Mr Peak.'

'And I can't reconcile anything else,' rejoined the other.

'He impresses you as a rationalist?'

'You not?'

'I confess I have taken his belief for granted. Oh, think! He couldn't keep up such a pretence. However you justify it, it implies conscious deception. It would be dishonourable. I am sure *he* would think it so.'

'How does your brother regard him?' Sylvia asked, smiling very slightly, but with direct eyes.

'Buckland can't credit anyone with sincerity except an aggressive agnostic.'

'But I think he allows honest credulity.'

Sidwell had no answer to this. After musing a little, she put a question which indicated how her thoughts had travelled.

'Have you met many women who declared themselves agnostics?'

'Several.'

Sylvia removed her hat, and began to fan herself gently with the brim. Here, in the shade, bees were humming; from the house came faint notes of a piano – Fanny practising a mazurka of Chopin.

'But never, I suppose, one who found a pleasure in attacking Christianity?'

'A girl who was at school with me in London,' Sylvia replied, with an air of amused reminiscence. 'Marcella Moxey. Didn't I ever speak to you of her?'

'I think not.'

'She was bitter against religion of every kind.'

'Because her mother made her learn collects, I dare say?' suggested Sidwell, in a tone of gentle satire.

'No, no. Marcella was about eighteen then, and had neither father nor mother. – (How Fanny's touch improves!) – She was a born atheist, in the fullest sense of the word.'

'And detestable?'

'Not to me – I rather liked her. She was remarkably honest, and

I have sometimes thought that in morals, on the whole, she stood far above most women. She hated falsehood – hated it with all her heart, and a story of injustice maddened her. When I think of Marcella it helps me to picture the Russian girls who propagate Nihilism.'

'You have lost sight of her?'

'She went abroad, I think. I should like to have known her fate. I rather think there will have to be many like her before women are civilised.'

'How I should like to ask her,' said Sidwell, 'on what she supported her morality?'

'Put the problem to Mr Peak,' suggested the other, gaily. 'I fancy he wouldn't find it insoluble.'

Mrs Warricombe and Mrs Moorhouse appeared in the distance, walking hither under parasols. The girls rose to meet them, and were presently engaged in less interesting colloquy.

IV

This summer Peak became a semi-graduate of London University. To avoid the risk of a casual meeting with acquaintances, he did not go to London, but sat for his examination at the nearest provincial centre. The revival of boyish tremors at the successive stages of this business was anything but agreeable; it reminded him, with humiliating force, how far he had strayed from the path indicated to his self-respecting manhood. Defeat would have strengthened in overwhelming revolt all the impulses which from time to time urged him to abandon his servile course. But there was no chance of his failing to satisfy the examiners. With 'Honours' he had now nothing to do; enough for his purpose that in another year's time he would write himself Bachelor of Arts, and thus simplify the clerical preliminaries. In what quarter he was to look for a curacy remained uncertain. Meanwhile his enterprise seemed to prosper, and success emboldened his hopes.

Hopes which were no longer vague, but had defined themselves in a way which circumstances made inevitable. Though he had consistently guarded himself against the obvious suggestions arising out of his intercourse with the Warricombe family, though he still emphasised every discouraging fact, and strove to regard it as axiomatic that nothing could be more perilous to his future than a hint of presumption or self-interest in word or deed beneath that friendly roof, it was coming to pass that he thought of Sidwell not only as the type of woman pursued by his imagination, but as herself the object of his converging desires. Comparison of her with others had no result but the deepening of that impression she had at first made upon him. Sidwell exhibited all the qualities which most appealed to him in her class; in addition, she had the charms of a personality which he could not think of common occurrence. He was yet far from understanding her; she exercised his powers of observation, analysis, conjecture, as no other person had ever done; each time he saw her (were it but for a moment) he came away with some new perception of her excellence, some hitherto unmarked grace of person or mind whereon to meditate. He had never approached a woman who possessed this power at once of fascinating his senses and controlling his intellect to a glad reverence. Whether in her presence or musing upon her in solitude, he found that the unsparing naturalism of his scrutiny was powerless to degrade that sweet, pure being.

Rare, under any circumstances, is the passionate love which controls every motive of heart and mind; rarer still that form of it which, with no assurance of reciprocation, devotes exclusive ardour to an object only approachable through declared obstacles. Godwin Peak was not framed for romantic languishment. In general, the more complex a man's mechanism, and the more pronounced his habit of introspection, the less capable is he of loving with vehemence and constancy. Heroes of passion are for the most part primitive natures, nobly tempered; in our time they tend to extinction. Growing vulgarism on the one hand, and on the other a development of the psychological conscience, are unfavourable to any relation between the sexes, save those which originate in pure animalism, or in reasoning less or more generous. Never having experienced any feeling which he could dignify with the name of love, Godwin had no criterion in himself whereby to test the emotions now besetting him. In a man of his age this was an unusual state of things, for when the ardour which will bear analysis has at length declared itself, it is wont to be moderated by the regretful memory of that fugacious essence which gave to the first frenzy of youth its irrecoverable delight. He could not say in reply to his impulses: If that was love which overmastered me, this must be something either more or less exalted. What he *did* say was something of this kind: If desire and tenderness, if frequency of dreaming rapture, if the calmest approval of the mind and the heart's most exquisite, most painful throbbing, constitute love, – then assuredly I love Sidwell. But if to love is to be possessed with madness, to lose all taste of life when hope refuses itself, to meditate frantic follies, to deem it inconceivable that this woman should ever lose her dominion over me, or another reign in her stead, – then my passion falls short of the true œstrum, and I am only dallying with fancies which might spring up as often as I encountered a charming girl.

All things considered, to encourage this amorous preoccupation was probably the height of unwisdom. The lover is ready at deluding himself, but Peak never lost sight of the extreme unlikelihood that he should ever become Martin Warricombe's son-in-law, of the thousand respects which forbade his hoping that Sidwell would ever lay her hand in his. That deep-rooted sense of class which had so much influence on his speculative and practical life asserted itself, with rigid consistency, even against his own aspirations; he attributed to the Warricombes more prejudice on this subject than really existed in them. He, it was true, belonged to no class whatever, acknowledged no subordination save that of the hierarchy of intelligence; but this could not obscure the fact that his brother sold seeds across a counter, that his sister had married a haberdasher, that his uncle (notoriously) was somewhere or other supplying the public with cheap repasts. Girls of Sidwell's delicacy do not misally themselves, for they take into account the fact that such misalliance is fraught with elements of unhappiness, affecting husband as much as wife. No need to dwell upon the scruples suggested by his moral attitude; he would never be called upon to combat them with reference to Sidwell's future.

What, then, was he about? For what advantage was he playing the hypocrite? Would he, after all, be satisfied with some such wife as the average curate may hope to marry?

A hundred times he reviewed the broad question, by the light of his six months' experience. Was Sidwell Warricombe his ideal woman, absolutely speaking? Why, no; not with all his glow of feeling could he persuade himself to declare her that. Satisfied up to a certain point, admitted to the sphere of wealthy refinement, he now had leisure to think of yet higher grades, of the women who are not only exquisite creatures by social comparison but rank by divine right among the foremost of their race. Sidwell was far from intolerant, and held her faiths in a sincerely ethical spirit. She judged nobly, she often saw with clear vision. But must not something of kindly condescension always blend with his admiring devotedness? Were it but possible to win the love of a woman who looked forth with eyes thoroughly purged from all mist of tradition and conventionalism, who was at home among arts and sciences, who, like himself, acknowledged no class and bowed to no authority but that of the supreme human mind!

Such women are to be found in every age, but how many of them shine with the distinctive ray of womanhood? These are so rare that they have a place in the pages of history. The truly emancipated woman – it was Godwin's conviction – is almost always asexual; to him, therefore, utterly repugnant. If, then, he were not content to waste his life in a vain search for the priceless jewel, which is won and worn only by fortune's supreme favourites, he must acquiesce in the imperfect marriage commonly the lot of men whose intellect allows them but little companionship even among their own sex: for that matter, the lot of most men, and necessarily so until the new efforts in female education shall have overcome the vice of wedlock as hitherto sanctioned. Nature provides the hallucination which flings a lover at his mistress's feet. For the chill which follows upon attainment she cares nothing – let society and individuals make their account with that as best they may. Even with a wife such as Sidwell the process of disillusion would doubtless have to be faced, however liberal one's allowances in the forecast.

Reflections of this colour were useful; they helped to keep within limits the growth of agitating desire. But there were seasons when Godwin surrendered himself to luxurious reverie, hours of summer twilight which forbade analysis and listened only to the harmonies of passion. Then was Sidwell's image glorified, and all the delights promised by such love as hers fired his imagination to intolerable ecstasy. O heaven! to see the smile softened by rosy warmth which would confess that she had given her heart – to feel her supple fingers intertwined with his that clasped them – to hear the words in which a mind so admirable, instincts so delicate, would make expression of their tenderness! To live with Sidwell – to breathe the fragrance of that flower of womanhood in wedded intimacy – to prove the devotion of a nature so profoundly chaste! The visionary transport was too poignant; in the end it drove him to a fierce outbreak of despairing wrath. How could he dream that such bliss would be the reward of despicable artifice, of calculated dishonour? Born a rebel, how could his be the fate of those happy men who are at one with the order of things? The prophecy of a heart wrung with anguish foretold too surely that for him was no rapturous love, no joy of noble wedlock. Solitude, now and for ever, or perchance some base alliance of the flesh, which would involve his later days in sordid misery.

In moods of discouragement he thought with envy of his old self, his life in London lodgings, his freedom in obscurity. It belongs to the pathos of human nature that only in looking back can one appreciate the true value of those long tracts of monotonous ease which, when we are living through them, seem of no account save in relation to past or future; only at a distance do we perceive that the exemption from painful shock was in itself a happiness, to be rated highly in comparison with most of those disturbances known as moments of joy. A wise man would have entertained no wish but that he might grow old in that same succession of days and weeks and years. Without anxiety concerning his material needs (certainly the most substantial of earthly blessings), his leisure not inadequate to the gratification of a moderate studiousness, with friends who offered him an ever-ready welcome, – was it not much? If he were condemned to bachelorhood, his philosophy was surely capable of teaching him that the sorrows and anxieties he thus escaped made more than an offset against the satisfactions he must forego. Reason had no part in the fantastic change to which his life had submitted, nor was he ever supported by a hope which would bear his cooler investigation.

And yet hope had her periods of control, for there are times when the mind wearies of rationality, and, as it were in self-defence, in obedience to the instinct of progressive life, craves a specious comfort. It seemed undeniable that Mr Warricombe regarded him with growth of interest, invited his conversation more unreservedly. He began to understand Martin's position with regard to religion and science, and thus could utter himself more securely. At length he ventured to discourse with some amplitude on his own convictions – the views, that is to say, which he thought fit to adopt in his character of a liberal Christian. It was on an afternoon of early August that this opportunity presented itself. They sat together in the study, and Martin was in a graver mood than usual, not much disposed to talk, but a willing listener. There had been mention of a sermon at the Cathedral, in which the preacher declared his faith that the maturity of science would dispel all antagonisms between it and revelation.

'The difficulties of the unbeliever,' said Peak, endeavouring to avoid a sermonising formality, though with indifferent success, 'are, of course, of two kinds; there's the theory of evolution, and there's modern biblical criticism. The more I study these objections, the less able I am to see how they come in conflict with belief in Christianity as a revealed religion.'

'Yet you probably had your time of doubt?' remarked the other, touching for the first time on this personal matter.

'Oh, yes; that was inevitable. It only means that one's development is imperfect. Most men who confirm themselves in agnosticism are kept at that point by arrested moral activity. They give up the intellectual question as wearisome, and accept the point of view which flatters their prejudices: thereupon follows a blunting of the sensibilities on the religious side.'

'There are men constitutionally unfitted for the reception of spiritual truth,' said Martin, in a troubled tone. He was playing with a piece of string, and did not raise his eyes.

'I quite believe that. There's our difficulty when we come to evidences. The evidences of science are wholly different in *kind* from those of religion. Faith cannot spring from any observation of phenomena, or scrutiny of authorities, but from the declaration made to us by the spiritual faculty. The man of science can only become a Christian by the way of humility – and that a kind of humility he finds it difficult even to conceive. One wishes to impress upon him the harmony of this faith with the spiritual voice that is in every man. He replies: I know nothing of that spiritual voice. And if that be true, one can't help him by argument.'

Peak had constructed for himself, out of his reading, a plausible system which on demand he could set forth with fluency. The tone of current apologetics taught him that, by men even of cultivated intellect, such a position as he was now sketching was deemed tenable; yet to himself it sounded so futile, so nugatory, that he had to harden his forehead as he spoke. Trial more severe to his conscience lay in the perceptible solicitude with which Mr Warricombe weighed these disingenuous arguments. It was a hateful thing to practise such deception on one who probably yearned for spiritual support. But he had committed himself to this course, and must brave it out.

'Christianity,' he was saying presently – appropriating a passage of which he had once made careful note – 'is an organism of such vital energy that it perforce assimilates whatever is good and true in the culture of each successive age. To understand this is to learn that we must depend rather on *constructive*, than on *defensive*, apology. That is to say, we must draw evidence of our faith from its latent capacities, its unsuspected affinities, its previsions, its adaptability, comprehensiveness, sympathy, adequacy to human needs.'

'That puts very well what I have always felt,' replied Mr Warricombe. 'Yet there will remain the objection that such a faith may be of purely human origin. If evolution and biblical criticism seem to overthrow all the historic evidences of Christianity, how convince the objectors that the faith itself was divinely given?'

'But I cannot hold for a moment,' exclaimed Peak, in the words which he knew his interlocutor desired to hear, 'that all the historic evidences have been destroyed. That indeed would shake our position.'

He enlarged on the point, with display of learning, yet studiously avoiding the tone of pedantry.

'Evolution,' he remarked, when the dialogue had again extended its scope, 'does not touch the evidence of design in the universe; at most it can correct our imperfect views (handed down from an age which had no scientific teaching because it was not ripe for it) of the mode in which that design was executed, or rather is still being executed. Evolutionists have not succeeded in explaining life; they have merely discovered a new law relating to life. If we must have an explanation, there is nothing for it but to accept the notion of a Deity. Indeed, how can there be religion without a divine author? Religion is based on the idea of a divine mind which reveals itself to us for moral ends. The Christian revelation, we hold, has been developed gradually, much of it in connection with secondary causes and human events. It has come down to us in anything but absolute purity – like a stream which has been made turbid by its earthly channel. The lower serves its purpose as a stage to the higher, then it falls away, the higher surviving. Hitherto, the final outcome of evolution is the soul in a bodily tenement. May it not be that the perfected soul alone survives in the last step of the struggle for existence?'

Peak had been talking for more than a quarter of an hour. Under stress of shame and intellectual self-criticism (for he could not help confuting every position as he stated it) his mind often wandered. When he ceased speaking there came upon him an uncomfortable dreaminess which he had already once or twice experienced when in colloquy with Mr Warricombe; a torment-ing metaphysical doubt of his own identity strangely beset him. With involuntary attempt to recover the familiar self he grasped his own wrist, and then, before he was aware, a laugh escaped him, an all but mocking laugh, unsuitable enough to the spirit of the moment. Mr Warricombe was startled, but looked up with a friendly smile.

'You fear,' he said, 'that this last speculation may seem rather fanciful to me?'

Godwin was biting his lip fiercely, and could not command himself to utterance of a word.

'By no means, I assure you,' added the other. 'It appeals to me very strongly.'

Peak rose from his chair.

'It struck me,' he said, 'that I had been preaching a sermon rather than taking part in a conversation. I'm afraid it is the habit of men who live a good deal alone to indulge in monologues.'

On his return home, the sight of *Bibel und Natur* and his sheets of laborious manuscript filled him with disgust. It was two or three days before he could again apply himself to the translation. Yet this expedient had undoubtedly been of great service to him in the matter of his relations with Mr Warricombe. Without the aid of Reusch he would have found it difficult to speak naturally on the theme which drew Martin into confidences and established an intimacy between them.

Already they had discussed in detail the first half of the book. How a man of Mr Warricombe's intelligence could take grave interest in an arid exegesis of the first chapter of Genesis, Godwin strove in vain to comprehend. Often enough the debates were perilously suggestive of burlesque, and, when alone, he relieved himself of the laughter he had scarce restrained. For instance, there was that terrible *thohu wabohu* of the second verse, a phrase preserved from the original, and tossed into all the corners of controversy. Was *thohu wabohu* the first condition of the earth, or was it merely a period of division between a previous state of things and creation as established by the Hexæmeron? Did light exist or not, previous to the *thohu wabohu*? Then, again, what kind of 'days' were the three which passed before the birth of the sun? Special interest, of course, attached to the successive theories of theology on the origin of geologic strata. First came the 'theory of restitution', which explained unbiblical antiquity by declaring that the strata belonged to a world before the Hexæmeron, a world which had been destroyed, and succeeded by the new creation. Less objectionable was the 'concordistic theory', which interprets the 'six days' as so many vast periods of creative activity. But Reusch himself gave preference to the 'ideal theory', the supporters whereof (diligently adapting themselves to the progress of science) hold that the six days are not to be understood as consecutive periods at all, but merely as six phases of the Creator's work.

By the exercise of watchfulness and dexterity, Peak managed for the most part to avoid expression of definite opinions. His attitude was that of a reverent (not yet reverend) student. Mr Warricombe was less guarded, and sometimes allowed himself to profess that he saw nothing but vain ingenuity in Reusch's argument: as, for example, where the theologian, convinced that the patriarchs did really live to an abnormal age, suggests that man's life was subsequently shortened in order that 'sin might not flourish with such exuberance'. This passage caused Martin to smile.

'It won't do, it won't do,' he said, quietly. 'Far better apply his rationalism here as elsewhere. These are wonderful old stories, not to be understood literally. Nothing depends upon them – nothing essential.'

Thereupon Peak mused anxiously. Not for the first time there occurred to him a thought which suited only too well with his ironic habits of mind. What if this hypocritic comedy were altogether superfluous? What if Mr Warricombe would have received him no less cordially had he avowed his sincere position, and contented himself with guarding against offensiveness? Buckland, it was true, had suffered in his father's esteem on account of his unorthodoxy, but that young man had been too aggressive, too scornful. With prudence, would it not have been possible to win Martin's regard by fortifying the scientific rather than the dogmatic side of his intellect? If so, what a hopeless error had he committed! – But Sidwell? Was *she* liberal enough to take a personal interest in one who had renounced faith in revelation? He could not decide this question, for of Sidwell he knew much less than of her father. And it was idle to torment himself with such debate of the irreversible.

And, indeed, there seemed much reason for believing that Martin, whatever the extent of his secret doubts, was by temperament armed against agnosticism. Distinctly it comforted him to hear the unbelievers assailed – the friends of whom he spoke most heartily were all on the orthodox side; if ever a hint of gentle malice occurred in his conversation, it was when he spoke of a fallacy, a precipitate conclusion, detected in works of science. Probably he was too old to overcome this bias.

His view of the Bible appeared to harmonise with that which Peak put forth in one of their dialogues. 'The Scriptures were meant to be literally understood in primitive ages, and spiritually when the growth of science made it possible. *Genesis* was never intended to teach the facts of natural history; it takes phenomena as they appear to uninstructed people, and uses them only for the inculcation of moral lessons; it presents to the childhood of the world a few great elementary truths. And the way in which phenomena are spoken of in the Old Testament is never really incompatible with the facts as we know them nowadays. Take the miracle of the sun standing still, which is supposed to be a safe subject of ridicule. Why, it merely means that light was miraculously prolonged; the words used are those which common people would at all times understand.'

(Was it necessary to have admitted the miracle? Godwin asked himself. At all events Mr Warricombe nodded approvingly.)

'Then the narrative of the creation of man; that's not at all incompatible with his slow development through ages. To teach the scientific fact – if we yet really know it – would have been worse than useless. The story is meant to express that spirit, and not matter, is the source of all existence. Indeed, our knowledge of the true meaning of the Bible has increased with the growth of science, and naturally that must have been intended from the first. Things which do not concern man's relation to the spiritual have no place in this book; they are not within its province. Such things were discoverable by human reason, and the knowledge which achieves has nothing to do with a divine revelation.'

To Godwin it was a grinding of the air, but the listener appeared to think it profitable.

With his clerical friend, Mr Lilywhite, he rarely touched on matters of religion. The vicar of St Ethelreda's was a man well suited to support the social dignity of his Church. A gentleman before everything, he seemed incapable of prying into the state of a parishioner's soul; you saw in him the official representative of a Divinity characterised by well-bred tolerance. He had written a pleasant little book on the by-ways of Devon and Cornwall, which brought about his intimacy with the Warricombe household. Peak liked him more the better he knew him, and in the course of the summer they had one or two long walks together, conversing exclusively of the things of earth. Mr Lilywhite troubled himself little about evolution; he spoke of trees and plants, of birds and animals, in a loving spirit, like the old simple naturalists. Geology did not come within his sphere.

'I'm very sorry,' he said, 'that I could never care much for it. Don't think I'm afraid of it – not I! I feel the grandeur of its scope, just as I do in the case of astronomy; but I have never brought myself to study either science. A narrowness of mind, no doubt. I can't go into such remote times and regions. I love the sunlight and the green fields of this little corner of the world – too well, perhaps: yes, perhaps too well.'

After one of these walks, he remarked to Mrs Lilywhite:

'It's my impression that Mr Peak has somehow been misled in his choice of a vocation. I don't think he'll do as a churchman.'

'Why not, Henry?' asked his wife, with gentle concern, for she still spoke of Peak's 'quiet moral force'.

'There's something too restless about him. I doubt whether he has really made up his mind on any subject whatever. Well, it's not easy to explain what I feel, but I don't think he will take Orders.'

Calling at the vicarage one afternoon in September, Godwin found Mrs Lilywhite alone. She startled him by saying at once:

'An old acquaintance of yours was with us yesterday, Mr Peak.'

'Who could that be, I wonder?'

He smiled softly, controlling his impulse to show quite another expression.

'You remember Mr Bruno Chilvers?'

'Oh, yes!'

There was a constriction in his throat. Struggling to overcome it, he added:

'But I should have thought he had no recollection of me.'

'Quite the contrary, I assure you. He is to succeed Mr Bell of St Margaret's, at Christmas; he was down here only for a day or two, and called upon my husband with a message from an old friend of ours. It appears he used to know the Warricombes, when they lived at Kingsmill, and he had been to see them before visiting us; it was there your name was mentioned to him.'

Godwin had seated himself, and leaned forward, his hands grasping the glove he had drawn off.

'We were contemporaries at Whitelaw College,' he observed.

'So we learnt from him. He spoke of you with the greatest interest; he was delighted to hear that you contemplated taking Orders. Of course we knew Mr Chilvers by reputation, but my husband had no idea that he was coming to Exeter. What an energetic man he is! In a few hours he seemed to have met everyone, and to have learnt everything. My husband says he felt quite rebuked by such a display of vigour!'

Even in his discomposure, graver than any that had affected

him since his talks with Buckland Warricombe, Peak was able to notice that the Rev. Bruno had not made a wholly favourable impression upon the Lilywhites. There was an amiable causticity in that mention of his 'display of vigour', such as did not often characterise Mrs Lilywhite's comments. Finding that the vicar would be away till evening, Godwin stayed for only a quarter of an hour, and when he had escaped it irritated and alarmed him to reflect how unusual his behaviour must have appeared to the good lady.

The blow was aimed at his self-possession from such an unlikely quarter. In Church papers he had frequently come across Chilvers's name, and the sight of it caused him a twofold disturbance: it was hateful to have memories of humiliation revived, and perhaps still more harassing to be forced upon acknowledgment of the fact that he stood as an obscure aspirant at the foot of the ladder which his old rival was triumphantly ascending. Bad enough to be classed in any way with such a man as Chilvers; but to be regarded as at one with him in religious faith, to be forbidden the utterance of scorn when Chilvers was extolled, stung him so keenly that he rushed into any distraction to elude the thought. When he was suffering shame under the gaze of Buckland Warricombe he remembered Chilvers, and shrank as before a merited scoff. But the sensation had not been abiding enough to affect his conduct. He had said to himself that he should never come in contact with the fellow, and that, after all, community of religious profession meant no more, under their respective circumstances, than if both were following law or physic.

But the unforeseen had happened. In a few months, the Rev. Bruno Chilvers would be a prominent figure about the streets of Exeter; would be frequently seen at the Warricombes', at the Lilywhites', at the houses of their friends. His sermons at St Margaret's would doubtless attract, and form a staple topic of conversation. Worse than all, his expressions of 'interest' and 'delight' made it probable that he would seek out his College competitor and offer the hand of brotherhood. These things were not to be avoided – save by abandonment of hopes, save by retreat, by yielding to a hostile destiny.

That Chilvers might talk here and there of Whitelaw stories was comparatively unimportant. The Warricombes must already know all that could be told, and what other people heard did not much matter. It was the man himself that Peak could not endure. Dissembling had hitherto been no light task. The burden had more than once pressed so gallingly that its permanent support seemed impossible; but to stand before Bruno Chilvers in the attitude of humble emulation, to give respectful ear whilst the popular cleric advised or encouraged, or bestowed pontifical praise, was comparable only to a searing of the flesh with red irons. Even with assured prospect of recompense in the shape of Sidwell Warricombe's heart and hand, he could hardly submit to such an ordeal. As it was, reason having so often convinced him that he clung to a visionary hope, the torture became gratuitous, and its mere suggestion inspired him with a fierce resentment destructive of all his purposes.

For several days he scarcely left the house. To wrath and dread had succeeded a wretched torpor, during which his mind kept revolving the thoughts prompted by his situation, turbidly and to no issue. He tasted all the bitterness of the solitude to which he had condemned himself; there was not a living soul with whom he could commune. At moments he was possessed with the desire of going straightway to London, and making Earwaker the confidant of all his folly. But that demanded an exertion of which he was physically incapable. He thought of the old home at Twybridge, and was tempted also in that direction. His mother would welcome him with human kindness; beneath her roof he could lie dormant until fate should again point his course. He even wrote a letter saying that in all probability he should pay a visit to Twybridge before long. But the impulse was only of an hour's duration, for he remembered that to talk with his mother would necessitate all manner of new falsehoods, a thickening of the atmosphere of lies which already oppressed him. No; if he quitted Exeter, it must be on a longer journey. He must resume his purpose of seeking some distant country, where new conditions of life would allow him to try his fortune at least as an honest adventurer. In many parts of colonial England his technical knowledge would have a value, and were there not women to be won beneath other skies — women perhaps of subtler charm than the old hidebound civilisation produced? Reminiscences of scenes and figures in novels he had read nourished the illusion. He pictured some thriving little town at the ends of the earth, where a young Englishman of good manners and unusual culture would easily be admitted to the intimacy of the richest families; he saw the ideal colonist (a man of good birth, but a sower of wild oats in his youth) with two or three daughters about him – beautiful girls, wondrously self-instructed – living amid romantic dreams of the old world, and of the lover who would some day carry them off (with a substantial share of papa's wealth) to Europe and the scenes of their imagination.

The mind has marvellous methods of self-defence against creeping lethargy of despair. At the point to which he had been reduced by several days of blank despondency, Peak was able to find genuine encouragement in visions such as this. He indulged his fancy until the vital force began to stir once more within him, and then, with one angry sweep, all his theological books and manuscripts were flung out of sight. Away with this detestable mummery! Now let Bruno Chilvers pour his eloquence from the pulpit of St Margaret's, and rear to what heights he could the edifice of his social glory; men of that stamp were alone fitted to thrive in England. Was not *he* almost certainly a hypocrite, masking his brains (for brains he had) under a show of broadest Anglicanism? But his career was throughout consistent. He trod in the footsteps of his father, and with inherited aptitude moulded antique traditions into harmony with the taste of the times. Compared with such a man, Peak felt himself a bungler. The wonder was that his clumsy lying had escaped detection.

Another day, and he had done nothing whatever, but was still buoyed up by the reaction of visionary hope. His need now was of communicating his change of purpose to some friendly hearer. A week had passed since he had exchanged a word with anyone but Mrs Roots, and converse he must. Why not with Mr Warricombe? That was plainly the next step: to see Martin and make known to him that after all he could not become a clergyman. No need of hinting a conscientious reason. At all events, nothing more definite than a sense of personal unfitness, a growing perception of difficulties inherent in his character. It would be very interesting to hear Mr Warricombe's replies.

A few minutes after this decision was taken, he set off towards the Old Tiverton Road, walking at great speed, flourishing his stick – symptoms of the nervous cramp (so to speak) which he was dispelling. He reached the house, and his hand was on the bell, when an unexpected opening of the door presented Louis Warricombe just coming forth for a walk. They exchanged amiabilities, and Louis made known that his father and mother were away on a visit to friends in Cornwall.

'But pray come in,' he added, offering to re-enter.

Peak excused himself, for it was evident that Louis made a sacrifice to courtesy. But at that moment there approached from the garden Fanny Warricombe and her friend Bertha Lilywhite, eldest daughter of the genial vicar; they shook hands with Godwin, Fanny exclaiming:

'Don't go away, Mr Peak. Have a cup of tea with us – Sidwell is at home. I want to show you a strange sort of spleenwort that I gathered this morning.'

'In that case,' said her brother, smiling, 'I may confess that I have an appointment. Pray forgive me for hurrying off, Mr Peak.'

Godwin was embarrassed, but the sprightly girl repeated her summons, and he followed into the house.

V

Having led the way to the drawing-room, Fanny retired again for a few moments, to fetch the fern of which she had spoken, leaving Peak in conversation with little Miss Lilywhite. Bertha was a rather shy girl of fifteen, not easily induced, under circumstances such as these, to utter more than monosyllables, and Godwin, occupied with the unforeseen results of his call, talked about the weather. With half-conscious absurdity he had begun to sketch a theory of his own regarding rain-clouds and estuaries (Bertha listening with an air of the gravest attention) when Fanny reappeared, followed by Sidwell. Peak searched the latter's face for indications of her mood, but could discover nothing save a spirit of gracious welcome. Such aspect was a matter of course, and he knew it. None the less, his nervousness and the state of mind engendered by a week's miserable solitude, tempted him to believe that Sidwell did not always wear that smile in greeting a casual caller. This was the first time that she had received him without the countenance of Mrs Warricombe. Observing her perfect manner, as she sat down and began to talk, he asked himself what her age really was. The question had never engaged his thoughts. Eleven years ago, when he saw her at the house near Kingsmill and again at Whitelaw College, she looked a very young girl, but whether of thirteen or sixteen he could not at the time have determined, and such a margin of possibility allowed her now to have reached – it might be – her twenty-seventh summer. But twenty-seven drew perilously near to thirty; no, no, Sidwell could not be more than twenty-five. Her eyes still had the dewy freshness of flowering maidenhood; her cheek, her throat, were so exquisitely young—

In how divine a calm must this girl have lived to show, even at five-and-twenty, features as little marked by inward perturbation as those of an infant! Her position in the world considered, one could forgive her for having borne so lightly the inevitable sorrows of life, for having dismissed so readily the spiritual doubts which were the heritage of her time; but was she a total stranger to passion? Did not the fact of her still remaining unmarried make probable such a deficiency in her nature? Had she a place among the women whom coldness of temperament preserves in a bloom like that of youth, until fading hair and sinking cheek betray them—?

Whilst he thought thus, Godwin was in appearance busy with the fern Fanny had brought for his inspection. He talked about it, but in snatches, with intervals of abstractedness.

Yet might he not be altogether wrong? Last year, when he observed Sidwell in the Cathedral and subsequently at home, his impression had been that her face was of rather pallid and dreamy cast; he recollected that distinctly. Had she changed, or did familiarity make him less sensible of her finer traits? Possibly she enjoyed better health nowadays, and, if so, it might result from influences other than physical. Her air of quiet happiness seemed to him especially noticeable this afternoon, and as he brooded there came upon him a dread which, under the circumstances, was quite irrational, but for all that troubled his views. Perhaps Sidwell was betrothed to some one? He knew of but one likely person – Miss Moorhouse's brother. About a month ago the Warricombes had been on a visit at Budleigh Salterton, and something might then have happened. Pangs of jealousy smote him, nor could he assuage them by reminding himself that he had no concern whatever in Sidwell's future.

'Will Mr Warricombe be long away?' he asked, coldly.

'A day or two. I hope you didn't wish particularly to see him to-day?'

'Oh, no.'

'Do you know, Mr Peak,' put in Fanny, 'that we are all going to London next month, to live there for half a year?'

Godwin exhibited surprise. He looked from the speaker to her sister, and Sidwell, as she smiled confirmation, bent very slightly towards him.

'We have made up our minds, after much uncertainty,' she said. 'My brother Buckland seems to think that we are falling behind in civilisation.'

'So we are,' affirmed Fanny, 'as Mr Peak would admit, if only he could be sincere.'

'Am I never sincere then, Miss Fanny?' Godwin asked.

'I only meant to say that nobody can be when the rules of politeness interfere. Don't you think it's a pity? We might tell one another the truth in a pleasant way.'

'I agree with you. But then we must be civilised indeed. How do you think of London, Miss Warricombe? Which of its aspects most impresses you?'

Sidwell answered rather indefinitely, and ended by mentioning that in *Villette*, which she had just re-read, Charlotte Brontë makes a contrast between the City and the West End, and greatly prefers the former.

'Do you agree with her, Mr Peak?'

'No, I can't. One understands the mood in which she wrote that; but a little more experience would have led her to see the contrast in a different light. That term, the West End, includes much that is despicable, but it means also the best results of civilisation. The City is hateful to me, and for a reason which I only understood after many an hour of depression in walking about its streets. It represents the ascendency of the average man.'

Sidwell waited for fuller explanation.

'A liberal mind,' Peak continued, 'is revolted by the triumphal procession that roars perpetually through the City highways. With myriad voices the City bellows its brutal scorn of everything but material advantage. There every humanising influence is contemptuously disregarded. I know, of course, that the trader may have his quiet home, where art and science and humanity are the first considerations; but the *mass* of traders, corporate and victorious, crush all such things beneath their heels. Take your stand (or try to do so) anywhere near the Exchange; the hustling and jolting to which you are exposed represents the very spirit of the life about you. Whatever is gentle and kindly and meditative must here go to the wall – trampled, spattered, ridiculed. Here the average man has it all his own way – a gross utilitarian power.'

'Yes, I can see that,' Sidwell replied, thoughtfully. 'And perhaps it also represents the triumphant forces of our time.'

He looked keenly at her, with a smile of delight.

'That also! The power which centres in the world's money-markets – plutocracy.'

In conversing with Sidwell, he had never before found an opportunity of uttering his vehement prejudices. The gentler side of his character had sometimes expressed itself, but those impulses which were vastly more significant lay hidden beneath the dissimulation he consistently practised. For the first time he was able to look into Sidwell's face with honest directness, and what he saw there strengthened his determination to talk on with the same freedom.

'You don't believe, then,' said Sidwell, 'that democracy is the proper name for the state into which we are passing?'

'Only if one can understand democracy as the opening of social privileges to free competition amongst men of trade. And social privilege is everything; home politics refer to nothing else.'

Fanny, true to the ingenuous principle of her years, put a direct question:

'Do you approve of real democracy, Mr Peak?'

He answered with another question:

'Have you read the "Life of Phokion" in Plutarch?'

'No, I'm sorry to say.'

'There's a story about him which I have enjoyed since I was your age. Phokion was once delivering a public speech, and at a certain point the majority of his hearers broke into applause; whereupon he turned to certain of his friends who stood near and asked, "What have I said amiss?"'

Fanny laughed.

'Then you despise public opinion?'

'With heart and soul!'

It was to Sidwell that he directed the reply. Though overcome by the joy of such an utterance, he felt that, considering the opinions and position of Buckland Warricombe, he was perhaps guilty of ill manners. But Sidwell manifested no disapproval.

'Did you know that story?' Fanny asked of her.

'It's quite new to me.'

'Then I'm sure you'll read the "Life of Phokion" as soon as possible. He will just suit you, Sidwell.'

Peak heard this with a shock of surprise which thrilled in him deliciously. He had the strongest desire to look again at Sidwell but refrained. As no one spoke, he turned to Bertha Lilywhite and put a commonplace question.

A servant entered with the tea-tray, and placed it on a small table near Fanny. Godwin looked at the younger girl; it seemed to him that there was an excess of colour in her cheeks. Had a glance from Sidwell rebuked her? With his usual rapidity of observation and inference he made much of this trifle.

Contrary to what he expected, Sidwell's next remark was in a tone of cheerfulness, almost of gaiety.

'One advantage of our stay in London will be that home will seem more delightful than ever when we return.'

'I suppose you won't be back till next summer?'

'I am afraid not.'

'Shall you be living here then?' Fanny inquired.

'It's very doubtful.'

He wished to answer with a decided negative, but his tongue refused. Sidwell was regarding him with calm but earnest eyes, and he knew, without caring to reflect, that his latest projects were crumbling.

'Have you been to see our friends at Budleigh Salterton yet?' she asked.

'Not yet. I hope to in a few days.'

Pursuing the subject, he was able to examine her face as she spoke of Mr Moorhouse. His conjecture was assuredly baseless.

Fanny and Bertha began to talk together of domestic affairs, and presently, when tea-cups were laid aside, the two girls went to another part of the room; then they withdrew altogether. Peak was monologising on English art as represented at the Academy, but finding himself alone with Sidwell (it had never before happened) he became silent. Ought he to take his leave? He must already have been sitting here more than half-an-hour. But the temptation of *tête-à-tête* was irresistible.

'You had a visit from Mr Chilvers the other day?' he remarked, abruptly.

'Yes; did he call to see you?'

Her tone gave evidence that she would not have introduced this topic.

'No; I heard from Mrs Lilywhite. He had been to the vicarage. Has he changed much since he was at Whitelaw?'

'So many years must make a difference at that time of life,' Sidwell answered, smiling.

'But does he show the same peculiarities of manner?'

He tried to put the question without insistency, in a tone quite compatible with friendliness. Her answer, given with a look of amusement, satisfied him that there was no fear of her taking Mr Chilvers too seriously.

'Yes. I think he speaks in much the same way.'

'Have you read any of his publications?'

'One or two. We have his lecture on *Altruism*.'

'I happen to know it. There are good things in it, I think. But I dislike his modern interpretation of old principles.'

'You think it dangerous?'

He no longer regarded her frankly, and in the consciousness of her look upon him he knit his brows.

'I think it both dangerous and offensive. Not a few clergymen nowadays, who imagine themselves free from the letter and wholly devoted to spirit, are doing their best in the cause of materialism. They surrender the very points at issue between religion and worldliness. They are so blinded by a vague humanitarian impulse as to make the New Testament an oracle of popular Radicalism.'

Sidwell looked up.

'I never quite understood, Mr Peak, how you regard Radicalism. You think it opposed to all true progress?'

'Utterly, as concerns any reasonable limit of time.'

'Buckland, as you know, maintains that spiritual progress is only possible by this way.'

'I can't venture to contradict him,' said Godwin; 'for it may be that advance is destined only to come after long retrogression and anarchy. Perhaps the way *does* lie through such miseries. But we can't foresee that with certainty, and those of us who hate the present tendency of things must needs assert their hatred as strongly as possible, seeing that we *may* have a more hopeful part to play than seems likely.'

'I like that view,' replied Sidwell, in an undertone.

'My belief,' pursued Godwin, with an earnestness very agreeable to himself, for he had reached the subject on which he could speak honestly, 'is that an instructed man can only hold views such as your brother's – hopeful views of the immediate future –if he has never been brought into close contact with the lower classes. Buckland doesn't know the people for whom he pleads.'

'You think them so degraded?'

'It is impossible, without seeming inhumanly scornful, to give a just account of their ignorance and baseness. The two things, speaking generally, go together. Of the ignorant, there are very few indeed who can think purely or aspiringly. You, of course, object the teaching of Christianity; but the lowly and the humble of whom it speaks scarcely exist, scarcely can exist, in our day and country. A ludicrous pretence of education is banishing every form of native simplicity. In the large towns, the populace sink deeper and deeper into a vicious vulgarity, and every rural district is being affected by the spread of contagion. To flatter the proletariat is to fight against all the good that still characterises educated England – against reverence for the beautiful, against magnanimity, against enthusiasm of mind, heart, and soul.'

He quivered with vehemence of feeling, and the flush which

rose to his hearer's cheek, the swimming brightness of her eye, proved that a strong sympathy stirred within her.

'I know nothing of the uneducated in towns,' she said, 'but the little I have seen of them in country places certainly supports your opinion. I could point to two or three families who have suffered distinct degradation owing to what most people call an improvement in their circumstances. Father often speaks of such instances, comparing the state of things now with what he can remember.'

'My own experience,' pursued Godwin, 'has been among the lower classes in London. I don't mean the very poorest, of whom one hears so much nowadays; I never went among them because I had no power of helping them, and the sight of their vileness would only have moved me to unjust hatred. But the people who earn enough for their needs, and whose spiritual guide is the Sunday newspaper – I know them, because for a long time I was obliged to lodge in their houses. Only a consuming fire could purify the places where they dwell. Don't misunderstand me; I am not charging them with what are commonly held vices and crimes, but with the consistent love of everything that is ignoble, with utter deadness to generous impulse, with the fatal habit of low mockery. And *these* are the people who really direct the democratic movement. They set the tone in politics; they are debasing art and literature; even the homes of wealthy people begin to show the effects of their influence. One hears men and women of gentle birth using phrases which originate with shopboys; one sees them reading print which is addressed to the coarsest million. They crowd to entertainments which are deliberately adapted to the lowest order of mind. When commercial interest is supreme, how can the tastes of the majority fail to lead and control?'

Though he spoke from the depths of his conviction, and was so moved that his voice rose and fell in tones such as a drawing-room seldom hears, he yet kept anxious watch upon Sidwell's countenance. That hint afforded him by Fanny was invaluable; it had enabled him to appeal to Sidwell's nature by the ardent expression of what was sincerest in his own. She too, he at length understood, had the aristocratic temperament. This explained her to him, supplied the key of doubts and difficulties which had troubled him in her presence. It justified, moreover, the feelings with which she had inspired him – feelings which this hour of intimate converse had exalted to passion. His heart thrilled with hope. Where sympathies so profound existed, what did it matter that there was variance on a few points between his intellect and hers? He felt the power to win her, and to defy every passing humiliation that lay in his course.

Sidwell raised her eyes with a look which signified that she was shaping a question diffidently.

'Have you always thought so hopelessly of our times?'

'Oh, I had my stage of optimism,' he answered, smiling. 'Though I never put faith in the masses, I once believed that the conversion of the educated to a purely human religion would set things moving in the right way. It was ignorance of the world.'

He paused a moment, then added:

'In youth one marvels that men remain at so low a stage of civilisation. Later in life, one is astonished that they have advanced so far.'

Sidwell met his look with appreciative intelligence and murmured:

'In spite of myself, I believe that expresses a truth.'

Peak was about to reply, when Fanny and her friend re-appeared. Bertha approached for the purpose of taking leave, and for a minute or two Sidwell talked with her. The young girls withdrew again together.

By the clock on the mantelpiece it was nearly six. Godwin did not resume his seat, though Sidwell had done so. He looked towards the window, and was all but lost in abstraction, when the soft voice again addressed him:

'But you have not chosen your life's work without some hope of doing good?'

'Do you think,' he asked, gently, 'that I shall be out of place in the Christian Church?'

'No – no, I certainly don't think that. But will you tell me what you have set before yourself?'

He drew nearer and leaned upon the back of a chair.

'I hope for what I shall perhaps never attain. Whatever my first steps may be – I am not independent; I must take the work that offers – it is my ambition to become the teacher of some rural parish which is still unpolluted by the influences of which we have been speaking – or, at all events, is still capable of being rescued. For work in crowded centres, I am altogether unfit; my prejudices are too strong; I should do far more harm than good. But among a few simple people I think my efforts mightn't be useless. I can't pretend to care for anything but individuals. The few whom I know and love are of more importance to me than all the blind multitude rushing to destruction. I hate the word *majority*; it is the few, the very few, that have always kept alive whatever of effectual good we see in the human race. There are individuals who outweigh, in every kind of value, generations of ordinary people. To some remote little community I hope to give the best energies of my life. My teaching will avoid doctrine and controversy. I shall take the spirit of the Gospels, and labour to make it a practical guide. No doubt you find inconsistencies in me; but remember that I shall not declare myself to those I instruct as I have done to you. I have been laying stress on my antipathies. In the future it will be a duty and a pleasure to forget these and foster my sympathies, which also are strong when opportunity is given them.'

Sidwell listened, her face bent downwards but not hidden from the speaker.

'My nature is intolerant,' he went on, 'and I am easily roused to an antagonism which destroys my peace. It is only by living apart, amid friendly circumstances, that I can cultivate the qualities useful to myself and others. The sense that my life was being wasted determined me a year ago to escape the world's uproar and prepare myself in quietness for this task. The resolve was taken here, in your house.'

'Are you quite sure,' asked Sidwell, 'that such simple duties and satisfactions'—

The sentence remained incomplete, or rather was finished in the timid glance she gave him.

'Such a life wouldn't be possible to me,' he replied, with unsteady voice, 'if I were condemned to intellectual solitude. But I have dared to hope that I shall not always be alone.'

A parched throat would have stayed his utterance, even if words had offered themselves. But sudden confusion beset his mind – a sense of having been guilty of monstrous presumption – a panic which threw darkness about him and made him grasp the chair convulsively. When he recovered himself and looked at Sidwell there was a faint smile on her lips, inexpressibly gentle.

'That's the rough outline of my projects,' he said, in his ordinary voice, moving a few steps away. 'You see that I count much on fortune; at the best, it may be years before I can get my country living.'

With a laugh, he came towards her and offered his hand for
good-bye. Sidwell rose.

'You have interested me very much. Whatever assistance it may
be in my father's power to offer you, I am sure you may count
upon.'

'I am already much indebted to Mr Warricombe's kindness.'

They shook hands without further speech, and Peak went his
way.

For an hour or two he was powerless to collect his thoughts. All he
had said repeated itself again and again, mixed up with turbid
comments, with deadly fears and frantic bursts of confidence,
with tumult of passion and merciless logic of self-criticism. Did
Sidwell understand that sentence: 'I have dared to hope that I shall
not always be alone'? Was it not possible that she might interpret
it as referring to some unknown woman whom he loved? If not, if
his voice and features had betrayed him, what could her
behaviour mean, except distinct encouragement? 'You have
interested me very much.' But could she have used such words if
his meaning had been plain to her? Far more likely that her frank
kindness came of misconception. She imagined him the lover of
some girl of his own 'station' – a toiling governess, or some such
person; it could not enter into her mind that he 'dared' so
recklessly as the truth implied.

But the glow of sympathy with which she heard his immeasurable scorn: there was the spirit that defies artificial distances. Why
had he not been bolder? At this rate he must spend a lifetime in
preparing for the decisive moment. When would another such
occasion offer itself?

Women are won by audacity; the poets have repeated it from
age to age, and some truth there must be in the saying. Suspicion
of self-interest could not but attach to him; that was inherent in
the circumstances. He must rely upon the sincerity of his passion,
which indeed was beginning to rack and rend him. A woman is
sensitive to that, especially a woman of Sidwell's refinement. In
matters of the intellect she may be misled, but she cannot mistake
quivering ardour for design simulating love. If it were impossible
to see her again in private before she left Exeter, then he must
write to her. Half a year of complete uncertainty, and of
counterfeiting face to face with Bruno Chilvers, would overtax his
resolution.

The evening went by he knew not how. Long after nightfall he was returning from an aimless ramble by way of the Old Tiverton Road. At least he would pass the house, and soothe or inflame his emotions by resting for a moment thus near to Sidwell.

What? He had believed himself incapable of erotic madness? And he pressed his forehead against the stones of the wall to relieve his sick dizziness.

It was Sidwell or death. Into what a void of hideous futility would his life be cast, if this desire proved vain, and he were left to combat alone with the memory of his dishonour! With Sidwell the reproach could be outlived. She would understand him, pardon him – and thereafter a glorified existence, rivalling that of whosoever has been most exultant among the sons of men!

PART THE FOURTH

I

Earwaker's struggle with the editor-in-chief of *The Weekly Post* and the journalist Kenyon came to its natural close about a month after Godwin Peak's disappearance. Only a vein of obstinacy in his character had kept him so long in a position he knew to be untenable. From the first his sympathy with Mr Runcorn's politics had been doubtful, and experience of the working of a Sunday newspaper, which appealed to the ignobly restive, could not encourage his adhesion to this form of Radicalism. He anticipated dismissal by retirement, and Kenyon, a man of coarsely vigorous fibre, at once stepped into his place.

Now that he had leisure to review the conflict, Earwaker understood that circumstances had but hastened his transition from a moderate ardour in the parliamentary cause of the people, to a regretful neutrality regarding all political movements. Birth allied him with the proletarian class, and his sentiment in favour of democracy was unendangered by the disillusions which must come upon every intellectual man brought into close contact with public affairs. The course of an education essentially aristocratic (Greek and Latin can have no other tendency so long as they are the privilege of the few) had not affected his natural bent, nor was he the man to be driven into reaction because of obstacles to his faith inseparable from human weakness. He had learnt that the emancipation of the poor and untaught must proceed more slowly than he once hoped – that was all. Restored to generous calm, he could admit that such men as Runcorn and Kenyon – the one with his polyarchic commercialism, the other with his demagogic violence – had possibly a useful part to play at the present stage of things. He, however, could have no place in that camp. Too indiscreetly he had hoisted his standard of idealism, and by stubborn resistance of insuperable forces he had merely brought forward the least satisfactory elements of his own character. 'Hold on!' cried Malkin. 'Fight the grovellers to the end!' But Earwaker had begun to see himself in a light of ridicule. There was just time to save his self-respect.

He was in no concern for his daily bread. With narrower resources in the world of print, he might have been compelled, like many another journalist, to swallow his objections and write as Runcorn dictated; for the humble folks at home could not starve to allow him the luxury of conscientiousness, whatever he might have been disposed to do on his own account. Happily, his pen had a scope beyond politics, and by working steadily for reviews, with which he was already connected, he would be able to keep his finances in reasonable order until, perchance, some hopeful appointment offered itself. In a mood of much cheerfulness he turned for ever from party uproar, and focused his mind upon those interests of humanity which so rarely coincide with the aims of any league among men.

Half a year went by, and at length he granted himself a short holiday, the first in a twelvemonth. It took the form of a voyage to Marseilles, and thence of a leisurely ramble up the Rhône. Before returning, he spent a day or two in Paris, for the most part beneath café awnings, or on garden seats – an indulgence of contented laziness.

On the day of his departure, he climbed the towers of Notre Dame, and lingered for half-an-hour in pleasant solitude among the stone monsters. His reverie was broken by an English voice, loud and animated:

'Come and look at this old demon of a bird; he has always been a favourite of mine. – Sure you're not tired, Miss Bella? When you want to rest, Miss Lily, mind you say so at once. What a day! – What a sky! – When I was last up here I had my hat blown away. I watched it as far as Montmartre. A fact! Never knew such a wind in my life – unless it was that tornado I told you about – Hollo! By the powers, if that isn't Earwaker! Confound you, old fellow! How the deuce do you do? What a glorious meeting! Hadn't the least idea where you were! – Let me have the pleasure of introducing you to Mrs Jacox – and to Miss Jacox – and to Miss Lily. They all know you thoroughly well. Now who would have thought of our meeting up here! Glorious!'

It was with some curiosity that Earwaker regarded the companions of his friend Malkin – whose proximity was the last thing he could have imagined, as only a few weeks ago he had heard of the restless fellow's departing, on business unknown, for Boston, US. Mrs Jacox, the widow whose wrongs had made such an impression on Malkin, announced herself, in a thin, mealy face and rag-doll figure, as not less than forty, though her irresponsible look made it evident that years profited her nothing, and suggested an explanation of the success with which she had been victimised. She was stylishly dressed, and had the air of enjoying an unusual treat. Her children were of more promising type, though Earwaker would hardly have supposed them so old as he knew them to be. Bella, just beyond her fourteenth year, had an intelligent prettiness, but was excessively shy; in giving her hand to the stranger she flushed over face and neck, and her bosom palpitated visibly. Her sister, two years younger, was a mere child, rather self-conscious, but of laughing temper. Their toilet suited ill with that of their mother; its plainness and negligence might have passed muster in London, but here, under the lucent sky, it seemed a wrong to their budding maidenhood.

'Mrs Jacox is on the point of returning to England,' Malkin explained. 'I happened to meet her, by chance – I'm always meeting my friends by chance; you, for instance, Earwaker. She is so good as to allow me to guide her and the young ladies to a few of the sights of Paris.'

'O Mr Malkin!' exclaimed the widow, with a stress on the exclamation peculiar to herself – two notes of deprecating falsetto. 'How can you say it is good of me, when I'm sure there are no words for your kindness to us all! If only you knew our debt to your friend, Mr Earwaker! To our dying day we must all remember it. It is entirely through Mr Malkin that we are able to leave that most disagreeable Rouen – a place I shall never cease to think of with horror. O Mr Earwaker! you have only to think of that wretched railway station, stuck between two black tunnels! O Mr Malkin!'

'What are you doing?' Malkin inquired of the journalist. 'How long shall you be here? Why haven't I heard from you?'

'I go to London to-night.'

'And we to-morrow. On Friday I'll look you up. Stay, can't you dine with me this evening? Anywhere you like. These ladies will be glad to be rid of me, and to dine in peace at their hotel.'

'O Mr Malkin!' piped the widow, 'you know how very far that is from the truth. But we shall be very glad indeed to know that you are enjoying yourself with Mr Earwaker.'

The friends made an appointment to meet near the Madeleine, and Earwaker hastened to escape the sound of Mrs Jacox's voice.

Punctual at the rendezvous, Malkin talked with his wonted effusiveness as he led towards the Café Anglais.

'I've managed it, my boy! The most complete success! I had to run over to Boston to get hold of a scoundrelly relative of that poor woman. You should have seen how I came over him – partly dignified sternness, partly justifiable cajolery. The affair only wanted some one to take it up in earnest. I have secured her about a couple of hundred a year – withheld on the most paltry and transparent pretences. They're going to live at Wrotham, in Kent, where Mrs Jacox has friends. I never thought myself so much of a man of business. Of course old Haliburton, the lawyer, had a hand in it, but without my personal energy it would have taken him a year longer. What do you think of the girls? How do you like Bella?'

'A pretty child.'

'Child? Well, yes, yes – immature of course; but I'm rather in the habit of thinking of her as a young lady. In three years she'll be seventeen, you know. Of course you couldn't form a judgment of her character. She's quite remarkably mature for her age; and, what delights me most of all, a sturdy Radical! She takes the most intelligent interest in all political and social movements, I assure you! There's a great deal of democratic fire in her.'

'You're sure it isn't reflected from your own fervour?'

'Not a bit of it! You should have seen her excitement when we were at the Bastille Column yesterday. She'll make a splendid woman, I assure you. Lily's very interesting, too – profoundly interesting. But then she is certainly very young, so I can't feel so sure of her on the great questions. She hasn't her sister's earnestness, I fancy.'

In the after-glow of dinner, Malkin became still more confidential.

'You remember what I said to you long since? My mind is made up – practically made up. I shall devote myself to Bella's education, in the hope – you understand me? Impossible to have found a girl who suited better with my aspirations. She has known the hardships of poverty, poor thing, and that will keep her for ever in sympathy with the downtrodden classes. She has a splendid intelligence, and it shall be cultivated to the utmost.'

'One word,' said Earwaker, soberly. 'We have heard before of men who waited for girls to grow up. Be cautious, my dear fellow, both on your own account and hers.'

'My dear Earwaker! Don't imagine for a moment that I take it for granted she will get to be fond of me. My attitude is one of the most absolute discretion. You must have observed how I behaved to them all – scrupulous courtesy, I trust; no more familiarity than any friend might be permitted. I should never dream of addressing the girls without ceremonious prefix – never! I talk of Bella's education, but be assured that I regard my own as a matter of quite as much importance. I mean, that I shall strive incessantly to make myself worthy of her. No laxity! For these next three years I shall live as becomes a man who has his eyes constantly on a high ideal – the pure and beautiful girl whom he humbly hopes to win for a wife.'

The listener was moved. He raised his wine-glass to conceal the smile which might have been misunderstood. In his heart he felt more admiration than had yet mingled with his liking for this strange fellow.

'And Mrs Jacox herself,' pursued Malkin; 'she has her weaknesses, as we all have. I don't think her a very strong-minded woman, to tell the truth. But there's a great deal of goodness in her. If there's one thing I desire in people, it is the virtue of gratitude, and Mrs Jacox is grateful almost to excess for the paltry exertions I have made on her behalf. You know that kind of thing costs me nothing; you know I like running about and getting things done. But the poor woman imagines that I have laid her under an eternal obligation. Of course I shall show her in time that it was nothing at all; that she might have done just as much for herself if she had known how to go about it.'

Earwaker was musing, a wrinkle of uneasiness at the corner of his eye.

'She isn't the kind of woman, you know, one can regard as a mother. But we are the best possible friends. She *may*, perhaps, think of me as a possible son-in-law. Poor thing; I hope she does. Perhaps it will help to put her mind at rest about the girls.'

'Then shall you often be down at Wrotham?' inquired the journalist, abstractedly.

'Oh, not often – that is to say, only once a month or so, just to look in. I wanted to ask you: do you think I might venture to begin a correspondence with Bella?'

'M–m–m! I can't say.'

'It would be so valuable, you know. I could suggest books for her reading; I could help her in her study of politics, and so on.'

'Well, think about it. But be cautious, I beg of you. Now I must be off. Only just time enough to get my traps to the station.'

'I'll come with you. Gare du Nord? Oh, plenty of time, plenty of time! Nothing so abominable as waiting for trains. I make a point of never getting to the station more than three minutes before time. Astonishing what one can do in three minutes! I want to tell you about an adventure I had in Boston. Met a fellow so devilish like Peak that I *couldn't* believe it wasn't he himself. I spoke to him, but he swore that he knew not the man. Never saw such a likeness!'

'Curious. It may have been Peak.'

'By all that's suspicious, I can't help thinking the same! He had an English accent, too.'

'Queer business, this of Peak's. I hope I may live to hear the end of the story.'

They left the restaurant, and in a few hours Earwaker was again on English soil.

At Staple Inn a pile of letters awaited him, among them a note from Christian Moxey, asking for an appointment as soon as possible after the journalist's return. Earwaker at once sent an invitation, and on the next evening Moxey came. An intimacy had grown up between the two, since the mysterious retreat of their common friend. Christian was at first lost without the companionship of Godwin Peak; he forsook his studies, and fell into a state of complete idleness which naturally fostered his tendency to find solace in the decanter. With Earwaker, he could not talk as unreservedly as with Peak, but on the other hand there was a tonic influence in the journalist's personality which he recognised as beneficial. Earwaker was steadily making his way in the world, lived a life of dignified independence. What was the secret of these strong, calm natures? Might it not be learnt by studious inspection?

'How well you look!' Christian exclaimed, on entering. 'We enjoyed your Provencal letter enormously. That's a ramble I have always meant to do. Next year perhaps.'

'Why not this? Haven't you got into a dangerous habit of postponement?'

'Yes, I'm afraid I have. But, by-the-bye, no news of Peak, I suppose?'

Earwaker related the story he had heard from Malkin, adding:

'You must remember that they met only once in London; Malkin might very well mistake another man for Peak.'

'Yes,' replied the other musingly. 'Yet it isn't impossible that Peak has gone over there. If so, what on earth can he be up to? Why *should* he hide from his friends?'

'*Cherchez la femme*,' said the journalist, with a smile. 'I can devise no other explanation.'

'But I can't see that it would be an explanation at all. Grant even – something unavowable, you know – are we Puritans? How could it harm him, at all events, to let us know his whereabouts? No such mystery ever came into my experience. It is too bad of Peak; it's confoundedly unkind.'

'Suppose he has found it necessary to assume a character wholly fictitious – or, let us say, quite inconsistent with his life and opinions as known to us?'

This was a fruitful suggestion, long in Earwaker's mind, but not hitherto communicated. Christian did not at once grasp its significance.

'How could that be necessary? Peak is no swindler. You don't imply that he is engaged in some fraud?'

'Not in the ordinary sense, decidedly. But picture some girl or woman of conventional opinions and surroundings. What if he resolved to win such a wife, at the expense of disguising his true self?'

'But what an extraordinary idea!' cried Moxey. 'Why Peak is all but a woman-hater!'

The journalist uttered croaking laughter.

'Have I totally misunderstood him?' asked Christian, confused and abashed.

'I think it not impossible.'

'You amaze me! – But no, no; you are wrong, Earwaker. Wrong in your suggestion, I mean. Peak could never sink to that. He is too uncompromising'—

'Well, it will be explained some day, I suppose.'

And with a shrug of impatience, the journalist turned to another subject. He, too, regretted his old friend's disappearance, and in a measure resented it. Godwin Peak was not a man to slip out of one's life and leave no appreciable vacancy. Neither of these men admired him, in the true sense of the word, yet had his voice sounded at the door both would have sprung up with eager welcome. He was a force – and how many such beings does one encounter in a lifetime?

II

In different ways, Christian and Marcella Moxey had both been lonely since their childhood. As a schoolgirl, Marcella seemed to her companions conceited and repellent; only as the result of reflection in after years did Sylvia Moorhouse express so favourable an opinion of her. In all things she affected singularity; especially it was her delight to utter democratic and revolutionary sentiments among hearers who, belonging to a rigidly conservative order, held such opinions impious. Arrived at womanhood, she affected scorn of the beliefs and habits cherished by her own sex, and shrank from association with the other. Godwin Peak was the first man with whom she conversed in the tone of friendship, and it took a year or more before that point was reached. As her intimacy with him established itself, she was observed to undergo changes which seemed very significant in the eyes of her few acquaintances. Disregard of costume had been one of her characteristics, but now she moved gradually towards the opposite extreme, till her dresses were occasionally more noticeable for richness than for good taste.

Christian, for kindred reasons, was equally debarred from the pleasures and profits of society. At school, his teachers considered him clever, his fellows for the most part looked down upon him as a sentimental weakling. The death of his parents, when he was still a lad, left him to the indifferent care of a guardian nothing akin to him. He began life in an uncongenial position, and had not courage to oppose the drift of circumstances. The romantic attachment which absorbed his best years naturally had a debilitating effect, for love was never yet a supporter of the strenuous virtues, save when it has survived fruition and been blessed by reason. In most men a fit of amorous mooning works its own cure; energetic rebound is soon inevitable. But Christian was so constituted that a decade of years could not exhaust his capacity for sentimental languishment. He made it a point of honour to seek no female companionship which could imperil his faith. Unfortunately, this avoidance of the society which would soon have made him a happy renegade, was but too easy. Marcella and he practically encouraged each other in a life of isolation, though to both of them such an existence was anything but congenial. Their difficulties were of the same nature as those

which had always beset Godwin Peak; they had no relatives with
whom they cared to associate, and none of the domestic friends
who, in the progress of time, establish and extend a sphere of
genuine intimacy.

Most people who are capable of independent thought rapidly
outgrow the stage when compromise is abhorred; they accept, at
first reluctantly, but ere long with satisfaction, that code of polite
intercourse which, as Steele says, is 'an expedient to make fools
and wise men equal'. It was Marcella's ill-fate that she could
neither learn tolerance nor persuade herself to affect it. The
emancipated woman has fewer opportunities of relieving her
mind than a man in corresponding position; if her temper be
aggressive she must renounce general society, and, if not content
to live alone, ally herself with some group of declared militants.
By correspondence, or otherwise, Marcella might have brought
herself into connection with women of a sympathetic type, but
this effort she had never made. And chiefly because of her
acquaintance with Godwin Peak. In him she concentrated her
interests; he was the man to whom her heart went forth with every
kind of fervour. So long as there remained a hope of moving him
to reciprocal feeling she did not care to go in search of female
companions. Year after year she sustained herself in solitude by
this faint hope. She had lost sight of the two or three schoolfellows who, though not so zealous as herself, would have
welcomed her as an interesting acquaintance; and the only
woman who assiduously sought her was Mrs Morton, the wife of
one of Christian's friends, a good-natured but silly person bent on
making known that she followed the 'higher law'.

Godwin's disappearance sank her in profound melancholy.
Through the black weeks of January and February she scarcely
left the house, and on the plea of illness refused to see any one but
her brother. Between Christian and her there was no avowed
confidence, but each knew the other's secret; their mutual
affection never spoke itself in words, yet none the less it was
indispensable to their lives. Deprived of his sister's company,
Christian must have yielded to the vice which had already too
strong a hold upon him, and have become a maudlin drunkard.
Left to herself, Marcella had but slender support against a grim
temptation already beckoning her in nights of sleeplessness. Of
the two, her nature was the more tragic. Circumstances aiding,
Christian might still forget his melancholy, abandon the whisky

bottle, and pass a lifetime of amiable uxoriousness, varied with scientific enthusiasm. But for Marcella, frustrate in the desire with which every impulse of her being had identified itself, what future could be imagined?

When a day or two of sunlight (the rays through a semi-opaque atmosphere which London has to accept with gratitude) had announced that the seven-months' winter was overcome, and when the newspapers began to speak, after their fashion, of pictures awaiting scrutiny, Christian exerted himself to rouse his sister from her growing indolence. He succeeded in taking her to the Academy. Among the works of sculpture, set apart for the indifference of the public, was a female head, catalogued as 'A Nihilist' – in itself interesting, and specially so to Marcella, because it was executed by an artist whose name she recognised as that of a schoolmate, Agatha Walworth. She spoke of the circumstance to Christian, and added:

'I should like to have that. Let us go and see the price.'

The work was already sold. Christian, happy that his sister could be aroused to this interest, suggested that a cast might be obtainable.

'Write to Miss Walworth,' he urged. 'Bring yourself to her recollection. – I should think she must be the right kind of woman.'

Though at the time she shook her head, Marcella was presently tempted to address a letter to the artist, who responded with friendly invitation. In this way a new house was opened to her; but, simultaneously, one more illusion was destroyed. Knowing little of life, and much of literature, she pictured Miss Walworth as inhabiting a delightful Bohemian world, where the rules of conventionalism had no existence, and everything was judged by the brain-standard. Modern French biographies supplied all her ideas of studio society. She prepared herself for the first visit with a joyous tremor, wondering whether she would be deemed worthy to associate with the men and women who lived for art. The reality was a shock. In a large house at Chiswick she found a gathering of most respectable English people, chatting over the regulation tea-cup; not one of them inclined to disregard the dictates of Mrs Grundy in dress, demeanour, or dialogue. Agatha Walworth lived with her parents and her sisters like any other irreproachable young woman. She had a nice little studio, and worked at modelling with a good deal of aptitude; but of Bohemia she knew nothing whatever, save by hearsay. Her 'Nihilist' was no indication of a rebellious spirit; some friend had happened to suggest that a certain female model, a Russian, would do very well for such a character, and the hint was tolerably well carried out – nothing more. Marcella returned in a mood of contemptuous disappointment. The cast she had desired to have was shortly sent to her as a gift, but she could take no pleasure in it.

Still, she saw more of the Walworths and found them not illiberal. Agatha was intelligent, and fairly well read in modern authors; no need to conceal one's opinions in conversation with her. Marcella happened to be spending the evening with these acquaintances whilst her brother was having his chat at Staple Inn; on her return, she mentioned to Christian that she had been invited to visit the Walworths in Devonshire a few weeks hence.

'Go, by all means,' urged her brother.

'I don't think I shall. They are too respectable.'

'Nonsense! They seem very open-minded; you really can't expect absolute unconventionality. Is it desirable? Really is it, now? – Suppose I were to marry some day, Marcella; do you think my household would be unconventional?'

His voice shook a little, and he kept his eyes averted. Marcella, to whom her brother's romance was anything but an agreeable subject, – the slight acquaintance she had with the modern Laura did not encourage her to hope for that lady's widowhood, – gave no heed to the question.

'They are going to have a house at Budleigh Salterton; do you know of the place? Somewhere near the mouth of the Exe. Miss Walworth tells me that one of our old school friends is living there – Sylvia Moorhouse. Did I ever mention Sylvia? She had gleams of sense, I remember; but no doubt society has drilled all that out of her.'

Christian sighed.

'Why?' he urged. 'Society is getting more tolerant than you are disposed to think. Very few well-educated people would nowadays object to an acquaintance on speculative grounds. Some one – who was it? – was telling me of a recent marriage between the daughter of some well-known Church people and a man who made no secret of his agnosticism; the parents acquiescing cheerfully. The one thing still insisted on is decency of behaviour.'

Marcella's eyes flashed.

'How can you say that? You know quite well that most kinds of immorality are far more readily forgiven by people of the world than sincere heterodoxy on moral subjects.'

'Well, well, I meant decency from *their* point of view. And there really must be such restrictions, you know. How very few people are capable of what you call sincere heterodoxy, in morals or religion! Your position is unphilosophical; indeed it is. Take the world as you find it, and make friends with kind, worthy people. You have suffered from a needless isolation. Do accept this opportunity of adding to your acquaintances! – Do, Marcella! I shall take it as a great kindness, dear girl.'

His sister let her head lie back against the chair, her face averted. A stranger seated in Christian's place, regarding Marcella whilst her features were thus hidden, would have thought it probable that she was a woman of no little beauty. Her masses of tawny hair, her arms and hands, the pose and outline of her figure, certainly suggested a countenance of corresponding charm, and the ornate richness of her attire aided such an impression. This thought came to Christian as he gazed at her; his eyes, always so gentle, softened to a tender compassion. As the silence continued, he looked uneasily about him; when at length he spoke, it was as though a matter of trifling moment had occurred to him.

'By-the-bye, I am told that Malkin (Earwaker's friend, you know) saw Peak not long ago – in America.'

Marcella did not change her position, but at the sound of Peak's name she stirred, as if with an intention, at once checked, of bending eagerly forward.

'In America?' she asked, incredulously.

'At Boston. He met him in the street – or thinks he did. There's a doubt. When Malkin spoke to the man, he declared that he was not Peak at all – said there was a mistake.'

Marcella moved so as to show her face; endeavouring to express an unemotional interest, she looked coldly scornful.

'That ridiculous man can't be depended upon,' she said.

There had been one meeting between Marcella and Mr Malkin, with the result that each thoroughly disliked the other – an antipathy which could have been foreseen.

'Well, there's no saying,' replied Christian. 'But of one thing I feel pretty sure: we have seen the last of Peak. He'll never come back to us.'

'Why not?'

'I can only say that I feel convinced he has broken finally with all his old friends. – We must think no more of him, Marcella.'

His sister rose slowly, affected to glance at a book, and in a few moments said good-night. For another hour Christian sat by himself in gloomy thought.

At breakfast next morning Marcella announced that she would be from home the whole day; she might return in time for dinner, but it was uncertain. Her brother asked no questions, but said that he would lunch in town. About ten o'clock a cab was summoned, and Marcella, without leave-taking, drove away.

Christian lingered as long as possible over the morning paper, unable to determine how he should waste the weary hours that lay before him. There was no reason for his remaining in London through this brief season of summer glow. Means and leisure were his, he could go whither he would. But the effort of decision and departure seemed too much for him. Worst of all, this lassitude (not for the first time) was affecting his imagination; he thought with a dull discontent of the ideal love to which he had bound himself. Could he but escape from it, and begin a new life! But he was the slave of his airy obligation; for very shame's sake his ten years' consistency must be that of a lifetime.

There was but one place away from London to which he felt himself drawn, and that was the one place he might not visit. This morning's sunshine carried him back to that day when he had lain in the meadow near Twybridge and talked with Godwin Peak. How distinctly he remembered his mood! 'Be practical – don't be led astray after ideals – concentrate yourself;' – yes, it was he who had given that advice to Peak: and had he but recked his own rede—! Poor little Janet! was she married? If so, her husband must be a happy man.

Why should he not go down to Twybridge? His uncle, undoubtedly still living, must by this time have forgotten the old resentment, perhaps would be glad to see him. In any case he might stroll about the town and somehow obtain news of the Moxey family.

With vague half-purpose he left the house and walked westward. The stream of traffic in Edgware Road brought him to a pause; he stood for five minutes in miserable indecision, all but resolving to go on as far as Euston and look for the next northward train. But the vice in his will prevailed; automaton-like he turned in another direction, and presently came out into Sussex Square. Here was the house to which his thoughts had perpetually gone forth ever since that day when Constance gave her hand to a thriving City man, and became Mrs Palmer. At present, he knew, it was inhabited only by domestics: Mr Palmer, recovering from illness that threatened to be fatal, had gone to Bournemouth, where Constance of course tended him. But he would walk past and look up at the windows.

All the blinds were down – naturally. Thrice he went by and retraced his steps. Then, still automaton-like, he approached the door, rang the bell. The appearance of the servant choked his voice for an instant, but he succeeded in shaping an inquiry after Mr Palmer's health.

'I'm sorry to say, sir,' was the reply, 'that Mr Palmer died last night. We received the news only an hour or two ago.'

Christian tottered on his feet and turned so pale that the servant regarded him with anxiety. For a minute or two he stared vacantly into the gloomy hall; then, without a word, he turned abruptly and walked away.

Unconcious of the intervening distance, he found himself at home, in his library. The parlour-maid was asking him whether he would have luncheon. Scarcely understanding the question, he muttered a refusal and sat down.

So, it had come at last. Constance was a widow. In a year or so she might think of marrying again.

He remained in the library for three or four hours. At first incapable of rejoicing, then ashamed to do so, he at length suffered from such a throbbing of the heart that apprehension of illness recalled him to a normal state of mind. The favourite decanter was within reach, and it gave him the wonted support. Then at length did heart and brain glow with exulting fervour.

Poor Constance! Noble woman! Most patient of martyrs! The hour of her redemption had struck. The fetters had fallen from her tender, suffering body. Of *him* she could not yet think. He did not wish it. The womanhood must pay its debt to nature before she could gladden in the prospect of a new life. Months must go by before he could approach her, or even remind her of his existence. But at last his reward was sure.

And he had thought of Twybridge, of his cousin Janet! O unworthy lapse!

He shed tears of tenderness. Dear, noble Constance! It was now nearly twelve years since he first looked upon her face. In those days he mingled freely with all the society within his reach. It was not very select, and Constance Markham shone to him like a divinity among creatures of indifferent clay. They said she was coquettish, that she played at the game of love with every presentable young man – envious calumny! No, she was single-hearted, inexperienced, a lovely and joyous girl of not yet twenty. It is so difficult for such a girl to understand her own emotions. Her parents persuaded her into wedding Palmer. That was all gone into the past, and now his concern – their concern – was only with the blessed future.

At three o'clock he began to feel a healthy appetite. He sent for a cab and drove towards the region of restaurants.

Had he yielded to the impulse which this morning directed him to Twybridge, he would have arrived in that town not very long after his sister.

For that was the aim of Marcella's journey. On reaching the station, she dropped a light veil over her face and set forth on foot to discover the abode of Mrs Peak. No inhabitant of Twybridge save her uncle and his daughters could possibly recognise her, but she shrank from walking through the streets with exposed countenance. Whether she would succeed in her quest was uncertain. Godwin Peak's mother still dwelt here, she knew, for less than a year ago she had asked the question of Godwin himself; but a woman in humble circumstances might not have a house of her own, and her name was probably unknown save to a few friends.

However, the first natural step was to inquire for a directory. A stationer supplied her with one, informing her, with pride, that he himself was the author of it – that this was only the second year of its issue, and that its success was 'very encouraging'. Retiring to a quiet street, Marcella examined her purchase, and came upon 'Peak, Oliver; seedsman' – the sole entry of the name. This was probably a relative of Godwin's. Without difficulty she found Mr Peak's shop; behind the counter stood Oliver himself, rubbing his hands. Was there indeed a family likeness between this fresh-looking young shopkeeper and the stern, ambitious, intellectual man whose lineaments were ever before her mind? Though with fear and repulsion, Marcella was constrained to recognise something in the commonplace visage. With an uncertain voice, she made known her business.

'I wish to find Mrs Peak – a widow – an elderly lady'—

'Oh yes, madam! My mother, no doubt. She lives with her sister, Miss Cadman – the milliner's shop in the first street to the left. Let me point it out.'

With a sinking of the heart, Marcella murmured thanks and walked away. She found the milliner's shop – and went past it.

Why should discoveries such as these be so distasteful to her? Her own origin was not so exalted that she must needs look down on trades-folk. Still, for the moment she all but abandoned her undertaking. Was Godwin Peak in truth of so much account to her? Would not the shock of meeting his mother be final? Having come thus far, she must go through with it. If the experience cured her of a hopeless passion, why, what more desirable?

She entered the shop. A young female assistant came forward with respectful smile, and waited her commands.

'I wish, if you please, to see Mrs Peak.'

'Oh yes, madam! Will you have the goodness to walk this way?'

Too late Marcella remembered that she ought to have gone to the house-entrance. The girl led her out of the shop into a dark passage, and thence into a sitting-room which smelt of lavender. Here she waited for a few moments; then the door opened softly, and Mrs Peak presented herself.

There was no shock. The widow had the air of a gentlewoman – walked with elderly grace – and spoke with propriety. She resembled Godwin, and this time it was not painful to remark the likeness.

'I have come to Twybridge,' began Marcella, gently and respectfully, 'that is to say, I have stopped in passing – to ask for the address of Mr Godwin Peak. A letter has failed to reach him.'

It was her wish to manage without either disclosing the truth about herself or elaborating fictions, but after the first words she felt it impossible not to offer some explanation. Mrs Peak showed a slight surprise. With the courage of cowardice, Marcella continued more rapidly:

'My name is Mrs Ward. My husband used to know Mr Peak, in London, a few years ago, but we have been abroad, and unfortunately have lost sight of him. We remembered that Mr Peak's relatives lived at Twybridge, and, as we wish very much to renew the old acquaintance, I took the opportunity – passing by rail. I made inquiries in the town, and was directed to you – I hope rightly'—

The widow's face changed to satisfaction. Evidently her straightforward mind accepted the story as perfectly credible. Marcella, with bitterness, knew herself far from comely enough to suggest perils. She looked old enough for the part she was playing, and the glove upon her hand might conceal a wedding-ring.

'Yes, you were directed rightly,' Mrs Peak made quiet answer. 'I shall be very glad to give you my son's address. He left London about last Christmas, and went to live at Exeter.'

'Exeter? We thought he might be out of England.'

'No; he has lived all the time at Exeter. The address is Longbrook Street' – she added the number. 'He is studying, and finds that part of the country pleasant. I am hoping to see him here before very long.'

Marcella did not extend the conversation. She spoke of having to catch a train, and veiled as well as she could beneath ordinary courtesies her perplexity at the information she had received.

When she again reached the house at Notting Hill, Christian was absent. He came home about nine in the evening. It was impossible not to remark his strange mood of repressed excitement; but Marcella did not question him, and Christian had resolved to conceal the day's event until he could speak of it without agitation. Before they parted for the night, Marcella said carelessly:

'I have decided to go down to Budleigh Salterton when the time comes.'

'That's right!' exclaimed her brother, with satisfaction. 'You couldn't do better – couldn't possibly. It will be a very good thing for you in several ways.'

And each withdrew to brood over a perturbing secret.

Three or four years ago, when already he had conceived the idea of trying his fortune in some provincial town, Peak persuaded himself that it would not be difficult to make acquaintances among educated people, even though he had no credentials to offer. He indulged his fancy and pictured all manner of pleasant accidents which surely, sooner or later, must bring him into contact with families of the better sort. One does hear of such occurrences, no doubt. In every town there is some one or other whom a stranger may approach: a medical man – a local antiquary – a librarian – a philanthropist; and with moderate advantages of mind and address, such casual connections may at times be the preface to intimacy, with all resulting benefits. But experience of Exeter had taught him how slight would have been his chance of getting on friendly terms with any mortal if he had depended solely on his personal qualities. After a nine months' residence, and with the friendship of such people as the Warricombes, he was daily oppressed by his isolation amid this community of English folk. He had done his utmost to adopt the tone of average polished life. He had sat at the tables of worthy men, and conversed freely with their sons and daughters; he exchanged greetings in the highways: but this availed him nothing. Now, as on the day of his arrival, he was an alien – a lodger. What else had he ever been, since boyhood? A lodger in Kingsmill, a lodger in London, a lodger in Exeter. Nay, even as a boy he could scarcely have been said to 'live at home', for from the dawn of conscious intelligence he felt himself out of place among familiar things and people, at issue with prevalent opinions. Was he never to win a right of citizenship, never to have a recognised place among men associated in the duties and pleasures of life?

Sunday was always a day of weariness and despondency, and at present he suffered from the excitement of his conversation with Sidwell, followed as it had been by a night of fever. Extravagant hope had given place to a depression which could see nothing beyond the immediate gloom. Until mid-day he lay in bed. After dinner, finding the solitude of his little room intolerable, he went out to walk in the streets.

Not far from his door some children had gathered in a quiet corner, and were playing at a game on the pavement with pieces of chalk. As he drew near, a policeman, observing the little group, called out to them in a stern voice:

'Now then! what are you doing there? Don't you know *what day* it is?'

The youngsters fled, conscious of shameful delinquency.

There it was! There spoke the civic voice, the social rule, the public sentiment! Godwin felt that the policeman had rebuked *him*, and in doing so had severely indicated the cause of that isolation which he was condemned to suffer. Yes, all his life he had desired to play games on Sunday; he had never been able to understand why games on Sunday should be forbidden. And the angry laugh which escaped him as he went by the guardian of public morals, declared the impossibility of his ever being at one with communities which made this point the prime test of worthiness.

He walked on at a great speed, chafing, talking to himself. His way took him through Heavitree (when Hooker saw the light here, how easy to believe that the Anglican Church was the noblest outcome of human progress!) and on and on, until by a lane with red banks of sandstone, thick with ferns, shadowed with noble boughs, he came to a hamlet which had always been one of his favourite resorts, so peacefully it lay amid the exquisite rural landscape. The cottages were all closed and silent; hark for the reason! From the old church sounded an organ prelude, then the voice of the congregation, joining in one of the familiar hymns.

A significant feature of Godwin's idiosyncrasy. Notwithstanding his profound hatred and contempt of multitudes, he could never hear the union of many voices in song but his breast heaved and a choking warmth rose in his throat. Even where prejudice wrought most strongly with him, it had to give way before this rush of emotion; he often hurried out of earshot when a group of Salvationists were singing, lest the involuntary sympathy of his senses should agitate and enrage him. At present he had no wish to draw away. He entered the churchyard, and found the leafy nook with a tombstone where he had often rested. And as he listened to the rude chanting of verse after verse, tears fell upon his cheeks.

This sensibility was quite distinct from religious feeling. If the note of devotion sounding in that simple strain had any effect upon him at all, it merely intensified his consciousness of pathos as he thought of the many generations that had worshipped here, living and dying in a faith which was at best a helpful delusion. He could appreciate the beautiful aspects of Christianity as a legend, its nobility as a humanising power, its rich results in literature, its grandeur in historic retrospect. But at no moment in his life had he felt it as a spiritual influence. So far from tending in that direction, as he sat and brooded here in the churchyard, he owed to his fit of tearfulness a courage which determined him to abandon all religious pretences, and henceforth trust only to what was sincere in him – his human passion. The future he had sketched to Sidwell was impossible; the rural pastorate, the life of moral endeavour which in his excitement had seemed so nearly a genuine aspiration that it might perchance become reality – dreams, dreams! He must woo as a man, and trust to fortune for his escape from a false position. Sidwell should hear nothing more of clerical projects. He was by this time convinced that she held far less tenaciously than he had supposed to the special doctrines of the Church; and, if he had not deceived himself in interpreting her behaviour, a mutual avowal of love would involve ready consent on her part to his abandoning a career which – as he would represent it – had been adopted under a mistaken impulse. He returned to the point which he had reached when he set forth with the intention of bidding good-bye to the Warricombes – except that in flinging away hypocrisy he no longer needed to trample his desires. The change need not be declared till after a lapse of time. For the present his task was to obtain one more private interview with Sidwell ere she went to London, or, if that could not be, somehow to address her in unmistakable language.

The fumes were dispelled from his brain, and as he walked homeward he plotted and planned with hopeful energy. Sylvia Moorhouse came into his mind; could he not in some way make use of her? He had never yet been to see her at Budleigh Salterton. That he would do forthwith, and perchance the visit might supply him with suggestions.

On the morrow he set forth, going by train to Exmouth, and thence by the coach which runs twice a day to the little seaside town. The delightful drive, up hill and down dale, with its magnificent views over the estuary, and its ever-changing wayside beauties, put him into the best of spirits. About noon, he alighted at the Rolle Arms, the hotel to which the coach conducts its passengers, and entered to take a meal. He would call upon the Moorhouses at the conventional hour. The intervening time was spent pleasantly enough in loitering about the pebbled beach. A south-west breeze which had begun to gather clouds drove on the rising tide. By four o'clock there was an end of sunshine, and spurts of rain mingled with flying foam. Peak turned inland, pursued the leafy street up the close-sheltered valley, and came to the house where his friends dwelt.

In crossing the garden he caught sight of a lady who sat in a room on the ground floor; her back was turned to the window, and before he could draw near enough to see her better she had moved away, but the glimpse he had obtained of her head and shoulders affected him with so distinct an alarm that his steps were checked. It seemed to him that he had recognised the figure, and if he were right. – But the supposition was ridiculous; at all events so vastly improbable, that he would not entertain it. And now he descried another face, that of Miss Moorhouse herself, and it gave him a reassuring smile. He rang the door bell.

How happy – he said to himself – those men who go to call upon their friends without a tremor! Even if he had not received that shock a moment ago, he would still have needed to struggle against the treacherous beating of his heart as he waited for admission. It was always so when he visited the Warricombes, or any other family in Exeter. Not merely in consequence of the dishonest part he was playing, but because he had not quite overcome the nervousness which so anguished him in earlier days. The first moment after his entering a drawing-room cost him pangs of complex origin.

His eyes fell first of all upon Mrs Moorhouse, who advanced to welcome him. He was aware of three other persons in the room. The nearest, he could perceive without regarding her, was Sidwell's friend; the other two, on whom he did not yet venture to cast a glance, sat – or rather had just risen – in a dim background. As he shook hands with Sylvia, they drew nearer; one of them was a man, and, as his voice at once declared, no other than Buckland Warricombe. Peak returned his greeting, and, in the same moment, gazed at the last of the party. Mrs Moorhouse was speaking.

'Mr Peak – Miss Moxey.'

A compression of the lips was the only sign of disturbance that anyone could have perceived on Godwin's countenance. Already he had strung himself against his wonted agitation, and the added trial did not sensibly enhance what he suffered. In discovering that he had rightly identified the figure at the window, he experienced no renewal of the dread which brought him to a stand-still.

Already half prepared for this stroke of fate, he felt a satisfaction in being able to meet it so steadily. Tumult of thought was his only trouble; it seemed as if his brain must burst with the stress of its lightning operations. In three seconds, he re-lived the past, made several distinct anticipations of the future, and still discussed with himself how he should behave this moment. He noted that Marcella's face was bloodless; that her attempt to smile resulted in a very painful distortion of brow and lips. And he had leisure to pity her. This emotion prevailed. With a sense of magnanimity, which afterwards excited his wonder, he pressed the cold hand and said in a cheerful tone:

'Our introduction took place long ago, if I'm not mistaken. I had no idea, Miss Moxey, that you were among Mrs Moorhouse's friends.'

'Nor I that you were, Mr Peak,' came the answer, in a steadier voice than Godwin had expected.

Mrs Moorhouse and her daughter made the pleasant exclamations that were called for. Buckland Warricombe, with a doubtful smile on his lips, kept glancing from Miss Moxey to her acquaintance and back again. Peak at length faced him.

'I hoped we should meet down here this autumn.'

'I should have looked you up in a day or two,' Buckland replied, seating himself. 'Do you propose to stay in Exeter through the winter?'

'I'm not quite sure – but I think it likely.'

Godwin turned to the neighbour of whose presence he was most conscious.

'I hope your brother is well, Miss Moxey?'

Their eyes encountered steadily.

'Yes, he is quite well, thank you. He often says that it seems very long since he heard from you.'

'I'm a bad correspondent. – Is he also in Devonshire?'

'No. In London.'

'What a storm we are going to have!' exclaimed Sylvia, looking to the window. 'They predicted it yesterday. I should like to be on the top of Westdown Beacon – wouldn't you, Miss Moxey?'

'I am quite willing to go with you.'

'And what pleasure do you look for up there?' asked Warricombe, in a blunt, matter-of-fact tone.

'Now, there's a question!' cried Sylvia, appealing to the rest of the company.

'I agree with Mr Warricombe,' remarked her mother. 'It's better to be in a comfortable room.'

'Oh, you Radicals! What a world you will make of it in time!'

Sylvia affected to turn away in disgust, and happening to glance through the window she saw two young ladies approaching from the road.

'The Walworths – struggling desperately with their umbrellas.'

'I shouldn't wonder if you think it unworthy of an artist to carry an umbrella,' said Buckland.

'Now you suggest it, I certainly do. They should get nobly drenched.'

She went out into the hall, and soon returned with her friends – Miss Walworth the artist, Miss Muriel Walworth, and a youth, their brother. In the course of conversation Peak learnt that Miss Moxey was the guest of this family, and that she had been at Budleigh Salterton with them only a day or two. For the time he listened and observed, endeavouring to postpone consideration of the dangers into which he had suddenly fallen. Marcella had made herself his accomplice, thus far, in disguising the real significance of their meeting, and whether she would betray him in her subsequent talk with the Moorhouses remained a matter of doubt. Of course he must have assurance of her disposition – but the issues involved were too desperate for instant scrutiny. He felt the gambler's excitement, an irrational pleasure in the consciousness that his whole future was at stake. Buckland Warricombe had a keen eye upon him, and doubtless was eager to strike a train of suspicious circumstances. His face, at all events, should give no sign of discomposure. Indeed, he found so much enjoyment in the bright gossip of this assembly of ladies that the smile he wore was perfectly natural.

The Walworths, he gathered, were to return to London in a week's time. This meant, in all probability, that Marcella's stay here would not be prolonged beyond that date. Perhaps he could find an opportunity of seeing her apart from her friends. In reply to a question from Mrs Moorhouse, he made known that he proposed staying at the Rolle Arms for several days, and when he had spoken he glanced at Marcella. She understood him; he felt sure. An invitation to lunch here on the morrow was of course accepted.

Before leaving, he exchanged a few words with Buckland.

'Your relatives will be going to town very soon, I understand.'

Warricombe nodded.

'Shall I see you at Exeter?' Godwin continued.

'I'm not sure. I shall go over to-morrow, but it's uncertain whether I shall still be there when you return.'

The Radical was distinctly less amicable than even on the last occasion of their meeting. They shook hands in rather a perfunctory way.

Early in the evening there was a temporary lull in the storm; rain no longer fell, and in spaces of the rushing sky a few stars showed themselves. Unable to rest at the hotel, Peak set out for a walk towards the cliff summit called Westdown Beacon; he could see little more than black vacancies, but a struggle with the wind suited his temper, and he enjoyed the incessant roar of surf in the darkness. After an hour of this buffeting he returned to the beach, and stood as close as possible to the fierce breakers. No person was in sight. But when he began to move towards the upper shore, three female figures detached themselves from the gloom and advanced in his direction. They came so near that their voices were audible, and thereupon he stepped up to them.

'Are you going to the Beacon after all, Miss Moorhouse?'

Sylvia was accompanied by Agatha Walworth and Miss Moxey. She explained laughingly that they had stolen out, by agreement, whilst the males of their respective households still lingered at the dinner-table.

'But Mr Warricombe was right after all. We shall be blown to pieces. A very little of the romantic goes a long way, nowadays.'

Godwin was determined to draw Marcella aside. Seemingly she met his wish, for as all turned to regain the shelter of houses she fell behind her female companions, and stood close by him.

'I want to see you before you go back to London,' he said, bending his head near to hers.

'I wrote a letter to you this morning,' was her reply.

'A letter? To what address?'

'Your address at Exeter.'

'But how did you know it?'

'I'll explain afterwards.'

'When can I see you?'

'Not here. It's impossible. I shall go to Exeter, and there write to you again.'

'Very well. You promise to do this?'

'Yes, I promise.'

There was danger even in the exchange of these hurried sentences. Miss Walworth had glanced back, and might possibly have caught a phrase that aroused curiosity. Having accompanied the girls to within view of their destination, Peak said good-night, and went home to spend the rest of the evening in thought which was sufficiently absorbing.

The next day he had no sight of Marcella. At luncheon the Moorhouses were alone. Afterwards Godwin accepted a proposal of the mathematician (who was generally invisible amid his formulæ) for a walk up the Otter valley. Naturally they talked of Coleridge, whose metaphysical side appealed to Moorhouse. Peak dwelt on the human and poetical, and was led by that peculiar recklessness of mood, which at times relieved his nervous tension, to defend opium eating, as a source of pleasurable experience.

'You will hardly venture on that paradox in the pulpit,' remarked his companion, with laughter.

'Perhaps not. But I have heard arguments from that place decidedly more immoral.'

'No doubt.'

Godwin corrected the impression he perhaps had made by turning with sudden seriousness to another subject. The ironic temptation was terribly strong in him just now. One is occasionally possessed by a desire to shout in the midst of a silent assembly; and impulse of the same kind kept urging him to utter words which would irretrievably ruin his prospects. The sense that life is an intolerable mummery can with difficulty be controlled by certain minds, even when circumstances offer no keen incitement to rebellion. But Peak's position to-day demanded an incessant effort to refrain from self-betrayal. What a joy to declare himself a hypocrite, and snap mocking fingers in the world's face! As a safeguard, he fixed his mind upon Sidwell, recalled her features and her voice as clearly as possible, stamped into his heart the conviction that she half loved him.

When he was alone again, he of a sudden determined to go to Exeter. He could no longer endure uncertainty as to the contents of Marcella's letter. As it was too late for the coach, he set off and walked five miles to Exmouth, where he caught a train.

The letter lay on his table, and with it one on which he recognised his mother's handwriting.

Marcella wrote in the simplest way, quite as if their intercourse had never been disturbed. As she happened to be staying with friends at Budleigh Salterton, it seemed possible for her to meet him. Might she hope that he would call at the hotel in Exeter, if she wrote again to make an appointment?

Well, that needed no reply. But how had she discovered the address? Was his story known in London? In a paroxysm of fury, he crushed the letter into a ball and flung it away. The veins of his forehead swelled; he walked about the room with senseless violence, striking his fist against furniture and walls. It would have relieved him to sob and cry like a thwarted child, but only a harsh sound, half-groan, half-laughter, burst from his throat.

The fit passed, and he was able to open the letter from Twybridge, the first he had received from his mother for more than a month. He expected to find nothing of interest, but his attention was soon caught by a passage, which ran thus:

'Have you heard from some friends of yours, called Ward? Some time ago a lady called here to ask for your address. She said her name was Mrs Ward, and that her husband, who had been abroad for a long time, very much wished to find you again. Of course I told her where you were to be found. It was just after I had written, or I should have let you know about it before.'

Ward? He knew no one of that name. Could it be Marcella who had done this? It looked more than likely; he believed her capable of strange proceedings.

In the morning he returned to the seaside. Prospect of pleasure there was none, but by moving about he made the time pass more quickly. Wandering in the lanes (which would have delighted him with their autumnal beauties had his mind been at rest), he came upon Miss Walworth, busy with a water-colour sketch. Though their acquaintance was so slight, he stopped for conversation, and the artist's manner appeared to testify that Marcella had as yet made no unfavourable report of him. By mentioning that he would return home on the morrow, he made sure that Marcella would be apprised of this. Perhaps she might shorten her stay, and his suspense.

Back in Longbrook Street once more, he found another letter. It was from Mrs Warricombe, who wrote to tell him of their coming removal to London, and added an invitation to dine four days hence. Then at all events he would speak again with Sidwell. But to what purpose? Could he let her go away for months, and perhaps all but forget him among the many new faces that would

surround her. He saw no feasible way of being with her in private.
To write was to run the gravest risk; things were not ripe for that. To
take Martin into his confidence? That asked too much courage.
Deliberate avowals of this kind seemed to him ludicrous and
humiliating, and under the circumstances – no, no; what force of
sincerity could make him appear other than a scheming adventurer?

He lived in tumult of mind and senses. When at length, on the
day before his engagement with the Warricombes, there came a
note from Marcella, summoning him to the interview agreed
upon, he could scarcely endure the hour or two until it was time to
set forth; every minute cost him a throb of pain. The torment must
have told upon his visage, for on entering the room where
Marcella waited he saw that she looked at him with a changing
expression, as if something surprised her.

They shook hands, but without a word. Marcella pointed to a
chair, yet remained standing. She was endeavouring to smile; her
eyes fell, and she coloured.

'Don't let us make each other uncomfortable,' Peak exclaimed
suddenly, in the off-hand tone of friendly intimacy. 'There's
nothing tragic in this affair, after all. Let us talk quietly.'

Marcella seated herself.

'I had reasons,' he went on, 'for going away from my old
acquaintances for a time. Why not, if I chose? You have found me
out. Very well; let us talk it over as we have discussed many
another moral or psychological question.'

He did not meditate these sentences. Something must of
necessity be said, and words shaped themselves for him. His
impulse was to avoid the emotional, to talk with this problematic
woman as with an intellectual friend of his own sex.

'Forgive me,' were the first sounds that came from Marcella's
lips. She spoke with bent head, and almost in a whisper.

'What have I to forgive?' He sat down and leaned sideways in
the easy chair. 'You were curious about my doings? What more
natural?'

'Do you know how I learnt where you were?'

She looked up for an instant.

'I have a suspicion. You went to Twybridge?'

'Yes.'

'But not in your own name?'

'I can hardly tell why not.'

Peak laughed. He was physically and mentally at rest in

comparison with his state for the past few days. Things had a simpler aspect all at once. After all, who would wish to interfere maliciously with him? Women like to be in secrets, and probably Marcella would preserve his.

'What conjectures had you made about me?' he asked, with an air of amusement.

'Many, of course. But I heard something not long ago which seemed so unlikely, yet was told so confidently, that at last I couldn't overcome my wish to make inquiries.'

'And what was that?'

'Mr Malkin has been to America, and he declared that he had met you in the streets of Boston – and that you refused to admit you were yourself.'

Peak laughed still more buoyantly. His mood was eager to seize on any point that afforded subject for jest.

'Malkin seems to have come across my *Doppelgänger*. One mustn't pretend to certainty in anything, but I am disposed to think I never was in Boston.'

'He was of course mistaken.'

Marcella's voice had an indistinctness very unlike her ordinary tone. As a rule she spoke with that clearness and decision which corresponds to qualities of mind not commonly found in women. But confidence seemed to have utterly deserted her; she had lost her individuality, and was weakly feminine.

'I have been here since last Christmas,' said Godwin, after a pause.

'Yes. I know.'

Their eyes met.

'No doubt your friends have told you as much as they know of me?'

'Yes – they have spoken of you.'

'And what does it amount to?'

He regarded her steadily, with a smile of indifference.

'They say' – she gazed at him as if constrained to do so – 'that you are going into the Church.' And as soon as she uttered the last word, a painful laugh escaped her.

'Nothing else? No comments?'

'I think Miss Moorhouse finds it difficult to understand.'

'Miss Moorhouse?' He reflected, still smiling. 'I shouldn't wonder. She has a sceptical mind, and she doesn't know me well enough to understand me.'

'Doesn't know you well enough?'

She repeated the words mechanically. Peak gave her a keen glance.

'Has she led you to suppose,' he asked, 'that we are on intimate terms?'

'No.' The word fell from her, absently, despondently.

'Miss Moxey, would anything be gained by our discussing my position? If you think it a mystery, hadn't we better leave it so?'

She made no answer.

'But perhaps,' he went on, 'you have told them – the Walworths and the Moorhouses – that I owe my friends an explanation? When I see them again, perhaps I shall be confronted with cold, questioning faces?'

'I haven't said a word that could injure you,' Marcella replied, with something of her usual self-possession, passing her eyes distantly over his face as she spoke.

'I knew the suggestion was unjust, when I made it.'

'Then why should you refuse me your confidence?'

She bent forward slightly, but with her eyes cast down. Tone and features intimated a sense of shame, due partly to the feeling that she offered complicity in deceit.

'What can I tell you more than you know?' said Godwin, coldly. 'I propose to become a clergyman, and I have acknowledged to you that my motive is ambition. As the matter concerns my conscience, that must rest with myself; I have spoken of it to no one. But you may depend upon it that I am prepared for every difficulty that may spring up. I knew, of course, that sooner or later some one would discover me here. Well, I have changed my opinions, that's all; who can demand more than that?'

Marcella answered in a tone of forced composure.

'You owe me no explanation at all. Yet we have known each other for a long time, and it pains me that – to be suddenly told that we are no more to each other than strangers.'

'Are we talking like strangers, Marcella?'

She flushed, and her eyes gleamed as they fixed themselves upon him for an instant. He had never before dreamt of addressing her so familiarly, and least of all in this moment was she prepared for it. Godwin despised himself for the impulse to which he had yielded, but its policy was justified. He had taken one more step in disingenuousness – a small matter.

'Let it be one of those things on which even friends don't open their minds to each other,' he pursued. 'I am living in solitude, and perhaps must do so for several years yet. If I succeed in my purposes, you will see me again on the old terms; if I fail, then too we shall be friends – if you are willing.'

'You won't tell me what those purposes are?'

'Surely you can imagine them.'

'Will you let me ask you – do you look for help to anyone that I have seen here?' She spoke with effort and with shame.

'To no one that you have met,' he answered, shortly.

'Then to some one in Exeter? I have been told that you have friends.'

He was irritated by her persistency, and his own inability to decide upon the most prudent way of answering.

'You mean the Warricombe family, I suppose?'

'Yes.'

'I think it very likely that Mr Warricombe may be able to help me substantially.'

Marcella kept silence. Then, without raising her eyes, she murmured:

'You will tell me no more?'

'There is nothing more to tell.'

She bit her lips, as if to compel them to muteness. Her breath came quickly; she glanced this way and that, like one who sought an escape. After eyeing her askance for a moment, Peak rose.

'You are going?' she said.

'Yes; but surely there is no reason why we shouldn't say good-bye in a natural and friendly way?'

'Can you forgive me for that deceit I practised?'

Peak laughed.

'What does it matter? We should in any case have met at Budleigh Salterton.'

'No. I had no serious thought of accepting their invitation.'

She stood looking away from him, endeavouring to speak as though the denial had but slight significance. Godwin stirred impatiently.

'I should never have gone to Twybridge,' Marcella continued, 'but for Mr Malkin's story.'

He turned to her.

'You mean that his story had a disagreeable sound?'

Marcella kept silence, her fingers working together.

'And is your mind relieved?' he added.

'I wish you were back in London. I wish this change had never come to pass.'

'I wish that several things in my life had never come to pass. But I am here, and my resolve is unalterable. One thing I must ask you — how shall you represent my position to your brother?'

For a moment Marcella hesitated. Then, meeting his look, she answered with nervous haste:

'I shall not mention you to him.'

Ashamed to give any sign of satisfaction, and oppressed by the feeling that he owed her gratitude, Peak stood gazing towards the windows with an air of half-indifferent abstractedness. It was better to let the interview end thus, without comment or further question; so he turned abruptly, and offered his hand.

'Good-bye. You will hear of me, or from me.'

'Good-bye!'

He tried to smile; but Marcella had a cold face, expressive of more dignity than she had hitherto shown. As he closed the door she was still looking towards him.

He knew what the look meant. In his position, a man of ordinary fibre would long ago have nursed the flattering conviction that Marcella loved him. Godwin had suspected it, but in a vague, unemotional way, never attaching importance to the matter. What he *had* clearly understood was, that Christian wished to inspire him with interest in Marcella, and on that account, when in her company, he sometimes set himself to display a deliberate negligence. No difficult undertaking, for he was distinctly repelled by the thought of any relations with her more intimate than had been brought about by his cold intellectual sympathy. Her person was still as disagreeable to him as when he first met her in her uncle's house at Twybridge. If a man sincerely hopes that a woman does not love him (which can seldom be the case where a suggestion of such feeling ever arises), he will find it easy to believe that she does not. Peak not only had the benefit of this principle; the constitution of his mind made it the opposite of natural for him to credit himself with having inspired affection. That his male friends held him in any warm esteem always appeared to him improbable, and as regards women his modesty was profound. The simplest explanation, that he was himself incapable of pure devotedness, perhaps hits the truth. Unsympathetic, however, he could with no justice be called, and now that the reality of Marcella's love was forced upon his consciousness he thought of her with sincere pity, – the emotion which had already possessed him (though he did not then analyse it) when he unsuspectingly looked into her troubled face a few days ago.

It was so hard to believe, that, on reaching home, he sat for a long time occupied with the thought of it, to the exclusion of his own anxieties. What! this woman had made of *him* an ideal such as he himself sought among the most exquisite of her sex? How was that possible? What quality of his, personal, psychical, had such magnetic force? What sort of being was he in Marcella's eyes? Reflective men must often enough marvel at the success of whiskered and trousered mortals in wooing the women of their desire, for only by a specific imagination can a person of one sex assume the emotions of the other. Godwin had neither that endowment nor the peculiar self-esteem which makes love-winning a matter of course to some intelligent males. His native arrogance signified a low estimate of mankind at large, rather than an overweening appreciation of his own qualities, and in his most presumptuous moments he had never claimed the sexual prefulgence which many a commonplace fellow so gloriously exhibits. At most, he had hoped that some woman might find him *interesting*, and so be led on to like him well enough for the venture of matrimony. Passion at length constrained him to believe that his ardour might be genuinely reciprocated, but even now it was only in paroxysms that he held this assurance; the hours of ordinary life still exposed him to the familiar self-criticism, sometimes more scathing than ever. He dreaded the looking-glass, consciously avoided it; and a like disparagement of his inner being tortured him through the endless labyrinths of erotic reverie.

Yet here was a woman who so loved him that not even a proud temper and his candid indifference could impose restraint upon her emotions. As he listened to the most significant of her words he was distressed with shame, and now, in recalling them, he felt that he should have said something, done something, to dis-illusion her. Could he not easily show himself in a contemptible light? But reflection taught him that the shame he had experienced on Marcella's behalf was blended with a gratification which forbade him at the moment to be altogether unamiable. It was not self-interest alone that prompted his use of her familiar name. In the secret places of his heart he was thankful to her for a most effective encouragement. She had confirmed him in the hope that he was loved by Sidwell.

And now that he no longer feared her, Marcella was gradually dismissed from mind. For a day or two he avoided the main streets of the town, lest a chance meeting with her should revive disquietude; but, by the time that Mrs Warricombe's invitation permitted him once more to follow his desire, he felt assured that Marcella was back in London, and the sense of distance helped to banish her among unrealities.

The hours had never pressed upon him with such demand for resolution. In the look with which Sidwell greeted him when he met her in the drawing-room, he seemed to read much more than wonted friendliness; it was as though a half secret already existed between them. But no occasion offered for a word other than trivial. The dinner-party consisted of about a score of people, and throughout the evening Peak found himself hopelessly severed from the one person whose presence was anything but an importunity to him. He maddened with jealousy, with fear, with ceaseless mental manœuvring. More than one young man of agreeable aspect appeared to be on dangerous terms with Sidwell, approaching her with that air of easy, well-bred intimacy which Godwin knew too well he would never be able to assume in perfection. Again he was humiliated by self-comparison with social superiors, and again reminded that in this circle he had a place merely on sufferance. Mrs Warricombe, when he chanced to speak with her, betrayed the slight regard in which she really held him, and Martin devoted himself to more important people. The evening was worse than lost.

Yet in two more days Sidwell would be beyond reach. He writhed upon his bed as the image of her loveliness returned again and again, – her face as she conversed at table, her dignity as she rose with the other ladies, her smile when he said good-night. A smile that meant more than civility; he was convinced of it. But memory would not support him through half-a-year of solitude and ill-divining passion.

He would write to her, and risk all. Two o'clock in the morning saw him sitting half-dressed at the table, raging over the difficulties of a composition which should express his highest self. Four o'clock saw the blotched letter torn into fragments. He could not write as he wished, could not hit the tone of manly appeal. At five o'clock he turned wretchedly into bed again.

A day of racking headache; then the long restful sleep which brings good counsel. It was well that he had not sent a letter, nor in any other way committed himself. If Sidwell were ever to be his wife, the end could only be won by heroic caution and patience. Thus far he had achieved notable results; to rush upon his aim would be the most absurd departure from a hopeful scheme gravely devised and pursued. To wait, to establish himself in the confidence of this family, to make sure his progress step by step, — that was the course indicated from the first by his calm reason. Other men might triumph by sudden audacity; for him was no hope save in slow, persevering energy of will. Passion had all but ruined him; now he had recovered self-control.

Sidwell's six months in London might banish him from her mind, might substitute some rival against whom it would be hopeless to contend. Yes; but a thousand possibilities stood with menace in the front of every great enterprise. Before next spring he might be dead.

Defiance, then, of every foreboding, of every shame; and a life that moulded itself in the ardour of unchangeable resolve.

IV

Martin Warricombe was reconciled to the prospect of a metropolitan winter by the fact that his old friend Thomas Gale,
formerly Geological Professor at Whitelaw College, had of late
returned from a three years' sojourn in North America, and now
dwelt in London. The breezy man of science was welcomed back
among his brethren with two-fold felicitation; his book on the
Appalachians would have given no insufficient proof of activity
abroad, but evidence more generally interesting accompanied him
in the shape of a young and beautiful wife. Not every geologist
whose years have entered the fifties can go forth and capture in
second marriage a charming New England girl, thirty years his
junior. Yet those who knew Mr Gale – his splendid physique, his
bluff cordiality, the vigour of his various talk – were scarcely
surprised. The young lady was no heiress; she had, in fact, been a
school teacher, and might have wearied through her best years in
that uncongenial pursuit. Transplanted to the richest English soil,
she developed remarkable aptitudes. A month or two of London
exhibited her as a type of all that is most attractive in American
womanhood.

Between Mrs Gale and the Warricombes intimacy was soon
established. Sidwell saw much of her, and liked her. To this
meditative English girl the young American offered an engrossing
problem, for she avowed her indifference to all religious dogmas,
yet was singularly tolerant and displayed a moral fervour which
Sidwell had believed inseparable from Christian faith. At the
Gales' house assembled a great variety of intellectual people, and
with her father's express approval (Martin had his reasons)
Sidwell made the most of this opportunity of studying the modern
world. Only a few days after her arrival in London, she became
acquainted with a Mr Walsh, a brother of that heresiarch, the
Whitelaw Professor, whose name was still obnoxious to her
mother. He was a well-favoured man of something between thirty
and forty, brilliant in conversation, personally engaging, and
known by his literary productions, which found small favour with
conservative readers. With surprise, Sidwell in a short time
became aware that Mr Walsh had a frank liking for her society.
He was often to be seen in Mrs Warricombe's drawing-room, and
at Mrs Gale's he yet more frequently obtained occasions of

talking with her. The candour with which he expressed himself on most subjects enabled her to observe a type of mind which at present had peculiar interest for her. Discretion often put restraint upon her curiosity, but none the less Mr Walsh had plausible grounds for believing that his advances were not unwelcome. He saw that Sidwell's gaze occasionally rested upon him with a pleasant gravity, and noted the mood of meditation which sometimes came upon her when he had drawn apart. The frequency of these dialogues was observed by Mrs Warricombe, and one evening she broached the subject to her daughter rather abruptly.

'I am surprised that you have taken such a liking to Mr Walsh.'

Sidwell coloured, and made answer in the quiet tone which her mother had come to understand as a reproof, a hint of defective delicacy:

'I don't think I have behaved in a way that should cause you surprise.'

'It seemed to me that you were really very – friendly with him.'

'Yes, I am always friendly. But nothing more.'

'Don't you think there's a danger of his misunderstanding you, Sidwell?'

'I don't, mother. Mr Walsh understands that we differ irreconcilably on subjects of the first importance. I have never allowed him to lose sight of that.'

Intellectual differences were of much less account to Mrs Warricombe than to her daughter, and her judgment in a matter such as this was consequently far more practical.

'If I may advise you, dear, you oughtn't to depend much on that. I am not the only one who has noticed something – I only mention it, you know.'

Sidwell mused gravely. In a minute or two she looked up and said in her gentlest voice:

'Thank you, mother. I will be more careful.'

Perhaps she had lost sight of prudence, forgetting that Mr Walsh could not divine her thoughts. Her interest in him was impersonal; when he spoke she was profoundly attentive, only because her mind would have been affected in the same way had she been reading his words instead of listening to them. She could not let him know that another face was often more distinct to her imagination than his to her actual sight, and that her thoughts were frequently more busy with a remembered dialogue than with this in which she was engaged. She had abundantly safe-guarded herself against serious misconstruction, but if gossip were making her its subject, it would be inconsiderate not to regard the warning.

It came, indeed, at a moment when she was very willing to rest from social activity. At the time of her last stay in London, three years ago, she had not been ripe for reflection on what she saw. Now her mind was kept so incessantly at strain, and her emotions answered so intensely to every appeal, that at length she felt the need of repose. It was not with her as with the young women who seek only to make the most of their time in agreeable ways. Sidwell's vital forces were concentrated in an effort of profound spiritual significance. The critical hour of her life was at hand, and she exerted every faculty in the endeavour to direct herself aright.

Having heard from his brother that Sidwell had not been out for several days, Buckland took an opportunity of calling at the house early one morning. He found her alone in a small drawing-room, and sat down with an expression of weary discontent. This mood had been frequent in the young man of late. Sidwell remarked a change that was coming over him, a gloominess unnatural to his character.

'Seen the Walworths lately?' he asked, when his sister had assured him that she was not seriously ailing.

'We called a few days ago.'

'Meet anyone there?'

'Two or three people. No one that interested me.'

'You haven't come across some friends of theirs called Moxey?'

'Oh yes! Miss Moxey was there one afternoon about a fortnight ago.'

'Did you talk to her at all?' Buckland asked.

'Yes; we hadn't much to say to each other, though. How do you know of her? Through Sylvia, I daresay.'

'Met her when I was last down yonder.'

Sidwell had long since heard from her friend of Miss Moxey's visit to Budleigh Salterton, but she was not aware that Buckland had been there at the same time. Sylvia had told her, however, of the acquaintance existing between Miss Moxey and Peak, a point of much interest to her, though it remained a mere unconnected fact. In her short conversation with Marcella, she had not ventured to refer to it.

'Do you know anything of the family?'

'I was going to ask you the same,' returned Buckland. 'I thought you might have heard something from the Walworths.'

Sidwell had in fact sought information, but, as her relations with the Walworths were formal, such inquiry as she could make from them elicited nothing more than she already knew from Sylvia.

'Are you anxious to discover who they are?' she asked.

'Oh, not particularly.'

Buckland moved uneasily, and became silent.

'I dined with Walsh yesterday,' he said, at length, struggling to shake off the obvious dreariness that oppressed him. 'He suits me; we can get on together.'

'No doubt.'

'But you don't dislike him, I think?'

'Implying that I dislike *you*,' said Sidwell, lightsomely.

'You have no affection for my opinions. – Walsh is an honest man.'

'I hope so.'

'He says what he thinks. No compromise with fashionable hypocrisy.'

'I despise that kind of thing quite as much as you do.'

They looked at each other. Buckland had a sullen air.

'Yes, in your own way,' he replied, 'you are sincere enough, I have no doubt. I wish all women were so.'

'What exception have you in mind?'

He did not seem inclined to answer.

'Perhaps it is your understanding of them that's at fault,' added Sidwell, gently.

'Not in one case, at all events,' he exclaimed. 'Suppose you were asked to define Miss Moorhouse's religious opinions, how would you do it?'

'I am not well enough acquainted with them.'

'Do you imagine for a moment that she has any more faith in the supernatural than I have?'

'I think there is a great difference between her position and yours.'

'Because she is hypocritical!' cried Buckland, angrily. 'She deceives you. She hasn't the courage to be honest.'

Sidwell wore a pained expression.

'You judge her,' she replied, 'far too coarsely. No one is called upon to make an elaborate declaration of faith as often as such subjects are spoken of. Sylvia thinks so differently from you about almost everything that, when she happens to agree with you, you are misled and misinterpret her whole position.'

'I understand her perfectly,' Buckland went on, in the same irritated voice. 'There are plenty of women like her – with brains enough, but utter and contemptible cowards. Cowards even to themselves, perhaps. What can you expect, when society is based on rotten shams?'

For several minutes he pursued this vein of invective, then took an abrupt leave. Sidwell had a piece of grave counsel ready to offer him, but he was clearly in no mood to listen, so she postponed it.

A day or two after this, she received a letter from Sylvia. Miss Moorhouse was anything but a good correspondent; she often confessed her inability to compose anything but the briefest and driest statement of facts. With no little surprise, therefore, Sidwell found that the envelope contained two sheets all but covered with her friend's cramped handwriting. The letter began with apology for long delay in acknowledging two communications.

'But you know well enough my dilatory disposition. I have written to you mentally at least once a day, and I hope you have mentally received the results – that is to say, have assured yourself of my goodwill to you, and I had nothing else to send.'

At this point Sylvia had carefully obliterated two lines, blackening the page into unsightliness. In vain Sidwell pored over the effaced passage, led to do so by a fancy that she could discern a capital P, which looked like the first letter of a name. The writer continued:

'Don't trouble yourself so much about insoluble questions. Try to be more positive – I don't say become a Positivist. Keep a receptive mind, and wait for time to shape your views of things. I see that London has agitated and confused you; you have lost your bearings amid the maze of contradictory finger-posts. If you were here I could soothe you with Sylvian (much the same as sylvan) philosophy, but I can't write.'

Here the letter was to have ended, for on the line beneath was legible 'Give my love to Fanny', but this again had been crossed out, and there followed a long paragraph:

'I have been reading a book about ants. Perhaps you know all the wonderful things about them, but I had neglected that branch of natural history. Their doings are astonishingly like those of an animal called man, and it seems to me that I have discovered onepoint of resemblance which perhaps has never been noted. Are you aware that at an early stage of their existence ants have wings? They fly – how shall I express it? – only for the brief time of their courtship and marriage, and when these important affairs are satisfactorily done with their wings wither away, and thenceforth they have to content themselves with running about on the earth. Now isn't this a remarkable parallel to one stage of human life? Do not men and women also soar and flutter – at a certain time? And don't their wings manifestly drop off as soon as the end of that skyward movement has been achieved? If the gods had made me poetical, I would sonnetise on this idea. Do you know any poet with a fondness for the ant-philosophy? If so, offer him this suggestion with liberty to "make any use of it he likes".

'But the fact of the matter is that some human beings are never winged at all. I am decidedly coming to the conclusion that I am one of those. Think of me henceforth as an apteryx – you have a dictionary at hand? Like the tailless fox, I might naturally maintain that my state is the more gracious, but honestly I am not assured of that. It may be (I half believe it is) a good thing to soar and flutter, and at times I regret that nature has forbidden me that experience. Decidedly I would never try *to persuade anyone else* to forego the use of wings. Bear this in mind, my dear girl. But I suspect that in time to come there will be an increasing number of female human creatures who from their birth are content with *walking*. Not long ago, I had occasion to hint that – though under another figure – to your brother Buckland. I hope he understood me – I think he did – and that he wasn't offended.

'I had something to tell you. I have forgotten it – never mind.'

And therewith the odd epistle was concluded. Sidwell perused the latter part several times. Of course she was at no loss to interpret it. Buckland's demeanour for the past two months had led her to surmise that his latest visit to Budleigh Salterton had finally extinguished the hopes which drew him in that direction. His recent censure of Sylvia might be thus explained. She grieved that her brother's suit should be discouraged, but could not persuade herself that Sylvia's decision was final. The idea of a match between those two was very pleasant to her. For Buckland she imagined it would be fraught with good results, and for Sylvia, on the whole, it might be the best thing.

Before she replied to her friend nearly a month passed, and Christmas was at hand. Again she had been much in society. Mr Walsh had renewed his unmistakable attentions, and, when her manner of meeting them began to trouble him with doubts, had cleared the air by making a formal offer of marriage. Sidwell's negative was absolute, much to her mother's relief. On the day of that event, she wrote rather a long letter to Sylvia, but Mr Walsh's name was not mentioned in it.

'Mother tells me [it began] that *your* mother has written to her from Salisbury, and that you yourself are going there for a stay of some weeks. I am sorry, for on the Monday after Christmas Day I shall be in Exeter, and hoped somehow to have seen you. We — mother and I — are going to run down together, to see after certain domestic affairs; only for three days at most.

'Your ant-letter was very amusing, but it saddened me, dear Sylvia. I can't make any answer. On these subjects it is very difficult even for the closest friends to open their minds to each other. I don't — and don't wish to — believe in the *apteryx* profession; that's all I must say.

'My health has been indifferent since I last wrote. We live in all but continuous darkness, and very seldom indeed breathe anything that can be called air. No doubt this state of things has its effect on me. I look forwards, not to the coming of spring, for here we shall see nothing of its beauties, but to the month which will release us from London. I want to smell the pines again, and to see the golden gorse in *our* road.

'By way of being more "positive", I have read much in the newspapers, supplementing from them my own experience of London society. The result is that I am more and more confirmed in the fears with which I have already worried you. Two movements are plainly going on in the life of our day. The decay of religious belief is undermining morality, and the progress of Radicalism in politics is working to the same end by overthrowing social distinctions. Evidence stares one in the face from every column of the papers. Of course you have read more or less about the recent "scandal" — I mean the *most* recent. — It isn't the kind of thing one cares to discuss, but we can't help knowing about it, and does it not strongly support what I say? Here is materialism sinking into brutal immorality, and high social rank degrading itself by intimacy with the corrupt vulgar. There are newspapers that make political capital out of these "revelations". I have read some of them, and they make me so *fiercely* aristocratic that I find it hard to care anything at all even for the humanitarian efforts of people I respect. You will tell me, I know, that this is quite the wrong way of looking at it. But the evils are so monstrous that it is hard to fix one's mind on the good that may long hence result from them.

'I cling to the essential (that is the *spiritual*) truths of Christianity as the only absolute good left in our time. I would say that I care nothing for forms, but some form there must be, else one's faith evaporates. It has become very easy for me to understand how men and women who know the world refuse to believe any longer in a directing Providence. A week ago I again met Miss Moxey at the Walworths', and talked with her more freely than before. This conversation showed me that I have become much more tolerant towards individuals. But though this or that person may be supported by moral sense alone, the world cannot dispense with religion. If it tries to – and it *will* – there are dreadful times before us.

'I wish I were a man! I would do something, however ineffectual. I would stand on the side of those who are fighting against mob-rule and mob-morals. How would you like to see Exeter Cathedral converted into a "coffee music-hall"? And that will come.'

Reading this, Sylvia had the sense of listening to an echo. Some of the phrases recalled to her quite a different voice from Sidwell's. She smiled and mused.

On the morning appointed for her journey to Exeter Sidwell rose early, and in unusually good spirits. Mrs Warricombe was less animated by the prospect of five hours in a railway carriage, for London had a covering of black snow, and it seemed likely that more would fall. Martin suggested postponement, but circumstances made this undesirable.

'Let Fanny go with me,' proposed Sidwell, just after breakfast. 'I can see to everything perfectly well, mother.'

But Fanny hastened to decline. She was engaged for a dance on the morrow.

'Then I'll run down with you myself, Sidwell,' said her father.

Mrs Warricombe looked at the weather and hesitated. There were strong reasons why she should go, and they determined her to brave discomforts.

It chanced that the morning post had brought Mr Warricombe a letter from Godwin Peak. It was a reply to one that he had written with Christmas greetings; a kindness natural in him, for he had remembered that the young man was probably hard at work in his lonely lodgings. He spoke of it privately to his wife.

'A very good letter – thoughtful and cheerful. You're not likely to see him, but if you happen to, say a pleasant word.'

'I shouldn't have written, if I were you,' remarked Mrs Warricombe.

'Why not? I was only thinking the other day that he contrasted very favourably with the younger generation as we observe it here. Yes, I have faith in Peak. There's the right stuff in him.'

'Oh, I daresay. But still'—

And Mrs Warricombe went away with an air of misgiving.

V

In volunteering a promise not to inform her brother of Peak's singular position, Marcella spoke with sincerity. She was prompted by incongrous feelings – a desire to compel Godwin's gratitude, and disdain of the circumstances in which she had discovered him. There seemed to be little likelihood of Christian's learning from any other person that she had met with Peak at Budleigh Salterton; he had, indeed, dined with her at the Walworths', and might improve his acquaintance with that family, but it was improbable that they would ever mention in his hearing the stranger who had casually been presented to them, or indeed ever again think of him. If she held her peace, the secret of Godwin's retirement must still remain impenetrable. He would pursue his ends as hitherto, thinking of *her*, if at all, as a weak woman who had immodestly betrayed a hopeless passion, and who could be trusted never to wish him harm.

That was Marcella's way of reading a man's thoughts. She did not attribute to Peak the penetration which would make him uneasy. In spite of masculine proverbs, it is the habit of women to suppose that the other sex regards them confidingly, ingenuously. Marcella was unusually endowed with analytic intelligence, but in this case she believed what she hoped. She knew that Peak's confidence in her must be coloured with contempt, but this mattered little so long as he paid her the compliment of feeling sure that she was superior to ignoble temptations. Many a woman would behave with treacherous malice. It was in her power to expose him, to confound all his schemes, for she knew the authorship of that remarkable paper in *The Critical Review*. Before receiving Peak's injunction of secrecy, Earwaker had talked of 'The New Sophistry' with Moxey and with Malkin; the request came too late. In her interview with Godwin at the Exeter hotel, she had not even hinted at this knowledge, partly because she was unconscious that Peak imagined the affair a secret between himself and Earwaker, partly because she thought it unworthy of her even to seem to threaten. It gratified her, however, to feel that he was at her mercy, and the thought preoccupied her for many days.

Passion which has the intellect on its side is more easily endured than that which offers sensual defiance to all reasoning, but on the other hand it lasts much longer. Marcella was not consumed by her emotions; she often thought calmly, coldly, of the man she loved. Yet he was seldom long out of her mind, and the instigation of circumstances at times made her suffering intense. Such an occasion was her first meeting with Sidwell Warricombe, which took place at the Walworths', in London. Down in Devonshire she had learnt that a family named Warricombe were Peak's intimate friends; nothing more than this, for indeed no one was in a position to tell her more. Wakeful jealousy caused her to fix upon the fact as one of significance; Godwin's evasive manner when she questioned him confirmed her suspicions; and as soon as she was brought face to face with Sidwell, suspicion became certainty. She knew at once that Miss Warricombe was the very person who would be supremely attractive to Godwin Peak.

An interval of weeks, and again she saw the face that in the meantime had been as present to her imagination as Godwin's own features. This time she conversed at some length with Miss Warricombe. Was it merely a fancy that the beautiful woman looked at her, spoke to her, with some exceptional interest? By now she had learnt that the Moorhouses and the Warricombes were connected in close friendship: it was all but certain, then, that Miss Moorhouse had told Miss Warricombe of Peak's visit to Budleigh Salterton, and its incidents. Could this in any way be explanatory of the steady, searching look in those soft eyes?

Marcella had always regarded the emotion of jealousy as characteristic of a vulgar nature. Now that it possessed her, she endeavoured to call it by other names; to persuade herself that she was indignant on abstract grounds, or anxious only with reference to Peak's true interests. She could not affect surprise. So intensely sympathetic was her reading of Godwin's character that she understood – or at all events recognised – the power Sidwell would possess over him. He did not care for enlightenment in a woman; he was sensual – though in a subtle way; the aristocratic vein in his temper made him subject to strong impressions from trivialities of personal demeanour, of social tone.

Yet all was mere conjecture. She had not dared to utter Peak's name, lest in doing so she should betray herself. Constantly planning to make further discoveries, she as constantly tried to dismiss all thought of the matter – to learn indifference. Already she had debased herself, and her nature must be contemptible indeed if anything could lure her forward on such a path.

None the less, she was assiduous in maintaining friendly relations with the Walworths. Christian, too, had got into the habit of calling there; it was significant of the noticeable change which was come upon him – a change his sister was at no loss to understand from the moment that he informed her (gravely, but without expressiveness) of Mr Palmer's death. Instead of shunning ordinary society, he seemed bent on extending the circle of his acquaintance. He urged Marcella to invite friendly calls, to have guests at dinner. There seemed to be a general revival of his energies, exhibited in the sphere of study as well as of amusement. Not a day went by without his purchasing books or scientific apparatus, and the house was brightened with works of art chosen in the studios which Miss Walworth advised him to visit. All the amiabilities of his character came into free play; with Marcella he was mirthful, affectionate, even caressing. He grew scrupulous about his neckties, his gloves, and was careful to guard his fingers against corroding acids when he worked in the laboratory. Such indications of hopefulness caused Marcella more misgiving than pleasure; she made no remark, but waited with anxiety for some light on the course of events.

Just before dinner, one evening, as she sat alone in the drawing-room, Christian entered with a look which portended some strange announcement. He spoke abruptly:

'I have heard something astonishing.'

'What is that?'

'This afternoon I went to the matinée at the Vaudeville, and found myself among a lot of our friends – the Walworths and the Hunters and the Mortons. Between the acts I was talking to Hunter, when a man came up to us, spoke to Hunter, and was introduced to me – a Mr Warricombe. What do you think he said? "I believe you know my friend Peak, Mr Moxey?" "Peak? To be sure! Can you tell me what has become of him?" He gave me an odd look. "Why, I met him last, some two months ago, in Devonshire." At that moment we were obliged to go to our places, and I couldn't get hold of the fellow again. Hunter told me something about him; he knows the Walworths, it seems – belongs to a good Devonshire family. What on earth can Peak be doing over there?'

Marcella kept silence. The event she had judged improbable had come to pass. The chance of its doing so had of course increased since Christian began to associate freely with the .

Walworths and their circle. Yet, considering the slightness of the
connection between that group of people and the Warricombe
family, there had seemed no great likelihood of Christian's getting
acquainted with the latter. She debated rapidly in her troubled
mind how to meet this disclosure. Curiosity would, of course,
impel her brother to follow up the clue; he would again encounter
Warricombe, and must then learn all the facts of Peak's position.
To what purpose should she dissemble her own knowledge?

Did she desire that Godwin should remain in security? A tremor
more akin to gladness than its opposite impeded her utterance. If
Warricombe became aware of all that was involved in Godwin
Peak's withdrawal from among his friends – if (as must follow) he
imparted the discovery to his sister—

The necessity of speaking enabled her to ignore these turbulent
speculations, which yet were anything but new to her.

'They met at Budleigh Salterton,' she said, quietly.

'Who did? Warricombe and Peak?'

'Yes. At the Moorhouses'. It was when I was there.'

Christian stared at her.

'When you were there? But – *you* met Peak?'

His sister smiled, turning from the astonished gaze.

'Yes, I met him.'

'But, why the deuce—? Why didn't you tell me, Marcella?'

'He asked me not to speak of it. He didn't wish you to know
that – that he has decided to become a clergyman.'

Christian was stricken dumb. In spite of his sister's obvious
agitation, he could not believe what she told him; her smile gave
him an excuse for supposing that she jested.

'Peak a clergyman?' He burst out laughing. 'What's the
meaning of all this? – Do speak intelligibly! What's the fellow up
to?'

'I am quite serious. He is studying for Orders – has been for this
last year.'

In desperation, Christian turned to another phase of the
subject.

'Then Malkin *was* mistaken?'

'Plainly.'

'And you mean to tell me that Peak—? Give me more details.
Where's he living? How has he got to know people like these
Warricombes?'

Marcella told all that she knew, and without injunction of

secrecy. The affair had passed out of her hands; destiny must fulfil itself. And again the tremor that resembled an uneasy joy went through her frame.

'But how,' asked Christian, 'did this fellow Warricombe come to know that *I* was a friend of Peak's?'

'That's a puzzle to me. I shouldn't have thought he would have remembered my name; and, even if he had, how could he conclude—'

She broke off, pondering. Warricombe must have made inquiries, possibly suggested by suspicions.

'I scarcely spoke of Mr Peak to anyone,' she added. 'People saw, of course, that we were acquaintances, but it couldn't have seemed a thing of any importance.'

'You spoke with him in private, it seems?'

'Yes, I saw him for a few minutes – in Exeter.'

'And you hadn't said anything to the Walworths that – that would surprise them?'

'Purposely not. – Why should I injure him?'

Christian knit his brows. He understood too well why his sister should refrain from such injury.

'You would have behaved in the same way,' Marcella added.

'Why really – yes, perhaps so. Yet I don't know. – In plain English, Peak is a wolf in sheep's clothing!'

'I don't know anything about that,' she replied, with gloomy evasion.

'Nonsense, my dear girl! – Had he the impudence to pretend to you that he was sincere?'

'He made no declaration.'

'But you are convinced he is acting the hypocrite, Marcella. You spoke of the risk of injuring him. – What are his motives? What does he aim at?'

'Scarcely a bishopric, I should think,' she replied, bitterly.

'Then, by Jove! Earwaker may be right!'

Marcella darted an inquiring look at him.

'What has he thought?'

'I'm ashamed to speak of it. He suggested once that Peak might disguise himself for the sake of – of making a good marriage.'

The reply was a nervous laugh.

'Look here, Marcella.' He caught her hand. 'This is a very awkward business. Peak is disgracing himself; he will be un-masked; there'll be a scandal. It was kind of you to keep silence –

when don't you behave kindly, dear girl? – but think of the possible results to *us*. We shall be something very like accomplices.'

'How?' Marcella exclaimed, impatiently. 'Who need know that we were so intimate with him?'

'Warricombe seems to know it.'

'Who can prove that he isn't sincere?'

'No one, perhaps. But it will seem a very odd thing that he hid away from all his old friends. You remember, I betrayed that to Warricombe, before I knew that it mattered.'

Yes, and Mr Warricombe could hardly forget the circumstance. He would press his investigation – knowing already, perhaps, of Peak's approaches to his sister Sidwell.

'Marcella, a man plays games like that at his own peril. I don't like this kind of thing. Perhaps he has audacity enough to face out any disclosure. But it's out of the question for you and me to nurse his secret. We have no right to do so.'

'You propose to denounce him?'

Marcella gazed at her brother with an agitated look.

'Not denounce. I am fond of Peak; I wish him well. But I can't join him in a dishonourable plot. – Then, we mustn't endanger our place in society.'

'I have no place in society,' Marcella answered, coldly.

'Don't say that, and don't think it. We are both going to make more of our lives; we are going to think very little of the past, and a great deal of the future. We are still young; we have happiness before us.'

'We?' she asked, with shaken voice.

'Yes – both of us! Who can say'—

Again he took her hand and pressed it warmly in both his own. Just then the door opened, and dinner was announced. Christian talked on, in low hurried tones, for several minutes, affectionately, encouragingly. After dinner, he wished to resume the subject, but Marcella declared that there was no more to be said; he must act as honour and discretion bade him; for herself, she should simply keep silence as hitherto. And she left him to his reflections.

Though with so little of ascertained fact to guide her, Marcella interpreted the hints afforded by her slight knowledge of the Warricombes with singular accuracy. Precisely as she had imagined, Buckland Warricombe was going about on Peak's track, learning all he could concerning the theological student, forming acquaintance with anyone likely to supplement his discoveries. And less than a fortnight after the meeting at the theatre, Christian made known to his sister that Warricombe and he had had a second conversation, this time uninterrupted.

'He inquired after you, Marcella, and – really I had no choice but to ask him to call here. I hardly think he'll come. He's not the kind of man I care for – though liberal enough, and all that.'

'Wasn't it rather rash to give that invitation?'

'The fact was, I so dreaded the appearance of – of seeming to avoid him,' Christian pleaded, awkwardly. 'You know, that affair – we won't talk any more of it; but, if there *should* be a row about it, you are sure to be compromised unless we have managed to guard ourselves. If Warricombe calls, we must talk about Peak without the least show of restraint. Let it appear that we thought his choice of a profession unlikely, but not impossible. Happily, we needn't know anything about that anonymous *Critical* article. – Indeed, I think I have acted wisely.'

Marcella murmured:

'Yes, I suppose you have.'

'And, by the way, I have spoken of it to Earwaker. Not of your part in the story, of course. I told him that I had met a man who knew all about Peak. – Impossible, you see, for me to keep silence with so intimate a friend.'

'Then Mr Earwaker will write to him?' said Marcella, reflectively.

'I couldn't give him any address.'

'How does Mr Warricombe seem to regard Mr Peak?'

'With a good deal of interest, and of the friendliest kind. Naturally enough; they were College friends, as you know, before I had heard of Peak's existence.'

'He has no suspicions?'

Christian thought not, but her brother's judgment had not much weight with Marcella.

She at once dreaded and desired Warricombe's appearance. If he thought it worth while to cultivate her acquaintance, she would henceforth have the opportunity of studying Peak's relations with the Warricombes; on the other hand, this was to expose herself to suffering and temptation from which the better part of her nature shrank with disdain. That she might seem to have broken the promise voluntarily made to Godwin was a small matter; not so the risk of being overcome by an ignoble jealousy. She had no overweening confidence in the steadfastness of her self-respect, if circumstances were all on the side of sensual impulse. And the longer she brooded on this peril, the more it allured her. For therewith was connected the one satisfaction which still remained to her: however little he desired to keep her constantly in mind, Godwin Peak must of necessity do so after what had passed between them. Had but her discovery remained her own secret, then the pleasure of commanding her less pure emotions, of proving to Godwin that she was above the weakness of common women, might easily have prevailed. Now that her knowledge was shared by others, she had lost that safeguard against lower motive. The argument that to unmask hypocrisy was in itself laudable she dismissed with contempt; let that be the resource of a woman who would indulge her rancour whilst keeping up the inward pretence of sanctity. If *she* erred in the ways characteristic of her sex, it should at all events be a conscious degradation.

'Have you seen that odd creature Malkin lately?' she asked of Christian, a day or two after.

'No, I haven't; I thought of him to make up our dinner on Sunday; but you had rather not have him here, I daresay?'

'Oh, he is amusing. Ask him by all means,' said Marcella, carelessly.

'He may have heard about Peak from Earwaker, you know. If he begins to talk before people'—

'Things have gone too far for such considerations,' replied his sister, with a petulance strange to her habits of speech.

'Well, yes,' admitted Christian, glancing at her. 'We can't be responsible.'

He reproached himself for this attitude towards Peak, but was heartily glad that Marcella seemed to have learnt to regard the intriguer with a wholesome indifference.

On the second day after Christmas, as they sat talking idly in the dusking twilight, the door of the drawing-room was thrown open, and a visitor announced. The name answered with such startling suddenness to the thought with which Marcella had been occupied that, for an instant, she could not believe that she had heard aright. Yet it was undoubtedly Mr Warricombe who presented himself. He came forward with a slightly hesitating air, but Christian made haste to smooth the situation. With the help of those commonplaces by which even intellectual people are at times compelled to prove their familiarity with social usages, conversation was set in movement.

Buckland could not be quite himself. The consciousness that he had sought these people not at all for their own sake made him formal and dry; his glances, his half-smile, indicated a doubt whether the Moxeys belonged entirely to the sphere in which he was at home. Hence a rather excessive politeness, such as the man who sets much store on breeding exhibits to those who may at any moment, even in a fraction of a syllable, prove themselves his inferiors. With men and women of the unmistakably lower orders, Buckland could converse in a genial tone that recommended him to their esteem; on the borderland of refinement, his sympathies were repressed, and he held the distinctive part of his mind in reserve.

Marcella desired to talk agreeably, but a weight lay upon her tongue; she was struck with the resemblance in Warricombe's features to those of his sister, and this held her in a troubled preoccupation, occasionally evident when she made a reply, or tried to diversify the talk by leading to a new topic. It was rather early in the afternoon, and she had slight hope that any other caller would appear; a female face would have been welcome to her, even that of foolish Mrs Morton, who might possibly look in before six o'clock. To her relief the door did presently open, but the sharp, creaking footstep which followed was no lady's; the servant announced Mr Malkin.

Marcella's eyes gleamed strangely. Not with the light of friendly welcome, though for that it could be mistaken. She rose quietly, and stepped forward with a movement which again seemed to betoken eagerness of greeting. In presenting the newcomer to Mr Warricombe, she spoke with an uncertain voice. Buckland was more than formal. The stranger's aspect impressed him far from favourably, and he resented as an impudence the hearty hand-grip to which he perforce submitted.

'I come to plead with you,' exclaimed Malkin, turning to Marcella, in his abrupt, excited way. 'After accepting your invitation to dine, I find that the thing is utterly and absolutely impossible. I had entirely forgotten an engagement of the very gravest nature. I am conscious of behaving in quite an unpardonable way.'

Marcella laughed down his excuses. She had suddenly become so mirthful that Christian looked at her in surprise, imagining that she was unable to restrain her sense of the ridiculous in Malkin's demeanour.

'I have hurried up from Wrotham,' pursued the apologist. 'Did I tell you, Moxey, that I had taken rooms down there, to be able to spend a day or two near my friends the Jacoxes occasionally? On the way here, I looked in at Staple Inn, but Earwaker is away somewhere. What an odd thing that people will go off without letting one know! It's such common ill-luck of mine to find people gone away – I'm really astonished to find you at home, Miss Moxey.'

Marcella looked at Warricombe and laughed.

'You must understand that subjectively,' she said, with nervous gaiety which again excited her brother's surprise. 'Please don't be discouraged by it from coming to see us again; I am very rarely out in the afternoon.'

'But,' persisted Malkin, 'it's precisely my ill fortune to hit on those rare moments when people *are* out! – Now, I never meet acquaintances in the streets of London; but, if I happen to be abroad, as likely as not I encounter the last person I should expect to find. Why, you remember, I rush over to America for scarcely a week's stay, and there I come across a man who has disappeared astonishingly from the ken of all his friends!'

Christian looked at Marcella. She was leaning forward, her lips slightly parted, her eyes wide as if in gaze at something that fascinated her. He saw that she spoke, but her voice was hardly to be recognised.

'Are you quite sure of that instance, Mr Malkin?'

'Yes, I feel quite sure, Miss Moxey. Undoubtedly it was Peak!'

Buckland Warricombe, who had been waiting for a chance of escape, suddenly wore a look of interest. He rapidly surveyed the trio. Christian, somewhat out of countenance, tried to answer Malkin in a tone of light banter.

'It happens, my dear fellow, that Peak has not left England since we lost sight of him.'

'What? He has been heard of? Where is he then?'

'Mr Warricombe can assure you that he has been living for a year at Exeter.'

Buckland, perceiving that he had at length come upon something important to his purposes, smiled genially.

'Yes, I have had the pleasure of seeing Peak down in Devon from time to time.'

'Then it was really an illusion!' cried Malkin. 'I was too hasty. Yet that isn't a charge that can be often brought against me, I think. Does Earwaker know of this?'

'He has lately heard,' replied Christian, who in vain sought for a means of checking Malkin's loquacity. 'I thought he might have told you.'

'Certainly not. The thing is quite new to me. And what is Peak doing down there, pray? Why did he conceal himself?'

Christian gazed appealingly at his sister. She returned the look steadily, but neither stirred nor spoke. It was Warricombe's voice that next sounded:

'Peak's behaviour seems mysterious,' he began, with ironic gravity. 'I don't pretend to understand him. What's *your* view of his character, Mr Malkin?'

'I know him very slightly indeed, Mr Warricombe. But I have a high opinion of his powers. I wonder he does so little. After that article of his in *The Critical*'—

Malkin became aware of something like agonised entreaty on Christian's countenance, but this had merely the effect of heightening his curiosity.

'In *The Critical?*' said Warricombe, eagerly. 'I didn't know of that. What was the subject?'

'To be sure, it was anonymous,' went on Malkin, without a suspicion of the part he was playing before these three excited people. 'A paper called "The New Sophistry", a tremendous bit of satire.'

Marcella's eyes closed as if a light had flashed before them; she drew a short sigh, and at once seemed to become quite at ease, the smile with which she regarded Warricombe expressing a calm interest.

'That article was Peak's?' Buckland asked, in a very quiet voice.

Christian at last found his opportunity.

'He never mentioned it to you? Perhaps he thought he had gone rather too far in his Broad Churchism, and might be misunderstood.'

'Broad Churchism?' cried Malkin. 'Uncommonly broad, I must say!'

And he laughed heartily; Marcella seemed to join in his mirth.

'Then it would surprise you,' said Buckland, in the same quiet tone as before, 'to hear that Peak is about to take Orders?'

'Orders? – For what?'

Christian laughed. The worst was over; after all, it came as a relief.

'Not for wines,' he replied. 'Mr Warricombe means that Peak is going to be ordained.'

Malkin's amazement rendered him speechless. He stared from one person to another, his features strangely distorted.

'You can hardly believe it?' pressed Buckland.

The reply was anticipated by Christian saying:

'Remember, Malkin, that you had no opportunity of studying Peak. It's not so easy to understand him.'

'But I don't see,' burst out the other, 'how I could possibly so *mis*understand him! What has Earwaker to say?'

Buckland rose from his seat, advanced to Marcella, and offered his hand. She said mechanically, 'Must you go?' but was incapable of another word. Christian came to her relief, performed the needful civilities, and accompanied his acquaintance to the foot of the stairs. Buckland had become grave, stiff, monosyllabic; Christian made no allusion to the scene thus suddenly interrupted, and they parted with a formal air.

Malkin remained for another quarter of an hour, when the muteness of his companions made it plain to him that he had better withdraw. He went off with a sense of having been mystified, half resentful, and vastly impatient to see Earwaker.

PART THE FIFTH

I

The cuckoo clock in Mrs Roots's kitchen had just struck three. A wind roared from the north-east, and light thickened beneath a sky which made threat of snow. Peak was in a mood to enjoy the crackling fire; he settled himself with a book in his easy-chair, and thought with pleasure of two hours' reading, before the appearance of the homely teapot.

Christmas was just over – one cause of the feeling of relief and quietness which possessed him. No one had invited him for Christmas Eve or the day that followed, and he did not regret it. The letter he had received from Martin Warricombe was assurance enough that those he desired to remember him still did so. He had thought of using this season for his long postponed visit to Twybridge, but reluctance prevailed. All popular holidays irritated and depressed him; he loathed the spectacle of multitudes in Sunday garb. It was all over, and the sense of that afforded him a brief content.

This book, which he had just brought from the circulating library, was altogether to his taste. The author, Justin Walsh, he knew to be a brother of Professor Walsh, long ago the object of his rebellious admiration. Matter and treatment rejoiced him. No intellectual delight, though he was capable of it in many forms, so stirred his spirit as that afforded him by a vigorous modern writer joyously assailing the old moralities. Justin Walsh was a modern of the moderns; at once man of science and man of letters; defiant without a hint of popular cynicism, scornful of English reticences yet never gross. '*Oui, répondit Pococurante, il est beau d'écrire ce qu'on pense; c'est le privilège de l'homme.*' This stood by way of motto on the title-page, and Godwin felt his nerves thrill in sympathetic response.

What a fine fellow he must be to have for a friend! Now a man like this surely had companionship enough and of the kind he wished? He wrote like one who associates freely with the educated classes both at home and abroad. Was he married? Where would *he* seek his wife? The fitting mate for him would doubtless be found among those women, cosmopolitan and emancipated, whose acquaintance falls only to men in easy circumstances and of good social standing, men who travel much, who are at home in all the great centres of civilisation.

As Peak meditated, the volume fell upon his knee. Had it not lain in his own power to win a reputation like that which Justin Walsh was achieving? His paper in *The Critical Review*, itself a decided success, might have been followed up by others of the same tenor. Instead of mouldering in a dull cathedral town, he might now be living and working in France or Germany. His money would have served one purpose as well as the other, and two or three years of determined effort—

Mrs Roots showed her face at the door.

'A gentleman is asking for you, sir, – Mr Chilvers.'

'Mr Chilvers? Please ask him to come up.'

He threw his book on to the table, and stood in expectancy. Someone ascended the stairs with rapid stride and creaking boots. The door was flung open, and a cordial but affected voice burst forth in greeting.

'Ha, Mr Peak! I hope you haven't altogether forgotten me? Delighted to see you again!'

Godwin gave his hand, and felt it strongly pressed, whilst Chilvers gazed into his face with a smiling wistfulness which could only be answered with a grin of discomfort. The Rev. Bruno had grown very tall, and seemed to be in perfect health; but the effeminacy of his brilliant youth still declared itself in his attitudes, gestures, and attire. He was dressed with marked avoidance of the professional pattern. A hat of soft felt but not clerical, fashionable collar and tie, a sweeping ulster, and beneath it a frock-coat, which was doubtless the pride of some West End tailor. His patent-leather boots were dandiacally diminutive; his glove fitted like that of a lady who lives but to be *bien gantée*. The feathery hair, which at Whitelaw he was wont to pat and smooth, still had its golden shimmer, and on his face no growth was permitted.

'I had heard of your arrival here, of course,' said Peak, trying to appear civil, though anything more than that was beyond his power. 'Will you sit down?'

'This is the "breathing time o' the day" with you, I hope? I don't disturb your work?'

'I was only reading this book of Walsh's. Do you know it?'

But for some such relief of his feelings, Godwin could not have sat still. There was a pleasure in uttering Walsh's name. Moreover, it would serve as a test of Chilvers' disposition.

'Walsh?' He took up the volume. 'Ha! Justin Walsh. I know him. A wonderful book! Admirable dialectic! Delicious style!'

'Not quite orthodox, I fancy,' replied Godwin, with a curling of the lips.

'Orthodox? Oh, of course not, of course not! But a rich vein of humanity. Don't you find that? – Pray allow me to throw off my overcoat. Ha, thanks! – A rich vein of humanity. Walsh is by no means to be confused with the nullifidians. A very broad-hearted, large-souled man; at bottom the truest of Christians. Now and then he effervesces rather too exuberantly. Yes, I admit it. In a review of his last book, which I was privileged to write for one of our papers, I ventured to urge upon him the necessity of *restraint*; it seems to me that in this new work he exhibits more self-control, an approach to the serene fortitude which I trust he may attain. A man of the broadest brotherliness. A most valuable ally of renascent Christianity.'

Peak was hardly prepared for this strain. He knew that Chilvers prided himself on 'breadth', but as yet he had enjoyed no intercourse with the broadest school of Anglicans, and was uncertain as to the limits of modern latitudinarianism. The discovery of such fantastic liberality in a man whom he could not but dislike and contemn gave him no pleasure, but at least it disposed him to amusement rather than antagonism. Chilvers' pronunciation and phraseology were distinguished by such original affectation that it was impossible not to find entertainment in listening to him. Though his voice was naturally thin and piping, he managed to speak in head notes which had a ring of robust utterance. The sound of his words was intended to correspond with their virile warmth of meaning. In the same way he had cultivated a habit of the muscles which conveyed an impression that he was devoted to athletic sports. His arms occasionally swung as if brandishing dumb-bells, his chest now and then spread itself to the uttermost, and his head was often thrown back in an attitude suggesting self-defence.

'So you are about to join us,' he exclaimed, with a look of

touching interest, much like that of a ladies' doctor speaking delicately of favourable symptoms. Then, as if consciously returning to the virile note, 'I think we shall understand each other. I am always eager to study the opinions of those among us who have scientific minds. I hear of you on all hands; already you have strongly impressed some of the thinking people in Exeter.'

Peak crossed his legs and made no reply.

'There is distinct need of an infusion of the scientific spirit into the work of the Church. The churchman hitherto has been, as a matter of course, of the literary stamp; hence much of our trouble during the last half-century. It behoves us to go in for science – physical, economic – science of every kind. Only thus can we resist the morbific influences which inevitably beset an Established Church in times such as these. I say it boldly. Let us throw aside our Hebrew and our Greek, our commentators ancient and modern! Let us have done with polemics and with compromises! What we have to do is to construct a spiritual edifice on the basis of scientific revelation. I use the word revelation advisedly. The results of science are the divine message to our age; to neglect them, to fear them, is to remain under the old law whilst the new is demanding our adherence, to repeat the Jewish error of bygone time. Less of St Paul, and more of Darwin! Less of Luther, and more of Herbert Spencer!'

'Shall I have the pleasure of hearing this doctrine at St Margaret's?' Peak inquired.

'In a form suitable to the intelligence of my parishioners, taken in the mass. Were my hands perfectly free, I should begin by preaching a series of sermons on *The Origin of Species*. Sermons! An obnoxious word! One ought never to use it. It signifies everything inept, inert.'

'Is it your serious belief, then, that the mass of parishioners – here or elsewhere – are ready for this form of spiritual instruction?'

'Most distinctly – given the true capacity in the teacher. Mark me; I don't say that they are capable of receiving much absolute knowledge. What I desire is that their minds shall be relieved from a state of harassing conflict – put at the right point of view. They are not to think that Jesus of Nazareth teaches faith and conduct incompatible with the doctrines of Evolutionism. They are not to spend their lives in kicking against the pricks, and regard as meritorious the punctures which result to them. The establish-

ment in their minds of a few cardinal facts – that is the first step.
Then let the interpretation follow – the solace, the encouragement, the hope for eternity!'

'You imagine,' said Godwin, with a calm air, 'that the mind of
the average church-goer is seriously disturbed on questions of
faith?'

'How can you ignore it, my dear Peak? – Permit me this
familiarity; we are old fellow-collegians. – The average church-
goer is the average citizen of our English commonwealth, – a man
necessarily aware of the great Radical movement, and all that it
involves. Forgive me. There has been far too much blinking of
actualities by zealous Christians whose faith is rooted in knowledge. We gain nothing by it; we lose immensely. Let us recognise
that our churches are filled with sceptics, endeavouring to believe
in spite of themselves.'

'Your experience is much larger than mine,' remarked the
listener, submissively.

'Indeed I have widely studied the subject.'

Chilvers smiled with ineffable self-content, his head twisted like
that of a sagacious parrot.

'Granting your average citizen,' said the other, 'what about the
average citizeness? The female church-goers are not insignificant
in number.'

'Ha! There we reach the core of the matter! Woman! woman!
Precisely *there* is the most hopeful outlook. I trust you are strong
for female emancipation?'

'Oh, perfectly sound on that question!'

'To be sure! Then it must be obvious to you that women are
destined to play the leading part in our Christian renascence,
precisely as they did in the original spreading of the faith. What
else is the meaning of the vast activity in female education? Let
them be taught, and forthwith they will rally to our Broad
Church. A man may be content to remain a nullifidian; women
cannot rest at that stage. They demand the spiritual significance of
everything. – I grieve to tell you, Peak, that for three years I have
been a widower. My wife died with shocking suddenness, leaving
me her two little children. Ah, but leaving me also the memory of a
singularly pure and noble being. I may say, with all humility, that I
have studied the female mind in its noblest modern type. I *know*
what can be expected of woman, in our day and in the future.'

'Mrs Chilvers was in full sympathy with your views?'

'Three years ago I had not yet reached my present standpoint. In several directions I was still narrow. But her prime characteristic was the tendency to spiritual growth. She would have accompanied me step by step. In very many respects I must regard myself as a man favoured by fortune, – I know it, and I trust I am grateful for it, – but that loss, my dear Peak, counterbalances much happiness. In moments of repose, when I look back on work joyously achieved, I often murmur to myself, with a sudden sigh, *Excepto quod non simul esses, cætera lætus!*'

He pronounced his Latin in the new-old way, with Continental vowels. The effect of this on an Englishman's lips is always more or less pedantic, and in his case it was intolerable.

'And when,' he exclaimed, dismissing the melancholy thought, 'do you present yourself for ordination?'

It was his habit to pay slight attention to the words of anyone but himself, and Peak's careless answer merely led him to talk on wide subjects with renewal of energy. One might have suspected that he had made a list of uncommon words wherewith to adorn his discourse, for certain of these frequently recurred. 'Nullifidian', 'morbific', 'renascent', were among his favourites. Once or twice he spoke of 'psychogenesis', with an emphatic enunciation which seemed to invite respectful wonder. In using Latin words which have become fixed in the English language, he generally corrected the common errors of quantity: '*minnus* the spiritual fervour', 'acting as his *loccum tennens*'. When he referred to Christian teachers with whom he was acquainted, they were seldom or never members of the Church of England. Methodists, Romanists, Presbyterians appeared to stand high in his favour, and Peak readily discerned that this was a way of displaying 'large-souled tolerance'. It was his foible to quote foreign languages, especially passages which came from heretical authors. Thus, he began to talk of Feuerbach for the sole purpose of delivering a German sentence.

'He has been of infinite value to me – quite infinite value. You remember his definition of God? It is constantly in my mind. "*Gott ist eine Träne der Liebe, in tiefster Verborgenheit vergossen über das menschliche Elend.*" Profoundly touching! I know nothing to approach it.'

Suddenly he inquired:

'Do you see much of the Exeter clergy?'

'I know only the Vicar of St Ethelreda's, Mr Lilywhite.'

'Ha! Admirable fellow! Large-minded, broad of sympathies. Has distinctly the scientific turn of thought.'

Peak smiled, knowing the truth. But he had hit upon a way of meeting the Rev. Bruno which promised greatly to diminish the suffering inherent in the situation. He would use the large-souled man deliberately for his mirth. Chilvers's self-absorption lent itself to persiflage, and by indulging in that mood Godwin tasted some compensation for the part he had to play.

'And I believe you know the Warricombes very well?' pursued Chilvers.

'Yes.'

'Ha! I hope to see much of them. They are people after my own heart. Long ago I had a slight acquaintance with them. I hear we shan't see them till the summer.'

'I believe not.'

'Mr Warricombe is a great geologist, I think? – Probably he frequents public worship as a mere tribute to social opinion?'

He asked the question in the airiest possible way, as if it mattered nothing to him what the reply might be.

'Mr Warricombe is a man of sincere piety,' Godwin answered, with grave countenance.

'That by no means necessitates church-going, my dear Peak,' rejoined the other, waving his hand.

'You think not? I am still only a student, you must remember. My mind is in suspense on not a few points.'

'Of course! Of course! Pray let me give you the results of my own thought on this subject.'

He proceeded to do so, at some length. When he had rounded his last period, he unexpectedly started up, swung on his toes, spread his chest, drew a deep breath, and with the sweetest of smiles announced that he must postpone the delight of further conversation.

'You must come and dine with me as soon as my house is in reasonable order. As yet, everything is *sens dessus-dessous*. Delightful old city, Exeter! Charming! Charming!'

And on the moment he was gone.

What were this man's real opinions? He had brains and literature; his pose before the world was not that of an ignorant charlatan. Vanity, no doubt, was his prime motive, but did it operate to make a cleric of a secret materialist, or to incite a display of excessive liberalism in one whose convictions were orthodox? Godwin could not answer to his satisfaction, but he preferred the latter surmise.

One thing, however, became clear to him. All his conscientious scruples about entering the Church were superfluous. Chilvers would have smiled pityingly at anyone who disputed his right to live by the Establishment, and to stand up as an authorised preacher of the national faith. And beyond a doubt he regulated his degree of 'breadth' by standards familiar to him in professional intercourse. To him it seemed all-sufficient to preach a gospel of moral progress, of intellectual growth, of universal fraternity. If this were the tendency of Anglicanism, then almost any man who desired to live a cleanly life, and to see others do the same, might without hesitation become a clergyman. The old formulæ of subscription were so symbolised, so volatilised, that they could not stand in the way of anyone but a combative nihilist. Peak was conscious of positive ideals by no means inconsistent with Christian teaching, and in his official capacity these alone would direct him.

He spent his evening pleasantly, often laughing as he recalled a phrase or gesture of the Rev. Bruno's.

In the night fell a sprinkling of snow, and when the sun rose it gleamed from a sky of pale, frosty blue. At ten o'clock Godwin set out for his usual walk, choosing the direction of the Old Tiverton Road. It was a fortnight since he had passed the Warricombes' house. At present he was disposed to indulge the thoughts which a sight of it would make active.

He had begun the ascent of the hill when the sound of an approaching vehicle caused him to raise his eyes – they were generally fixed on the ground when he walked alone. It was only a hired fly. But, as it passed him, he recognised the face he had least expected to see, – Sidwell Warricombe sat in the carriage, and unaccompanied. She noticed him – smiled – and bent forward. He clutched at his hat, but it happened that the driver had turned to look at him, and, instead of the salute he had intended, his hand waved to the man to stop. The gesture was scarcely voluntary; when he saw the carriage pull up, his heart sank; he felt guilty of monstrous impudence. But Sidwell's face appeared at the window, and its expression was anything but resentful; she offered her hand, too. Without preface of formal phrase he exclaimed:

'How delightful to see you so unexpectedly! Are you all here?'

'Only mother and I. We have come for a day or two.'

'Will you allow me to call? If only for a few minutes'—

'We shall be at home this afternoon.'

'Thank you! Don't you enjoy the sunshine after London?'

'Indeed I do!'

He stepped back and signed to the driver. Sidwell bent her head and was out of sight.

But the carriage was visible for some distance, and even when he could no longer see it he heard the horse's hoofs on the hard road. Long after the last sound had died away his heart continued to beat painfully, and he breathed as if recovering from a hard run.

How beautiful were these lanes and hills, even in mid-winter! Once more he sang aloud in his joyous solitude. The hope he had nourished was not unreasonable; his boldness justified itself. Yes, he was one of the men who succeed, and the life before him would be richer for all the mistakes and miseries through which he had passed. Thirty, forty, fifty – why, twenty years hence he would be in the prime of manhood, with perhaps yet another twenty years of mental and bodily vigour. One of the men who succeed!

On the morning after her journey down from London, Mrs Warricombe awoke with the conviction that she had caught a cold. Her health was in general excellent, and she had no disposition to nurse imaginary ailments, but when some slight disorder broke the routine of her life she made the most of it, enjoying – much as children do – the importance with which for the time it invested her. At such seasons she was wont to regard herself with a mildly despondent compassion, to feel that her family and her friends held her of slight account; she spoke in a tone of conscious resignation, often with a forgiving smile. When the girls redoubled their attentions, and soothed her with gentle words, she would close her eyes and sigh, seeming to remind them that they would know her value when she was no more.

'You are hoarse, mother,' Sidwell said to her, when they met at breakfast.

'Am I, dear? You know I felt rather afraid of the journey. I hope I shan't be laid up.'

Sidwell advised her not to leave the house to-day. Having seen the invalid comfortably established in an upper room, she went into the city on business which could not be delayed. On her way occurred the meeting with Peak, but of this, on her return, she made no mention. Mother and daughter had luncheon upstairs, and Sidwell was full of affectionate solicitude.

'This afternoon you had better lie down for an hour or two,' she said.

'Do you think so? Just drop a line to father, and warn him that we may kept here for some time.'

'Shall I send for Dr Endacott?'

'Just as you like, dear.'

But Mrs Warricombe had eaten such an excellent lunch, that Sidwell could not feel uneasy.

'We'll see how you are this evening. At all events, it will be safer for you not to go downstairs. If you lie quiet for an hour or two, I can look for those pamphlets that father wants.'

'Just as you like, dear.'

By three o'clock the invalid was calmly slumbering. Having entered the bedroom on tiptoe and heard regular breathing, Sidwell went down and for a few minutes lingered about the hall.

A servant came to her for instructions on some domestic matter; when this was dismissed she mentioned that, if anyone called, she would be found in the library.

The pamphlets of which her father had spoken were soon discovered. She laid them aside, and seated herself by the fire, but without leaning back. At any sound within or outside the house she moved her head to listen. Her look was anxious, but the gleam of her eyes expressed pleasurable agitation.

At half-past three she went into the drawing-room, where all the furniture was draped, and the floor bare. Standing where she could look from a distance through one of the windows, at which the blind had been raised, she waited for a quarter of an hour. Then the chill atmosphere drove her back to the fireside. In the study, evidences of temporary desertion were less oppressive, but the windows looked only upon a sequestered part of the garden. Sidwell desired to watch the approach from the high-road, and in a few minutes she was again in the drawing-room. But scarcely had she closed the door behind her when a ringing of the visitors' bell sounded with unfamiliar distinctness. She started, hastened from the room, fled into the library, and had time to seat herself before she heard the footsteps of a servant moving in answer to the summons.

The door opened, and Peak was announced.

Sidwell had never known what it was to be thus overcome with emotion. Shame at her inability to command the calm features with which she would naturally receive a caller flushed her cheeks and neck; she stepped forward with downcast eyes, and only in offering her hand could at length look at him who stood before her. She saw at once that Peak was unlike himself; he too had unusual warmth in his countenance, and his eyes seemed strangely large, luminous. On his forehead were drops of moisture.

This sight restored her self-control, or such measure of it as permitted her to speak in the conventional way.

'I am sorry that mother can't leave her room. She had a slight cold this morning, but I didn't think it would give her any trouble.'

Peak was delighted, and betrayed the feeling even whilst he constrained his face into a look of exaggerated anxiety.

'It won't be anything serious, I hope? The railway journey, I'm afraid.'

'Yes, the journey. She has a slight hoarseness, but I think we shall prevent it from'—

Their eyes kept meeting, and with more steadfastness. They were conscious of mutual scrutiny, and, on both sides, of changes since they last met. When two people have devoted intense study to each other's features, a three months' absence not only revives the old impressions but subjects them to sudden modification which engrosses thought and feeling. Sidwell continued to utter commonplaces, simply as a means of disguising the thoughts that occupied her; she was saying to herself that Peak's face had a purer outline than she had believed, and that his eyes had gained in expressiveness. In the same way Godwin said and replied he knew not what, just to give himself time to observe and enjoy the something new – the increased animation or subtler facial movements – which struck him as often as he looked at his companion. Each wondered what the other had been doing, whether the time had seemed long or short.

'I hope you have kept well?' Sidwell asked.

Godwin hastened to respond with civil inquiries.

'I was very glad to hear from Mr Warricombe a few days ago,' he continued. Sidwell was not aware that her father had written, but her pleased smile seemed to signify the contrary.

'She looks younger,' Peak said in his mind. 'Perhaps that London dress and the new way of arranging her hair have something to do with it. But no, she looks younger in herself. She must have been enjoying the pleasures of town.'

'You have been constantly occupied, no doubt,' he added aloud, feeling at the same time that this was a clumsy expression of what he meant. Though he had unbuttoned his overcoat, and seated himself as easily as he could, the absurd tall hat which he held embarrassed him; to deposit it on the floor demanded an effort of which he was yet incapable.

'I have seen many things and heard much talk,' Sidwell was replying, in a gay tone. It irritated him; he would have preferred her to speak with more of the old pensiveness. Yet perhaps she was glad simply because she found herself again talking with him?

'And you?' she went on. 'It has not been all work, I hope?'

'Oh no! I have had many pleasant intervals.'

This was in imitation of her vivacity. He felt the words and the manner to be ridiculous, but could not restrain himself. Every moment increased his uneasiness; the hat weighed in his hands like a lump of lead, and he was convinced that he had never looked so clownish. Did her smile signify criticism of his attitude?

With a decision which came he knew not how, he let his hat drop to the floor and pushed it aside. There, that was better; he felt less of a bumpkin.

Sidwell glanced at the glossy grotesque, but instantly averted her eyes, and asked rather more gravely:

'Have you been in Exeter all the time?'

'Yes.'

'But you didn't spend your Christmas alone, I hope?'

'Oh, I had my books.'

Was there not a touch of natural pathos in this? He hoped so; then mocked at himself for calculating such effects.

'I think you don't care much for ordinary social pleasures, Mr Peak?'

He smiled bitterly.

'I have never known much of them, – and you remember that I look forward to a life in which they will have little part. Such a life,' he continued, after a pause, 'seems to you unendurably dull? I noticed that, when I spoke of it before.'

'You misunderstood me.' She said it so undecidedly that he gazed at her with puzzled look. Her eyes fell.

'But you like society?'

'If you use the word in its narrowest meaning,' she answered, 'then I not only dislike society, but despise it.'

She had raised her eyebrows, and was looking coldly at him. Did she mean to rebuke him for the tone he had adopted? Indeed, he seemed to himself presumptuous. But if they were still on terms such as these, was it not better to know it, even at the cost of humiliation? One moment he believed that he could read Sidwell's thoughts, and that they were wholly favourable to him; at another he felt absolutely ignorant of all that was passing in her, and disposed to interpret her face as that of a conventional woman who had never regarded him as on her own social plane. These uncertainties, these frequent reversions to a state of mind which at other times he seemed to have long outgrown, were a singular feature of his relations with Sidwell. Could such experiences consist with genuine love? Never had he felt more willing to answer the question with a negative. He felt that he was come here to act a part, and that the end of the interview, be it what it might, would only affect him superficially.

'No,' he replied, with deliberation; 'I never supposed that you had any interest in the most foolish class of wealthy people. I meant that you recognise your place in a certain social rank, and regard intercourse with your equals as an essential of happiness.'

'If I understood why you ask'— she began abruptly, but ceased as she met his glance. Again he thought she was asserting a distant dignity.

'The question arose naturally out of a train of thought which always occupies me when I talk with you. I myself belong to no class whatever, and I can't help wondering how – if the subject ever occurred to you – you would place me.'

He saw his way now, and, having said thus much, could talk on defiantly. This hour must decide his fortune with Sidwell, yet his tongue utterly refused any of the modes of speech which the situation would have suggested to an ordinary mind. He could not 'make love'. Instead of humility, he was prompted to display a rough arrogance; instead of tender phrases, he uttered what sounded like deliberate rudeness. His voice was less gently tuned than Sidwell had been wont to hear it. It all meant that he despaired of wooing successfully, and more than half wished to force some word from Sidwell which would spare him the necessity of a plain avowal.

But before he had finished speaking, her face changed. A light of sudden understanding shone in her eyes; her lips softened to a smile of exquisite gentleness.

'The subject never *did* occur to me,' she answered. 'How should it? A friend is a friend.'

It was not strictly true, but in the strength of her emotion she could forget all that contradicted it.

'A friend – yes.'

Godwin began with the same note of bluntness. But of a sudden he felt the influence of Sidwell's smile. His voice sank into a murmur, his heart leapt, a thrill went through his veins.

'I wish to be something more than a friend.'

He felt that it was bald, inadequate. Yet the words had come of their own accord, on an impulse of unimpaired sincerity. Sidwell's head was bent.

'That is why I can't take simple things for granted,' he continued, his gaze fixed upon her. 'If I thought of nothing but friendship, it would seem rational enough that you should accept me for what I am – a man of education, talking your own language. Because I have dared to hope something more, I suffer from the thought that I was not born into your world, and that you must be always remembering this difference.'

'Do you think me so far behind the age?' asked Sidwell, trying to laugh.

'Classes are getting mixed, confused. Yes, but we are so conscious of the process that we talk of class distinctions more than of anything else, – talk and think of them incessantly. You have never heard me make a profession of Radicalism; *I* am decidedly behind the age. Be what I may – and I have spiritual pride more than enough – the fact that I have relatives in the lower, even the lowest, social class must necessarily affect the whole course of my life. A certain kind of man declares himself proud of such an origin – and most often lies. Or one may be driven by it into rebellion against social privilege. To me, my origin is simply a grave misfortune, to be accepted and, if possible, overcome. Does that sound mean-spirited? I can't help it; I want you to know me.'

'I believe I know you very well,' Sidwell replied.

The consciousness that she was deceived checked the words which were rising to his lips. Again he saw himself in a pitiful light, and this self-contempt reflected upon Sidwell. He could not doubt that she was yielding to him; her attitude and her voice declared it; but what was the value of love won by imposture? Why had she not intelligence enough to see through his hypocrisy, which at times was so thin a veil? How defective must her sympathy be!

'Yet you have seen very little of me,' he said, smiling.

There was a short silence; then he exclaimed in a voice of emotion:

'How I wish we had known each other ever since that day when your brother brought me to your house near Kingsmill! If we had met and talked through all those years! But that was impossible for the very reason which makes me inarticulate now that I wish to say so much. When you first saw me I was a gawky schoolboy, learning to use my brains, and knowing already that life had nothing to offer me but a false position. Whether I remained with my kith and kin, or turned my back upon them in the hope of finding my equals, I was condemned to a life of miserable incompleteness. I was born in exile. It took a long time before I had taught myself how to move and speak like one of the class to which I belonged by right of intellect. I was living alone in London, in mean lodging-houses. But the day came when I felt more confidence in myself. I had saved money, and foresaw that in a year or two I should be able to carry out a plan, make one serious attempt to win a position among educated people.'

He stopped. Had he intended a full confession, it was thus he might have begun it. Sidwell was regarding him, but with a gentle look, utterly unsuspecting. She was unable to realise his character and his temptations.

'And have you not succeeded?' she asked, in a low voice.

'Have I? Let me put it to the test. I will set aside every thought of presumption; forget that I am a penniless student looking forward to a country curacy; and say what I wished to when we had our last conversation. Never mind how it sounds. I have dared to hope that some day I shall ask you to be my wife, and that you won't refuse.'

The word 'wife' reverberated on his ears. A whirl of emotion broke the defiant calm he had supported for the last few minutes. The silence seemed to be endless; when he looked at Sidwell, her head was bent, the eyes concealed by their drooping lids. Her expression was very grave.

'Such a piece of recklessness,' he said at length, 'deserves no answer.'

Sidwell raised her eyes and spoke gently, with voice a little shaken.

'Why should you call it recklessness? I have never thought of the things that seem to trouble you so much. You were a friend of ours. Wasn't that enough?'

It seemed to him an evasive reply. Doubtless it was much that she showed neither annoyance nor prudish reserve. He had won the right of addressing her on equal terms, but she was not inclined to anticipate that future day to which he pointed.

'You have never thought of such things, because you have never thought of me as I of you. Every day of your absence in London has caused me torments which were due most often to the difference between your social position and mine. You have been among people of leisure and refinement and culture. Each evening you have talked with men whom it cost no effort to make themselves liked and respected. I think of that with bitterness.'

'But why? I have made many acquaintances; have met very interesting people. I am glad of it; it enables me to understand you better than I could before.'

'You are glad on that account?'

'Yes; indeed I am.'

'Dare I think you mean more than a civil phrase?'

'I mean quite simply all that my words imply. I have thought of you, though certainly without bitterness. No one's conversation in London interested me so much as yours.'

Soothed with an exquisite joy, Godwin felt his eyes moisten. For a moment he was reconciled to all the world, and forgot the hostilities of a lifetime.

'And will it still be so, now, when you go back?' he asked, in a soft tone.

'I am sure it will.'

'Then it will be strange if I ever feel bitterly again.'

Sidwell smiled.

'You could have said nothing that could please me more. Why should your life be troubled by these dark moods? I could understand it if you were still struggling with – with doubts, with all manner of uncertainties about your course'—

She hesitated, watching his face.

'You think I have chosen well?' said Godwin, meeting her look.

Sidwell's eyes were at once averted.

'I hope,' she said, 'we may talk of that again very soon. You have told me much of yourself, but I have said little or nothing of my own – difficulties. It won't be long before we come back from London, and then'—

Once more their eyes met steadily.

'You think,' Godwin asked, 'that I am right in aiming at a life of retirement?'

'It is one of my doubts. Your influence would be useful anywhere; but most useful, surely, among people of active mind.'

'Perhaps I shan't be able to choose. Remember that I am seeking for a livelihood as well as for a sphere of usefulness.'

His eyes fell as he spoke. Hitherto he had had no means of learning whether Sidwell would bring her husband a dowry substantial enough to be considered. Though he could not feel that she had betrothed herself to him, their talk was so nearly that of avowed lovers that perchance she would disclose whatever might help to put his mind at rest. The thought revived his painful self-consciousness; it was that of a schemer, yet would not the curse of poverty have suggested it to any man?

'Perhaps you won't be able to choose – at first,' Sidwell

assented, thereby seeming to answer his unspoken question. 'But I am sure my father will use whatever influence he has.'

Had he been seated near enough, he would have been tempted to the boldness of taking her hand. What more encouragement did he await? But the distance between them was enough to check his embarrassed impulses. He could not even call her 'Sidwell'; it would have been easier a few minutes ago, before she had begun to speak with such calm friendliness. Now, in spite of everything, he felt that to dare such a familiarity must needs call upon him the reproof of astonished eyes.

'You return to-morrow?' he asked, suddenly.

'I think so. You have promised me to be cheerful until we are home again.'

'A promise to be cheerful wouldn't mean much. But it *does* mean much that I can think of what you have said to-day.'

Sidwell did not speak, and her silence seemed to compel him to rise. It was strange how remote he still felt from her pure, grave face, and the flowing outlines of her figure. Why could he not say to her, 'I love you; give me your hands; give me your lips'? Such words seemed impossible. Yet passion thrilled in him as he watched the grace of her movements, the light and shadow upon her features. She had risen and come a step or two forward.

'I think you look taller – in that dress.'

The words rather escaped him than were spoken. His need was to talk of common things, of trifles, that so he might come to feel humanly.

Sidwell smiled with unmistakable pleasure.

'Do I? Do you like the dress?'

'Yes. It becomes you.'

'Are you critical in such things?'

'Not with understanding. But I should like to see you every day in a new and beautiful dress.'

'Oh, I couldn't afford it!' was the laughing reply.

He offered his hand; the touch of her warm, soft fingers fired his blood.

'Sidwell!'

It was spoken at last, involuntarily, and he stood with his eyes on hers, her hand crushed in his.

'Some day!' she whispered.

If their lips met, the contact was so slight as to seem

accidental; it was the mere timorous promise of a future kiss. And both were glad of the something that had imposed restraint.

When Sidwell went up to her mother's sitting-room, a servant had just brought tea.

'I hear that Mr Peak has been,' said Mrs Warricombe, who looked puffy and uncomfortable after her sleep. 'Emma was going to take tea to the study, but I thought it unnecessary. How could he know that we were here?'

'I met him this morning on my way into the town.'

'Surely it was rather inconsiderate of him to call.'

'He asked if he might.'

Mrs Warricombe turned her head and examined Sidwell.

'Oh! And did he stay long?'

'Not very long,' replied Sidwell, who was in quiet good-humour.

'I think it would have been better if you had told him by the servant that I was not well enough to see callers. You didn't mention that he might be coming.'

Mrs Warricombe's mind worked slowly at all times, and at present she was suffering from a cold.

'Why didn't you speak of it, Sidwell?'

'Really – I forgot,' replied the daughter, lightly.

'And what had he to say?'

'Nothing new, mother. Is your head better, dear?'

There was no answer. Mrs Warricombe had conceived a vague suspicion which was so alarming that she would not press inquiries alluding to it. The encouragement given by her husband to Godwin Peak in the latter's social progress had always annoyed her, though she could not frame solid objections. To be sure, to say of a man that he is about to be ordained meets every possible question that society can put; but Mrs Warricombe's uneasiness was in part due to personal dislike. Oftener than not, she still thought of Peak as he appeared some eleven years ago – an evident plebeian, without manners, without a redeeming grace. She knew the story of his relative who had opened a shop in Kingsmill; thinking of that now, she shuddered.

Sidwell began to talk of indifferent matters, and Peak was not again mentioned.

Her throat being still troublesome, Mrs Warricombe retired very soon after dinner. About nine o'clock Sidwell went to the library, and sat down at her father's writing-table, purposing a letter to Sylvia. She penned a line or two, but soon lapsed into reverie, her head on her hands. Of a sudden the door was thrown open, and there stood Buckland, fresh from travel.

'What has brought you?' exclaimed his sister, starting up anxiously, for something in the young man's look seemed ominous.

'Oh, nothing to trouble about. I had to come down – on business. Mother gone to bed?'

Sidwell explained.

'All right; doesn't matter. I suppose I can sleep here? Let them get me a mouthful of something; cold meat, anything will do.'

His needs were quickly supplied, and before long he was smoking by the library fire.

'I was writing to Sylvia,' said his sister, glancing at her fragmentary letter.

'Oh!'

'You know she is at Salisbury?'

'Salisbury? No, I didn't.'

His carelessness proved to Sidwell that she was wrong in conjecturing that his journey had something to do with Miss Moorhouse. Buckland was in no mood for conversation; he smoked for a quarter of an hour whilst Sidwell resumed her writing.

'Of course you haven't seen Peak?' fell from him at length.

His sister looked at him before replying.

'Yes. He called this afternoon.'

'But who told him you were here?'

His brows were knitted, and he spoke very abruptly. Sidwell gave the same explanation as to her mother, and had further to reply that she alone received the caller.

'I see,' was Buckland's comment.

Its tone troubled Sidwell.

'Has your coming anything to do with Mr Peak?'

'Yes, it has. I want to see him the first thing to-morrow.'

'Can you tell me what about?'

He searched her face, frowning.

'Not now. I'll tell you in the morning.'

Sidwell saw herself doomed to a night of suspense. She could not confess how nearly the mystery concerned her. Had Buckland made some discovery that irritated him against Peak? She knew he was disposed to catch at anything that seemed to tell against

Godwin's claims to respectful treatment, and it surely must be a grave affair to hurry him on so long a journey. Though she could imagine no ground of fear, the situation was seriously disturbing.

She tried to go on with her letter, but failed. As Buckland smoked in silence, she at length rose and said she would go upstairs.

'All right! Shall see you at breakfast. Good-night!'

At nine next morning Mrs Warricombe sent a message to Buckland that she wished to see him in her bedroom. He entered hurriedly.

'Cold better, mother? I have only just time to drink a cup of coffee. I want to catch Peak before he can have left home.'

'Mr Peak? Why? I was going to speak about him.'

'What were you going to say?' Buckland asked, anxiously.

His mother began in a roundabout way which threatened long detention. In a minute or two Buckland had gathered enough to interrupt her with the direct inquiry:

'You don't mean that there's anything between him and Sidwell?'

'I do hope not; but I can't imagine why she should – really, almost make a private appointment. I am very uneasy, Buckland. I have hardly slept. Sidwell is rather – you know'—

'The deuce! I can't stop now. Wait an hour or two, and I shall have seen the fellow. You needn't alarm yourself. He will probably have disappeared in a few days.'

'What do you mean?' Mrs Warricombe asked, with nervous eagerness.

'I'll explain afterwards.'

He hurried away. Sidwell was at the breakfast-table. Her eyes seemed to declare that she had not slept well. With an insignificant word or two, the young man swallowed his cup of coffee, and had soon left the house.

III

The wrath which illumined Buckland's countenance as he strode rapidly towards Longbrook Street was not unmingled with joy. In the deep pocket of his ulster lay something heavy which kept striking against his leg, and every such contact spurred him with a sense of satisfaction. All his suspicions were abundantly justified. Not only would his father and Sidwell be obliged to confess that his insight had been profounder than theirs, but he had the pleasure of standing justified before his own conscience. The philosophy by which he lived was strikingly illustrated and confirmed.

He sniffed the morning air, enjoyed the firmness of the frozen ground, on which his boots made a pleasant thud. To be sure, the interview before him would have its disagreeableness, but Buckland was not one of those over-civilised men who shrink from every scene of painful explanation. The detection of a harmful lie was decidedly congenial to him – especially when he and his had been made its victims. He was now at liberty to indulge that antipathetic feeling towards Godwin Peak which sundry considerations had hitherto urged him to repress. Whatever might have passed between Peak and Sidwell, he could not doubt that his sister's peace was gravely endangered; the adventurer (with however much or little sincerity) had been making subtle love to her. Such a thought was intolerable. Buckland's class-prejudice asserted itself with brutal vigour now that it had moral indignation for an ally.

He had never been at Peak's lodgings, but the address was long since noted. Something of disdain came into his eyes as he approached the row of insignificant houses. Having pulled the bell, he stood at his full height, looking severely at the number painted on the door.

Mrs Roots opened to him, and said that her lodger was at home. He gave his name, and after waiting for a moment was led to the upper floor. Godwin, who had breakfasted later than usual, still sat by the table. On Warricombe's entrance, he pushed back his chair and rose, but with deliberate movement, scarcely smiling. That Buckland made no offer of a friendly hand did not surprise him. The name of his visitor had alarmed him with a sudden presentiment. Hardening his features, he stood in expectancy.

'I want to have a talk with you,' Buckland began. 'You are at leisure, I hope?'

'Pray sit down.'

Godwin pointed to a chair near the fire, but Warricombe, having thrown his hat on to a side table, seated himself by one of the windows. His motions proved that he found it difficult to support a semblance of courtesy.

'I have come down from London on purpose to see you. Unless I am strangely misinformed you have been guilty of conduct which I shouldn't like to call by its proper name.'

Remembering that he was in a little house, with thin partitions, he kept his voice low, but the effort this cost him was obvious. He looked straight at Peak, who did not return the gaze.

'Indeed?' said Godwin, coldly. 'What is my crime?'

'I am told that you have won the confidence of my relatives by what looks like a scheme of gross dishonesty.'

'Indeed? Who has told you so?'

'No one in so many words. But I happened to come across certain acquaintances of yours in London – people who know you very well indeed; and I find that they regard your position here as altogether incredible. You will remember I had much the same feeling myself. In support of their view it was mentioned to me that you had published an article in *The Critical* – the date less than a year ago, observe. The article was anonymous, but I remember it very well. I have re-read it, and I want you to tell me how the views it expresses can be reconciled with those you have maintained in conversation with my father.'

He drew from his pocket the incriminating periodical, turned it back at the article headed 'The New Sophistry', and held it out for inspection.

'Perhaps you would like to refresh your memory.'

'Needless, thank you,' returned Godwin, with a smile – in which the vanity of an author had its part.

Had Marcella betrayed him? He had supposed she knew nothing of this article, but Earwaker had perhaps spoken of it to Moxey before receiving the injunction of secrecy. On the other hand, it might be Earwaker himself from whom Warricombe had derived his information. Not impossible for the men to meet, and Earwaker's indignation might have led him to disregard a friend's confidence.

The details mattered little. He was face to face with the most serious danger that could befall him, and already he had strung himself to encounter it. Yet even in the same moment he asked, 'Is it worth while?'

'Did you write this?' Buckland inquired.

'Yes, I wrote it.'

'Then I wait for your explanation.'

'You mustn't expect me to enter upon an elaborate defence,' Godwin replied, taking his pipe from the mantelpiece and beginning to fill it. 'A man charged with rascality can hardly help getting excited – and that excitement, to one in your mood, seems evidence against him. Please to bear in mind that I have never declared myself an orthodox theologian. Mr Warricombe is well acquainted with my views; to you I have never explained them.'

'You mean to say that my father knew of this article?'

'No. I have not spoken of it.'

'And why not?'

'Because, for one thing, I shouldn't write in that way now; and, for another, the essay seems to imply more than I meant when I did write it.'

'"Seems to imply"—? I understand. You wish to represent that this attack on M'Naughten involves no attack on Christianity?'

'Not on Christianity as I understand it.'

Buckland's face expressed profound disgust, but he controlled his speech.

'Well, I foresaw this. You attacked a new sophistry, but there is a newer sophistry still, and uncommonly difficult it is to deal with. Mr Peak, I have a plain word to say to you. More than a year ago you asked me for my goodwill, to aid you in getting a social position. Say what you like, I see now that you dealt with me dishonestly. I can no longer be your friend in any sense, and I shall do my best to have you excluded from my parents' house. My father will re-read this essay – I have marked the significant passages throughout – and will form his own judgment; I know what it will be.'

'You are within your rights.'

'Undoubtedly,' replied Buckland, with polished insolence, as he rose from his seat. 'I can't forbid you to go to the house again, but – I hope we mayn't meet there. It would be very unpleasant.'

Godwin was still pressing down the tobacco in the bowl of his pipe. He smiled, and glanced about the room. Did Warricombe know how far things had gone between him and Sidwell?

Whether or no, it was certain now that Sidwell would be informed of this disastrous piece of authorship – and the result?

What did it matter? There is no struggling against destiny. If he and Sidwell were ever fated to come together, why, these difficulties would all be surmounted. If, as seemed more than likely, he was again to be foiled on the point of success – he could bear it, perhaps even enjoy the comedy.

'There is no possibility of arguing against determined anger,' he said, quietly. 'I am not at all inclined to plead for justice: one only does that with a friend who desires to be just. My opinions are utterly distasteful to you, and personal motives have made you regard me as – a scoundrel to be got rid of. Well, there's an end of it. I don't see what is to be gained by further talk.'

This was a dismissal. Godwin felt the necessity of asserting himself thus far.

'One question,' said Warricombe, as he put the periodical back into his pocket. 'What do you mean by my "personal motives"?'

Their eyes met for an instant.

'I mean the motives which you have spoken of.'

It was Buckland's hope that Peak might reveal his relations with Sidwell, but he shrank from seeming to know anything of the matter. Clearly, no light was to be had from this source.

'I am afraid,' he said, moving to the door, 'that you will find my motives shared by all the people whose acquaintance you have made in Exeter.'

And without further leave-taking he departed.

There was a doubt in his mind. Peak's coolness might be the audacity of rascaldom; he preferred to understand it so; but it *might* have nothing to do with baseness.

'Confound it!' he muttered to himself, irritably. 'In our times life is so deucedly complicated. It used to be the easiest thing to convict a man of religious hypocrisy; nowadays, one has to bear in mind such a multiplicity of fine considerations. There's that fellow Bruno Chilvers: mightn't anyone who had personal reasons treat him precisely as I have treated Peak? Both of them *may* be honest. Yet in Peak's case all appearances are against him – just because he is of low birth, has no means, and wants desperately to get into society. The fellow is a scoundrel; I am convinced of it. Yet his designs may be innocent. How, then, a scoundrel?—

'Poor devil! Has he really fallen in love with Sidwell?—

'Humbug! He wants position, and the comfort it brings. And if he hadn't acted like a blackguard – if he had come among us telling the truth – who knows? Sidwell wouldn't then have thought of him, but for my own part I would willingly have given him a hand. There are plenty of girls who have learned to think for themselves.'

This was an unhappy line of reflection. It led to Sylvia Moorhouse – and to grinding of the teeth. By the time he reached the house, Buckland was again in remorseless mood.

He would have it out with Sidwell. The desire of proving to her that he had been right from the first overrode all thought of the pain he might inflict.

She was in the library. At breakfast he had noticed her heavy eyes, and that she made only a pretence of eating. She was now less unlike herself, but her position at the window showed that she had been waiting impatiently.

'Isn't mother coming down to-day?' he asked.

'Yes; after luncheon she will go out for an hour, if it keeps fine.'

'And to-morrow you return?'

'If mother feels able to travel.'

He had *The Critical* in his hand, and stood rustling the pages with his fingers.

'I have been to see Peak.'

'Have you?'

She moved a few steps and seated herself sideways on a small chair.

'My business with him was confoundedly unpleasant. I'm glad it's over. I wish I had known what I now do half a year ago.'

'Let me hear what it is.'

'You remember that I told you to be on your guard against Peak?'

Sidwell smiled faintly, and glanced at him, but made no answer.

'I knew he wasn't to be trusted,' pursued her brother, with gloomy satisfaction. 'And I had far better means of judging than father or you; but, of course, my suspicions were ungenerous and cynical.'

'Will you come to the point?' said Sidwell, in an irritated tone.

'I think you read this article in *The Critical*?' He approached and showed it to her. 'We spoke of it once, *à propos* of M'Naughten's book.'

She raised her eyes, and met his with a look of concern she could not disguise.

'What of that?'

'Peak is the author of it. It seems to have been written just about the time when I met him and brought him here as a visitor, and it was published after he had begun to edify you with his zeal for Christianity.'

She held out her hand.

'You remember the tone of the thing?' Buckland added. 'I'll leave it with you; but just glance at one or two of the passages I have marked. The Anglicanism of their writer is decidedly "broad", it seems to me.'

He moved apart and watched his sister as she bent over the pages. There was silence for five minutes. Seeing that Sidwell had ceased to read, he ejaculated, 'Well?'

'Has Mr Peak admitted the authorship?' she asked, slowly and distinctly.

'Yes, and with a cool impudence I hardly expected.'

'Do you mean that he has made no attempt to justify himself?'

'None worth listening to. Practically, he refused an explanation.'

Sidwell rested her forehead lightly upon the tips of her fingers; the periodical slipped from her lap and lay open on the floor.

'How did you find this out?'

'In the simplest way. Knowing perfectly well that I had only to get familiar with some of his old friends to obtain proof that he was an impostor, I followed up my acquaintance with Miss Moxey – got hold of her brother – called upon them. Whilst I was there, a man named Malkin came in, and somehow or other he began talking of Peak. I learned at once precisely what I expected, that Peak was known to all these people as a violent anti-Christian. Malkin refused to believe the story of his going in for the Church – it sounded to him a mere joke. Then came out the fact that he had written this article. They all knew about it.'

He saw a flush of shame upon Sidwell's half-hidden face. It gratified him. He was resolved to let her taste all the bitterness of her folly.

'It seems pretty clear that the Moxeys – at all events Miss Moxey – knew the rascally part he was playing. Whether they wished to unmask him, or not, I can't say. Perhaps not. Yet I caught an odd look on Miss Moxey's face when that man Malkin began to talk of Peak's characteristics and achievements. It came out, by-the-bye, that he had given all his acquaintances the slip;

they had completely lost sight of him – I suppose until Miss Moxey met him by chance at Budleigh Salterton. There's some mystery still. She evidently kept Peak's secret from the Moorhouses and the Walworths. A nice business, altogether!'

Again there was a long silence. Then Sidwell raised her face and said, abruptly:

'You may be quite mistaken.'

'How?'

'You went to Mr Peak in a spirit of enmity and anger. It is not likely he would explain himself. You may have quite misunderstood what he said.'

'Ridiculous! You mean that he was perhaps "converted" after writing this article? – Then why did he allow it to be published?'

'He did not sign it. He may have been unable to withdraw it from the editor's hands.'

'Bosh! He didn't sign it, because the idea of this Exeter campaign came between the reception and the appearance of his paper. In the ordinary course of things, he would have been only too glad to see his name in *The Critical*. The scoundrelly project was conceived perhaps the very day that I brought him here – perhaps in that moment – at lunch, do you remember? – when he began to talk of the sermon at the Cathedral?'

'Why did he go to the Cathedral and hear that sermon?'

'To amuse a Sunday morning, I suppose.'

'That is not very likely in a man who hates and ridicules religion.'

'It is decidedly more probable than the idea of his conversion.'

Sidwell fell back again into her brooding attitude.

'The reason of your mistake in judging him,' resumed Buckland, with emphasis, 'is that you have undervalued his intellect. I told you long ago that a man of Peak's calibre could not possibly be a supporter of dogmas and churches. No amount of plausible evidence would have made me believe in his sincerity. Let me beg you to appreciate the simple fact, that *no* young man of brains and education is nowadays an honest defender of mediæval Christianity – the Christianity of your churches. Such fellows may transact with their conscience, and make a more or less decent business of the clerical career; or, in rare cases, they may believe that society is served by the maintenance of a national faith, and accordingly preach with all manner of mental reserves and symbolical interpretations. These are in reality politicians, not priests. But Peak belongs to neither class. He is an acute cynic, bent on making the best of this world, since he believes in no other. How he must have chuckled after every visit to this house! He despises you, one and all. Believe me, he regards you with profound contempt.'

Buckland's obtuseness on the imaginative side spared him the understanding of his sister's state of mind. Though in theory he recognised that women were little amenable to reasoning, he took it for granted that a clear demonstration of Peak's duplicity must at once banish all thought of him from Sidwell's mind. Therefore he was unsparing in his assaults upon her delusion. It surprised him when at length Sidwell looked up with flashing, tear-dewed eyes and addressed him indignantly:

'In all this there is not one word of truth! You know that in representing the clergy as a body of ignorant and shallow men you speak out of prejudice. If you believed what you say, you would be yourself both ignorant and shallow. I can't trust your judgment of anyone whatever.'

She paused, but in a moment added the remark which would have come first had she spoken in the order of her thoughts.

'It is because the spirit of contempt is so familiar to you that you are so ready to perceive it in others. I consider that habit of mind worse than hypocrisy – yes, worse, far worse!'

Buckland was sorry for the pain he had given. The retort did not affect him, but he hung his head and looked uncomfortable. His next speech was in a milder strain:

'I feel it a duty, Sidwell, to represent this man to you in what I verily believe to be the true light. To be despised by one who is immeasurably contemptible surely can't distress you. If a butler gets into your house by means of a forged character, and then lays his plans for a great burglary, no doubt he scorns you for being so easily taken in, – and that is an exact parallel to Peak's proceedings. He has somehow got the exterior of a gentleman; you could not believe that one who behaved so agreeably and talked so well was concealing an essentially base nature. But I must remind you that Peak belongs by origin to the lower classes, which is as much as to say that he lacks the sense of honour generally inherited by men of our world. A powerful intellect by no means implies a corresponding development of the moral sense.'

Sidwell could not close her ears against the argument. But her features were still set in an expression of resentment, and she kept silence lest her voice should sound tearful.

'And don't be tempted by personal feeling,' pursued her brother, 'to make light of hypocrisy – especially this kind. The man who can act such a part as Peak's has been for the last twelve months must be capable of any depravity. It is difficult for you to estimate his baseness, because you are only half convinced that any one can really be an enemy of religious faith. You suspect a lurking belief even in the minds of avowed atheists. But take the assurance from me that a man like Peak (and I am at one with him in this matter) regards with absolute repugnance every form of supernaturalism. For him to affect belief in *your* religion, is a crime against conscience. Peak has committed this crime with a mercenary motive, – what viler charge could be brought against him?'

Without looking at him, his sister replied:

'Whether he is guilty or not, I can't yet determine. But the motive of his life here was not mercenary.'

'Then how would you describe it?' Buckland asked, in astonishment.

'I only know that it can't be called mercenary.'

'Then the distinction you draw must be a very fine one. – He has abandoned the employment by which he lived, and by his own admission he looks to the Church for means of support. It was necessary for him to make interest with people of social position; the closer his relations with them the better. From month to month he has worked skilfully to establish his footing in this house, and among your friends. What do you call this?'

She had no verbal answer to make, but her look declared that she held to another interpretation.

'Well,' Buckland added, impatiently, 'we will hear father's opinion. He, remember, has been deceived in a very gross and cruel way. Possibly he may help you to see the thing in all its hatefulness.'

Sidwell turned to him.

'You go to London this afternoon?'

'In an hour or two,' he replied, consulting his watch.

'Is it any use my asking you to keep silence about everything until I am back in town?'

Buckland frowned and hesitated.

'To mother as well as father, you mean?'

'Yes. Will you do me this kindness?'

'Answer me a question, Sidwell. Have you any thought of seeing Peak?'

'I can't say,' she replied, in agitation. 'I must leave myself free. I have a right to use my own judgment.'

'Don't see him! I beg you not to see him!'

He was so earnest that Sidwell suspected some other reason in his request than regard for her dignity.

'I must leave myself free,' she repeated, with shaking voice. 'In any case I shall be back in London to-morrow evening – that is, if – but I am sure mother will wish to go. Grant me this one kindness; say nothing here or there till I am back and have seen you again.'

He turned a deaf ear, for the persistency with which she resisted proof of Peak's dishonour had begun to alarm him. Who could say what miserable folly she might commit in the next four-and-twenty hours? The unavoidable necessity of his own return exasperated him; he wished to see her safe back in London, and under her father's care.

'No,' he exclaimed, with a gesture of determination; 'I can't keep such a thing as this secret for another hour. Mother must know at once – especially as you mean to invite that fellow into the house again. – I have half a mind to telegraph to Godolphin that I can't possibly be with him to-night.'

Sidwell regarded him and spoke with forced composure.

'Do as seems right to you, Buckland. But don't think that by remaining here you would prevent me from seeing Mr Peak, if I wish to do so. That is treating me too much like a child. You have done your part – doubtless your duty; now I must reflect and judge for myself. Neither you nor anyone else has authority over me in such circumstances.'

'Very well. I have no authority, as you say, but common sense bids me let mother know how the case stands.'

And angrily he left the room.

The Critical still lay where it had fallen. When Sidwell had stood a while in confused thought, her eye turned to it, and she went hurriedly to take it up. Yes, that was the first thing to be done, to read those pages with close care. For this she must have privacy. She ran upstairs and shut herself in her bedroom.

But did not at once begin to read. It concerned her deeply to know whether Peak had so expressed himself in this paper, that no room was left for doubt as to his convictions; but another question pressed upon her with even more urgency – could it be true that he did not love her? If Buckland were wholly right, then it mattered little in what degree she had been misled by intellectual hypocrisy.

It was impossible to believe that Peak had made love to her in cold blood, with none but sordid impulses. The thought was so humiliating that her mind resolutely rejected it; and she had no difficulty in recalling numberless minutiæ of behaviour – nuances of look and tone such as abide in a woman's memory – any one of which would have sufficed to persuade her that he felt genuine emotion. How had it come to pass that a feeling of friendly interest, which did not for a moment threaten her peace, changed all at once to an agitation only the more persistent the more she tried to subdue it, – how, if it were not that her heart responded to a passionate appeal, effectual as only the sincerest love can prove? Prior to that long talk with Godwin, on the eve of her departure for London, she had not imagined that he loved her; when they said good-bye to each other, she knew by her own sensations all that the parting meant to him. She felt glad, instead of sorry, that they were not to meet again for several months; for she wished to think of him calmly and prudently, now that he presented himself to her imagination in so new an aspect. The hand-clasp was a mutual assurance of fidelity.

'I should never have loved him, if he had not first loved me. Of that I am as firmly convinced as of my own existence. It is not in my nature to dream romances. I never did so even as a young girl, and at this age I am not likely to fall into a foolish self-deception. I had often thought about him. He seemed to me a man of higher and more complex type than those with whom I was familiar; but most surely I never attributed to him even a corresponding interest in me. I am neither vain, nor very anxious to please; I never suffered because men did not woo me; I have only moderate good looks, and certainly no uncommon mental endowments. – If he had been attracted by Sylvia, I should have thought it natural; and I more than once suspected that Sylvia was disposed to like him. It seemed strange at first that his choice should have fallen upon me; yet when I was far away from him, and longed so to sit once more by him and hear him talk, I understood that it might be in my power to afford him the companionship he needed. – Mercenary? If I had been merely a governess in the house, he would have loved me just the same!'

Only by a painful effort could she remind herself that the ideal which had grown so slowly was now defaced. He loved her, but it was not the love of an honest man. After all, she had no need to peruse this writing of his; she remembered so well how it had impressed her when she read it on its first appearance, how her father had spoken of it. Buckland's manifold evidence was irresistible. Why should Peak have concealed his authorship? Why had he disappeared from among the people who thoroughly knew him?

She had loved a dream. What a task would it be to distinguish between those parts of Peak's conversation which represented his real thoughts, and those which were mockery of his listeners! The plan of a retired life which he had sketched to her – was it all falsehood? Impossible, for his love was inextricably blended with the details. Did he imagine that the secret of his unbelief could be preserved for a lifetime, and that it would have no effect whatever upon his happiness as a man? This seemed a likely reading of the problem. But what a multitude of moral and intellectual obscurities remained! The character which had seemed to her nobly simple was become a dark and dread enigma.

She knew so little of his life. If only it could all be laid bare to her, the secret of his position would be revealed. Buckland's violence altogether missed its mark; the dishonour of such a man as Godwin Peak was due to no gross incentive.

It was probable that, in talk with her father, he had been guilty of more deliberate misrepresentation than had marked his intercourse with the rest of the family. Her father, she felt sure, had come to regard him as a valuable source of argument in the battle against materialism. Doubtless the German book, which Peak was translating, bore upon that debate, and consequently was used as an aid to dissimulation. Thinking of this, she all but shared her brother's vehement feeling. It pained her to the inmost heart that her father's generous and candid nature should thus have been played upon. The deceit, as it concerned herself alone, she could forgive; at least she could suspend judgment until the accused had offered his defence – feeling that the psychology of the case must till then be beyond her powers of analysis. But the wrong done to her father revolted her.

A tap at the door caused her to rise, trembling. She remembered that by this time her mother must be aware of the extraordinary disclosure, and that a new scene of wretched agitation had to be gone through.

'Sidwell!'

It was Mrs Warricombe's voice, and the door opened.

'Sidwell! – What *does* all this mean? I don't understand half that Buckland has been telling me.'

The speaker's face was mottled, and she stood panting, a hand pressed against her side.

'How very, very imprudent we have been! How wrong of father not to have made inquiries! To think that such a man should have sat at our table!'

'Sit down, mother; don't be so distressed,' said Sidwell, calmly. 'It will all very soon be settled.'

'Of course not a word must be said to anyone. How very fortunate that we shall be in London till the summer! Of course he must leave Exeter.'

'I have no doubt he will. Let us talk as little of it as possible, mother. We shall go back to-morrow'—

'This afternoon! We will go back with Buckland. That is decided. I couldn't sleep here another night.'

'We must remain till to-morrow,' Sidwell replied, with quiet determination.

'Why? What reason can there be?'

Mrs Warricombe's voice was suspended by a horrible surmise.

'Of course we shall go to-day, Sidwell,' she continued, in nervous haste. 'To think of that man having the impudence to call and sit talking with you! If I could have dreamt'—

'Mother,' said Sidwell, gravely, 'I am obliged to see Mr Peak, either this evening or to-morrow morning.'

'To – to *see* him—? Sidwell! What can you mean?'

'I have a reason for wishing to hear from his own lips the whole truth.'

'But we *know* the whole truth! – What can you be thinking of, dear? Who is this Mr Peak that you should ask him to come and see you, under *any* circumstances?'

It would never have occurred to Sidwell to debate with her mother on subtle questions of character and motive, but the agitation of her nerves made it difficult for her to keep silence under these vapid outcries. She desired to be alone; commonplace discussion of the misery that had come upon her was impossible. A little more strain, and she would be on the point of tears, a weakness she was resolute to avoid.

'Let me think quietly for an hour or two,' she said, moving

away. 'It's quite certain that I must stay here till to-morrow. When Buckland has gone, we can talk again.'

'But, Sidwell'—

'If you insist, I must leave the house, and find a refuge somewhere else.'

Mrs Warricombe tossed her head.

'Oh, if I am not permitted to speak to you! I only hope you won't have occasion to remember my warning! Such extraordinary behaviour was surely never known! I should have thought'—

Sidwell was by this time out of the room. Safe in privacy she sat down as if to pen a letter. From an hour's agitated thought, the following lines resulted:

> 'My brother has told me of a conversation he held with you this morning. He says you admit the authorship of an article which seems quite inconsistent with what you have professed in our talks. How am I to understand this contradiction? I beg that you will write to me at once. I shall anxiously await your reply.'

This, with her signature, was all. Having enclosed the note in an envelope, she left it on her table and went down to the library, where Buckland was sitting alone in gloomy reverie. Mrs Warricombe had told him of Sidwell's incredible purpose. Recognising his sister's independence, and feeling sure that if she saw Peak it could only be to take final leave of him, he had decided to say no more. To London he must perforce return this afternoon, but he had done his duty satisfactorily, and just in time. It was plain that things had gone far between Peak and Sidwell; the latter's behaviour avowed it. But danger there could be none, with 'The New Sophistry' staring her in the eyes. Let her see the fellow, by all means. His evasions and hairsplittings would complete her deliverance.

'There's a train at 1.53,' Buckland remarked, rising, 'and I shall catch it if I start now. I can't stay for the discomfort of luncheon. You remain here till to-morrow, I understand?'

'Yes.'

'It's a pity you are angry with me. It seems to me I have done you a kindness.'

'I am not angry with you, Buckland,' she replied, gently. 'You have done what you were plainly obliged to do.'

'That's a sensible way of putting it. Let us say goodbye with friendliness then.'

Sidwell gave her hand, and tried to smile. With a look of pained affection, Buckland went silently away.

Shortly after, Sidwell fetched her note from upstairs, and gave it to the housekeeper to be delivered by hand as soon as possible. Mrs Warricombe remained invisible, and Sidwell went back to the library, where she sat with *The Critical* open before her at Godwin's essay.

Hours went by; she still waited for an answer from Longbrook Street.

At six o'clock she went upstairs and spoke to her mother.

'Shall you come down to dinner?'

'No, Sidwell,' was the cold reply. 'Be so good as to excuse me.'

Towards eight, a letter was brought to her; it could only be from Godwin Peak. With eyes which endeavoured to take in all at once, and therefore could at first distinguish nothing, she scanned what seemed to be hurriedly written lines.

'I have tried to answer you in a long letter, but after all I can't send it. I fear you wouldn't understand. Better to repeat simply that I wrote the article you speak of. I should have told you about it some day, but now my intentions and hopes matter nothing. Whatever I said now would seem dishonest pleading. Good-bye.'

She read this so many times that at length she had but to close her eyes to see every word clearly traced on the darkness. The meanings she extracted from each sentence were scarcely less numerous than her perusals. In spite of reason, this enigmatic answer brought her some solace. He *could* defend himself; that was the assurance she had longed for. Impossible (she again and again declared to herself with emphasis) for their intimacy to be resumed. But in secret she could hold him, if not innocent, at all events not base. She had not bestowed her love upon a mere impostor.

But now a mournful, regretful passion began to weigh upon her heart. She shed tears, and presently stole away to her room for a night of sorrow.

What must be her practical course? If she went back to London without addressing another word to him, he must understand her silence as a final farewell. In that case his departure from Exeter would, no doubt, speedily follow, and there was little likelihood that she would ever again see him. Were Godwin a vulgar schemer, he would not so readily relinquish the advantage he had gained; he would calculate upon the weakness of a loving woman, and make at least one effort to redeem his position. As it was, she could neither hope nor fear that he would try to see her again. Yet she wished to see him, desired it ardently.

And yet — for each impulse of ardour was followed by a cold fit of reasoning — might not his abandonment of the position bear a meaning such as Buckland would of course attribute to it? If he were hopeless of the goodwill of her parents, what profit would it be to him to retain her love? She was no heiress; supposing him actuated by base motive, her value in his eyes came merely of his regarding her as a means to an end.

But this was to reopen the question of whether or not he truly loved her. No; he was forsaking her because he thought it impossible for her to pardon the deceit he had undeniably practised — with whatever palliating circumstances. He was overcome with shame. He imagined her indignant, scornful.

Why had she written such a short, cold note, the very thing to produce in his mind a conviction of her resentment?

Hereupon came another paroxysm of tearful misery. It was intensified by a thought she had half consciously been repressing ever since the conversation with her brother. Was it true that Miss Moxey had had it in her power to strip Godwin of a disguise? What, then, were the relations existing between him and that strangely impressive woman? How long had they known each other? It was now all but certain that a strong intellectual sympathy united their minds — and perhaps there had been something more.

She turned her face upon the pillow and moaned.

IV

And from the Moxeys Buckland had derived his information. What was it he said – something about 'an odd look' on Miss Moxey's face when that friend of theirs talked of Peak? Might not such a look signify a conflict between the temptation to injure and the desire to screen?

Sidwell constructed a complete romance. Ignorance of the past of both persons concerned allowed her imagination free play. There was no limit to the possibilities of self-torment.

The desire to see Godwin took such hold upon her, that she had already begun to think over the wording of another note to be sent to him the first thing in the morning. His reply had been insufficient: simple justice required that she should hear him in his own defence before parting with him for ever. If she kept silence, he would always remember her with bitterness, and this would make her life-long sorrow harder to bear. Sidwell was one of those few women whose love, never demonstrative, never exigent, only declares itself in all its profound significance when it is called upon to pardon. What was likely to be the issue of a meeting with Godwin she could not foresee. It seemed all but impossible for their intercourse to continue, and their coming face to face might result in nothing but distress to both, better avoided; yet judgment yielded to emotion. Yesterday – only yesterday – she had yielded herself to the joy of loving, and before her consciousness had had time to make itself familiar with its new realm, before her eyes had grown accustomed to the light suddenly shed about her, she was bidden to think of what had happened as only a dream. Her heart refused to make surrender of its hope. Though it could be held only by an encouragement of recognised illusion, she preferred to dream yet a little longer. Above all, she must taste the luxury of forgiving her lover, of making sure that her image would not dwell in his mind as that of a self-righteous woman who had turned coldly from his error, perhaps from his repentance.

A little after midnight, she rose from bed, slipped on her dressing-gown, and sat down by the still burning lamp to write what her passion dictated:

'Why should you distrust my ability, or my willingness to understand you? It would have been so much better if you had sent what you first wrote. These few lines do not even let me know whether you think yourself to blame. Why do you leave me to form a judgment of things as they appear on the surface? If you *wish* to explain, if you sincerely feel that I am in danger of wronging you by misconstruction, come to me as soon as you have received this note. If you will not come, then at least write to me – the letter you at first thought of sending. This afternoon (Friday) I return to London, but you know my address there. Don't think because I wrote so briefly that I have judged you.

S. W.'

To have committed this to paper was a relief. In the morning she would read it over and consider again whether she wished to send it.

On the table lay *The Critical*. She opened it once more at the page that concerned her, and glanced over the first few lines. Then, having put the lamp nearer to the bed, she again lay down, not to sleep but to read.

This essay was not so repugnant to her mind or her feelings as when she first became acquainted with it. Its bitterness no longer seemed to be directed against herself. There was much in it with which she could have agreed at any time during the last six months, and many strokes of satire, which till the other day would have offended her, she now felt to be legitimate. As she read on, a kind of anger such as she had never experienced trembled along her nerves. Was it not flagrantly true that English society at large made profession of a faith which in no sense whatever it could be said sincerely to hold? Was there not every reason to believe that thousands of people keep up an ignoble formalism, because they feared the social results of declaring their severance from the religion of the churches? This was a monstrous evil; she had never till this moment understood the scope of its baneful effects. But for the prevalence of such a spirit of hypocrisy, Godwin Peak would never have sinned against his honour. Why was it not declared in trumpet-tones of authority, from end to end of the Christian world, that Christianity, as it has been understood through the ages, can no longer be accepted? For that was the truth, the truth, the *truth*!

She lay back, quivering as if with terror. For an instant her soul had been filled with hatred of the religion for which she could once have died. It had stood before her as a power of darkness and ignorance, to be assailed, crushed, driven from the memory of man.

Last night she had hardly slept, and now, though her body was numb with weariness, her mind kept up a feverish activity. She was bent on excusing Godwin, and the only way in which she could do so was by arraigning the world for its huge dishonesty. In a condition between slumber and waking, she seemed to plead for him before a circle of Pharisaic accusers. Streams of silent eloquence rushed through her brain, and the spirit which prompted her was closely akin to that of 'The New Sophistry'. Now and then, for a few seconds, she was smitten with a consciousness of extraordinary change in her habits of thought. She looked about her with wide, fearful eyes, and endeavoured to see things in the familiar aspect. As if with physical constraint her angry imagination again overcame her, until at length from the penumbra of sleep she passed into its profoundest gloom.

To wake when dawn was pale at the window. A choking odour reminded her that she had not extinguished the lamp, which must have gone out for lack of oil. She opened the window, took a draught of water, and addressed herself to sleep again. But in recollecting what the new day meant for her, she had spoilt the chances of longer rest. Her head ached; all worldly thoughts were repulsive, yet she could not dismiss them. She tried to repeat the prayers she had known since childhood, but they were meaningless, and a sense of shame attached to their utterance.

When the first gleam of sun told her that it was past eight o'clock, she made an effort and rose.

At breakfast Mrs Warricombe talked of the departure for London. She mentioned an early train; by getting ready as soon as the meal was over, they could easily reach the station in time. Sidwell made no direct reply and seemed to assent; but when they rose from the table, she said, nervously:

'I couldn't speak before the servants. I wish to stay here till the afternoon.'

'Why, Sidwell?'

'I have asked Mr Peak to come and see me this morning.'

Her mother knew that expostulation was useless, but could not refrain from a long harangue made up of warning and reproof.

'You have very little consideration for me,' was her final remark. 'Now we shan't get home till after dark, and of course my throat will be bad again.'

Glad of the anti-climax, Sidwell replied that the day was much warmer, and that with care no harm need come of the journey.

'It's easy to say that, Sidwell. I never knew you to behave so selfishly, never!'

'Don't be angry with me, mother. You don't know how grieved I am to distress you so. I can't help it, dear; indeed, I can't. Won't you sacrifice a few hours to put my mind at rest?'

Mrs Warricombe once more gave expression to her outraged feelings. Sidwell could only listen silently with bent head.

If Godwin were coming at all, he would be here by eleven o'clock. Sidwell had learnt that her letter was put into his hands. She asked him to come at once, and nothing but a resolve not to meet her could delay him more than an hour or two.

At half-past ten the bell sounded. She was sitting in the library with her back turned to the door. When a voice announced 'Mr Peak', she did not at once rise, and with a feeling akin to terror she heard the footstep slowly approaching. It stopped at some distance from her; then, overcoming a weakness which threatened to clog her as in a nightmare, she stood up and looked round.

Peak wore neither overcoat nor gloves, but otherwise was dressed in the usual way. As Sidwell fixed her eyes upon him, he threw his hat into a chair and came a step or two nearer. Whether he had passed the night in sleep or vigil could not be determined; but his look was one of shame, and he did not hold himself so upright as was his wont.

'Will you come and sit down?' said Sidwell, pointing to a chair not far from that on which one of her hands rested.

He moved forward, and was about to pass near her, when Sidwell involuntarily held her hand to him. He took it and gazed into her face with a melancholy smile.

'What does it mean?' she asked, in a low voice.

He relinquished her fingers, which he had scarcely pressed, and stood with his arms behind his back.

'Oh, it's all quite true,' was his reply, wearily spoken.

'What is true?'

'All that you have heard from your brother.'

'All? – But how can you know what he has said?'

They looked at each other. Peak's lips were set as if in resistance of emotion, and a frown wrinkled his brows. Sidwell's gaze was one of fear and appeal.

'He said, of course, that I had deceived you.'

'But in what? – Was there no truth in anything you said to me?'

'To you I have spoken far more truth than falsehood.'

A light shone in her eyes, and her lips quivered.

'Then,' she murmured, 'Buckland was not right in everything.'

'I understand. He wished you to believe that my love was as much a pretence as my religion?'

'He said that.'

'It was natural enough. – And you were disposed to believe it?'

'I thought it impossible. But I should have thought the same of the other things.'

Peak nodded, and moved away. Watching him, Sidwell was beset with conflicting impulses. His assurance had allayed her worst misgiving, and she approved the self-restraint with which he bore himself, but at the same time she longed for a passionate declaration. As a reasoning woman, she did her utmost to remember that Peak was on his defence before her, and that nothing could pass between them but grave discussion of the motives which had impelled him to dishonourable behaviour. As a woman in love, she would fain have obscured the moral issue by indulgence of her heart's desire. She was glad that he held aloof, but if he had taken her in his arms, she would have forgotten everything in the moment's happiness.

'Let us sit down, and tell me – tell me all you can.'

He delayed a moment, then seated himself opposite to her. She saw now that his movements were those of physical fatigue; and the full light from the window, enabling her to read his face more distinctly, revealed the impress of suffering. Instead of calling upon him to atone in such measure as was possible for the wrong he had done her, she felt ready to reproach herself for speaking coldly when his need of solace was so great.

'What can I tell you,' he said, 'that you don't know, or that you can't conjecture?'

'But you wrote that there was so much I could not be expected to understand. And I can't, can't understand you. It still seems impossible. Why did you hide the truth from me?'

'Because if I had begun by telling it, I should never have won a kind look or a kind thought from you.'

Sidwell reflected.

'But what did you care for me then – when it began?'

'Not so much as I do now, but enough to overthrow all the results of my life up to that time. Before I met you in this house I had seen you twice, and had learned who you were. I was sitting in the Cathedral when you came there with your sister and Miss Moorhouse – do you remember? I heard Fanny call you by your name, and that brought to my mind a young girl whom I had known in a slight way years before. And the next day I again saw you there, at the service; I waited about the entrance only to see you. I cared enough for you then to conceive a design which for a long time seemed too hateful really to be carried out, but – at last it was, you see.'

Sidwell breathed quickly. Nothing he could have urged for himself would have affected her more deeply than this. To date back and extend the period of his love for her was a flattery more subtle than Peak imagined.

'Why didn't you tell me that the day before yesterday?' she asked, with tremulous bosom.

'I had no wish to remind myself of baseness in the midst of a pure joy.'

She was silent, then exclaimed, in accents of pain:

'Why should you have thought it necessary to be other than yourself? Couldn't you see, at first meeting with us, that we were not bigoted people? Didn't you know that Buckland had accustomed us to understand how common it is nowadays for people to throw off the old religion? Would father have looked coldly on you if he had known that you followed where so many good and thoughtful men were leading?'

He regarded her anxiously.

'I had heard from Buckland that your father was strongly prejudiced; that you also were quite out of sympathy with the new thought.'

'He exaggerated – even then.'

'Exaggerated? But on what plea could I have come to live in this neighbourhood? How could I have kept you in sight – tried to win your interest? I had no means, no position. The very thought of encouraging my love for you demanded some extraordinary step. What course was open to me?'

Sidwell let her head droop.

'I don't know. You might perhaps have discovered a way.'

'But what was the use, when the mere fact of my heresy would have forbidden hope from the outset?'

'Why should it have done so?'

'Why? You know very well that you could never even have been friendly with the man who wrote that thing in the review.'

'But here is the proof how much better it is to behave truthfully! In this last year I have changed so much that I find it difficult to understand the strength of my former prejudices. What is it to me now that you speak scornfully of attempts to reconcile things that can't be reconciled? I understand the new thought, and how natural it is for you to accept it. If only I could have come to know you well, your opinions would not have stood between us.'

Peak made a slight gesture, and smiled incredulously.

'You think so now.'

'And I have such good reason for my thought,' rejoined Sidwell, earnestly, 'that when you said you loved me, my only regret in looking to the future was – that you had resolved to be a clergyman.'

He leaned back in the chair, and let a hand fall on his knee. The gesture seemed to signify a weary relinquishment of concern in what they were discussing.

'How could I foresee that?' he uttered, in a corresponding tone.

Sidwell was made uneasy by the course upon which she had entered. To what did her words tend? If only to a demonstration that fate had used him as the plaything of its irony – if, after all, she had nothing to say to him but 'See how your own folly has ruined you', then she had better have kept silence. She not only appeared to be offering him encouragement, but was in truth doing so. She wished him to understand that his way of thinking was no obstacle to her love, and with that purpose she was even guilty of a slight misrepresentation. For it was only since the shock of this disaster that she had clearly recognised the change in her own mind. True, the regret of which she spoke had for an instant visited her, but it represented a mundane solicitude rather than an intellectual scruple. It had occurred to her how much brighter would be their prospect if Peak were but an active man of the world, with a career before him distinctly suited to his powers.

His contention was undeniably just. The influence to which she had from the first submitted was the same that her father felt so strongly. Godwin interested her as a self-reliant champion of the old faiths, and his personal characteristics would never have awakened such sympathy in her but for that initial recommendation. Natural prejudice would have prevented her from perceiving the points of kindred between his temperament and her own. His low origin, the ridiculous stories connected with his youth – why had she, in spite of likelihood, been able to disregard these things? Only because of what she then deemed his spiritual value.

But for the dishonourable part he had played, this bond of love would never have been formed between them. The thought was a new apology for his transgression; she could not but defy her conscience, and look indulgently on the evil which had borne such fruit.

Godwin had begun to speak again.

'This is quite in keeping with the tenor of my whole life. Whatever I undertake ends in frustration at a point where success seems to have just come within my reach. Great things and trifles – it's all the same. My course at College was broken off at the moment when I might have assured my future. Later, I made many an effort to succeed in literature, and when at length something of mine was printed in a leading review, I could not even sign it, and had no profit from the attention it excited. Now – well, you see. Laughable, isn't it?'

Sidwell scarcely withheld herself from bending forward and giving him her hand.

'What shall you do?' she asked.

'Oh, I am not afraid. I have still enough money left to support me until I can find some occupation of the old kind. Fortunately, I am not one of those men whose brains have no marketable value.'

'If you knew how it pains me to hear you!'

'If I didn't believe that, I couldn't speak to you like this. I never thought you would let me see you again, and if you hadn't asked me to come, I could never have brought myself to face you. But it would have been a miserable thing to go off without even knowing what you thought of me.'

'Should you never have written to me?'

'I think not. You find it hard to imagine that I have any pride, no doubt; but it is there, explain it how one may.'

'It would have been wrong to leave me in such uncertainty.'

'Uncertainty?'

'About you – about your future.'

'Did you quite mean that? Hadn't your brother made you doubt whether I loved you at all?'

'Yes. But no, I didn't doubt. Indeed, indeed, I didn't doubt! But I felt such a need of hearing from your own lips that – Oh, I can't explain myself!'

Godwin smiled sadly.

'I think I understand. But there was every reason for my believing that *your* love could not bear such a test. You must regard me as quite a different man – one utterly unknown to you.'

He had resolved to speak not a word that could sound like an appeal to her emotions. When he entered the room he felt a sincere indifference as to what would result from the interview, for to his mind the story was ended, and he had only to retire with the dignity still possible to a dishonoured man. To touch the note of pathos would be unworthy; to exert what influence might be left to him, a wanton cruelty. But he had heard such unexpected things, that it was not easy for him to remember how complete had seemed the severance between him and Sidwell. The charm of her presence was reasserting itself, and when avowal of continued love appeared so unmistakably in her troubled countenance, her broken words, he could not control the answering fervour. He spoke in a changed voice, and allowed his eyes to dwell longingly upon hers.

'I felt so at first,' she answered. 'And it would be wrong to pretend that I can still regard you as I did before.'

It cost her a great effort to add these words. When they were spoken, she was at once glad and fearful.

'I am not so foolish, as to think it possible,' said Peak, half turning away.

'But that is no reason,' she pursued, 'why we should become strangers. You are still so young a man; life must be so full of possibilities for you. This year has been wasted, but when you leave Exeter'—

An impatient movement of Godwin's checked her.

'You are going to encourage me to begin the struggle once more,' he said, bitterly. 'Where? How? It is so easy to talk of "possibilities".'

'You are not without friends – I mean friends whose sympathy is of real value to you.'

Saying this, she looked keenly at him.

'Friends,' he replied, 'who perhaps at this moment are laughing over my disgrace.'

'How do they know of – what has happened?'

'How did your brother get his information? I didn't care to ask him. – No, I don't even wish you to say anything about that.'

'But surely there is no reason for keeping it secret. Why may I not speak freely? Buckland told me that he had heard you spoken of at the house of people named Moxey.'

She endeavoured to understand the smile which rose to his lips.

'Now it is clear to me,' he said. 'Yes, I suppose that was inevitable, sooner or later.'

'You knew that he had become acquainted with the Moxeys?'

Her tone was more reserved than hitherto.

'Yes, I knew he had. He met Miss Moxey by chance at Budleigh Salterton, and I happened to be there – at the Moorhouses' – on the same day.'

Sidwell glanced at him inquiringly, and waited for something more.

'I saw Miss Moxey in private,' he added, speaking more quickly, 'and asked her to keep my secret. I ought to be ashamed to tell you this, but it is better you should know how far my humiliation has gone.'

He saw that she was moved with strong feeling. The low tone in which she answered had peculiar significance.

'Did you speak of me to Miss Moxey?'

'I must forgive you for asking that,' Peak replied, coldly. 'It may well seem to you that I have neither honour nor delicacy left.'

There had come a flush on her cheeks. For some moments she was absorbed in thought.

'It seems strange to you,' he continued at length, 'that I could ask Miss Moxey to share such a secret. But you must understand on what terms we were – she and I. We have known each other for several years. She has a man's mind, and I have always

thought of her in much the same way as of my male companions.
– Your brother has told you about her, perhaps?'

'I have met her in London.'

'Then that will make my explanation easier,' said Godwin,
disregarding the anxious questions that at once suggested themselves to him. 'Well, I misled her, or tried to do so. I allowed her
to suppose that I was sincere in my new undertakings, and that I
didn't wish – Oh!' he exclaimed, suddenly breaking off, 'Why
need I go any further in confession? It must be as miserable for
you to hear as for me to speak. Let us make an end of it. I can't
understand how I have escaped detection so long.'

Remembering every detail of Buckland's story, Sidwell felt
that she had possibly been unjust in representing the Moxeys as
her brother's authority; in strictness, she ought to mention that a
friend of theirs was the actual source of information. But she
could not pursue the subject; like Godwin, she wished to put it
out of her mind. What question could there be of honour or
dishonour in the case of a person such as Miss Moxey, who had
consented to be party to a shameful deceit? Strangely, it was a
relief to her to have heard this. The moral repugnance which
threatened to estrange her from Godwin, was now directed in
another quarter; unduly restrained by love, it found scope under
the guidance of jealousy.

'You have been trying to adapt yourself,' she said, 'to a world
for which you are by nature unfitted. Your place is in the new
order; by turning back to the old, you condemned yourself to a
wasted life. Since we have been in London, I have come to
understand better the great difference between modern intellectual life and that which we lead in these far-away corners. You
must go out among your equals, go and take your part with men
who are working for the future.'

Peak rose with a gesture of passionate impatience.

'What is it to me, new world or old? My world is where *you*
are. I have no life of my own; I think only of you, live only by
you.'

'If I could help you!' she replied, with emotion. 'What can I do
– but be your friend at a distance? Everything else has become
impossible.'

'Impossible for the present – for a long time to come. But is
there no hope for me?'

She pressed her hands together, and stood before him unable to answer.

'Remember,' he continued, 'that you are almost as much changed in my eyes as I in yours. I did not imagine that you had moved so far towards freedom of mind. If my love for you was profound and absorbing, think what it must now have become! Yours has suffered by my disgrace, but is there no hope of its reviving – if I live worthily – if I—?'

His voice failed.

'I have said that we can't be strangers,' Sidwell murmured brokenly. 'Wherever you go, I must hear of you.'

'Everyone about you will detest my name. You will soon wish to forget my existence.'

'If I know myself, never! – Oh, try to find your true work! You have such abilities, powers so much greater than those of ordinary men. You will always be the same to me, and if ever circumstances'—

'You would have to give up so much, Sidwell. And there is little chance of my ever being well-to-do; poverty will always stand between us, if nothing else.'

'It must be so long before we can think of that.'

'But can I ever see you? – No, I won't ask that. Who knows? I may have to go too far away. But I *may* write to you – after a time?'

'I shall live in the hope of good news from you,' she replied, trying to smile and to speak cheerfully. 'This will always be my home. Nothing will be changed.'

'Then you don't think of me as irredeemably base?'

'If I thought you base,' Sidwell answered, in a low voice, 'I should not now be speaking with you. It is because I feel and know that you have erred only – that is what makes it impossible for me to think of your fault as outweighing the good in your nature.'

'The good? I wonder how you understand that. What is there *good* in me? You don't mean mere intellect?'

He waited anxiously for what she would say. A necessity for speaking out his inmost thoughts had arisen with the emotion, scarcely to be called hope, excited by Sidwell's magnanimity. Now, or never, he must stand before this woman as his very self, and be convinced that she loved him for his own sake.

'No, I don't mean intellect,' she replied, with hesitation.

'What then? Tell me of one quality in me strong enough to justify a woman's love.'

Sidwell dropped her eyes in confusion.

'I can't analyse your character – I only know'—

She became silent.

'To myself,' pursued Godwin, with the modulated, moving voice which always expressed his genuine feeling, 'I seem anything but lovable. I don't underrate my powers – rather the opposite, no doubt; but what I always seem to lack is the gift of pleasing – moral grace. My strongest emotions seem to be absorbed in revolt; for once that I feel tenderly, I have a hundred fierce, resentful, tempestuous moods. To be suave and smiling in common intercourse costs me an effort. I have to act the part, and this habit makes me sceptical, whenever I am really prompted to gentleness. I criticise myself ceaselessly; expose without mercy all those characteristics which another man would keep out of sight. Yes, and for this very reason, just because I think myself unlovable – the gift of love means far more to me than to other men. If you could conceive the passion of gratitude which possessed me for hours after I left you the other day! You cannot!'

Sidwell regarded him fixedly.

'In comparison with this sincerity, what becomes of the pretence you blame in me? If you knew how paltry it seems – that accusation of dishonesty! I believed the world round, and pretended to believe it flat: that's what it amounts to! Are you, on such an account as that, to consider worthless the devotion which has grown in me month by month? You – I was persuaded – thought the world flat, and couldn't think kindly of any man who held the other hypothesis. Very well; why not concede the trifle, and so at least give myself a chance? I did so – that was all.'

In vain her conscience strove to assert itself. She was under the spell of a nature infinitely stronger than hers; she saw and felt as Godwin did.

'You think, Sidwell, that I stand in need of forgiveness. Then be great enough to forgive me, wholly – once and for all. Let your love be strengthened by the trial it has passed through. That will mean that my whole life is yours, directed by the ever-present thought of your beauty, face and soul. Then there *will* be good in me, thanks to you. I shall no longer live a life of hypocrisy, of suppressed rage and scorn. I know how much I am asking; perhaps it means that for my sake you give up everything else that is dear to you'—

The thought checked him. He looked at her despondently.

'You can trust me,' Sidwell answered, moving nearer to him, tears on her cheeks. 'I must hear from you, and I will write.'

'I can ask no more than that.'

He took her hands, held them for a moment, and turned away. At the door he looked round. Sidwell's head was bowed, and, on her raising it, he saw that she was blinded with tears.

So he went forth.

PART THE SIXTH

I

For several days after the scene in which Mr Malkin un-
consciously played an important part, Marcella seemed to be ill.
She appeared at meals, but neither ate nor conversed. Christian
had never known her so sullen and nervously irritable; he did not
venture to utter Peak's name. Upon seclusion followed restless
activity. Marcella was rarely at home between breakfast and
dinner-time, and her brother learnt with satisfaction that she went
much among her acquaintances. Late one evening, when he had
just returned from he knew not where, Christian tried to put an
end to the unnatural constraint between them. After talking
cheerfully for a few minutes, he risked the question:

'Have you seen anything of the Warricombes?'

She replied with a cold negative.

'Nor heard anything?'

'No. Have you?'

'Nothing at all. I have seen Earwaker. Malkin had told him
about what happened here the other day.'

'Of course.'

'But he had no news. – Of Peak, I mean.'

Marcella smiled, as if the situation amused her; but she would
not discuss it. Christian began to hope that she was training
herself to a wholesome indifference.

A month of the new year went by, and Peak seemed to be
forgotten. Marcella had returned to her studious habits, was
fenced around with books, seldom left the house. Another month
and the brother and sister were living very much in the old way,
seeing few people, conversing only of intellectual things. But
Christian concealed an expectation which enabled him to pass
hours of retirement in the completest idleness. Since the death of
her husband, Mrs Palmer had been living abroad. Before the end

of March, as he had been careful to discover, she would be back in London, at the house in Sussex Square. By that time he might venture, without indelicacy, to call upon her. And after the first interview—

The day came, when, ill with agitation, he set forth to pay this call. For two or three nights he had scarcely closed his eyes; he looked ghastly. The weather was execrable, and on that very account he made choice of this afternoon, hoping that he might find his widowed Laura alone. Between ringing the bell and the opening of the door, he could hardly support himself. He asked for Mrs Palmer in a gasping voice which caused the servant to look at him with surprise.

The lady was at home. At the drawing-room door, before his name could be announced, he caught the unwelcome sound of voices in lively conversation. It seemed to him that a score of persons were assembled. In reality there were six, three of them callers.

Mrs Palmer met him with the friendliest welcome. A stranger would have thought her pretty, but by no means impressive. She was short, anything but meagre, fair-haired, brisk of movement, idly vivacious in look and tone. The mourning she wore imposed no restraint upon her humour, which at present was not far from gay.

'Is it really Mr Moxey?' she exclaimed. 'Why, I had all but forgotten you, and positively it is your own fault! It must be a year or more since you came to see me. No? Eight months? – But I have been through so much trouble, you know.' She sighed mechanically. 'I thought of you one day at Bordighera, when we were looking at some funny little sea-creatures – the kind of thing you used to know all about. How is your sister?'

A chill struck upon his heart. Assuredly he had no wish to find Constance sunk in the semblance of dolour; such hypocrisy would have pained him. But her sprightliness was a shock. Though months had passed since Mr Palmer's decease, a decent gravity would more have become her condition. He could reply only in broken phrases, and it was a relief to him when the widow, as if tiring of his awkwardness, turned her attention elsewhere.

He was at length able to survey the company. Two ladies in mourning he faintly recognised, the one a sister of Mr Palmer's, comely but of dull aspect; the other a niece, whose laugh was too frequent even had it been more musical, and who talked of athletic sports with a young man evidently better fitted to excel in that kind of thing than in any pursuit demanding intelligence. This gentleman Christian had never met. The two other callers, a grey-headed, military-looking person, and a lady, possibly his wife, were equally strangers to him.

The drawing-room was much changed in appearance since Christian's last visit. There was more display, a richer profusion of ornaments not in the best taste. The old pictures had given place to showily-framed daubs of the most popular school. On a little table at his elbow, he remarked the photograph of a jockey who was just then engrossing public affection. What did all this mean? Formerly, he had attributed every graceful feature of the room to Constance's choice. He had imagined that to her Mr Palmer was indebted for guidance on points of aesthetic propriety. Could it be that—?

He caught a glance which she cast in his direction, and instantly forgot the troublesome problem. How dull of him to misunderstand her! Her sportiveness had a double significance. It was the expression of a hope which would not be subdued, and at the same time a means of disguising the tender interest with which she regarded *him*. If she had been blithe before his appearance, how could she suddenly change her demeanour as soon as he entered? It would have challenged suspicion and remark. For the same reason she affected to have all but forgotten him. Of course! how could he have failed to see that? 'I thought of you one day at Bordighera' – was not that the best possible way of making known to him that he had never been out of her mind?

Sweet, noble, long-suffering Constance!

He took a place by her sister, and began to talk of he knew not what, for all his attention was given to the sound of Constance's voice.

'Yes,' she was saying to the man of military appearance, 'it's very early to come back to London, but I did get so tired of those foreign places.'

(In other words, of being far from her Christian – thus he interpreted.)

'No, we didn't make a single pleasant acquaintance. A shockingly tiresome lot of people wherever we went.'

(In comparison with the faithful lover, who waited, waited.)

'Foreigners are so stupid – don't you think so? Why should they always expect you to speak *their* language? – Oh, of course

I speak French; but it is such a disagreeable language – don't you think so?'

(Compared with the accents of English devotion, of course.)

'Do you go in for cycling, Mr Moxey?' inquired Mrs Palmer's laughing niece, from a little distance.

'For cycling?' With a great effort he recovered himself and grasped the meaning of the words. 'No, I – I'm sorry to say I don't. Capital exercise!'

'Mr Dwight has just been telling me such an awfully good story about a friend of his. Do tell it again, Mr Dwight! It'll make you laugh no end, Mr Moxey.'

The young man appealed to was ready enough to repeat his anecdote, which had to do with a bold cyclist, who, after dining more than well, rode his machine down a steep hill and escaped destruction only by miracle. Christian laughed desperately, and declared that he had never heard anything so good.

But the tension of his nerves was unendurable. Five minutes more of anguish, and he sprang up like an automaton.

'Must you really go, Mr Moxey?' said Constance, with a manner which of course was intended to veil her emotion. 'Please don't be another year before you let us see you again.'

Blessings on her tender heart! What more could she have said, in the presence of all those people? He walked all the way to Notting Hill through a pelting rain, his passion aglow.

Impossible to be silent longer concerning the brilliant future. Arrived at home, he flung off hat and coat, and went straight to the drawing-room, hoping to find Marcella alone. To his annoyance, a stranger was sitting there in conversation, a very simply dressed lady, who, as he entered, looked at him with a grave smile and stood up. He thought he had never seen her before.

Marcella wore a singular expression; there was a moment of silence, for Christian decidedly embarrassing, since it seemed to be expected that he should greet the stranger.

'Don't you remember Janet?' said his sister.

'Janet?' He felt his face flush. 'You don't mean to say—? But how you have altered! And yet, no; really, you haven't. It's only my stupidity.' He grasped her hand, and with a feeling of genuine pleasure, despite awkward reminiscences.

'One does alter in eleven years,' said Janet Moxey, in a very pleasant, natural voice – a voice of habitual self-command, conveying the idea of a highly cultivated mind, and many other agreeable things.

'Eleven years? Yes, yes! How very glad I am to see you! And I'm sure Marcella was. How very kind of you to call on us!'

Janet was as far as ever from looking handsome or pretty, but it must have been a dullard who proclaimed her face unpleasing. She had eyes of remarkable intelligence, something like Marcella's but milder, more benevolent. Her lips were softly firm; they would not readily part in laughter; their frequent smile meant more than that of the woman who sets herself to be engaging.

'I am on my way home,' she said, 'from a holiday in the South, — an enforced holiday, I'm sorry to say.'

'You have been ill?'

'Overworked a little. I am practising medicine in Kingsmill.'

Christian did not disguise his astonishment.

'Medicine?'

'You don't remember that I always had scientific tastes?'

If it was a reproach, none could have been more gently administered.

'Of course — of course I do! Your botany, your skeletons of birds and cats and mice — of course! But where did you study?'

'In London. The Women's Medical School. I have been in practice for nearly four years.'

'And have overworked yourself. — But why are we standing? Let us sit down and talk. How is your father?'

Marcella was watching her brother closely, and with a curious smile.

Janet remained for another hour. No reference was made to the long rupture of intercourse between her family and these relatives. Christian learnt that his uncle was still hale, and that Janet's four sisters all lived, obviously unmarried. To-day he was disposed to be almost affectionate with anyone who showed him a friendly face: he expressed grief that his cousin must leave for Twybridge early in the morning.

'Whenever you pass through the Midlands,' was Janet's indirect reply, addressed to Marcella, 'try to stop at Kingsmill.'

And a few minutes after that she took her leave. There lingered behind her that peculiar fragrance of modern womanhood, refreshing, inspiriting, which is so entirely different from the merely feminine perfume, however exquisite.

'What a surprising visit!' was Christian's exclamation, when he and his sister were alone. 'How did she find us?'

'Directory, I suppose.'

'A lady doctor!' he mused.

'And a very capable one, I fancy,' said Marcella. 'We had nearly an hour's talk before you came. But she won't be able to stand the work. There'll be another breakdown before long.'

'Has she a large practice, then?'

'Not very large, perhaps; but she studies as well. I never dreamt of Janet becoming so interesting a person.'

Christian had to postpone till after dinner the talk he purposed about Mrs Palmer. When that time came, he was no longer disposed for sentimental confessions; it would be better to wait until he could announce a settled project of marriage. Through the evening, his sister recurred to the subject of Janet with curious frequency, and on the following day her interest had suffered no diminution. Christian had always taken for granted that she understood the grounds of the breach between him and his uncle; without ever unbosoming himself, he had occasionally, in his softer moments, alluded to the awkward subject in language which he thought easy enough to interpret. Now at length, in reply to some remark of Marcella's, he said with significant accent:

'Janet was very friendly to me.'

'She has studied science for ten years,' was his sister's comment.

'Yes, and can forgive a boy's absurdities.'

'Easier to forgive, certainly, than those of a man,' said Marcella, with a curl of the lip.

Christian became silent, and went thoughtfully away.

A week later, he was again in Mrs Palmer's drawing-room, where again he met an assemblage of people such as seemed to profane this sanctuary. To be sure – he said to himself – Constance could not at once get rid of the acquaintances forced upon her by her husband; little by little she would free herself. It was a pity that her sister and her niece – persons anything but intelligent and refined – should be permanent members of her household; for their sake, no doubt, she felt constrained to welcome men and women for whose society she herself had little taste. But when the year of her widowhood was past—

Petrarch's Laura was the mother of eleven children; Constance had had only three, and one of these was dead. The remaining two, Christian now learnt, lived with a governess in a little house at Bournemouth, which Mrs Palmer had taken for that purpose.

'I'm going down to see them to-morrow,' she informed Christian, 'and I shall stay there over the next day. It's so quiet and restful.'

These words kept repeating themselves to Christian's ear, as he went home, and all through the evening. Were they not an invitation? Down there at Bournemouth, Constance would be alone the day after to-morrow. 'It is so quiet and restful;' that was to say, no idle callers would break upon her retirement; she would be able to welcome a friend, and talk reposefully with him. Surely she must have meant that; for she spoke with a peculiar intonation – a look—

By the second morning he had worked himself up to a persuasion that yonder by the seaside Constance was expecting him. To miss the opportunity would be to prove himself dull of apprehension, a laggard in love. With trembling hands, he hurried through his toilet and made haste downstairs to examine a railway time-table. He found it was possible to reach Bournemouth by about two o'clock, a very convenient hour; it would allow him to take refreshment, and walk to the house shortly after three.

His conviction strong as ever, he came to the journey's end, and in due course discovered the pleasant little house of which Constance had spoken. At the door, his heart failed him; but retreat could not now be thought of. Yes, Mrs Palmer was at home. The servant led him into a sitting-room on the ground floor, took his name, and left him.

It was nearly ten minutes before Constance appeared. On her face he read a frank surprise.

'I happened to – to be down here; couldn't resist the temptation'—

'Delighted to see you, Mr Moxey. But how did you know I was here?'

He gazed at her.

'You – don't you remember? The day before yesterday – in Sussex Square – you mentioned'—

'Oh, did I?' She laughed. 'I had quite forgotten.'

Christian sank upon his chair. He tried to convince himself that she was playing a part; perhaps she thought that she had been premature in revealing her wish to talk with him.

Mrs Palmer was good-natured. This call evidently puzzled her, but she did not stint her hospitality. When Christian asked after the children, they were summoned; two little girls daintily dressed, pretty, affectionate with their mother. The sight of them tortured Christian, and he sighed deeply with relief when they left the room. Constance appeared rather absent; her quick glance at him signified something, but he could not determine what. In agony of constraint, he rose as if to go.

'Oh, you will have a cup of tea with me,' said Mrs Palmer. 'It will be brought in a few minutes.'

Then she really wished him to stop. Was he not behaving like an obtuse creature? Why, everything was planned to encourage him.

He talked recklessly of this and that, and got round to the years long gone by. When the tea came, he was reviving memories of occasions on which he and she had met as young people. Constance laughed merrily, declared she could hardly remember.

'Oh, what a time ago! – But I was quite a child.'

'No – indeed, no! You were a young lady, and a brilliant one.'

The tea seemed to intoxicate him. He noticed again that Constance glanced at him significantly. How good of her to allow him this delicious afternoon!

'Mr Moxey,' she said, after meditating a little, 'why haven't you married? I should have thought you would have married long ago.'

He was stricken dumb. Her jerky laugh came as a shock upon his hearing.

'Married—?'

'What is there astonishing in the idea?'

'But – I – how can I answer you?'

The pretty, characterless face betrayed some unusual feeling. She looked at him furtively; seemed to suppress a tendency to laugh.

'I mustn't pry into secrets,' she simpered.

'But there is no secret!' Christian panted, laying down his teacup for fear he should drop it. 'Whom should I – could I have married?'

Constance also put aside her cup. She was bewildered, and just a little abashed. With courage which came he knew not whence, Christian bent forward and continued speaking:

'Whom could I marry after that day when I met you in the little drawing-room at the Robinsons'?'

She stared in genuine astonishment, then was embarrassed.

'You cannot – cannot have forgotten—?'

'You surely don't mean to say, Mr Moxey, that *you* have remembered? Oh, I'm afraid I was a shocking flirt in those days!'

'But I mean *after* your marriage – when I found you in tears'—

'Please, please don't remind me!' she exclaimed, giggling nervously. 'Oh how silly! – of me, I mean. To think that – but you are making fun of me, Mr Moxey?'

Christian rose and went to the window. He was not only shaken by his tender emotions – something very like repugnance had begun to affect him. If Constance were feigning, it was in very bad taste; if she spoke with sincerity – what a woman had he worshipped! It did not occur to him to lay the fault upon his own absurd romanticism. After eleven years' persistence in one point of view, he could not suddenly see the affair with the eyes of common sense.

He turned and approached her again.

'Do you not know, then,' he asked, with quiet dignity, 'that ever since the day I speak of, I have devoted my life to the love I then felt? All these years, have you not understood me?'

Mrs Palmer was quite unable to grasp ideas such as these. Neither her reading nor her experience prepared her to understand what Christian meant. Courtship of a married woman was intelligible enough to her; but a love that feared to soil itself, a devotion from afar, encouraged by only the faintest hope of reward other than the most insubstantial – of that she had as little conception as any woman among the wealthy vulgar.

'Do you really mean, Mr Moxey, that you – have kept unmarried for *my* sake?'

'You don't know that?' he asked, hoarsely.

'How could I? How was I to imagine such a thing? Really, was it proper? How could you expect me, Mr Moxey—?'

For a moment she looked offended. But her real feelings were astonishment and amusement, not unmingled with an idle gratification.

'I must ask you to pardon me,' said Christian, whose forehead gleamed with moisture.

'No, don't say that. I am really so sorry! What an odd mistake!'

'And I have hoped in vain – since you were free—?'

'Oh, you mustn't say such things! I shall never dream of marrying again – never!'

There was a matter-of-fact vigour in the assertion which proved that Mrs Palmer spoke her genuine thought. The tone could not be interpreted as devotion to her husband's memory; it meant, plainly and simply, that she had had enough of marriage, and delighted in her freedom.

Christian could not say another word. Disillusion was complete. The voice, the face, were those of as unspiritual a woman as he could easily have met with, and his life's story was that of a fool.

He took his hat, held out his hand, with 'Good-bye, Mrs Palmer.' The cold politeness left her no choice but again to look offended, and with merely a motion of the head she replied, 'Good-bye, Mr Moxey.'

And therewith permitted him to leave the house.

II

On calling at Earwaker's chambers one February evening, Malkin became aware, from the very threshold of the outer door, that the domicile was not as he had known it. With the familiar fragrance of Earwaker's special 'mixture' blended a suggestion of new upholstery. The little vestibule had somehow put off its dinginess, and an unwontedly brilliant light from the sitting-room revealed changes of the interior which the visitor remarked with frank astonishment.

'What the deuce! Has it happened at last? Are you going to be married?' he cried, staring about him at unrecognised chairs, tables, and bookcases, at whitened ceiling and pleasantly papered walls, at pictures and ornaments which he knew not.

The journalist shook his head, and smiled contentedly.

'An idea that came to me all at once. My editorship seemed to inspire it.'

After a year of waiting upon Providence, Earwaker had received the offer of a substantial appointment much more to his taste than those he had previously held. He was now literary editor of a weekly review which made no kind of appeal to the untaught multitude.

'I have decided to dwell here for the rest of my life,' he added, looking round the walls. 'One must have a homestead, and this shall be mine; here I have set up my penates. It's a portion of space, you know; and what more can be said of Longleat or Chatsworth? A house I shall never want, because I shall never have a wife. And on the whole I prefer this situation to any other. I am well within reach of everything urban that I care about, and as for the country, that is too good to be put to common use; let it be kept for holiday. There's an atmosphere in the old Inns that pleases me. The new flats are insufferable. How can one live sandwiched between a music-hall singer and a female politician? For lodgings of any kind no sane man had ever a word of approval. Reflecting on all these things, I have established myself in perpetuity.'

'Just what I can't do,' exclaimed Malkin, flinging himself into a broad, deep, leather-covered chair. 'Yet I have leanings that way. Only a few days ago I sat for a whole evening with the map of England open before me, wondering where would be the best

place to settle down – a few years hence, I mean, you know; when
Bella is old enough. – That reminds me. Next Sunday is her
birthday, and do you know what? I wish you'd go down to
Wrotham with me.'

'Many thanks, but I think I had better not.'

'Oh, but do! I want you to see how Bella is getting on. She's
grown wonderfully since you saw her in Paris – an inch taller, I
should think. I don't go down there very often, you know, so I
notice these changes. Really, I think no one could be more discreet
than I am, under the circumstances. A friend of the family; that's
all. Just dropping in for a casual cup of tea now and then. Sunday
will be a special occasion, of course. I say, what are your views
about early marriage? Do you think seventeen too young?'

'I should think seven-and-twenty much better.'

Malkin broke into fretfulness.

'Let me tell you, Earwaker, I don't like the way you habitually
speak of this project of mine. Plainly, I don't like it. It's a very
serious matter indeed – eh? What? Why are you smiling?'

'I agree with you as to its seriousness.'

'Yes, yes; but in a very cynical and offensive way. It makes me
confoundedly uncomfortable, let me tell you. I don't think that's
very friendly on your part. And the fact is, if it goes on I'm very
much afraid we shan't see so much of each other as we have done.
I like you, Earwaker, and I respect you; I think you know that. But
occasionally you seem to have too little regard for one's feelings.
No, I don't feel able to pass it over with a joke. – There! The deuce
take it! I've bitten off the end of my pipe.'

He spat out a piece of amber, and looked ruefully at the broken
stem.

'Take a cigar,' said Earwaker, fetching a box from a
cupboard.

'I don't mind. – Well – what was I saying? Oh yes; I was
quarrelling with you. Now, look here, what fault have you to find
with Bella Jacox?'

'None whatever. She seemed to me a very amiable child.'

'Child! Pooh! pshaw! And fifteen next Sunday, I tell you. She's a
young lady, and to tell you the confounded plain truth, I'm in love
with her. I am, and there's nothing to be ashamed of. If you smile,
we shall quarrel. I warn you, Earwaker, we shall quarrel.'

The journalist, instead of smiling, gave forth his deepest laugh.
Malkin turned very red, scowled, and threw his cigar aside.

'You really wish me to go on Sunday?' Earwaker asked, in a pleasant voice.

The other's countenance immediately cleared.

'I shall take it as a great kindness. Mrs Jacox will be delighted. Meet me at Holborn Viaduct at 1.25. No, to make sure I'll come here at one o'clock.'

In a few minutes he was chatting as unconcernedly as ever.

'Talking of settling down, my brother Tom and his wife are on the point of going to New Zealand. Necessity of business; may be out there for the rest of their lives. Do you know that I shall think very seriously of following them some day? With Bella, you know. The fact of the matter is, I don't believe I could ever make a solid home in England. Why, I can't quite say; partly, I suppose, because I have nothing to do. Now there's a good deal to be said for going out to the colonies. A man feels that he is helping the spread of civilisation; and that's something, you know. I should compare myself with the Greek and Roman colonists – something inspiriting in that thought – what? Why shouldn't I found a respectable newspaper, for instance? Yes, I shall think very seriously of this.'

'You wouldn't care to run over with your relatives, just to have a look?'

'It occurred to me,' Malkin replied, thoughtfully. 'But they sail in ten days, and – well, I'm afraid I couldn't get ready in time. And then I've promised to look after some little affairs for Mrs Jacox – some trifling money matters. But later in the year – who knows?'

Earwaker half repented of his promise to visit the Jacox household, but there was no possibility of excusing himself. So on Sunday he journeyed with his friend down to Wrotham. Mrs Jacox and her children were very comfortably established in a small new house. When the companions entered they found the mother alone in her sitting-room, and she received them with an effusiveness very distasteful to Earwaker.

'Now you shouldn't!' was her first exclamation to Malkin. 'Indeed you shouldn't! It's really very naughty of you. O Mr Earwaker! Who ever took so much pleasure in doing kindnesses? Do look at this *beautiful* book that Mr Malkin has sent as a present to my little Bella. O Mr Earwaker!'

The journalist was at once struck with her tone and manner as she addressed Malkin. He remarked that phrase, 'my little Bella', and it occurred to him that Mrs Jacox had been growing younger since he made her acquaintance on the towers of Notre Dame. When the girls presented themselves, they also appeared to him more juvenile; Bella, in particular, was dressed with an exaggeration of childishness decidedly not becoming. One had but to look into her face to see that she answered perfectly to Malkin's description; she was a young lady, and no child. A very pretty young lady, moreover; given to colouring, but with no silly simper; intelligent about the eyes and lips; modest, in a natural and sweet way. He conversed with her, and in doing so was disagreeably affected by certain glances she occasionally cast towards her mother. One would have said that she feared censure, though it was hard to see why.

On the return journey Earwaker made known some of his impressions, though not all.

'I like the girls,' he said, 'Bella especially. But I can't say much good of their mother.'

They were opposite each other in the railway carriage. Malkin leaned forward with earnest, anxious face.

'That's my own trouble,' he whispered. 'I'm confoundedly uneasy about it. I don't think she's bringing them up at all in a proper way. Earwaker, I would pay down five thousand pounds for the possibility of taking Bella away altogether.'

The other mused.

'But, mind you,' pursued Malkin, 'she's not a *bad* woman. By no means! Thoroughly good-hearted I'm convinced; only a little weak here.' He tapped his forehead. 'I respect her, for all she has suffered, and her way of going through it. But she isn't the ideal mother, you know.'

On his way home, Malkin turned into his friend's chambers 'for five minutes'. At two in the morning he was still there, and his talk in the meanwhile had been of nothing but schemes for protecting Bella against her mother's more objectionable influences. On taking leave, he asked:

'Any news of Peak yet?'

'None. I haven't seen Moxey for a long time.'

'Do you think Peak will look you up again, if he's in London?'

'No, I think he'll keep away. And I half hope he will; I shouldn't quite know how to behave. Ten to one he's in London now. I suppose he couldn't stay at Exeter. But he may have left England.'

They parted, and for a week did not see each other. Then, on Monday evening, when Earwaker was very busy with a mass of manuscript, the well-known knock sounded from the passage, and Malkin received admission. The look he wore was appalling, a look such as only some fearful catastrophe could warrant.

'Are you busy?' he asked, in a voice very unlike his own.

Earwaker could not doubt that the trouble was this time serious. He abandoned his work, and gave himself wholly to his friend's service.

'An awful thing has happened,' Malkin began. 'How the deuce shall I tell you? Oh, the ass I have made of myself! But I couldn't help it; there seemed no way out of it.'

'Well? What?'

'It was last night, but I couldn't come to you till now. By Jove! I veritably thought of sending you a note, and then killing myself. Early this morning I was within an ace of suicide. Believe me, old friend. This is no farce.'

'I'm waiting.'

'Yes, yes; but I can't tell you all at once. Sure you're not busy? I know I pester you. I was down at Wrotham yesterday. I hadn't meant to go, but the temptation was too strong. I got there at five o'clock, and found that the girls were gone to have tea with some young friends. Well, I wasn't altogether sorry; it was a good opportunity for a little talk with their mother. And I *had* the talk. But, oh, ass that I was!'

He smote the side of his head savagely.

'Can you guess, Earwaker? Can you give a shot at what happened?'

'Perhaps I might,' replied the other, gravely.

'Well?'

'That woman asked you to marry her.'

Malkin leapt from his chair, and sank back again.

'It came to that. Yes, upon my word, it came to that. She said she had fallen in love with me – that was the long and short of it. And I had never said a word that could suggest – Oh, confound it! What a frightful scene it was!'

'You took a final leave of her?'

Malkin stared with eyes of anguish into his friend's face, and at length whispered thickly:

'I said I would!'

'What? Take leave?'

'Marry her!'

Earwaker had much ado to check an impatiently remonstrant

laugh. He paused awhile, then began his expostulation, at first treating the affair as too absurd for grave argument.

'My boy,' he concluded, 'you have got into a preposterous scrape, and I see only one way out of it. You must flee. When does your brother start for the Antipodes?'

'Thursday morning.'

'Then you go with him; there's an end of it.'

Malkin listened with the blank, despairing look of a man condemned to death.

'Do you hear me?' urged the other. 'Go home and pack. On Thursday I'll see you off.'

'I can't bring myself to that,' came in a groan from Malkin. 'I've never yet done anything to be seriously ashamed of, and I can't run away after promising marriage. It would weigh upon me for the rest of my life.'

'Humbug! Would it weigh upon you less to marry the mother, and all the time be in love with the daughter? To my mind, there's something peculiarly loathsome in the suggestion.'

'But, look here; Bella is very young, really very young indeed. It's possible that I have deluded myself. Perhaps I don't really care for her in the way I imagined. It's more than likely that I might be content to regard her with fatherly affection.'

'Even supposing that, with what sort of affection do you regard Mrs Jacox?'

Malkin writhed on his chair before replying.

'You mustn't misjudge her!' he exclaimed. 'She is no heartless schemer. The poor thing almost cried her eyes out. It was a frightful scene. She reproached herself bitterly. What *could* I do? I have a tenderness for her, there's no denying that. She has been so vilely used, and has borne it all so patiently. How abominable it would be if I dealt her another blow!'

The journalist raised his eyebrows, and uttered inarticulate sounds.

'Was anything said about Bella?' he asked, abruptly.

'Not a word. I'm convinced she doesn't suspect that I thought of Bella like that. The fact is, I have misled her. She thought all along that my chief interest was in *her*.'

'Indeed? Then what was the ground of her self-reproach that you speak of?'

'How defective you are in the appreciation of delicate feeling!' cried Malkin frantically, starting up and rushing about the room.

'She reproached herself for having permitted me to get entangled with a widow older than myself, and the mother of two children. What could be simpler?'

Earwaker began to appreciate the dangers of the situation. If he insisted upon his view of Mrs Jacox's behaviour (though it was not the harshest that the circumstances suggested, for he was disposed to believe that the widow had really lost her heart to her kind, eccentric champion), the result would probably be to confirm Malkin in his resolution of self-sacrifice. The man must be saved, if possible, from such calamity, and this would not be effected by merely demonstrating that he was on the highroad to ruin. It was necessary to try another tack.

'It seems to me, Malkin,' he resumed, gravely, 'that it is you who are deficient in right feeling. In offering to marry this poor woman, you did her the gravest wrong.'

'What? How?'

'You know that it is impossible for you to love her. You know that you will repent, and that she will be aware of it. You are not the kind of man to conceal your emotions. Bella will grow up, and – well, the state of things won't tend to domestic felicity. For Mrs Jacox's own sake, it is your duty to put an end to this folly before it has gone too far.'

The other gave earnest ear, but with no sign of shaken conviction.

'Yes,' he said. 'I know this is one way of looking at it. But it assumes that a man can't control himself, that his sense of honour isn't strong enough to keep him in the right way. I don't think you quite understand me. I am not a passionate man; the proof is that I have never fallen in love since I was sixteen. I think a great deal of domestic peace, a good deal more than of romantic enthusiasm. If I marry Mrs Jacox, I shall make her a good and faithful husband, – so much I can safely say of myself.'

He waited, but Earwaker was not ready with a rejoinder.

'And there's another point. I have always admitted the defect of my character – an inability to settle down. Now, if I run away to New Zealand, with the sense of having dishonoured myself, I shall be a mere Wandering Jew for the rest of my life. All hope of redemption will be over. Of the two courses now open to me, that of marriage with Mrs Jacox is decidedly the less disadvantageous. Granting that I have made a fool of myself, I must abide by the result, and make the best of it. And the plain fact is, I *can't* treat her so disgracefully; I *can't* burden my conscience in this way. I believe it would end in suicide; I do, indeed.'

'This sounds all very well, but it is weakness and selfishness.'

'How can you say so?'

'There's no proving to so short-sighted a man the result of his mistaken course. I've a good mind to let you have your way just for the satisfaction of saying afterwards, "Didn't I tell you so?" You propose to behave with abominable injustice to two people, putting yourself aside. Doesn't it occur to you that Bella may already look upon you as her future husband? Haven't you done your best to plant that idea in her mind?'

Malkin started, but quickly recovered himself.

'No, I haven't! I have behaved with the utmost discretion. Bella thinks of me only as of a friend much older than herself.'

'I don't believe it!'

'Nonsense, Earwaker! A child of fifteen!'

'The other day you had quite a different view, and after seeing her again I agreed with you. She is a young girl, and if not already in love with you, is on the way to be so.'

'That will come to nothing when she hears that I am going to be her step-father.'

'Far more likely to develop into a grief that will waste the best part of her lifetime. She will be shocked and made miserable. But do as you like. I am tired of arguing.'

Earwaker affected to abandon the matter in disgust. For several minutes there was silence, then a low voice sounded from the corner where Malkin stood leaning.

'So it is your honest belief that Bella has begun to think of me in that way?'

'I am convinced of it.'

'But if I run away, I shall never see her again.'

'Why not? *She* won't run away. Come back when things have squared themselves. Write to Mrs Jacox from the ends of the earth, and let her understand that there is no possibility of your marrying her.'

'Tell her about Bella, you mean?'

'No, that's just what I don't mean. Avoid any mention of the girl. Come back when she is seventeen, and, if she is willing, carry her off to be happy ever after.'

'But she may have fallen in love with someone else.'

'I think not. You must risk it, at all events.'

'Look here!' Malkin came forward eagerly. 'I'll write to Mrs Jacox to-night, and make a full confession. I'll tell her exactly how the case stands. She's a good woman; she'll gladly sacrifice herself for the sake of her daughter.'

Earwaker was firm in resistance. He had no faith whatever in the widow's capacity for self-immolation, and foresaw that his friend would be drawn into another 'frightful scene', resulting probably in a marriage as soon as the licence could be obtained.

'When are you to see her again?' he inquired.

'On Wednesday.'

'Will you undertake to do nothing whatever till Wednesday morning, and then to have another talk with me? I'll come and see you about ten o'clock.'

In the end Malkin was constrained into making this engagement, and not long after midnight the journalist managed to get rid of him.

On Tuesday afternoon arrived a distracted note. 'I shall keep my promise, and I won't try to see you till you come here to-morrow. But I am sore beset. I have received *three* letters from Mrs Jacox, all long and horribly pathetic. She seems to have a presentiment that I shall forsake her. What a beast I shall be if I do! Tom comes here to-night, and I think I shall tell him all.'

The last sentence was a relief to the reader; he knew nothing of Mr Thomas Malkin, but there was a fair presumption that this gentleman would not see his brother bent on making such a notable fool of himself without vigorous protest.

At the appointed hour next morning, Earwaker reached his friend's lodgings, which were now at Kilburn. On entering the room he saw, not the familiar figure, but a solid, dark-faced, black-whiskered man, whom a faint resemblance enabled him to identify as Malkin the younger.

'I was expecting you,' said Thomas, as they shook hands. 'My brother is completely floored. When I got here an hour ago, I insisted on his lying down, and now I think he's asleep. If you don't mind, we'll let him rest for a little. I believe he has hardly closed his eyes since this unfortunate affair happened.'

'It rejoiced me to hear that he was going to ask your advice. How do matters stand?'

'You know Mrs Jacox?'

Thomas was obviously a man of discretion, but less intellectual than his brother; he spoke like one who is accustomed to the management of affairs. At first he was inclined to a polite reserve, but Earwaker's conversation speedily put him more at ease.

'I have quite made up my mind,' he said presently, 'that we must take him away with us to-morrow. The voyage will bring him to his senses.'

'Of course he resists?'

'Yes, but if you will give me your help, I think we can manage him. He is not very strong-willed. In a spasmodic way he can defy everyone, but the steady pressure of common sense will prevail with him, I think.'

They had talked for half-an-hour, when the door opened and the object of their benevolent cares stood before them. He was clad in a dressing-gown, and his disordered hair heightened the look of illness which his features presented.

'Why didn't you call me?' he asked his brother, irritably. 'Earwaker, I beg a thousand pardons! I'm not very well; I've overslept myself.'

'Yes, yes; come and sit down.'

Thomas made an offer to leave them.

'Don't go,' said Malkin. 'No need whatever. You know why Earwaker has been so kind as to come here. We may as well talk it over together.'

He sat on the table, swinging a tassel of his dressing-gown round and round.

'Now, what do you really think of doing?' asked the journalist, in a kind voice.

'I don't know. I absolutely do not know. I'm unutterably wretched.'

'In that case, will you let your brother and me decide for you? We have no desire but for your good, and we are perfectly at one in our judgment.'

'Of course I know what you will propose!' cried the other, excitedly. 'From the prudential point of view, you are right, I have no doubt. But how can you protect me against remorse? If you had received letters such as these three,' he pulled them out of a pocket, 'you would be as miserable as I am. If I don't keep my promise, I shall never know another moment of peace.'

'You certainly won't if you *do* keep it,' remarked Thomas.

'No,' added Earwaker, 'and one if not two other persons will be put into the same case. Whereas by boldly facing these reproaches of conscience, you do a great kindness to the others.'

'If only you could assure me of that!'

'I *can* assure you. That is to say, I can give it as my unassailable conviction.'

And Earwaker once more enlarged upon the theme, stating it from every point of view that served his purpose.

'You're making a mountain out of a mole-heap,' was the confirmatory remark that came from Thomas. 'This respectable lady will get over her sorrows quickly enough, and some day she'll be only too glad to have you for a son-in-law, if Miss Bella still pleases you.'

'It's only right,' urged Earwaker, in pursuance of his subtler intention, 'that you should bear the worst of the suffering, for the trouble has come out of your own thoughtlessness. You are fond of saying that you have behaved with the utmost discretion; so far from that you have been outrageously indiscreet. I foresaw that something of this kind might come to pass'—

'Then why the devil didn't you warn me?' shouted Malkin, in an agony of nervous strain.

'It would have been useless. In fact, I foresaw it too late.'

The discussion continued for an hour. By careful insistence on the idea of self-sacrifice, Earwaker by degrees demolished the arguments his friend kept putting forward. Thomas, who had gone impatiently to the window, turned round with words that were meant to be final.

'It's quite decided. You begin your preparations at once, and to-morrow morning you go on board with us.'

'But if I don't go to Wrotham this afternoon, she'll be here either to-night or the first thing to-morrow. I'm sure of it!'

'By four or five o'clock,' said Earwaker, 'you can have broken up the camp. You've often done it at shorter notice. Go to an hotel for the night.'

'I must write to the poor woman.'

'Do as you like about that.'

'Who is to help her, if she gets into difficulties – as she's always doing? Who is to advise her about Bella's education? Who is to pay – I mean, who will see to—? Oh, confound it!'

The listeners glanced at each other.

'Are her affairs in order?' asked Earwaker. 'Has she a sufficient income?'

'For ordinary needs, quite sufficient. But'—

'Then you needn't be in the least uneasy. Let her know where you are, when the equator is between you. Watch over her interests from a distance, if you like. I can as good as promise you that Bella will wait hopefully to see her friend again.'

Malkin succumbed to argument and exhaustion. Facing Earwaker with a look of pathetic appeal, he asked hoarsely:

'Will you stand by me till it's over? Have you time?'

'I can give you till five o'clock.'

'Then I'll go and dress. Ring the bell, Tom, and ask them to bring up some beer.'

Before three had struck, the arrangements for flight were completed. A heavily-laden cab bore away Malkin's personal property; within sat the unhappy man and his faithful friend.

The next morning Earwaker went down to Tilbury, and said farewell to the travellers on board the steamship *Orient*. Mrs Thomas had already taken her brother-in-law under her special care.

'It's only three children to look after, instead of two,' she remarked, in a laughing aside to the journalist. 'How grateful he will be to you in a few days! And I'm sure *we* are already.'

Malkin's eyes were no longer quite lustreless. At the last moment he talked with animation of 'two years hence', and there was vigour in the waving of his hand as the vessel started seaward.

Peak lost no time in leaving Exeter. To lighten his baggage, and to get rid of possessions to which hateful memories attached, he sold all his books that had any bearing on theology. The incomplete translation of *Bibel und Natur* he committed to the flames in Mrs Roots's kitchen, scattering its black remnants with savage thrusts of the poker. Whilst engaged in packing, he debated with himself whether or not he should take leave of the few acquaintances to whom he was indebted for hospitality and other kindness. The question was: Had Buckland Warricombe already warned these people against him? Probably it had seemed to Buckland the wiser course to be content with driving the hypocrite away; and, if this were so, regard for the future dictated a retirement from Exeter which should in no way resemble secret flight. Sidwell's influence with her parents would perhaps withhold them from making his disgrace known, and in a few years he might be glad that he had behaved with all possible prudence. In the end, he decided to write to Mr Lilywhite, saying that he was obliged to go away at a moment's notice, and that he feared it would be necessary altogether to change the scheme of life which he had had in view. This was the best way. From the Lilywhites, other people would hear of him, and perchance their conjectures would be charitable.

Without much hesitation he had settled his immediate plans. To London he would not return, for he dreaded the temptations to which the proximity of Sidwell would expose him, and he had no mind to meet with Moxey or Earwaker. As it was now imperative that he should find work of the old kind, he could not do better than go to Bristol, where, from the safe ground of a cheap and obscure lodging, he might make inquiries, watch advertisements, and so on. He already knew of establishments in Bristol where he might possibly obtain employment. Living with the utmost economy, he need not fall into difficulties for more than a year, and before then his good repute with the Rotherhithe firm would ensure him some position or other; if not in Bristol, then at Newcastle, St Helen's – any great centre of fuming and malodorous industry. He was ready to work, would delight in work. Idleness was now the intolerable thing.

So to Bristol he betook himself, and there made his temporary abode. After spending a few weeks in fruitless search for an engagement, he at length paid his oft-postponed visit to Twybridge. In the old home he felt completely a stranger, and his relatives strengthened the feeling by declaring him so changed in appearance that they hardly knew his face. With his mother only could he talk in anything like an intimate way, and the falsehoods with which he was obliged to answer her questions all but destroyed the pleasure he would otherwise have found in being affectionately tended. His sister, Mrs Cusse, was happy in her husband, her children, and a flourishing business. Oliver was making money, and enjoyed distinction among the shopkeeping community. His aunt still dealt in millinery, and kept up her acquaintance with respectable families. To Godwin all was like a dream dreamt for the second time. He could not acknowledge any actual connection between these people and himself. But their characteristics no longer gravely offended him, and he willingly recognised the homespun worth which their lives displayed. It was clear to him that by no possible agency of circumstances could he have been held in normal relations with his kinsfolk. However smooth his career, it must have wafted him to an immeasurable distance from Twybridge. Nature had decreed that he was to resemble the animals which, once reared, go forth in complete independence of birthplace and the ties of blood. It was a harsh fate, but in what had not fate been harsh to him? The one consolation was that he alone suffered. His mother was no doubt occasionally troubled by solicitude on his account, but she could not divine his inward miseries, and an assurance that he had no material cares sufficed to set her mind at ease.

'You are very like your father, Godwin,' she said, with a sigh. 'He couldn't rest, however well he seemed to be getting on. There was always something he wanted, and yet he didn't know what it was.'

'Yes, I must be like him,' Godwin replied, smiling.

He stayed five days, then returned to Bristol. A week after that, his mother forwarded to him a letter which had come to Twybridge. He at once recognised the writing, and broke the envelope with curiosity.

'If you should be in London [the note began], I beg you to let me see you. There is something I have to say. To speak to you for a few minutes I would come any distance. Don't accuse me of behaving treacherously; it was not my fault. I

know you would rather avoid me, but do consent to hear
what I have to say. If you have no intention of coming to
London, will you write and let me know where you are
living?

M. M.'

What could Marcella have to say to him? Nothing surely that
he at all cared to hear. No doubt she imagined that he might be in
ignorance of the circumstances which had led to Buckland
Warricombe's discovery; she wished to defend herself against the
suspicion of 'treachery'. He laughed carelessly, and threw her
note aside.

Two months passed, and his efforts to find employment were
still vain, though he had received conditional promises. The
solitude of his life grew burdensome. Several times he began a
letter to Sidwell, but his difficulty in writing was so great that he
destroyed the attempt. In truth, he knew not how to address her.
The words he penned were tumid, meaningless. He could not send
professions of love, for his heart seemed to be suffering a
paralysis, and the laborious artificiality of his style must have been
evident. The only excuse for breaking silence would be to let her
know that he had resumed honest work; he must wait till the
opportunity offered. It did not distress him to be without news of
her. If she wished to write, and was only withheld by ignorance of
his whereabouts, it was well; if she had no thought of sending him
a word, it did not matter. He loved her, and consciously nourished
hope, but for the present there was nothing intolerable in
separation. His state of mind resulted partly from nervous
reaction, and in part from a sense that only by silent suffering
could his dignity in Sidwell's eyes be ultimately restored. Between
the evil past and the hopeful future must be a complete break.

His thoughts kept turning to London, though not because
Sidwell might still be there. He felt urgent need of speaking with a
friend. Moxey was perhaps no longer to be considered one; but
Earwaker would be tolerant of human weaknesses. To have a
long talk with Earwaker would help him to recover his mental
balance, to understand himself and his position better. So one
morning in March, on the spur of the moment, he took train and
was once more in the metropolis. On his way he had determined
to send a note to Earwaker before calling at Staple Inn. He wrote it
at a small hotel in Paddington, where he took a room for the night,

and then spent the evening at a theatre, as the best way of killing time.

By the first post next morning came a card, whereon Earwaker had written: 'Be here, if you can, at two o'clock. Shall be glad to see you.'

'So you have been new-furnishing!' Godwin remarked, as he was admitted to the chambers. 'You look much more comfortable.'

'I'm glad you think so. It is the general opinion.'

They had shaken hands as though this were one of the ordinary meetings of old time, and their voices scarcely belied the appearance. Peak moved about the study, glancing at pictures and books, Earwaker eyeing him the while with not unfriendly expression. They were sincerely glad to see each other, and when Peak seated himself it was with an audible sigh of contentment.

'And what are you doing?' he inquired.

The journalist gave a brief account of his affairs, and Peak brightened with pleasure.

'This is good news. I knew you would shake off the ragamuffins before long. Give me some of your back numbers, will you? I shall be curious to examine your new style.'

'And you? – Come to live in London?'

'No; I am at Bristol, but only waiting. There's a chance of an analyst's place in Lancashire; but I may give the preference to an opening I have heard of in Belgium. Better to go abroad, I think.'

'Perhaps so.'

'I have a question to ask you. I suppose you talked about that *Critical* article of mine *before* you received my request for silence?'

'That's how it was,' Earwaker replied, calmly.

'Yes; I understood. It doesn't matter.'

The other puffed at his pipe, and moved uneasily.

'I am taking for granted,' Peak continued, 'that you know how I have spent my time down in Devonshire.'

'In outline. Need we trouble about the details?'

'No. But don't suppose that I should feel any shame in talking to you about them. That would be a confession of base motive. You and I have studied each other, and we can exchange thoughts on most subjects with mutual understanding. You know that I have only followed my convictions to their logical issue. An opportunity offered of achieving the supreme end to which my life is directed, and what scruple could stand in my way? We have nothing to do with names and epithets. *Here* are the facts of life as I had known it; *there* is the existence promised as the reward of successful artifice. To live was to pursue the object of my being. I could not feel otherwise; therefore, could not act otherwise. You imagine me defeated, flung back into the gutter.' His words came more quickly, and the muscles of his face worked under emotion. 'It isn't so. I have a great and reasonable hope. Perhaps I have gained everything I really desired. I could tell you the strangest story, but there a scruple *does* interpose. If we live another twenty years – but now I can only talk about myself.'

'And this hope of which you speak,' said Earwaker, with a grave smile, 'points you at present to sober work among your retorts and test-tubes?'

'Yes, it does.'

'Good. Then I can put faith in the result.'

'Yet the hope began in a lie,' rejoined Peak, bitterly. 'It will always be pleasant to look back upon that, won't it? You see: by no conceivable honest effort could I have gained this point. Life utterly denied to me the satisfaction of my strongest instincts, so long as I plodded on without cause of shame; the moment I denied my faith, and put on a visage of brass, great possibilities opened before me. Of course I understand the moralist's position. It behoved me, though I knew that a barren and solitary track would be my only treading to the end, to keep courageously onward. If I can't *believe* that any such duty is imposed upon me, where is the obligation to persevere, the morality of doing so? That is the worst hypocrisy. I have been honest, inasmuch as I have acted in accordance with my actual belief.'

'M–m–m,' muttered Earwaker, slowly. 'Then you have never been troubled with a twinge of conscience?'

'With a thousand! I have been racked, martyred. What has that to do with it? Do you suppose I attach any final significance to those torments? Conscience is the same in my view as an inherited disease which may possibly break out on any most innocent physical indulgence. – What end have I been pursuing? Is it criminal? Is it mean? I wanted to win the love of a woman – nothing more. To do that, I have had to behave like the grovelling villain who has no desire but to fill his pockets. And with success! – You understand that, Earwaker? I have succeeded! What respect can I have for the common morality, after this?'

'You have succeeded?' the other asked, thoughtfully. 'I could have imagined that you had been in appearance successful'—

He paused, and Peak resumed with vehemence:

'No, not in appearance only. I can't tell you the story'—

'I don't wish you to'—

'But what I have won is won for ever. The triumph no longer rests on deceit. What I insist upon is that by deceit only was it rendered possible. If a starving man succeeds in stealing a loaf of bread, the food will benefit him no less than if he had purchased it; it is good, true sustenance, no matter how he got it. To be sure, the man may prefer starvation; he may have so strong a metaphysical faith that death is welcome in comparison with what he calls dishonour. I – I have no such faith; and millions of other men in this country would tell the blunt truth if they said the same. I have *used means*, that's all. The old way of candour led me to bitterness and cursing; by dissimulation I have won something more glorious than tongue can tell.'

It was in the endeavour to expel the subtlest enemy of his peace that Godwin dwelt so defiantly upon this view of the temptation to which he had yielded. Since his farewell interview with Sidwell, he knew no rest from the torment of a mocking voice which bade him bear in mind that all his dishonour had been superfluous, seeing that whilst he played the part of a zealous Christian, Sidwell herself was drifting further and further from the old religion. This voice mingled with his dreams, and left not a waking hour untroubled. He refused to believe it, strove against the suggestion as a half-despairing man does against the persistent thought of suicide. If only he could obtain Earwaker's assent to the plan he put forward, it would support him in disregard of idle regrets.

'It is impossible,' said the journalist, 'for anyone to determine whether that is true or not – for you, as much as for anyone else. Be glad that you have shaken off the evil and retained the good, – no use in saying more than that.'

'Yes,' declared the other, stubbornly, 'there is good in exposing false views of life. I ought to have come utterly to grief and shame, and instead'—

'Instead—? Well?'

What I have told you.'

'Which I interpret thus: that you have permission to redeem your character, if possible, in the eyes of a woman you have grievously misled.'

Godwin frowned.

'Who suggested this to you, Earwaker?'

'You; no one else. I don't even know who the woman is of whom you speak.'

'Grant you are right. As an honest man, I should never have won her faintest interest.'

'It is absurd for us to talk about it. Think in the way that is most helpful to you, – that, no doubt, is a reasonable rule. Let us have done with all these obscurities, and come to a practical question. Can I be of any use to you? Would you care, for instance, to write an article now and then on some scientific matter that has a popular interest? I think I could promise to get that kind of thing printed for you. Or would you review an occasional book that happened to be in your line?'

Godwin reflected.

'Thank you,' he replied, at length. 'I should be glad of such work – if I can get into the mood for doing it properly. That won't be just yet; but perhaps when I have found a place'—

'Think it over. Write to me about it.'

Peak glanced round the room.

'You don't know how glad I am,' he said, 'that your prosperity shows itself in this region of bachelordom. If I had seen you in a comfortable house, married to a woman worthy of you – I couldn't have been sincere in my congratulations: I should have envied you so fiercely.'

'You're a strange fellow. Twenty years hence – as you said just now – you will one way or another have got rid of your astounding illusions. At fifty – well, let us say at sixty – you will have a chance of seeing things without these preposterous sexual spectacles.'

'I hope so. Every stage of life has its powers and enjoyments. When I am old, I hope to perceive and judge without passion of any kind. But is that any reason why my youth should be frustrated? We have only one life, and I want to live mine throughout.'

Soon after this Peak rose. He remembered that the journalist's time was valuable, and that he no longer had the right to demand more of it than could be granted to any casual caller. Earwaker behaved with all friendliness, but their relations had necessarily suffered a change. More than a year of separation, spent by the one in accumulating memories of dishonour, had given the other an enviable position among men; Earwaker had his place in the social system, his growing circle of friends, his congenial labour; perhaps – notwithstanding the tone in which he spoke of marriage – his hopes of domestic happiness. All this with no sacrifice of principle. He was fortunate in his temper, moral and intellectual; partly directing circumstances, partly guided by their pressure, he advanced on the way of harmonious development. Nothing great would come of his endeavours, but what he aimed at he steadily perfected. And this in spite of the adverse conditions under which he began his course. Nature had been kind to him; what more could one say?

When he went forth into the street again, Godwin felt his heart sink. His solitude was the more complete for this hour of friendly dialogue. No other companionship offered itself; if he lingered here, it must be as one of the drifting crowd, as an idle and envious spectator of the business and pleasure rife about him. He durst not approach that quarter of the town where Sidwell was living – if indeed she still remained here. Happily, the vastness of London enabled him to think of her as at a great distance; by keeping to the district in which he now wandered he was practically as remote from her as when he walked the streets of Bristol.

Yet there was one person who would welcome him eagerly if he chose to visit her. And, after all, might it not be as well if he heard what Marcella had to say to him? He could not go to the house, for it would be disagreeable to encounter Moxey; but, if he wrote, Marcella would speedily make an appointment. After an hour or two of purposeless rambling, he decided to ask for an interview. He might learn something that really concerned him; in any case, it was a final meeting with Marcella, to whom he perhaps owed this much courtesy.

The reply was as prompt as that from Earwaker. By the morning post came a letter inviting him to call upon Miss Moxey as soon as possible before noon. She added, 'My brother is away in the country; you will meet no one here.'

By eleven o'clock he was at Notting Hill; in the drawing-room, he sat alone for two or three minutes. Marcella entered silently, and came towards him without a smile; he saw that she read his face eagerly, if not with a light of triumph in her eyes. The expression might signify that she rejoiced at having been an instrument of his discomfiture; perhaps it was nothing more than gladness at seeing him again.

'Have you come to live in London?' she asked, when they had shaken hands without a word.

'I am only here for a day or two.'

'My letter reached you without delay?'

'Yes. It was sent from Twybridge to Bristol. I didn't reply then, as I had no prospect of being in London.'

'Will you sit down? You can stay for a few minutes?'

He seated himself awkwardly. Now that he was in Marcella's presence, he felt that he had acted unaccountably in giving occasion for another scene between them which could only end as painfully as that at Exeter. Her emotion grew evident; he could not bear to meet the look she had fixed upon him.

'I want to speak of what happened in this house about Christmas time,' she resumed. 'But I must know first what you have been told.'

'What have *you* been told?' he replied, with an uneasy smile. 'How do you know that anything which happened here had any importance for me?'

'I don't know that it had. But I felt sure that Mr Warricombe meant to speak to you about it.'

'Yes, he did.'

'But did he tell you the exact truth? Or were you led to suppose that I had broken my promise to you?'

Unwilling to introduce any mention of Sidwell, Peak preferred to simplify the story by attributing to Buckland all the information he had gathered.

'I understood,' he replied, 'that Warricombe had come here in the hope of learning more about me, and that certain facts came out in general conversation. What does it matter how he learned what he did? From the day when he met you down in Devonshire, it was of course inevitable that the truth should sooner or later come out. He always suspected me.'

'But I want you to know,' said Marcella, 'that I had no willing part in it. I promised you not to speak even to my brother, and I should never have done so but that Christian somehow met Mr Warricombe, and heard him talk of you. Of course he came to me in astonishment, and for your own interest I thought it best to tell Christian what I knew. When Mr Warricombe came here, neither Christian nor I would have enlightened him about – about your past. It happened most unfortunately that Mr Malkin was

present, and he it was who began to speak of the *Critical* article –
and other things. I was powerless to prevent it.'

'Why trouble about it? I quite believe your account.'

'You *do* believe it? You know I would not have injured you?'

'I am sure you had no wish to,' Godwin replied, in as
unsentimental a tone as possible. And, he added after a moment's
pause, 'Was this what you were so anxious to tell me?'

'Yes. Chiefly that.'

'Let me put your mind at rest,' pursued the other, with quiet
friendliness. 'I am disposed to turn optimist; everything has
happened just as it should have done. Warricombe relieved me
from a false position. If *he* hadn't done so, I must very soon have
done it for myself. Let us rejoice that things work together for
such obvious good. A few more lessons of this kind, and we shall
acknowledge that the world is the best possible.'

He laughed, but the tense expression of Marcella's features did
not relax.

'You say you are living in Bristol?'

'For a time.'

'Have you abandoned Exeter?'

The word implied something that Marcella could not utter
more plainly. Her face completed the question.

'And the clerical career as well,' he answered.

But he knew that she sought more than this, and his voice again
broke the silence.

'Perhaps you have heard that already? Are you in communication with Miss Moorhouse?'

She shook her head.

'But probably Warricombe has told your brother—?'

'What?'

'Oh, of his success in ridding Exeter of my objectionable
presence.'

'Christian hasn't seen him again, nor have I.'

'I only wish to assure you that I have suffered no injury. My
experiment was doomed to failure. What led me to it, how I
regarded it, we won't discuss; I am as little prepared to do so now
as when we talked at Exeter. That chapter in my life is happily
over. As soon as I am established again in a place like that I had at
Rotherhithe, I shall be quite contented.'

'Contented?' She smiled incredulously. 'For how long?'

'Who can say? I have lost the habit of looking far forward.'

Marcella kept silence so long that he concluded she had nothing more to say to him. It was an opportunity for taking leave without emotional stress, and he rose from his chair.

'Don't go yet,' she said at once. 'It wasn't only this that I'— Her voice was checked.

'Can I be of any use to you in Bristol?' Peak asked, determined to avoid the trial he saw approaching.

'There is something more I wanted to say,' she pursued, seeming not to hear him. 'You pretend to be contented, but I know that is impossible. You talk of going back to a dull routine of toil, when what you most desire is freedom. I want – if I can – to help you.'

Again she failed to command her voice. Godwin raised his eyes, and was astonished at the transformation she had suddenly undergone. Her face, instead of being colourless and darkly vehement, had changed to a bright warmth, a smiling radiance such as would have become a happy girl. His look seemed to give her courage.

'Only hear me patiently. We are such old friends – are we not? We have so often proclaimed our scorn of conventionality, and why should a conventional fear hinder what I want to say? You know – don't you? – that I have far more money than I need or am ever likely to. I want only a few hundreds a year, and I have more than a thousand.' She spoke more and more quickly, fearful of being interrupted. 'Why shouldn't I give you some of my superfluity? Let me help you in this way. Money can do so much. Take some from me, and use it as you will – just as you will. It is useless to *me*. Why shouldn't someone whom I wish well benefit by it?'

Godwin was not so much surprised as disconcerted. He knew that Marcella's nature was of large mould, and that whether she acted for good or evil its promptings would be anything but commonplace. The ardour with which she pleaded, and the magnitude of the benefaction she desired to bestow upon him, so affected his imagination that for the moment he stood as if doubting what reply to make. The doubt really in his mind was whether Marcella had calculated upon his weakness, and hoped to draw him within her power by the force of such an obligation, or if in truth she sought only to appease her heart with the exercise of generosity.

'You will let me?' she panted forth, watching him with brilliant eyes. 'This shall be a secret for ever between you and me. It imposes no debt of gratitude – how I despise the thought! I give you what is worthless to me, – except that it can do *you* good. But you can thank me if you will. I am not above being thanked.' She laughed unnaturally. 'Go and travel at first, as you wished to. Write me a short letter every month – every two months, just that I may know you are enjoying your life. It is agreed, isn't it?'

She held her hand to him, but Peak drew away, his face averted.

'How can you give me the pain of refusing such an offer?' he exclaimed, with remonstrance which was all but anger. 'You know the thing is utterly impossible. I should be ridiculous if I argued about it for a moment.'

'I can't see that it is impossible.'

'Then you must take my word for it. But I have no right to speak to you in that way,' he added, more kindly, seeing the profound humiliation which fell upon her. 'You meant to come to my aid at a time when I seemed to you lonely and miserable. It was a generous impulse, and I do indeed thank you. I shall always remember it and be grateful to you.'

Marcella's face was again in shadow. Its lineaments hardened to an expression of cold, stern dignity.

'I have made a mistake,' she said. 'I thought you above common ways of thinking.'

'Yes, you put me on too high a pedestal,' Peak answered, trying to speak humorously. 'One of my faults is that I am apt to mistake my own position in the same way.'

'You think yourself ambitious. Oh, if you knew really great ambition! Go back to your laboratory, and work for wages. I would have saved you from that.'

The tone was not vehement, but the words bit all the deeper for their unimpassioned accent. Godwin could make no reply.

'I hope,' she continued, 'we may meet a few years hence. By that time you will have learnt that what I offered was not impossible. You will wish you had dared to accept it. I know what your *ambition* is. Wait till you are old enough to see it in its true light. How you will scorn yourself! Surely there was never a man who united such capacity for great things with so mean an ideal. You will never win even the paltry satisfaction on which you have set your mind – never! But you can't be made to understand that. You will throw away all the best part of your life. Meet me in a few years, and tell me the story of the interval.'

'I will engage to do that, Marcella.'

'You will? But not to tell me the truth. You will not dare to tell the truth.'

'Why not?' he asked, indifferently. 'Decidedly I shall owe it you in return for your frankness to-day. Till then – good-bye.'

She did not refuse her hand, and as he moved away she watched him with a smile of slighting good-nature.

On the morrow Godwin was back in Bristol, and there he dwelt for another six months, a period of mental and physical lassitude. Earwaker corresponded with him, and urged him to attempt the work that had been proposed, but such effort was beyond his power.

He saw one day in a literary paper an announcement that Reusch's *Bibel und Natur* was about to be published in an English translation. So someone else had successfully finished the work he undertook nearly two years ago. He amused himself with the thought that he could ever have persevered so long in such profitless labour, and with a contemptuous laugh he muttered '*Thohu wabohu.*'

Just when the winter had set in, he received an offer of a post in chemical works at St Helen's, and without delay travelled northwards. The appointment was a poor one, and seemed unlikely to be a step to anything better, but his resources would not last more than another half year, and employment of whatever kind came as welcome relief to the tedium of his existence. Established in his new abode, he at length wrote to Sidwell. She answered him at once in a short letter which he might have shown to anyone, so calm were its expressions of interest, so uncompromising its words of congratulation. It began 'Dear Mr Peak', and ended with 'Yours sincerely'. Well, he had used the same formalities, and had uttered his feelings with scarcely more of warmth. Disappointment troubled him for a moment, and for a moment only. He was so far from Exeter, and further still from the life that he had led there. It seemed to him all but certain that Sidwell wrote coldly, with the intention of discouraging his hopes. What hope was he so foolish as to entertain? His position poorer than ever, what could justify him in writing love-letters to a girl who, even if willing to marry him, must not do so until he had a suitable home to offer her?

Since his maturity, he had never known so long a freedom from passion. One day he wrote to Earwaker: 'I begin to understand your independence with regard to women. It would be a strange thing if I became a convert to that way of thinking, but once or twice of late I have imagined that it was happening. My mind has all but recovered its tone, and I am able to read, to think – I mean really to *think*, not to muse. I get through big and solid books. Presently, if your offer still hold good, I shall send you a scrap of writing on something or other. The pestilent atmosphere of this place seems to invigorate me. Last Saturday evening I took train, got away into the hills, and spent the Sunday geologising. And a curious experience befell me, – one I had long, long ago, in the Whitelaw days. Sitting down before some interesting strata, I lost myself in something like nirvana, grew so subject to the idea of vastness in geological time that all human desires and purposes shrivelled to ridiculous unimportance. Awaking for a minute, I tried to realise the passion which not long ago rent and racked me, but I was flatly incapable of understanding it. Will this philosophic state endure? Perhaps I have used up all my emotional energy? I hardly know whether to hope or fear it.'

About midsummer, when his short holiday (he would only be released for a fortnight) drew near, he was surprised by another letter from Sidwell.

'I am anxious [she wrote] to hear that you are well. It is more than half a year since your last letter, and of late I have been constantly expecting a few lines. The spring has been a time of trouble with us. A distant relative, an old and feeble lady who has passed her life in a little Dorsetshire village, came to see us in April, and in less than a fortnight she was seized with illness and died. Then Fanny had an attack of bronchitis, from which even now she is not altogether recovered. On her account we are all going to Royat, and I think we shall be away until the end of September. Will you let me hear from you before I leave England, which will be in a week's time? Don't refrain from writing because you think you have no news to send. Anything that interests you is of interest to me. If it is only to tell me what you have been reading, I shall be glad of a letter.'

It was still 'Yours sincerely'; but Godwin felt that the letter meant more. In re-reading it he was pleasantly thrilled with a stirring of the old emotions. But his first impulse, to write an ardent reply, did not carry him away; he reflected and took counsel of the experience gained in his studious solitude. It was evident that by keeping silence he had caused Sidwell to throw off something of her reserve. The course dictated by prudence was to maintain an attitude of dignity, to hold himself in check. In this way he would regain what he had so disastrously lost, Sidwell's respect. There was a distinct pleasure in this exercise of self-command; it was something new to him; it flattered his pride. 'Let her learn that, after all, I am her superior. Let her fear to lose me. Then, if her love is still to be depended upon, she will before long find a way to our union. It is in her power, if only she wills it.'

So he sat down and wrote a short letter which seemed to him a model of dignified expression.

IV

Sidwell took no one into her confidence. The case was not one for counsel; whatever her future action, it must result from the maturing of self-knowledge, from the effect of circumstance upon her mind and heart. For the present she could live in silence.

'We hear,' she wrote from London to Sylvia Moorhouse, 'that Mr Peak has left Exeter, and that he is not likely to carry out his intention of being ordained. You, I daresay, will feel no surprise.' Nothing more than that; and Sylvia's comments in reply were equally brief.

Martin Warricombe, after conversations with his wife and with Buckland, felt it impossible not to seek for an understanding of Sidwell's share in the catastrophe. He was gravely perturbed, feeling that with himself lay the chief responsibility for what had happened. Buckland's attitude was that of the man who can only keep repeating 'I told you so'; Mrs Warricombe could only lament and upbraid in the worse than profitless fashion natural to women of her stamp. But in his daughter Martin had every kind of faith, and he longed to speak to her without reserve. Two days after her return from Exeter, he took Sidwell apart, and, with a distressing sense of the delicacy of the situation, tried to persuade her to frank utterance.

'I have been hearing strange reports,' he began, gravely, but without show of displeasure. 'Can you help me to understand the real facts of the case, Sidwell? — What is your view of Peak's behaviour?'

'He has deceived you, father,' was the quiet reply.

'You are convinced of that? — It allows of no—?'

'It can't be explained away. He pretended to believe what he did not and could not believe.'

'With interested motives, then?'

'Yes. — But not motives in themselves dishonourable.'

There was a pause. Sidwell had spoken in a steady voice, though with eyes cast down. Whether her father could understand a position such as Godwin's, she felt uncertain. That he would honestly endeavour to do so, there could be no doubt, especially since he must suspect that her own desire was to distinguish between the man and his fault. But a revelation of all that had passed between her and Peak was not possible; she had the support neither of intellect nor of passion; it would be asking for guidance, the very thing she had determined not to do. Already she found it difficult to recover the impulses which had directed her in that scene of parting; to talk of it would be to see her action in such a doubtful light that she might be led to some premature and irretrievable resolve. The only trustworthy counsellor was time; on what time brought forth must depend her future.

'Do you mean, Sidwell,' resumed her father, 'that you think it possible for us to overlook this deception?'

She delayed a moment, then said:

'I don't think it possible for you to regard him as a friend.'

Martin's face expressed relief.

'But will he remain in Exeter?'

'I shouldn't think he can.'

Again a pause. Martin was of course puzzled exceedingly, but he began to feel some assurance that Peak need not be regarded as a danger.

'I am grieved beyond expression,' he said at length. 'So deliberate a fraud – it seems to me inconsistent with any of the qualities I thought I saw in him.'

'Yes – it must.'

'Not – perhaps – to you?' Martin ventured, anxiously.

'His nature is not base.'

'Forgive me, dear. – I understand that you spoke with him after Buckland's call at his lodgings—?'

'Yes, I saw him.'

'And – he strove to persuade you that he had some motive which justified his conduct?'

'Excused, rather than justified.'

'Not – it seems – to your satisfaction?'

'I can't answer that question, father. My experience of life is too slight. I can only say that untruthfulness in itself is abhorrent to me, and that I could never try to make it seem a light thing.'

'That, surely, is a sound view, think as we may on speculative points. But allow me one more question, Sidwell. Does it seem to you that I have no choice but to break off all communication with Mr Peak?'

It was the course dictated by his own wish, she knew. And what could be gained by any middle way between hearty goodwill and complete repudiation? Time – time alone must work out the problem.

'Yes, I think you have no choice,' she answered.

'Then I must make inquiries – see if he leaves the town.'

'Mr Lilywhite will know, probably.'

'I will write before long.'

So the dialogue ended, and neither sought to renew it.

Martin enjoined upon his wife a discreet avoidance of the subject. The younger members of the family were to know nothing of what had happened, and, if possible, the secret must be kept from friends at Exeter. When a fortnight had elapsed, he wrote to Mr Lilywhite, asking whether it was true that Peak had gone away. 'It seems that private circumstances have obliged him to give up his project of taking Orders. Possibly he has had a talk with you?' The clergyman replied that Peak had left Exeter. 'I have had a letter from him, explaining in general terms his change of views. It hardly surprises me that he has reconsidered the matter. I don't think he was cut out for clerical work. He is far more likely to distinguish himself in the world of science. I suspect that conscientious scruples may have something to do with it; if so, all honour to him!'

The Warricombes prolonged their stay in London until the end of June. On their return home, Martin was relieved to find that scarcely an inquiry was made of him concerning Peak. The young man's disappearance excited no curiosity in the good people who had come in contact with him, and who were so far from suspecting what a notable figure had passed across their placid vision. One person only was urgent in his questioning. On an afternoon when Mrs Warricombe and her daughters were alone, the Rev. Bruno Chilvers made a call.

'Oh!' he exclaimed, after a few minutes' conversation, 'I am so anxious to ask you what has become of Mr Peak. Soon after my arrival in Exeter, I went to see him, and we had a long talk – a most interesting talk. Then I heard all at once that he was gone, and that we should see no more of him. Where is he? What is he doing?'

There was a barely appreciable delay before Mrs Warricombe made answer.

'We have quite lost sight of him,' she said, with an artificial smile. 'We know only that he was called away on some urgent business – family affairs, I suppose.'

Chilvers, in the most natural way, glanced from the speaker to Sidwell, and instantly, without the slightest change of expression, brought his eyes back again.

'I hope most earnestly,' he went on, in his fluty tone, 'that he will return. A most interesting man! A man of *large* intellectual scope, and really *broad* sympathies. I looked forward to many a chat with him. Has he, I wonder, been led to change his views? Possibly he would find a secular sphere more adapted to his special powers.'

Mrs Warricombe had nothing to say. Sidwell, finding that Mr Chilvers' smile now beamed in her direction, replied to him with steady utterance:

'It isn't uncommon, I think, nowadays, for doubts to interfere with the course of study for ordination?'

'Far from uncommon!' exclaimed the Rector of St Margaret's, with almost joyous admission of the fact. 'Very far from uncommon. Such students have my profound sympathy. I know from experience exactly what it means to be overcome in a struggle with the modern spirit. Happily for myself, I was enabled to recover what for a time I lost. But charity forbid that I should judge those who think they must needs voyage for ever in "sunless gulfs of doubt", or even absolutely deny that the human intellect can be enlightened from above.'

At a loss even to follow this rhetoric, Mrs Warricombe, who was delighted to welcome the Rev. Bruno, and regarded him as a gleaming pillar of the Church, made haste to introduce a safer topic. After that, Mr Chilvers was seen at the house with some frequency. Not that he paid more attention to the Warricombes than to his other acquaintances. Relieved by his curate from the uncongenial burden of mere parish affairs, he seemed to regard himself as an apostle at large, whose mission directed him to the households of well-to-do people throughout the city. His brother clergymen held him in slight esteem. In private talk with Martin Warricombe, Mr Lilywhite did not hesitate to call him 'a mountebank', and to add other depreciatory remarks.

'My wife tells me – and I can trust her judgment in such things – that his sole object just now is to make a good marriage. Rather disagreeable stories seem to have followed him from the other side of England. He makes love to all unmarried women – never going beyond what is thought permissible, but doing a good deal of mischief, I fancy. One lady in Exeter – I won't mention names – has already pulled him up with a direct inquiry as to his intentions; at her house, I imagine, he will no more be seen.'

The genial parson chuckled over his narrative, and Martin, by no means predisposed in the Rev. Bruno's favour, took care to report these matters to his wife.

'I don't believe a word of it!' exclaimed Mrs Warricombe. 'All the clergy are jealous of Mr Chilvers.'

'What? Of his success with ladies?'

'Martin! It is something new for you to be profane! – They are jealous of his high reputation.'

'Rather a serious charge against our respectable friends.'

'And the stories are all nonsense,' pursued Mrs Warricombe. 'It's very wrong of Mr Lilywhite to report such things. I don't believe any other clergyman would have done so.'

Martin smiled – as he had been accustomed to do all through his married life – and let the discussion rest there. On the next occasion of Mr Chilvers being at the house, he observed the reverend man's behaviour with Sidwell, and was not at all pleased. Bruno had a way of addressing women which certainly went beyond the ordinary limits of courtesy. At a little distance, anyone would have concluded that he was doing his best to excite Sidwell's affectionate interest. The matter of his discourse might be unobjectionable, but the manner of it was not in good taste.

Mrs Warricombe was likewise observant, but with other emotions. To her it seemed a subject for pleasurable reflection, that Mr Chilvers should show interest in Sidwell. The Rev. Bruno had bright prospects. With the colour of his orthodoxy she did not concern herself. He was ticketed 'broad', a term which carried with it no disparagement; and Sidwell's sympathies were altogether with the men of 'breadth'. The time drew near when Sidwell must marry, if she ever meant to do so, and in comparison with such candidates as Mr Walsh and Godwin Peak, the Rector of St Margaret's would be an ideal husband for her. Sidwell's attitude towards Mr Chilvers was not encouraging, but Mrs Warricombe suspected that a lingering regard for the impostor, so lately unmasked, still troubled her daughter's mind: a new suitor, even if rejected, would help the poor girl to dismiss that shocking infatuation.

Sidwell and her father nowadays spent much time together, and in the autumn days it became usual for them to have an afternoon ramble about the lanes. Their talk was of science and literature, occasionally skirting very close upon those questions which both feared to discuss plainly – for a twofold reason. Sidwell read much more than had been her wont, and her choice of authors would alone have indicated a change in her ways of thinking, even if she had not allowed it to appear in the tenor of her talk. The questions she put with reference to Martin's favourite studies were sometimes embarrassing.

One day they happened to meet Mr Chilvers, who was driving with his eldest child, a boy of four. The narrowness of the road made it impossible – as Martin would have wished – to greet and pass on. Chilvers stopped the carriage and jumped out. Sidwell could not but pay some attention to the youthful Chilvers.

'Till he is ten years old,' cried Bruno, 'I shall think much more of his body than of his mind. In fact, at this age the body *is* the mind. Books, books – oh, we attach far too much importance to them. Over-study is one of the morbific tendencies of our time. Some one or other has been trying to frown down what he calls the excessive athleticism of our public schools. No, no! Let us rejoice that our lads have such an opportunity of vigorous physical development. The culture of the body is a great part of religion.' He always uttered remarks of this kind as if suggesting that his hearers should note them in a collection of aphorisms. 'If to labour is to pray, so also is the practice of open-air recreation.'

When they had succeeded in getting away, father and daughter walked for some minutes without speaking. At length Sidwell asked, with a smile:

'How does this form of Christianity strike you?'

'Why, very much like a box on the ear with a perfumed glove,' replied Martin.

'That describes it very well.'

They walked a little further, and Sidwell spoke in a more serious tone.

'If Mr Chilvers were brought before the ecclesiastical authorities and compelled to make a clear statement of his faith, what sect, in all the history of heresies, would he really seem to belong to?'

'I know too little of him, and too little of heresies.'

'Do you suppose for a moment that he sincerely believes the dogmas of his Church?'

Martin bit his lip and looked uneasy.

'We can't judge him, Sidwell.'

'I don't know,' she persisted. 'It seems to me that he does his best to give us the means of judging him. I half believe that he often laughs in himself at the success of his audacity.'

'No, no. I think the man is sincere.'

This was very uncomfortable ground, but Sidwell would not avoid it. Her eyes flashed, and she spoke with a vehemence such as Martin had never seen in her.

'Undoubtedly sincere in his determination to make a figure in the world. But a Christian, in any intelligible sense of that much-abused word, – no! He is one type of the successful man of our day. Where thousands of better and stronger men struggle vainly for fair recognition, he and his kind are glorified. In comparison with a really energetic man, he is an acrobat. The crowd stares at him and applauds, and there is nothing he cares for so much as that kind of admiration.'

Martin kept silence, and in a few minutes succeeded in broaching a wholly different subject.

Not long after this, Mr Chilvers paid a call at the conventional hour. Sidwell, hoping to escape, invited two girls to step out with her on to the lawn. The sun was sinking, and, as she stood with eyes fixed upon it, the Rev. Bruno's voice disagreeably broke her reverie. She was perforce involved in a dialogue, her companions moving aside.

'What a magnificent sky!' murmured Chilvers. '"There sinks the nebulous star." Forgive me, I have fallen into a tiresome trick of quoting. How differently a sunset is viewed nowadays from what it was in old times! Our impersonal emotions are on a higher plane – don't you think so? Yes, scientific discovery has done more for religion than all the ages of pious imagination. A theory of Galileo or Newton is more to the soul than a psalm of David.'

'You think so?' Sidwell asked, coldly.

In everyday conversation she was less suave than formerly. This summer she had never worn her spray of sweet-brier, and the omission might have been deemed significant of a change in herself. When the occasion offered, she no longer hesitated to express a difference of opinion; at times she uttered her dissent with a bluntness which recalled Buckland's manner in private.

'Does the comparison seem to you unbecoming?' said Chilvers, with genial condescension. 'Or untrue?'

'What do you mean by "the soul"?' she inquired, still gazing away from him.

'The principle of conscious life in man – that which understands and worships.'

'The two faculties seem to me so different that'— She broke off. 'But I mustn't talk foolishly about such things.'

'I feel sure you have thought of them to some purpose. I wonder whether you ever read Francis Newman's book on *The Soul?*'

'No, I never saw it.'

'Allow me to recommend it to you. I believe you would find it deeply interesting.'

'Does the Church approve it?'

'The Church?' He smiled. 'Ah! what Church? Churchmen there are, unfortunately, who detest the name of its author, but I hope you have never classed me among them. The Church, rightly understood, comprehends every mind and heart that is striving upwards. The age of intolerance will soon be as remote from us as that of persecution. Can I be mistaken in thinking that this broader view has your sympathy, Miss Warricombe?'

'I can't sympathise with what I don't understand, Mr Chilvers.'

He looked at her with tender solicitude, bending slightly from his usual square-shouldered attitude.

'Do let me find an opportunity of talking over the whole matter with you – by no means as an instructor. In my view, a clergyman may seek instruction from the humblest of those who are called his flock. The thoughtful and high-minded among them will often assist him materially in his endeavour at self-development. To my "flock",' he continued, playfully, 'you don't belong; but may I not count you one of that circle of friends to whom I look for the higher kind of sympathy?'

Sidwell glanced about her in the hope that some one might be approaching. Her two friends were at a distance, talking and laughing together.

'You shall tell me some day,' she replied, with more attention to courtesy, 'what the doctrines of the Broad Church really are. But the air grows too cool to be pleasant; hadn't we better return to the drawing-room?'

The greater part of the winter went by before she had again to submit to a *tête-à-tête* with the Rev. Bruno. It was seldom that she thought of him save when compelled to do so by his exacting presence, but in the meantime he exercised no small influence on her mental life. Insensibly she was confirmed in her alienation from all accepted forms of religious faith. Whether she wished it or not, it was inevitable that such a process should keep her constantly in mind of Godwin Peak. Her desire to talk with him at times became so like passion that she appeared to herself to love him more truly than ever. Yet such a mood was always followed by doubt, and she could not say whether the reaction distressed or soothed her. These months that had gone by brought one result, not to be disguised. Whatever the true nature of her feeling for Godwin, the thought of marrying him was so difficult to face that it seemed to involve impossibilities. He himself had warned her that marriage would mean severance from all her kindred. It was practically true, and time would only increase the difficulty of such a determination.

The very fact that her love (again, if love it were) must be indulged in defiance of universal opinion tended to keep emotion alive. A woman is disposed to cling to a lover who has disgraced himself, especially if she can believe that the disgrace was incurred as a result of devotion to her. Could love be separated from thought of marriage, Sidwell would have encouraged herself in fidelity, happy in the prospect of a life-long spiritual communion – for she would not doubt of Godwin's upward progress, of his eventual purification. But this was a mere dream. If Godwin's passion were steadfast, the day would come when she must decide either to cast in her lot with his, or to bid him be free. And could she imagine herself going forth into exile?

There came a letter from him, and she was fortunate enough to receive it without the knowledge of her relatives. He wrote that he had obtained employment. The news gave her a troubled joy, lasting for several days. That no emotion appeared in her reply was due to a fear lest she might be guilty of misleading him. Perhaps already she had done so. Her last whisper – 'Some day!' – was it not a promise and an appeal? Now she had not the excuse of profound agitation, there must be no word her conscience could not justify. But in writing those formal lines she felt herself a coward. She was drawing back – preparing her escape.

Often she had the letter beneath her pillow. It was the first she had ever received from a man who professed to love her. So long without romance in her life, she could not but entertain this semblance of it, and feel that she was still young.

It told much in Godwin's favour that he had not ventured to write before there was this news to send her. It testified to the force of his character, the purity of his purpose. A weaker man, she knew, would have tried to excite her compassion by letters of mournful strain, might even have distressed her with attempts at clandestine meeting. She had said rightly – his nature was not base. And she loved him! She was passionately grateful to him for proving that her love had not been unworthily bestowed.

When he wrote again, her answer should not be cowardly.

The life of the household went on as it had been wont to do for years, but with the spring came events. An old lady died whilst on a visit to the house (she was a half-sister of Mrs Warricombe), and by a will executed a few years previously she left a thousand pounds, to be equally divided between the children of this family. Sidwell smiled sadly on finding herself in possession of this bequest, the first sum of any importance that she had ever held in her own right. If she married a man of whom all her kith and kin so strongly disapproved that they would not give her even a wedding present, two hundred and fifty pounds would be better than no dowry at all. One could furnish a house with it.

Then Fanny had an attack of bronchitis, and whilst she was recovering Buckland came down for a few days, bringing with him a piece of news for which no one was prepared. As if to make reparation to his elder sister for the harshness with which he had behaved in the affair of Godwin Peak, he chose her for his first confidante.

'Sidwell, I am going to be married. Do you care to hear about it?'

'Certainly I do.'

Long ago she had been assured of Sylvia Moorhouse's sincerity in rejecting Buckland's suit. That was still a grief to her, but she acknowledged her friend's wisdom, and was now very curious to learn who it was that the Radical had honoured with his transferred affections.

'The lady's name,' Buckland began, 'is Miss Matilda Renshaw. She is the second daughter of a dealer in hides, tallow, and that kind of thing. Both her parents are dead; she has lived of late with her married sister at Blackheath.'

Sidwell listened with no slight astonishment, and her countenance looked what she felt.

'That's the bald statement of the cause,' pursued her brother, seeming to enjoy the consternation he had excited. 'Now, let me fill up the outline. Miss Renshaw is something more than good-looking, has had an admirable education, is five-and-twenty, and for a couple of years has been actively engaged in humanitarian work in the East End. She has published a book on social questions, and is a very good public speaker. Finally, she owns property representing between three and four thousand a year.'

'The picture has become more attractive,' said Sidwell.

'You imagined a rather different person? If I persuade mother to invite her down here presently, do you think you could be friendly with her?'

'I see no reason why I should not be.'

'But I must warn you. She has nothing to do with creeds and dogmas.'

He tried to read her face. Sidwell's mind was a mystery to him.

'I shall make no inquiry about her religious views,' his sister replied, in a dispassionate tone, which conveyed no certain meaning.

'Then I feel sure you will like her, and equally sure that she will like you.'

His parents had no distinct fault to find with this choice, though they would both greatly have preferred a daughter-in-law whose genealogy could be more freely spoken of. Miss Renshaw was invited to Exeter, and the first week of June saw her arrival. Buckland had in no way exaggerated her qualities. She was a dark-eyed beauty, perfect from the social point of view, a very interesting talker, – in short, no ordinary woman. That Buckland should have fallen in love with her, even after Sylvia, was easily understood; it seemed likely that she would make him as good a wife as he could ever hope to win.

Sidwell was expecting another letter from the north of England. The silence which during those first months had been justifiable was now a source of anxiety. But whether fear or hope predominated in her expectancy, she still could not decide. She had said to herself that her next reply should not be cowardly, yet she was as far as ever from a courageous resolve.

Mental harassment told upon her health. Martin, watching her with solicitude, declared that for her sake as much as for Fanny's they must have a thorough holiday abroad.

Urged by the approaching departure, Sidwell overcame her reluctance to write to Godwin before she had a letter to answer. It was done in a mood of intolerable despondency, when life looked barren before her, and the desire of love all but triumphed over every other consideration. The letter written and posted, she would gladly have recovered it – reserved, formal as it was. Cowardly still; but then Godwin had not written.

She kept a watch upon the postman, and again, when Godwin's reply was delivered, escaped detection.

Hardly did she dare to open the envelope. Her letter had perchance been more significant than she supposed; and did not the mere fact of her writing invite a lover's frankness?

But the reply was hardly more moving than if it had come from a total stranger. For a moment she felt relieved; in an hour's time she suffered indescribable distress. Godwin wrote – so she convinced herself after repeated perusals – as if discharging a task; not a word suggested tenderness. Had the letter been unsolicited, she could have used it like the former one; but it was the answer to an appeal. The phrases she had used were still present in her mind. 'I am anxious … it is more than half a year since you wrote … I have been expecting … anything that is of interest to you will interest me …' How could she imagine that this was reserved and formal? Shame fell upon her; she locked herself from all companionship, and wept in rebellion against the laws of life.

A fortnight later, she wrote from Royat to Sylvia Moorhouse. It was a long epistle, full of sunny descriptions, breathing renewed vigour of body and mind. The last paragraph ran thus:

'Yesterday was my birthday; I was twenty-eight. At this age, it is wisdom in a woman to remind herself that youth is over. I don't regret it; let it go with all its follies! But I am sorry that I have no serious work in life; it is not cheerful to look forward to perhaps another eight-and-twenty years of elegant leisure – that is to say, of wearisome idleness. What can I do? Try and think of some task for me, something that will last a lifetime.'

PART THE SEVENTH

I

At the close of a sultry day in September, when factory fumes hung low over the town of St Helen's, and twilight thickened luridly, and the air tasted of sulphur, and the noises of the streets, muffled in their joint effect, had individually an ominous distinctness, Godwin Peak walked with languid steps to his lodgings and the meal that there awaited him. His vitality was at low ebb. The routine of his life disgusted him; the hope of release was a mockery. What was to be the limit of this effort to redeem his character? How many years before the past could be forgotten, and his claim to the style of honourable be deemed secure? Rubbish! It was an idea out of old-fashioned romances. What he was, he was, and no extent of dogged duration at St Helen's or elsewhere, could affect his personality. What, practically, was to be the end? If Sidwell had no money of her own, and no expectations from her father, how could she ever become his wife? Women liked this kind of thing, this indefinite engagement to marry when something should happen, which in all likelihood never would happen – this fantastic mutual fidelity with only the airiest reward. Especially women of a certain age.

A heavy cart seemed to be rumbling in the next street. No, it was thunder. If only a good rattling storm would sweep the bituminous atmosphere, and allow a breath of pure air before midnight.

She could not be far from thirty. Of course there prevails much conventional nonsense about women's age; there are plenty of women who reckon four decades, and yet retain all the essential charm of their sex. And as a man gets older, as he begins to persuade himself that at forty one has scarce reached the prime of life—

The storm was coming on in earnest. Big drops began to fall. He quickened his pace, reached home, and rang the bell for a light.

His landlady came in with the announcement that a gentleman had called to see him, about an hour ago; he would come again at seven o'clock.

'What name?'

None had been given. A youngish gentleman, speaking like a Londoner.

It might be Earwaker, but that was not likely. Godwin sat down to his plain meal, and after it lit a pipe. Thunder was still rolling, but now in the distance. He waited impatiently for seven o'clock.

To the minute, sounded a knock at the house-door. A little delay, and there appeared Christian Moxey.

Godwin was surprised and embarrassed. His visitor had a very grave face, and was thinner, paler, than three years ago; he appeared to hesitate, but at length offered his hand.

'I got your address from Earwaker. I was obliged to see you – on business.'

'Business?'

'May I take my coat off? We shall have to talk.'

They sat down, and Godwin, unable to strike the note of friendship lest he should be met with repulse, broke silence by regretting that Moxey should have had to make a second call.

'Oh, that's nothing! I went and had dinner. – Peak, my sister is dead.'

Their eyes met; something of the old kindness rose to either face.

'That must be a heavy blow to you,' murmured Godwin, possessed with a strange anticipation which he would not allow to take clear form.

'It is. She was ill for three months.' Whilst staying in the country last June she met with an accident. She went for a long walk alone one day, and in a steep lane she came up with a carter who was trying to make a wretched horse drag a load beyond its strength. The fellow was perhaps half drunk; he stood there beating the horse unmercifully. Marcella couldn't endure that kind of thing – impossible for her to pass on and say nothing. She interfered, and tried to persuade the man to lighten his cart. He was insolent, attacked the horse more furiously than ever, and kicked it so violently in the stomach that it fell. Even then he wouldn't stop his brutality. Marcella tried to get between him and the animal – just as it lashed out with its heels. The poor girl was so badly injured that she lay by the roadside until another carter took her up and brought her back to the village. Three months of accursed suffering, and then happily came the end.'

A far, faint echoing of thunder filled the silence of their voices. Heavy rain splashed upon the pavement.

'She said to me just before her death,' resumed Christian, '"I have ill luck when I try to do a kindness – but perhaps there is one more chance." I didn't know what she meant till afterwards. Peak, she has left nearly all her money to you.'

Godwin knew it before the words were spoken. His heart leaped, and only the dread of being observed enabled him to control his features. When his tongue was released he said harshly:

'Of course I can't accept it.'

The words were uttered independently of his will. He had no such thought, and the sound of his voice shook him with alarm.

'Why can't you?' returned Christian.

'I have no right – it belongs to you, or to some other relative – it would be'—

His stammering broke off. Flushes and chills ran through him; he could not raise his eyes from the ground.

'It belongs to no one but you,' said Moxey, with cold persistence. 'Her last wish was to do you a kindness, and I, at all events, shall never consent to frustrate her intention. The legacy represents something more than eight hundred a year, as the investments now stand. This will make you independent – of everything and everybody.' He looked meaningly at the listener. 'Her own life was not a very happy one; she did what she could to save yours from a like doom.'

Godwin at last looked up.

'Did she speak of me during her illness?'

'She asked me once, soon after the accident, what had become of you. As I knew from Earwaker, I was able to tell her.'

A long silence followed. Christian's voice was softer when he resumed.

'You never knew her. She was the one woman in ten thousand – at once strong and gentle; a fine intellect, and a heart of rare tenderness. But because she had not the kind of face that'—

He checked himself.

'To the end her mind kept its clearness and courage. One day she reminded me of Heine – how we had talked of that "conversion" on the mattress-grave, and had pitied the noble intellect subdued by disease. "I shan't live long enough," she said, "to incur that danger. What I have thought ever since I could study, I think now, and shall to the last moment." I buried her without forms of any kind, in the cemetery at Kingsmill. That was what she wished. I should have despised myself if I had lacked that courage.'

'It was right,' muttered Godwin.

'And I wear no mourning, you see. All that kind of thing is ignoble. I am robbed of a priceless companionship, but I don't care to go about inviting people's pity. If only I could forget those months of suffering! Some day I shall, perhaps, and think of her only as she lived.'

'Were you alone with her all the time?'

'No. Our cousin Janet was often with us.' Christian spoke with averted face. 'You don't know, of course, that she has gone in for medical work – practises at Kingsmill. The accident was at a village called Lowton, ten miles or more from Kingsmill. Janet came over very often.'

Godwin mused on this development of the girl whom he remembered so well. He could not direct his thoughts; a languor had crept over him.

'Do you recollect, Peak,' said Christian, presently, 'the talk we had in the fields by Twybridge, when we first met?'

The old friendliness was reappearing in his manner, He was yielding to the impulse to be communicative, confidential, which had always characterised him.

'I remember,' Godwin murmured.

'If only my words then had had any weight with you! And if only I had acted upon my own advice! Just for those few weeks I was sane; I understood something of life; I saw my true way before me. You and I have both gone after ruinous ideals, instead of taking the solid good held out to us. Of course, I know your story in outline. I don't ask you to talk about it. You are independent now, and I hope you can use your freedom. – Well, and I too am free.'

The last words were in a lower tone. Godwin glanced at the speaker, whose sadness was not banished, but illumined with a ray of calm hope.

'Have you ever thought of me and my infatuation?' Christian asked.

'Yes.'

'I have outlived that mawkish folly. I used to drink too much; the two things went well together. It would shame me to tell you all about it. But, happily, I have been able to go back about thirteen years – recover my old sane self – and with it what I then threw away.'

'I understand.'

'Do you? Marcella knew of it, just before her death, and it made her glad. But the waste of years, the best part of a lifetime! It's incredible to me as I look back. Janet called on us one day in London. Heaven be thanked that she was forgiving enough to do so! What would have become of me now?'

'How are you going to live, then?' Godwin asked, absently.

'How? My income is sufficient'—

'No, no; I mean, where and how will you live in your married life?'

'That's still uncertain. Janet mustn't go on with professional work. In any case, I don't think she could for long; her strength isn't equal to it. But I shouldn't wonder if we settle in Kingsmill. To you it would seem intolerable? But why should we live in London? At Kingsmill Janet has a large circle of friends; in London we know scarcely half-a-dozen people – of the kind it would give us any pleasure to live with. We shall have no lack of intellectual society; Janet knows some of the Whitelaw professors. The atmosphere of Kingsmill isn't illiberal, you know; we shan't be fought shy of because we object to pass Sundays in a state of coma. But the years that I have lost! The irrecoverable years!'

'There's nothing so idle as regretting the past,' said Godwin, with some impatience. 'Why groan over what couldn't be otherwise? The probability is, Janet and you are far better suited to each other now than you ever would have been if you had married long ago.'

'You think that?' exclaimed the other, eagerly. 'I have tried to see it in that light. If I didn't feel so despicable!'

'She, I take it, doesn't think you so,' Godwin muttered.

'But how can she understand? I have tried to tell her everything, but she refused to listen. Perhaps Marcella told her all she cared to know.'

'No doubt.'

Each brooded for a while over his own affairs, then Christian reverted to the subject which concerned them both.

'Let us speak frankly. You will take this gift of Marcella's as it was meant?'

How *was* it meant? Critic and analyst as ever, Godwin could not be content to see in it the simple benefaction of a woman who died loving him. Was it not rather the last subtle device of jealousy? Marcella knew that the legacy would be a temptation he could scarcely resist – and knew at the same time that, if he accepted it, he practically renounced his hope of marrying Sidwell Warricombe. Doubtless she had learned as much as she needed to know of Sidwell's position. Refusing this bequest, he was as far as ever from the possibility of asking Sidwell to marry him. Profiting by it, he stood for ever indebted to Marcella, must needs be grateful to her, and some day, assuredly, would reveal the truth to whatever woman became his wife. Conflict of reasonings and emotions made it difficult to answer Moxey's question.

'I must take time to think of it,' he said, at length.

'Well, I suppose that is right. But – well, I know so little of your circumstances'—

'Is that strictly true?' Peak asked.

'Yes. I have only the vaguest idea of what you have been doing since you left us. Of course I have tried to find out.'

Godwin smiled, rather gloomily.

'We won't talk of it. I suppose you stay in St Helen's for the night?'

'There's a train at 10.20. I had better go by it.'

'Then let us forget everything but your own cheerful outlook. At ten, I'll walk with you to the station.'

Reluctantly at first, but before long with a quiet abandonment to the joy that would not be suppressed, Christian talked of his future wife. In Janet he found every perfection. Her mind was something more than the companion of his own. Already she had begun to inspire him with a hopeful activity, and to foster the elements of true manliness which he was conscious of possessing, though they had never yet had free play. With a sense of luxurious safety, he submitted to her influence, knowing none the less that it was in his power to complete her imperfect life. Studiously he avoided the word 'ideal'; from such vaporous illusions he had turned to the world's actualities; his language dealt with concretes, with homely satisfactions, with prospects near enough to be soberly examined.

A hurry to catch the train facilitated parting. Godwin promised to write in a few days.

He took a roundabout way back to his lodgings. The rain was over, the sky had become placid. He was conscious of an effect from Christian's conversation which half counteracted the mood he would otherwise have indulged, – the joy of liberty and of an outlook wholly new. Sidwell might perchance be to him all that Janet was to Christian. Was it not the luring of 'ideals' that prompted him to turn away from his long hope?

There must be no more untruthfulness. Sidwell must have all the facts laid before her, and make her choice.

Without a clear understanding of what he was going to write, he sat down at eleven o'clock, and began, 'Dear Miss Warricombe'. Why not 'Dear Sidwell'? He took another sheet of paper.

'Dear Sidwell, – To-night I can remember only your last word to me when we parted. I cannot address you coldly, as though half a stranger. Thus long I have kept silence about everything but the outward events of my life; now, in telling you of something that has happened, I must speak as I think.

'Early this evening I was surprised by a visit from Christian Moxey – a name you know. He came to tell me that his sister (she of whom I once spoke to you) was dead, and had bequeathed to me a large sum of money. He said that it represented an income of eight hundred pounds.

'I knew nothing of Miss Moxey's illness, and the news of her will came to me as a surprise. In word or deed, I never sought more than her simple friendship – and even *that* I believed myself to have forfeited.

'If I were to refuse this money, it would be in consequence of a scruple which I do not in truth respect. Christian Moxey tells me that his sister's desire was to enable me to live the life of a free man, and if I have any duty at all in the matter, surely it does not constrain me to defeat her kindness. No condition whatever is attached. The gift releases me from the necessity of leading a hopeless existence – leaves me at liberty to direct my life how I will.

'I wish, then, to put aside all thoughts of how this opportunity came to me, and to ask you if you are willing to be my wife.

'Though I have never written a word of love, my love is unchanged. The passionate hope of three years ago still rules my life. Is *your* love strong enough to enable you to disregard all hindrances? I cannot of course know whether, in your sight, dishonour still clings to me, or whether you understand me well enough to have forgiven and forgotten those hateful things in the past. Is it yet too soon? Do you wish me still to wait, still to prove myself? Is your interest in the free man less than in the slave? For my life has been one of slavery and exile – exile, if you know what I mean by it, from the day of my birth.

'Dearest, grant me this great happiness! We can live where we will. I am not rich enough to promise all the comforts and refinements to which you are accustomed, but we should be safe from sordid anxieties. We can travel; we can make a home in any European city. It would be idle to speak of the projects and ambitions that fill my mind – but surely I may do something worth doing, win some position among intellectual men of which you would not be ashamed. You yourself urged me to hope that. With you at my side – Sidwell, grant me this chance, that I may know the joy of satisfied love! I am past the age which is misled by vain fancies. I have suffered unspeakably, longed for the calm strength, the pure, steady purpose which would result to me from a happy marriage. There is no fatal divergence between our minds; did you not tell me that? You said that if I had been truthful from the first, you might have loved me with no misgiving. Forget the madness into which I was betrayed. There is no soil upon my spirit. I offer you love as noble as any man is capable of. Think – think well – before replying to me; let your true self prevail. You *did* love me, dearest.—

Yours ever,
Godwin Peak.'

At first he wrote slowly, as though engaged on a literary composition, with erasions, insertions. Facts once stated, he allowed himself to forget how Sidwell would most likely view them, and thereafter his pen hastened: fervour inspired the last paragraph. Sidwell's image had become present to him, and exercised all – or nearly all – its old influence.

The letter must be copied, because of that laboured beginning.

Copying one's own words is at all times a disenchanting drudgery, and when the end was reached Godwin signed his name with hasty contempt. What answer could he expect to such an appeal? How vast an improbability that Sidwell would consent to profit by the gift of Marcella Moxey!

Yet how otherwise could he write? With what show of sincerity could he offer to refuse the bequest? Nay, in that case he must not *offer* to do so, but simply state the fact that his refusal was beyond recall. Logically, he had chosen the only course open to him, – for to refuse independence was impossible.

A wheezy clock in his landlady's kitchen was striking two. For very fear of having to revise his letter in the morning, he put it into its envelope, and went out to the nearest pillar-post.

That was done. Whether Sidwell answered with 'Yes' or with 'No', he was a free man.

On the morrow he went to his work as usual, and on the day after that. The third morning might bring a reply – but did not. On the evening of the fifth day, when he came home, there lay the expected letter. He felt it; it was light and thin. That hideous choking of suspense – Well, it ran thus:

'I cannot. It is not that I am troubled by your accepting the legacy. You have every right to do so, and I know that your life will justify the hopes of her who thus befriended you. But I am too weak to take this step. To ask you to wait yet longer, would only be a fresh cowardice. You cannot know how it shames me to write this. In my very heart I believe I love you, but what is such love worth? You must despise me, and you will forget me. I live in a little world; in the greater world where your place is, you will win a love very different.

S. W.'

Godwin laughed aloud as the paper dropped from his hand.

Well, she was not the heroine of a romance. Had he expected her to leave home and kindred – the 'little world' so infinitely dear to her – and go forth with a man deeply dishonoured? Very young girls have been known to do such a thing; but a thoughtful mature woman—! Present, his passion had dominated her: and perhaps her nerves only. But she had had time to recover from that weakness.

A woman, like most women, of cool blood, temperate fancies.

A domestic woman; the ornament of a typical English home.

Most likely it was true that the matter of the legacy did not trouble her. In any case she would not have consented to marry him, and *therefore* she knew no jealousy. Her love! why, truly, what was it worth?

(Much, much! of no less than infinite value. He knew it, but this was not the moment for such a truth.)

A cup of tea to steady the nerves. Then thoughts, planning, world-building.

He was awake all night, and Sidwell's letter lay within reach. – Did *she* sleep calmly? Had she never stretched out her hand for *his* letter, when all was silent? There were men who would not take such a refusal. A scheme to meet her once more – the appeal of passion, face to face, heart to heart – the means of escape ready – and then the 'greater world'—

But neither was he cast in heroic mould. He had not the self-confidence, he had not the hot, youthful blood. A critic of life, an analyst of moods and motives; not the man who dares and acts. The only important resolve he had ever carried through was a scheme of ignoble trickery – to end in frustration.

'The greater world'. It was a phrase that had been in his own mind once or twice since Moxey's visit. To point him thither was doubtless the one service Sidwell could render him. And in a day or two, that phrase was all that remained to him of her letter.

On a Sunday afternoon at the end of October, Godwin once more climbed the familiar stairs at Staple Inn, and was welcomed by his friend Earwaker. The visit was by appointment. Earwaker knew all about the legacy; that it was accepted; and that Peak had only a few days to spend in London, on his way to the Continent.

'You are regenerated,' was his remark as Godwin entered.

'Do I look it? Just what I feel. I have shaken off a good (or a bad) ten years.'

The speaker's face, at all events in this moment, was no longer that of a man at hungry issue with the world. He spoke cheerily.

'It isn't often that fortune does a man such a kind turn. One often hears it said: If only I could begin life again with all the experience I have gained! That is what I *can* do. I can break utterly with the past, and I have learnt how to live in the future.'

'Break utterly with the past?'

'In the practical sense. And even morally to a great extent.'

Earwaker pushed a box of cigars across the table. Godwin accepted the offer, and began to smoke. During these moments of silence, the man of letters had been turning over a weekly paper, as if in search of some paragraph; a smile announced his discovery.

'Here is something that will interest you – possibly you have seen it.'

He began to read aloud:

'"On the 23rd inst. was celebrated at St Bragg's, Torquay, the marriage of the Rev. Bruno Leathwaite Chilvers, late Rector of St Margaret's, Exeter, and the Hon. Bertha Harriet Cecilia Jute, eldest daughter of the late Baron Jute. The ceremony was conducted by the Hon. and Rev. J. C. Jute, uncle of the bride, assisted by the Rev. F. Miller, the Very Rev. Dean Pinnock, the Rev. H. S. Crook, and the Rev. William Tomkinson. The bride was given away by Lord Jute. Mr Horatio Dukinfield was best man. The bridal dress was of white brocade, draped with Brussels lace, the corsage being trimmed with lace and adorned with orange blossoms. The tulle veil, fastened with three diamond stars, the gifts of"— Well, shall I go on?'

'The triumph of Chilvers!' murmured Godwin. 'I wonder whether the Hon. Bertha is past her fortieth year?'

'A blooming beauty, I dare say. But Lord! how many people it takes to marry a man like Chilvers! How sacred the union must be! – Pray take a paragraph more: "The four bridesmaids – Miss – etc., etc. – wore cream crépon dresses trimmed with turquoise blue velvet, and hats to match. The bridegroom's presents to them were diamond and ruby brooches."'

'Chilvers *in excelsis*! – So he is no longer at Exeter; has no living, it seems. What does he aim at next, I wonder?'

Earwaker cast meaning glances at his friend.

'I understand you,' said Godwin, at length. 'You mean that this merely illustrates my own ambition. Well, you are right, I confess my shame – and there's an end of it.'

He puffed at his cigar, resuming presently:

'But it would be untrue if I said that I regretted anything. Constituted as I am, there was no other way of learning my real needs and capabilities. Much in the past is hateful to me, but it all had its use. There are men – why, take your own case. You look back on life, no doubt, with calm and satisfaction.'

'Rather, with resignation.'

Godwin let his cigar fall, and laughed bitterly.

'Your resignation has kept pace with life. I was always a rebel. My good qualities – I mean what I say – have always wrecked me. Now that I haven't to fight with circumstances, they may possibly be made subservient to my happiness.'

'But what form is your happiness to take?'

'Well, I am leaving England. On the Continent I shall make no fixed abode, but live in the places where cosmopolitan people are to be met. I shall make friends; with money at command, one may hope to succeed in that. Hotels, boarding-houses, and so on, offer the opportunities. It sounds oddly like the project of a swindler, doesn't it? There's the curse I can't escape from! Though my desires are as pure as those of any man living, I am compelled to express myself as if I were about to do something base and underhand. Simply because I have never had a social place. I am an individual merely; I belong to no class, town, family, club'—

'Cosmopolitan people,' mused Earwaker. 'Your ideal is transformed.'

'As you know. Experience only could bring that about. I seek now only the free, intellectual people – men who have done with the old conceptions – women who'—

His voice grew husky, and he did not complete the sentence.

'I shall find them in Paris, Rome. – Earwaker, think of my being able to speak like this! No day-dreams, but actual sober plans, their execution to begin in a day or two. Paris, Rome! And a month ago I was a hopeless slave in a vile manufacturing town. – I wish it were possible for me to pray for the soul of that poor dead woman. I don't speak to you of her; but do you imagine I am brutally forgetful of her to whom I owe all this?'

'I do you justice,' returned the other, quietly.

'I believe you can and do.'

'How grand it is to go forth as I am now going!' Godwin resumed, after a long pause. 'Nothing to hide, no shams, no pretences. Let who will inquire about me. I am an independent Englishman, with so and so much a year. In England I have one friend only – that is you. The result, you see, of all these years' savage striving to knit myself into the social fabric.'

'Well, you will invite me some day to your villa at Sorrento,' said Earwaker, encouragingly.

'That I shall!' Godwin's eyes flashed with imaginative delight. 'And before very long. Never to a home in England!'

'By-the-bye, a request. I have never had your portrait. Sit before you leave London.'

'No. I'll send you one from Paris – it will be better done.'

'But I am serious. You promise?'

'You shall have the thing in less than a fortnight.'

The promise was kept. Earwaker received an admirable photograph, which he inserted in his album with a curious sense of satisfaction. A face by which every intelligent eye must be arrested; which no two observers would interpret in the same way.

'His mate must be somewhere,' thought the man of letters, 'but he will never find her.'

II

In his acceptance of Sidwell's reply, Peak did not care to ask himself whether the delay of its arrival had any meaning one way or another. Decency would hardly have permitted her to answer such a letter by return of post; of course she waited a day or so.

But the interval meant more than this.

Sylvia Moorhouse was staying with her friend. The death of Mrs Moorhouse, and the marriage of the mathematical brother, had left Sylvia homeless, though not in any distressing sense; her inclination was to wander for a year or two, and she remained in England only until the needful arrangements could be concluded.

'You had better come with me,' she said to Sidwell, as they walked together on the lawn after luncheon.

The other shook her head.

'Indeed, you had better. — What are you doing here? What are you going to make of your life?'

'I don't know.'

'Precisely. Yet one ought to live on some kind of plan. I think it is time you got away from Exeter; it seems to me you are finding its atmosphere *morbific*.'

Sidwell laughed at the allusion.

'You know,' she said, 'that the reverend gentleman is shortly to be married?'

'Oh yes, I have heard all about it. But is he forsaking the Church?'

'Retiring only for a time, they say.'

'Forgive the question, Sidwell — did he honour you with a proposal?'

'Indeed, no!'

'Some one told me it was imminent, not long ago.'

'Quite a mistake,' Sidwell answered, with her grave smile. 'Mr Chilvers had a singular manner with women in general. It was meant, perhaps, for subtle flattery; he may have thought it the most suitable return for the female worship he was accustomed to receive.'

Mr Warricombe was coming towards them. He brought a new subject of conversation, and as they talked the trio drew near to the gate which led into the road. The afternoon postman was just entering; Mr Warricombe took from him two letters.

'One for you, Sylvia, and – one for you, Sidwell.'

A slight change in his voice caused Sidwell to look at her father as he handed her the letter. In the same moment she recognised the writing of the address. It was Godwin Peak's, and undoubtedly her father knew it.

With a momentary hesitation Mr Warricombe continued his talk from the point at which he had broken off, but he avoided his daughter's look, and Sidwell was too well aware of an uneasiness which had fallen upon him. In a few minutes he brought the chat to an end, and walked away towards the house.

Sidwell held her letter tightly. Conversation was no longer possible for her; she had a painful throbbing of the heart, and felt that her face must be playing traitor. Fortunately, Sylvia found it necessary to write a reply to the missive she had received, and her companion was soon at liberty to seek solitude.

For more than an hour she remained alone. However un-emotional the contents of the letter, its arrival would have perturbed her seriously, as in the two previous instances; what she found on opening the envelope threw her into so extreme an agitation that it was long before she could subdue the anguish of disorder in all her senses. She had tried to believe that Godwin Peak was henceforth powerless to affect her in this way, write what he would. The romance of her life was over; time had brought the solution of difficulties to which she looked forward; she recognised the inevitable, as doubtless did Godwin also. But all this was self-deception. The passionate letter delighted as much as it tortured her; in secret her heart had desired this, though reason suppressed and denied the hope. No longer need she remember with pangs of shame the last letter she had written, and the cold response; once again things were as they should be – the lover pleading before her – she with the control of his fate. The injury to her pride was healed, and in the thought that perforce she must answer with a final 'No', she found at first more of solace than of distress.

Subsidence of physical suffering allowed her to forget this emotion, in its nature unavowable. She could think of the news Godwin sent, could torment herself with interpretations of Marcella Moxey's behaviour, and view in detail the circum-stances which enabled Godwin to urge a formal suit. Among her various thoughts there recurred frequently a regret that this letter had not reached her, like the other two, unobserved. Her father

had now learnt that she was in correspondence with the
disgraced man; to keep silence would be to cause him grave
trouble; yet how much better if fortune had only once more
favoured her, so that the story might have remained her secret,
from beginning to end.

For was not this the end?—

At the usual time she went to the drawing-room, and somehow succeeded in conversing as though nothing had disturbed
her. Mr Warricombe was not seen till dinner. When he came
forth, Sidwell noticed his air of preoccupation, and that he
avoided addressing her. The evening asked too much of her self-
command; she again withdrew, and only came back when the
household was ready for retiring. In bidding her father good-
night, she forced herself to meet his gaze; he looked at her with
troubled inquiry, and she felt her cheek redden.

'Do you want to get rid of me?' asked Sylvia, with wonted
frankness, when her friend drew near.

'No. Let us go to the glass-house.'

Up there on the roof Sidwell often found a retreat when her
thoughts were troublesome. Fitfully, she had resumed her water-
colour drawing, but as a rule her withdrawal to the glass-house
was for reading or reverie. Carrying a small lamp, she led the
way before Sylvia, and they sat down in the chairs which on one
occasion had been occupied by Buckland Warricombe and Peak.

The wind, rarely silent in this part of Devon, blew boisterously
from the south-west. A far-off whistle, that of a train speeding
up the valley on its way from Plymouth, heightened the sense of
retirement and quietude always to be enjoyed at night here under
the stars.

'Have you been thinking over my suggestion?' asked Sylvia,
when there had been silence awhile.

'No,' was the murmured reply.

'Something has happened, I think.'

'Yes. I should like to tell you, Sylvia, but'—

'But'—

'I *must* tell you! I can't keep it in my own mind, and you are
the only one'—

Sylvia was surprised at the agitation which suddenly revealed
itself in her companion's look and voice. She became serious, her
eyes brightening with intellectual curiosity. Feminine expressions of sympathy were not to be expected from Miss

Moorhouse; far more reassuring to Sidwell was the kind attentiveness with which her friend bent forward.

'That letter father handed me to-day was from Mr Peak.'

'You hear from him?'

'This is the third time – since he went away. At our last meeting' – her voice dropped – 'I pledged my faith to him. – Not absolutely. The future was too uncertain'—

The gleam in Sylvia's eyes grew more vivid. She was profoundly interested, and did not speak when Sidwell's voice failed.

'You never suspected this?' asked the latter, in a few moments.

'Not exactly that. What I did suspect was that Mr Peak's departure resulted from – your rejection of him.'

'There is more to be told,' pursued Sidwell, in tremulous accents. 'You must know it all – because I need your help. No one here has learnt what took place between us. Mr Peak did not go away on that account. But – you remember being puzzled to explain his orthodoxy in religion?'

She paused. Sylvia gave a nod, signifying much.

'He never believed as he professed,' went on Sidwell, hurriedly. 'You were justified in doubting him. He concealed the truth – pretended to champion the old faiths'—

For an instant she broke off, then hastened through a description of the circumstances which had brought about Peak's discovery. Sylvia could not restrain a smile, but it was softened by the sincere kindliness of her feeling.

'And it was after this,' she inquired impartially, 'that the decisive conversation between you took place?'

'No; just before Buckland's announcement. We met again, after that. – Does it seem incredible to you that I should have let the second meeting end as it did?'

'I think I understand. Yes, I know you well enough to follow it. I can even guess at the defence he was able to urge.'

'You can?' asked Sidwell, eagerly. 'You see a possibility of his defending himself?'

'I should conjecture that it amounted to the old proverb, "All's fair in love and war". And, putting aside a few moral prejudices, one can easily enough absolve him. – The fact is, I had long ago surmised that his motives in taking to such a career had more reference to this world than the next. You know, I had several long talks with him; I told you how he interested me. Now I can piece together my conclusions.'

'Still,' urged Sidwell, 'you must inevitably regard him as ignoble – as guilty of base deceit. I must hide nothing from you, having told so much. Have you heard from anyone about his early life?'

'Your mother told me some old stories.'

Sidwell made an impatient gesture. In words of force and ardour, such as never before had been at her command, she related all she knew of Godwin's history prior to his settling at Exeter, and depicted the mood, the impulses, which, by his own confession, had led to that strange enterprise. Only by long exercise of an impassioned imagination could she thus thoroughly have identified herself with a life so remote from her own. Peak's pleading for himself was scarcely more impressive. In listening, Sylvia understood how completely Sidwell had cast off the beliefs for which her ordinary conversation seemed still to betray a tenderness.

'I know,' the speaker concluded, 'that he cannot in that first hour have come to regard me with a feeling strong enough to determine what he then undertook. It was not I as an individual, but all of us here, and the world we represented. Afterwards, he persuaded himself that he had felt love for me from the beginning. And I, I tried to believe it – because I wished it true; for his sake, and for my own. However it was, I could not harden my heart against him. A thousand considerations forbade me to allow him further hope; but I refused to listen – no, I *could* not listen. I said I would remain true to him. He went away to take up his old pursuits, and if possible to make a position for himself. It was to be our secret. And in spite of everything. I hoped for the future.'

Silence followed, and Sidwell seemed to lose herself in distressful thought.

'And now,' asked her friend, 'what has come to pass?'

'Do you know that Miss Moxey is dead?'

'I haven't heard of it.'

'She is dead, and has left Mr Peak a fortune. – His letter of to-day tells me this. And at the same time he claims my promise.'

Their eyes met. Sylvia still had the air of meditating a most interesting problem. Impossible to decide from her countenance how she regarded Sidwell's position.

'But why in the world,' she asked, 'should Marcella Moxey have left her money to Mr Peak?'

'They were friends,' was the quick reply. 'She knew all that had befallen him, and wished to smooth his path.'

Sylvia put several more questions, and to all of them Sidwell replied with a peculiar decision, as though bent on making it clear that there was nothing remarkable in this fact of the bequest. The motive which impelled her was obscure even to her own mind, for ever since receiving the letter she had suffered harassing doubts where now she affected to have none.

'She knew, then,' was Sylvia's last inquiry, 'of the relations between you and Mr Peak?'

'I am not sure – but I think so. Yes, I think she must have known.'

'From Mr Peak himself, then?'

Sidwell was agitated.

'Yes – I think so. But what does that matter?'

The other allowed her face to betray perplexity.

'So much for the past,' she said at length. 'And now?'—

'I have not the courage to do what I wish.'

There was a long silence.

'About your wish,' asked Sylvia at length, 'you are not at all doubtful?'

'Not for one moment. – Whether I err in my judgment of him could be proved only by time; but I know that if I were free, if I stood alone'—

She broke off and sighed.

'It would mean, I suppose,' said the other, 'a rupture with your family?'

'Father would not abandon me, but I should darken the close of his life. Buckland would utterly cast me off; mother would wish to do so. – You see, I cannot think and act simply as a woman, as a human being. I am bound to a certain sphere of life. The fact that I have outgrown it, counts for nothing. I cannot free myself without injury to people whom I love. To act as I wish would be to outrage every rule and prejudice of the society to which I belong. You yourself – you know how you would regard me.'

Sylvia replied deliberately.

'I am seeing you in a new light, Sidwell. It takes a little time to reconstruct my conception of you.'

'You think worse of me than you did.'

'Neither better nor worse, but differently. There has been too much reserve between us. After so long a friendship, I ought to have known you more thoroughly. To tell the truth, I have thought now and then of you and Mr Peak; that was inevitable.

But I went astray; it seemed to me the most unlikely thing that you should regard him with more than a doubtful interest. I knew, of course, that he had made you his ideal, and I felt sorry for him.'

'I seemed to you unworthy?'—

'Too placid, too calmly prudent. – In plain words, Sidwell, I do think better of you.'

Sidwell smiled.

'Only to know me henceforth as the woman who did not dare to act upon her best impulses.'

'As for "best" – I can't say. I don't glorify passion, as you know; and on the other hand I have little sympathy with the people who are always crying out for self-sacrifice. I don't know whether it would be "best" to throw over your family, or to direct yourself solely with regard to their comfort.'

Sidwell broke in.

'Yes, that is the true phrase – "their comfort". No higher word should be used. That is the ideal of the life to which I have been brought up. Comfort, respectability. – And has *he* no right? If I sacrifice myself to father and mother, do I not sacrifice *him* as well? He has forfeited all claim to consideration – that is what people say. With my whole soul, I deny it! If he sinned against anyone, it was against me, and the sin ended as soon as I understood him. That episode in his life is blotted out; by what law must it condemn to imperfection the whole of his life and of my own? Yet because people will not, cannot, look at a thing in a spirit of justice, I must wrong myself and him.'

'Let us think of it more quietly,' said Sylvia, in her clear, dispassionate tones. 'You speak as though a decision must be taken at once. Where is the necessity for that? Mr Peak is now independent. Suppose a year or two be allowed to pass, may not things look differently?'

'A year or two!' exclaimed Sidwell, with impatience. 'Nothing will be changed. What I have to contend against is unchangeable. If I guide myself by such a hope as that, the only reasonable thing would be for me to write to Mr Peak, and ask him to wait until my father and mother are dead.'

'Very well. On that point we are at rest, then. The step must be taken at once, or never.'

The wind roared, and for some minutes no other sound was audible. By this, all the inmates of the house save the two friends were in bed, and most likely sleeping.

'You must think it strange,' said Sidwell, 'that I have chosen to tell you all this, just when the confession is most humiliating to me. I want to feel the humiliation, as one only can when another is witness of it. I wish to leave myself no excuse for the future.'

'I'm not sure that I quite understand you. You have made up your mind to break with him?'

'Because I am a coward.'

'If my feeling in any matter were as strong as that, I should allow it to guide me.'

'Because your will is stronger. You, Sylvia, would never (in my position) have granted him that second interview. You would have known that all was at an end, and have acted upon the knowledge. I knew it, but yielded to temptation – at *his* expense. I could not let him leave me, though that would have been kindest. I held him by a promise, basely conscious that retreat was always open to me. And now I shall have earned his contempt'—

Her voice failed. Sylvia, affected by the outbreak of emotion in one whom she had always known so strong in self-command, spoke with a deeper earnestness.

'Dear, do you wish me to help you against what you call your cowardice? I cannot take it upon me to encourage you until your own will has spoken. The decision must come from yourself. Choose what course you may, I am still your friend. I have no idle prejudices, and no social bonds. You know how I wish you to come away with me; now I see only more clearly how needful it is for you to breathe new air. Yes, you have outgrown these conditions, just as your brothers have, just as Fanny will – indeed has. Take to-night to think of it. If you can decide to travel with me for a year, be frank with Mr Peak, and ask him to wait so long – till you have made up your mind. He cannot reasonably find fault with you, for he knows all you have to consider. Won't this be best?'

Sidwell was long silent.

'I will go with you,' she said at last, in a low voice. 'I will ask him to grant me perfect liberty for a year.'

When she came down next morning it was Sidwell's intention to seek a private interview with her father, and make known her resolve to go abroad with Sylvia; but Mr Warricombe anticipated her.

'Will you come to the library after breakfast, Sidwell?' he said, on meeting her in the hall.

She interpreted his tone, and her heart misgave her. An hour later she obeyed the summons. Martin greeted her with a smile, but hardly tried to appear at ease.

'I am obliged to speak to you,' were his first words. 'The letter you had yesterday was from Mr Peak?'

'Yes, father.'

'Is he' – Mr Warricombe hesitated – 'in these parts again?'

'No; in Lancashire.'

'Sidwell, I claim no right whatever to control your correspondence; but it was a shock to me to find that you are in communication with him.'

'He wrote,' Sidwell replied with difficulty, 'to let me know of a change that has come upon his prospects. By the death of a friend, he is made independent.'

'For his own sake, I am glad to hear that. But how could it concern *you*, dear?'

She struggled to command herself.

'It was at my invitation that he wrote, father.'

Martin's face expressed grave concern.

'Sidwell! Is this right?'

She was very pale, and kept her eyes unmovingly directed just aside from her father.

'What can it mean?' Mr Warricombe pursued, with sad remonstrance. 'Will you not take me into your confidence, Sidwell?'

'I can't speak of it,' she replied, with sudden determination. 'Least of all with you, father.'

'Least of all? – I thought we were very near to each other.'

'For that very reason, I can't speak to you of this. I *must* be left free! I am going away with Sylvia, for a year, and for so long I must be absolutely independent. Father, I entreat you not to'—

A sob checked her. She turned away, and fought against the hysterical tendency; but it was too strong to be controlled. Her father approached, beseeching her to be more like herself. He held her in his arms, until tears had their free course, and a measure of calmness returned.

'I can't speak to you about it,' she repeated, her face hidden from him. 'I must write you a long letter, when I have gone. You shall know everything in that way.'

'But, my dearest, I can't let you leave us under these circumstances. This is a terrible trial to me. You cannot possibly go until we understand each other!'

'Then I will write to you here – to-day or to-morrow.'

With this promise Martin was obliged to be contented, Sidwell left him, and was not seen, except by Sylvia, during the whole day.

Nor did she appear at breakfast on the morning that followed. But when this meal was over, Sylvia received a message, summoning her to the retreat on the top of the house. Here Sidwell sat in the light and warmth, a glass door wide open to the west, the rays of a brilliant sun softened by curtains which fluttered lightly in the breeze from the sea.

'Will you read this?' she said, holding out a sheet of notepaper on which were a few lines in her own handwriting.

It was a letter, beginning – 'I cannot.'

Sylvia perused it carefully, and stood in thought.

'After all?' were the words with which she broke silence. They were neither reproachful nor regretful, but expressed grave interest.

'In the night,' said Sidwell, 'I wrote to father, but I shall not give him the letter. Before it was finished, I knew that I must write *this*. There's no more to be said, dear. You will go abroad without me – at all events for the present.'

'If that is your resolve,' answered the other, quietly, 'I shall keep my word, and only do what I can to aid it.' She sat down shielding her eyes from the sunlight with a Japanese fan. 'After all, Sidwell, there's much to be said for a purpose formed on such a morning as this; one can't help distrusting the midnight.'

Sidwell was lying back in a low chair, her eyes turned to the woody hills on the far side of the Exe.

'There's one thing I should like to say,' her friend pursued. 'It struck me as curious that you were not at all affected, by what to me would have been the one insuperable difficulty.'

'I know what you mean – the legacy.'

'Yes. It still seems to you of no significance?'

'Of very little,' Sidwell answered wearily, letting her eyelids droop.

'Then we won't talk about it. From the higher point of view, I believe you are right; but – still let it rest.'

In the afternoon, Sidwell penned the following lines which she enclosed in an envelope and placed on the study table, when her father was absent.

'The long letter which I promised you, dear father, is needless. I have to-day sent Mr Peak a reply which closes our correspondence. I am sure he will not write again; if he were to do so, I should not answer.

'I have given up my intention of going away with Sylvia. Later, perhaps, I shall wish to join her somewhere on the Continent, but by that time you will be in no concern about me.'

To this Mr Warricombe replied only with the joyous smile which greeted his daughter at their next meeting. Mrs Warricombe remained in ignorance of the ominous shadow which had passed over her house. At present, she was greatly interested in the coming marriage of the Rev. Bruno Chilvers, whom she tried *not* to forgive for having disappointed her secret hope.

Martin had finally driven into the background those uneasy questionings, which at one time it seemed likely that Godwin Peak would rather accentuate than silence. With Sidwell, he could never again touch on such topics. If he were still conscious of a postponed debate, the adjournment was *sine die*. Martin rested in the faith that, without effort of his own, the mysteries of life and time would ere long be revealed to him.

III

Earwaker spent Christmas with his relatives at Kingsmill. His father and mother both lived; the latter very infirm, unable to leave the house; the former a man of seventy, twisted with rheumatism, his face rugged as a countenance picked out by fancy on the trunk of a big old oak, his hands scarred and deformed with labour. Their old age was restful. The son who had made himself a 'gentleman', and who in London sat at the tables of the high-born, the wealthy, the famous, saw to it that they lacked no comfort.

A bright, dry morning invited the old man and the young to go forth together. They walked from the suburb countrywards, and their conversation was of the time when a struggle was being made to bear the expense of those three years at Whitelaw – no bad investment, as it proved. The father spoke with a strong Midland accent, using words of dialect by no means disagreeable to the son's ear – for dialect is a very different thing from the bestial jargon which on the lips of the London vulgar passes for English. They were laughing over some half grim reminiscence, when Earwaker became aware of two people who were approaching along the pavement, they also in merry talk. One of them he knew; it was Christian Moxey.

Too much interested in his companion to gaze about him, Christian came quite near before his eyes fell on Earwaker. Then he started with a pleasant surprise, changed instantly to something like embarrassment when he observed the aged man. Earwaker was willing to smile and go by, had the other consented; but a better impulse prevailed in both. They stopped and struck hands together.

'My father,' said the man of letters, quite at his ease.

Christian was equal to the occasion; he shook hands heartily with the battered toiler, then turned to the lady at his side.

'Janet, you guess who this is. – My cousin, Earwaker, Miss Janet Moxey.'

Doubtless Janet was aware that her praises had suffered no diminution when sung by Christian to his friends. Her eyes just fell, but in a moment were ready with their frank, intelligent smile. Earwaker experienced a pang – ever so slight – suggesting a revision of his philosophy.

They talked genially, and parted with good wishes for the New Year.

Two days later, on reaching home, Earwaker found in his letter-box a scrap of paper on which were scribbled a few barely legible lines. 'Here I am!' he at length deciphered. 'Got into Tilbury at eleven this morning. Where the devil are you? Write to Charing Cross Hotel.' No signature, but none was needed. Malkin's return from New Zealand had been signalled in advance.

That evening the erratic gentleman burst in like a whirlwind. He was the picture of health, though as far as ever from enduing the comfortable flesh which accompanies robustness in men of calmer temperament. After violent greetings, he sat down with abrupt gravity, and began to talk as if in continuance of a dialogue just interrupted.

'Now, don't let us have any misunderstanding. You will please remember that my journey to England is quite independent of what took place two years and a half ago. It has *nothing whatever* to do with those circumstances.'

Earwaker smiled.

'I tell you,' pursued the other, hotly, 'that I am here to see *you* – and one or two other old friends; and to look after some business matters. You will oblige me by giving credit to my assertion!'

'Don't get angry. I am convinced of the truth of what you say.'

'Very well! It's as likely as not that, on returning to Auckland, I shall marry Miss Maccabe – of whom I have written to you. I needn't repeat the substance of my letters. I am not in love with her, you understand, and I needn't say that my intercourse with that family has been guided by extreme discretion. But she is a very sensible young lady. My only regret is that I didn't know her half-a-dozen years ago, so that I could have directed her education. She might have been even more interesting than she is. But – you are at leisure, I hope, Earwaker?'

'For an hour or two.'

'Oh, confound it! When a friend comes back from the ends of the earth! – Yes, yes; I understand. You are a busy man; forgive my hastiness. Well now, I was going to say that I shall probably call upon Mrs Jacox.' He paused, and gave the listener a stern look, forbidding misconstruction. 'Yes, I shall probably go down to Wrotham. I wish to put my relations with that family on a proper footing. Our correspondence has been very satisfactory, especially of late. The poor woman laments more sincerely her – well, let us say, her folly of two years and a half ago. She has outlived it; she regards me as a friend. Bella and Lily seem to be getting on very well indeed. That governess of theirs – we won't have any more mystery; it was I who undertook the trifling expense. A really excellent teacher, I have every reason to believe. I am told that Bella promises to be a remarkable pianist, and Lily is uncommonly strong in languages. But my interest in them is merely that of a friend; let it be understood.'

'Precisely. You didn't say whether the girls have been writing to you?'

'No, no, no! Not a line. I have exchanged letters only with their mother. Anything else would have been indiscreet. I shall be glad to see them, but my old schemes are things of the past. There is not the faintest probability that Bella has retained any recollection of me at all.'

'I daresay not,' assented Earwaker.

'You think so? Very well; I have acted wisely. Bella is still a child, you know – compared with a man of my age. She is seventeen and a few months; quite a child! Miss Maccabe is just one-and-twenty; the proper age. When we are married, I think I shall bring her to Europe for a year or two. Her education needs that; she will be delighted to see the old countries.'

'Have you her portrait?'

'Oh no! Things haven't got so far as that. What a hasty fellow you are, Earwaker! I told you distinctly'—

He talked till after midnight, and at leave-taking apologised profusely for wasting his friend's valuable time.

Earwaker awaited with some apprehension the result of Malkin's visit to Wrotham. But the report of what took place on that occasion was surprisingly commonplace. Weeks passed, and Malkin seldom showed himself at Staple Inn; when he did so, his talk was exclusively of Miss Maccabe; all he could be got to say of the young ladies at Wrotham was, 'Nice girls; very nice girls. I hope they'll marry well.' Two months had gone by, and already the journalist had heard by letter of his friend's intention to return to New Zealand, when, on coming home late one night, he found Malkin sitting on the steps.

'Earwaker, I have something very serious to tell you. Give me just a quarter of an hour.'

What calamity did this tone portend? The eccentric man seated himself with slow movement. Seen by a good light, his face was not gloomy, but very grave.

'Listen to me, old friend,' he began, sliding forward to the edge of his chair. 'You remember I told you that my relations with the Maccabe family had been marked throughout with extreme discretion.'

'You impressed that upon me.'

'Good! I have never made love to Miss Maccabe, and I doubt whether she has ever thought of me as a possible husband.'

'Well?'

'Don't be impatient. I want you to grasp the fact. It is important, because – I am going to marry Bella Jacox.'

'You don't say so?'

'Why not?' cried Malkin, suddenly passing to a state of excitement. 'What objection can you make? I tell you that I am absolutely free to choose'—

The journalist calmed him, and thereupon had to hear a glowing account of Bella's perfections. All the feeling that Malkin had suppressed during these two months rushed forth in a flood of turbid eloquence.

'And now,' he concluded, 'you will come down with me to Wrotham. I don't mean to-night; let us say the day after to-morrow, Sunday. You remember our last joint visit! Ha, ha!'

'Mrs Jacox is reconciled?'

'My dear fellow, she rejoices! A wonderful nobility in that poor little woman! She wept upon my shoulder! But you must see Bella! I shan't take her to New Zealand, at all events not just yet. We shall travel about Europe, completing her education. Don't you approve of that?'

On Sunday, the two travelled down into Kent. This time they were received by Lily, now a pretty, pale, half-developed girl of fifteen. In a few minutes her sister entered. Bella was charming; nervousness made her words few, and it could be seen that she was naturally thoughtful, earnest, prone to reverie; her beauty had still to ripen, and gave much promise for the years between twenty and thirty. Last of all appeared Mrs Jacox, who blushed as she shook hands with Earwaker, and for a time was ill at ease; but her vocatives were not long restrained, and when all sat down to the tea-table she chattered away with astonishing vivacity. After tea the company was joined by a lady of middle age, who, for about two years, had acted as governess to the girls. Earwaker formed his conclusions as to the 'trifling expense' which her services represented; but it was probably a real interest in her pupils which had induced a person of so much refinement to bear so long with the proximity of Mrs Jacox.

'A natural question occurs to me,' remarked Earwaker, as they were returning. 'Who and what was *Mr* Jacox?'

'Ah! Bella was talking to me about him the other day. He must have been distinctly an interesting man. Bella had a very clear recollection of him, and she showed me two or three photographs. Engaged in some kind of commerce. I didn't seek particulars. But a remarkable man, one can't doubt.'

He resumed presently.

'Now don't suppose that this marriage entirely satisfies me. Bella has been fairly well taught, but not, you see, under my supervision. I ought to have been able to watch and direct her month by month. As it is, I shall have to begin by assailing her views on all manner of things. Religion, for example. Well, I have no religion, that's plain. I might call myself this or that for the sake of seeming respectable, but it all comes to the same thing. I don't mind Bella going to church if she wishes, but I must teach her that there's no merit whatever in doing so. It isn't an ideal marriage, but perhaps as good as this imperfect world allows. If I have children, I can then put my educational theories to the test.'

By way of novel experience, Earwaker, not long after this, converted his study into a drawing-room, and invited the Jacox family to taste his tea and cake. With Malkin's assistance, the risky enterprise was made a great success. When Mrs Jacox would allow her to be heard, Bella talked intelligently, and showed eager interest in the details of literary manufacture.

'O Mr Earwaker!' cried her mother, when it was time to go. 'What a delightful afternoon you have given us! We must think of you from now as one of our very best friends. Mustn't we, Lily?'

But troubles were yet in store. Malkin was strongly opposed to a religious marriage; he wished the wedding to be at a registrar's office, and had obtained Bella's consent to this, but Mrs Jacox would not hear of such a thing. She wept and bewailed herself. 'How *can* you think of being married like a costermonger? O Mr Malkin, you will break my heart, indeed you will!' And she wrote an ejaculatory letter to Earwaker, imploring his intercession. The journalist took his friend in hand.

'My good fellow, don't make a fool of yourself. Women are

born for one thing only, the Church of England marriage service. How can you seek to defeat the end of their existence? Give in to the inevitable. Grin and bear it.'

'I can't! I won't! It shall be a runaway match! I had rather suffer the rack than go through an ordinary wedding!'

Dire was the conflict. Down at Wrotham there were floods of tears. In the end, Bella effected a compromise; the marriage was to be at a church, but in the greatest possible privacy. No carriages, no gala dresses, no invitations, no wedding feast; the bare indispensable formalities. And so it came to pass. Earwaker and the girl's governess were the only strangers present, when, on a morning of June, Malkin and Bella were declared by the Church to be henceforth one and indivisible. The bride wore a graceful travelling costume; the bridegroom was in corresponding attire.

'Heaven be thanked, that's over!' exclaimed Malkin, as he issued from the portal. 'Bella, we have twenty-three minutes to get to the railway station. Don't cry!' he whispered to her. 'I can't stand that!'

'No, no; don't be afraid,' she whispered back. 'We have said good-bye already.'

'Capital! That was very thoughtful of you. – Goodbye, all! Shall write from Paris, Earwaker. Nineteen minutes; we shall just manage it!'

He sprang into the cab, and away it clattered.

A letter from Paris, a letter from Strasburg, from Berlin, Munich – letters about once a fortnight. From Bella also came an occasional note, a pretty contrast to the incoherent enthusiasm of her husband's compositions. Midway in September she announced their departure from a retreat in Switzerland.

'We are in the utmost excitement, for it is now decided that in three days we start for Italy! The heat has been terrific, and we have waited on what seems to me the threshold of Paradise until we could hope to enjoy the delights beyond. We go first to Milan. My husband, of course, knows Italy, but he shares my impatience. I am to entreat you to write to Milan, with as much news as possible. Especially have you heard anything more of Mr Peak?'

November the pair spent in Rome, and thence was despatched the following in Malkin's hand:

'This time I am *not* mistaken! I have seen Peak. He didn't see me;

perhaps wouldn't have known me. It was in Piale's reading-room. I had sat down to *The Times*, when a voice behind me sounded in such a curiously reminding way that I couldn't help looking round. It was Peak; not a doubt of it. I might have been uncertain about his face, but the voice brought back that conversation at your rooms too unmistakably – long ago as it was. He was talking to an American, whom evidently he had met somewhere else, and had now recognised. "I've had a fever," he said, "and can't quite shake off the results. Been in Ischia for the last month. I'm going north to Vienna." Then the two walked away together. He looked ill, sallow, worn out. Let me know if you hear.'

On that same day, Earwaker received another letter, with the Roman post-mark. It was from Peak.

'I have had nothing particular to tell you. A month ago I thought I should never write to you again; I got malarial fever, and lay desperately ill at the *Ospedale Internazionale* at Naples. It came of some monstrous follies there's no need to speak of. A new and valuable experience. I know what it is to look steadily into the eyes of Death.

'Even now, I am far from well. This keeps me in low spirits. The other day I was half decided to start for London. I am miserably alone, want to see a friend. What a glorious place Staple Inn seemed to me as I lay in the hospital! Proof how low I had sunk: I thought longingly of Exeter, of a certain house there – never mind!

'I write hastily. An invitation from some musical people has decided me to strike for Vienna. Up there, I shall get my health back. The people are of no account – boarding-house acquaintances – but they may lead to better. I never in my life suffered so from loneliness.'

This was the eighteenth of November. On the twenty-eighth the postman delivered a letter of an appearance which puzzled Earwaker. The stamp was Austrian, the mark 'Wien'. From Peak, therefore. But the writing was unknown, plainly that of a foreigner.

The envelope contained two sheets of paper. The one was covered with a long communication in German; on the other stood a few words of English, written, or rather scrawled, in a hand there was no recognising:

'Ill again, and alone. If I die, act for me. Write to Mrs Peak, Twybridge.'

Beneath was added, 'J. E. Earwaker, Staple Inn, London.'

He turned hurriedly to the foreign writing. Earwaker read a German book as easily as an English, but German manuscript was a terror to him. And the present correspondent wrote so execrably that beyond *Geehrter Herr*, scarcely a word yielded sense to his anxious eyes. Ha! One he had made out – *gestorben*.

Crumpling the papers into his pocket, he hastened out, and knocked at the door of an acquaintance in another part of the Inn. This was a man who had probably more skill in German cursive. Between them, they extracted the essence of the letter.

He who wrote was the landlord of an hotel in Vienna. He reported that an English gentleman, named Peak, just arrived from Italy, had taken a bedroom at that house. In the night, the stranger became very ill, sent for a doctor, and wrote the lines enclosed, the purport whereof he at the same time explained to his attendants. On the second day Mr Peak died. Among his effects were found circular notes, and a sum of loose money. The body was about to be interred. Probably Mr Earwaker would receive official communications, as the British consul had been informed of the matter. To whom should *bills* be sent?

The man of letters walked slowly back to his own abode.

'Dead, too, in exile!' was his thought. 'Poor old fellow!'

THE END

EXPLANATORY NOTES

3 **Caesar's privilege**: in 45 BC the Senate granted Julius Caesar the right to wear permanently a triumphal crown or laurel wreath.

3 *homalonotus*: genus of trilobites found in British rocks of the Upper Silurian; type of fossil. (In the manuscript Gissing wrote 'Hamalonotus'; previous editions follow his spelling, though not the upper case 'H'. There is no root *hamalo-* from which 'hamalonotus' could regularly be derived, and the error is corrected in the text.)

8 **First BA**: an intermediate stage in the curriculum for the degree of Bachelor of Arts (also referred to on p. 35).

8 **Mill's *Logic***: *A System of Logic* (1843) by John Stuart Mill (1806–73) became a standard textbook.

9 **estrade**: a slightly raised platform; a dais.

11 **imputation ... English college**: the most notorious case of an English academic suffering on account of such an imputation was that of F. D. Maurice (1805–72), Professor of Theology at King's College, London. In 1853 he was forced to resign for rejecting belief in eternal punishment (in his *Theological Essays*, 1853).

12 **inability to carry ... won**: perhaps based on Gissing's own experience at Owens College. In 1874 he won so many prize volumes that he had to take them home in a cab (*The Collected Letters of George Gissing*, ed. P. F. Mattheisen, A. C. Young and P. Coustillas, vol. 1, p. 32).

15 **But, I say ... nothing to it**: this passage is based on an entry in Gissing's *Commonplace Book* (ed. Jacob Korg, 1962), p. 47.

17 **Spiers & Pond**: pioneering restaurant chain, founded in the 1860s. The firm owned 'The Criterion', a luxurious restaurant in Piccadilly Circus, as well as buffets at Holborn Viaduct and Mansion House stations.

21 **Robert Burns ... irascibility**: a quotation (omitting the word 'ungovernable' before 'irascibility') from Burns's letter to Dr John Moore of 2 August 1787 (*The Letters of Robert Burns*, ed. J. Logie Robertson, 1887, p. 67).

21 **military outbreak**: the Crimean War (1854–6).

21 **Godwin's Political Justice**: in his *Enquiry Concerning Political Justice* (1793) William Godwin (1756–1836) attacked organised religion and expressed his sympathy with the French Revolution and English Radicalism.

22 **the Protector**: Oliver Cromwell, Lord Protector (1653–8), evidently admired by Nicholas Peak as a symbol of anti-royalism.

23 **the historic earl**: Godwin, or Godwine (*c.*990–*c.*1053), Earl of Wessex, father of King Harold.

26 **Figuier**: *The World before the Deluge* (1865), first published as *La Terre avant le Déluge* (1863), by Louis Figuier (1819–94). It contains the 'fanciful' illustrations mentioned.

27 **sequaciousness**: slavish or unreasoning following of others, especially in matters of thought or opinion.

33 **committing to memory lists of dates**: this incident recalls Gissing's own memorising practices during Church services as a schoolboy. See *George Gissing at Alderley Edge* (1969), ed. Pierre Coustillas, p. 22.

33 **try for something in the Civil Service**: since 1870 administrative grades in the Civil Service had been open to competitive examination.

34 **Medicean patronage**: the earlier Medici, Cosimo (1389–1464) and his grandson Lorenzo the Magnificent (1448–92), were munificent patrons of the arts, literature and scholarship; their patronage helped to make Florence the centre of European culture.

36 **the negligence which left him ... utter inexperience**: Gissing expressed similar sentiments about his own isolation as a student in Manchester. See Morley Roberts, *The Private Life of Henry Maitland*, ed. Morchard Bishop (1958), p. 28.

44 **spiritual company of Charles Lamb**: Lamb (1775–1834) was a keen playgoer. In his essay 'My First Play' (*Elia*, 1823) he describes queuing at the theatre door in Drury Lane to see his first plays.

45 *O mihi præteritos referat si Jupiter annos!*: If only Jupiter would bring me back lost years (Virgil, *Aeneid*, VIII, 560) – the old King Evander's lament for his lost youth. Also quoted in *The Private Papers of Henry Ryecroft*, Winter XVI. For Gissing's use of Virgil in his fiction, see *George Gissing at Work: a Study of his Notebook 'Extracts from my Reading'*, ed. Pierre Coustillas and Patrick Bridgwater (1988), pp. 155–6.

51 **what is meant by inherited tendencies**: Gissing, like many late Victorian novelists, was keenly interested in heredity. In 1889 he made extensive notes on Théodule Ribot's *L'hérédité psychologique* (1873). See the *Commonplace Book*, pp. 59–62.

56 **right hand knew nothing of what the left performed**: 'But when thou doest alms, let not thy left hand know what thy right hand doeth' (Matthew, VI, 3).

58 **Brummagem**: local vulgar form of the name of Birmingham; used contemptuously of articles of Birmingham manufacture.

58 **natural supernatural**: allusion to Book III, Chap. VIII, of *Sartor Resartus* (1836) by Thomas Carlyle (1795–1881).

63 **The silly buckits, etc.**: (mis)quotation from Coleridge's *Ancient Mariner*, Part V. The incident is derived from a note in Gissing's unpublished scrapbook beginning, 'A board-school child repeating a verse she has to learn by heart' (all extracts from the scrapbook are quoted with the kind permission of the Lilly Library, Indiana University, Bloomington, Indiana.

73 **But me no buts!**: from Mrs Centlivre's *The Busie Bodie* (1709), II, i, 28 (Sir Francis Gripe to his son Charles).

85 **the London *Weekly Post***: probably based on the *Weekly Dispatch*, a Radical periodical (1801–1928), whose editor had invited Gissing to write a serial story for the paper in September 1888 (see Gissing's *Diary*, ed. Pierre Coustillas, p. 43).

85 **Staple Inn**: situated in Holborn, originally one of the Inns of Chancery, places of residence for law students.

86 **survival among the fittest**: the phrase 'survival of the fittest' (an alternative to Darwin's 'natural selection') originated with Herbert Spencer (1820–1903), *The Principles of Biology* (1864), vol. I, p. 444.

90 *diatomaceæ*: the order of the diatoms, microscopic unicellular algae with the power of locomotion, on which account they were formerly placed by many naturalists in the animal kingdom. They are found at the bottom of the sea and in fresh water.

93 **Hafiz**: Persian poet (*c.*1326–*c.*1390), born at Shiraz. His fame rests on the *Diwan*, a collection of short odes.

94 **Bradlaugh, Darwin, Huxley**: Charles Bradlaugh (1833–91), British politician, social reformer and free-thinker who campaigned for women's suffrage and birth control. Elected an MP in 1880, he aroused opposition by asserting the right of an unbeliever to make an affirmation rather than take a Bible oath, and was refused his seat until 1886. Gissing admired his principled stand, though aware of his reputation for 'dogmatic Atheism' (see the *Collected Letters*, vols. I and II). Charles Darwin (1809–82) published *The Origin of Species* in 1859 and *The Descent of Man* in 1871. Thomas Huxley (1825–95), Darwin's champion, was the originator (in 1869) of the term 'agnostic', used by Sidwell Warricombe on p. 242.

95 **Lyell**: Sir Charles Lyell (1797–1875), British geologist, author of the seminal *Principles of Geology* (1830–3). In a late book, *The Geological Evidence of the Antiquity of Man* (1863), he tentatively accepted the theory of Darwinian evolution.

100 **vasculum**: case used by botanists for carrying newly collected specimens; usually made of tin in the form of a flattened cylinder, with a lid on one side opening lengthwise.

106 **Malkin never was intoxicated . . . vivacity**: an allusion to Disraeli on Gladstone (1878): 'A sophistical rhetorician, inebriated with the exuberance of his own verbosity.'

106 **Sir Thomas Brown**: *Pseudodoxia Epidemica* (also known as *Vulgar Errors*) was published in 1646 by Sir Thomas Browne (1605–82). The spelling of Browne's name without the final 'e' was apparently taken by Gissing from the title-page of the 1686 edition he owned (now in the hands of his great-grandson). *Nos numerus sumus*: We are the (greater) number. On the use of this quotation, see *George Gissing at Work*, pp. 164–5.

108 **I was reading Burns**: based on an entry in Gissing's scrapbook: 'The curious feeling of exultation I have when I read Burns's "Highland Mary" poems. To think that a servant girl can be glorified to heights that the aristocratic lady can never attain. It satisfies my instinct of revolt. Must put this into a character. Note how entirely wrong it is to call such a man a "Democrat".'

109 **That book of M'Naughten's**: no title is given here or later, but one may infer that it is the book referred to earlier (p. 105) as *Spiritual Aspects of Evolution*. Author and title appear to be fictional, though it has been suggested (*Gissing Journal*, XXVIII, 2, April 1992, pp. 10–18) that the original may be a collection of articles entitled *Science and Revelation* sometimes catalogued under the name of one of the contributors, the Rev. John MacNaughtan, and based on lectures given in Belfast in 1874–5. However, this proposes a publication date about ten years before the fictional conversation and no textual echoes of the lectures have been found in *Born in Exile*. Another possibility is that 'M'Naughten' refers in general terms to the Scottish-American writer James McCosh (1811–94), who published *The Religious Aspect of Evolution* in 1888. But the figure is probably fictional – hardly surprising in view of his treatment in the text.

109 **Jeremy Taylor**: Anglican divine (1613–67), imprisoned as a royalist under the Commonwealth. His books include *Holy Living* (1650) and *Holy Dying* (1651).

110 **nictitating membrane**: third or inner eyelid in many animals, serving to protect the eye from dust and to keep it moist.

112 **a Rachel or a Charlotte Brontë**: Rachel was the stage-name of the French classical and tragic actress Elisabeth Félix (1821–58). Gissing noted that she was the original of Vashti in Brontë's *Villette* (*Collected Letters*, vol. 3, p. 115, 170). Charlotte Brontë (1816–55) was revered by Gissing as novelist, stylist and personality: 'No page of her is without genius'; 'A great & glorious woman!' (*Collected Letters*, vol. 3, pp. 101, 105).

112 **St James's Gazette**: London evening paper (1880–1905) offering news reports and political, social and literary articles. Its editorial

tendency in the 1880s (when Gissing took it regularly) was Tory and imperialist.

114 **'Dear, had the world', etc.:** the opening lines of 'Respectability' by Robert Browning. First published in *Men and Women* (1855), the poem mocks the judgments of the respectable world, especially as regards sexual morality.

114 **Murger and Musset:** Henri Murger (1822–61), French novelist, noted especially for *Scènes de la Vie de Bohème* (1848). Louis Charles Alfred de Musset (1810–57), French poet, novelist and playwright. Gissing was fascinated by the bohemian world of both authors. For his attitudes see *The Private Life of Henry Maitland*, chapters X, XIV; *Commonplace Book* pp. 31, 35–6; and *George Gissing at Work*, pp. 36–7, 104–6.

116 *Pereunt et imputantur:* '*Bonosque,/Soles effugere atque abire sentit,/Qui nobis pereunt et imputantur*': 'And he feels the good days are fleeing and passing away, our days that perish and are scored to our account' (Martial, *Epigrammata*, V, xx). One of many references in the novel to the passing of time: see, for example, pp. 47, 120, 147, 162, 370, 389.

116 **those two Greek dramatists:** Posidippos (b. *c.*310 BC) and Menander (*c.*342–291 BC). On 12 December 1888 Gissing noted of a visit to the Vatican: '*Gallerìa delle Statue.* The two seated statues of Poseilippos [*sic*] and Menandros. [. . .] Baedeker says that these two were long worshipped as Saints at San Lorenzo in Panisperna. One chuckles to think of it' (*Diary*, p. 96).

117 **dedicated to St Sidwell:** Sidwell (Latin: Sativola), virgin saint, possibly of British origin. The church is just outside Exeter's east gate.

117 **William Buckland:** geologist (1784–1856), Dean of Westminster. Author of *Reliquiae Diluvianae; or, Observations on the Organic Remains [. . .] Attesting the Action of an Universal Deluge* (1823), 'he returned natural history to the explicit service of religious truth' (Charles Coulston Gillispie, *Genesis and Geology*, 1951, p. 98). See also note on p. 184.

120 **azimuth compass, clinometer:** the first is a minutely divided mariner's compass, fitted with vertical sights, used for taking the magnetic azimuth of a heavenly body; the second, an instrument for measuring slopes and altitudes, especially the dip of mineral strata.

120 **to buy one of Hardy's:** the only reference to Thomas Hardy (1840–1928) in Gissing's fiction, but from 1886 onwards he and Gissing corresponded and occasionally met. Gissing's comments on Hardy and his works are recorded in his diary and letters.

129 **the ship canal: the story of the countess:** the history of the Exeter canal (built in the late sixteenth century) began with attempts to remove the weirs that blocked the Exe; the conflict began in the

thirteenth century when Isabella, Countess of Devon, constructed two weirs in the river to serve the manor mill. See Wallace T. MacCaffrey, *Exeter, 1540–1640* (1975), pp. 126ff.

130 **Sir Stafford Northcote**: Henry Stafford Northcote (1846–1911), Conservative MP for Exeter, 1880–99. Later, Governor-General of Australia (1903–8).

135 **elvans**: Cornish name for hard rocks of igneous origin.

135 **sciolist**: superficial pretender to knowledge.

135 **Professor Pfaff of Erlangen**: Alexius Pfaff (1825–86), Professor of Geology at Erlangen from 1859.

136 *Pereant qui ante nos nostra dixerunt!*: May they perish who have expressed our (ideas) before us! From Aelius Donatus, St Jerome's teacher, quoted in Jerome's *Commentaries on Ecclesiastes*, chap. I.

136 **first sentence of the *Annals* is a hexameter**: the opening of the *Annales* (AD 115–17) by the Roman historian Tacitus is '*Urbem Romam a principio reges habuere*' (At the beginning kings held the city of Rome). Gissing noted this point about its scansion in his *Commonplace Book*, p. 30.

144 **Bishop Blougram**: speaker in Browning's 'Bishop Blougram's Apology' (*Men and Women*, 1855), who offers casuistical and worldly arguments in support of religious belief.

145 **Newman's *Apologia***: *Apologia pro Vita sua* (1864) by John Henry Newman (1801–90). A comment on the book's circular argument similar to Buckland Warricombe's was made by Thomas Hardy in a journal entry of 2 July 1865: 'there is no first link to his excellent chain of reasoning, and down you come headlong' (F. E. Hardy, *The Life of Thomas Hardy 1840–1928*, 1962, p. 48).

149 *Tuissimus*: Entirely yours (non-standard Latin form, used light-heartedly).

149 **Reusch's *Bibel und Natur***: *Bibel und Natur* (Freiburg, 1862) by F. H. Reusch, Professor of Catholic Theology at Bonn, translated as *Nature and the Bible*, 2 vols (Edinburgh, 1886) by Kathleen Lyttelton. The passages referred to later (p. 207) are from Reusch, pp. 85–97, 124–48, 347–59; in the translation they are at Vol. I, pp. 111–12, 165–88, Vol. II, p. 250. Gissing read Reusch on 31 December 1890 (Diary, p. 234). Though he knew of the translation (*Born in Exile*, p. 369), he may not have consulted it: his translations differ markedly from Lyttelton's.

158 *Foris ut moris, intus ut libet*: In public (behave) according to custom; in private, as you please. Quoted in the *Commonplace Book*, p. 58, as 'The motto of liberals of the late Renaissance'. A similar sentiment occurs in Seneca, *Epistulae ad Lucilium*, Epistle V, 2.

159 **envy of its fate**: the passage is based on an entry in Gissing's scrapbook: 'I always have a distinct feeling of envy when I crush an insect, its end seems to me so blessed. This is the truest pessimism.'

162 **Laura of the voiceless Petrarch**: Petrarch (1304–74), Italian poet and humanist, whose sonnets were a major influence on the lyric poetry of the Renaissance. Laura, whom he recorded as first seeing in 1327, and who died in 1348, was his ideal love and chief inspirer of his sonnets. For Gissing's knowledge of Petrarch, see *George Gissing at Work*, pp. 67–8.

163 **'fate, free-will, foreknowledge absolute'**: 'and reasoned high/Of providence, foreknowledge, will, and fate,/Fix'd fate, freewill, foreknowledge absolute' (Milton, *Paradise Lost*, Book II, 558–60).

172 **Davidson's superb work on the *Brachiopoda***: Thomas Davidson (1817–85) published *British Fossil Brachiopoda* in 6 vols, 1851–86.

173 *La Grèce, Rome, et Dante*: published in 1848 by Jean-Jacques Ampère (1800–64), writer and philologist and member of the French Academy. The passage occurs at the beginning not of the book but of the section '*Voyage Dantesque*' (p. 211). Ampère is deploring the vulgar fashion of admiration for Dante. The significance of the quotation is discussed in *George Gissing at Work*, pp. 122–3.

173 *'Il faut souvent'*, etc.: 'It often takes real courage to persist in upholding a just opinion, its supporters notwithstanding.' In the manuscript, as in his notebook, Gissing wrote *'un'* for *'une opinion'*.

179 **'He either fears'**, etc.: 'He either fears his fate too much,/Or his deserts are small,/That dares not put it to the touch,/To gain or lose it all': James Graham, Marquis of Montrose (1612–50), 'Lines Written on the Window of his Jail the Night before his Execution'.

181 **Northernhay [. . .] Rougemont Castle**: the first is a street in Exeter; the second, built by William the Conqueror, derives its name from the red, elevated rock on which its inner fortress was built.

183 *Calceola sandalina*: solitary coral of the extinct order Rugosa, dating from the Devonian period; so called because shaped like an eastern sandal (from Latin *calceolus*, small shoe).

184 **Buckland's Bridgewater Treatise**: the Reverend Francis Henry Egerton, eighth Earl of Bridgewater (1756–1829), left £8,000 for an eight-author work on 'the Power, Wisdom, and Goodness of God, as manifested in the Creation'. The treatise on 'Geology and Mineralogy' (1836) was by William Buckland (see note on p. 117). See Gillispie, *Geology and Genesis*, pp. 209–16 and *passim*.

184 **Hugh Miller**: Scottish geologist and writer (1802–56), author of *Foot-Prints of the Creator* (1847) and *The Testimony of the Rocks* (1857), which is quoted from on p. 197. The passages alluded to are on pp. 331 and 335 (in the chapter 'The Noachian Deluge. Part II').

188 **Tartufe**: hypocritical hero of *Le Tartuffe* (1664) by Molière (1622–73).

193 **I would quote the Master of Trinity**: the contemporary Master of Trinity College, Cambridge, was William Hepworth Thompson

(1810–86). His 'capital epigram' was 'We are none of us infallible – not even the youngest of us'. See G. W. E. Russell, *Collections and Recollections* (1904), chap. 18.

195 *woman* in the abstract [. . .] individuals: compare Gissing's letter of 18 December 1898: 'I much dislike generalisations about women [. . .] A woman is an individual' (*The Letters of George Gissing to Gabrielle Fleury*, ed. Pierre Coustillas, 1964, p. 89).

196 Bedford College: school of London University founded in 1849 to provide a liberal education for women.

196 Hugh Miller's *Testimony of the Rocks*: see note on p. 184.

203 exemption from painful shock [. . .] happiness: the sentiment derives from Schopenhauer, *Parerga and Paralipomena*, trans. E. F. J. Payne, 2 vols (1974), vol. II, pp. 285–6, 291. Schopenhauer's influence can be traced in Gissing's essay of 1882, 'The Hope of Pessimism' (in *George Gissing: Essays and Fiction*, ed. Pierre Coustillas, 1970). See also Patrick Bridgwater, *Gissing and Germany* (1981), pp. 36–57.

205 a passage of which [. . .] careful note: Peak's apologetics here rely on an interweaving of passages from Frederick Temple, *The Relations between Religion and Science* (1884), p. 114 (and cf. pp. 61–2, 232), and Asa Gray, *Natural Science and Religion* (1880), pp. 105–7. Gissing read these books in December 1890 (*Diary*, pp. 233–4).

207 *thohu wabohu*: without form and void (also used, ironically, on p. 369).

208 'sin might not flourish [. . .] exuberance': for the sources in Reusch, see note on p. 149.

217 *Villette*: Charlotte Brontë, *Villette* (1853), vol. I, chap. 6, 'London', beginning.

217 The City is hateful, etc.: compare the *Commonplace Book* (p. 44): 'The "City" is so oppressive to the spirit because it represents the *triumph* of the vulgar man.'

218 the 'Life of Phokion': Plutarch (*c.*AD 46–120), Greek biographer, historian and philosopher, author of the *Parallel Lives* of Greeks and Romans. The anecdote, recorded in Gissing's *Commonplace Book* (p. 52), is from the 'Life of Phokion', VIII, 3.

222 In youth one marvels [. . .] advanced so far: from the *Commonplace Book* (p. 25). See also *The Private Papers of Henry Ryecroft*, Spring, XVI, and Schopenhauer, *Essays and Aphorisms*, trans. R. J. Hollingdale (1970), p. 152.

227 polyarchic: having the characteristics of a polyarchy, i.e. government by many.

233 *Cherchez la femme*: look for the woman. Catch-phrase first used (as *cherchons la femme*) by Alexandre Dumas (*Les Mohicans de Paris*, 1864, vol. II, chap. 2).

236 as Steele says, etc.: Sir Richard Steele (1672–1729), *The Tatler*, no.

30 (18 June 1709): 'As Ceremony is the Invention of wise Men to keep Fools at a Distance, so good Breeding is an Expedient to make Fools and wise Men equals.'

237 **Mrs Grundy**: symbol of conventional propriety in Thomas Morton's play *Speed the Plough* (1798).

240 **left the house and walked westward**: both Gissing's manuscript and previous editions read 'westward', yet the context seems to demand 'eastward' (Moxey's house is in Notting Hill).

246 **Hooker**: Richard Hooker (1554–1600), theologian, born at Heavitree, near Exeter, author of the *Laws of Ecclesiastical Politie*, the classic defence of the Anglican church as established in Elizabethan I's reign.

252 **Otter valley [. . .] Coleridge**: among the poems of S. T. Coleridge (1772–1834) is 'Sonnet to the River Otter'.

267 **an apteryx**: New Zealand bird with rudimentary wings and no tail; a kiwi.

268 **the recent 'scandal'**: probably an allusion to the case of Sir Charles Dilke (1843–1911), English Radical politician, whose career was damaged in 1885–6 by his involvement in the Crawford divorce case. Though denying adultery with Mrs Crawford, he admitted to an affair with her mother; it was also alleged that he had forced Mrs Crawford to go to bed with himself and his maidservant. The reference to Radicalism and materialism is doubtless based on Dilke's record of republicanism; that to the debasement of high social rank, on the fact that Dilke was a baronet. See Roy Jenkins, *Sir Charles Dilke: a Victorian Tragedy* (1958).

283 *Oui, répondit Pococurante*, etc.: 'Yes, replied Pococurante, it is a noble thing to write what one thinks; it is man's privilege.' From Voltaire, *Candide* (1759), chap. 35. (Corrected from Gissing's manuscript, where *'privilège'*, is written with an acute accent.)

284 *bien gantée*: well gloved.

285 **'breathing time o' the day'**: 'If it please his Majesty, it is the breathing time of day with me' (*Hamlet*, V, ii, 170–1).

288 *Excepto quod non simul*, etc.: 'Except that you were not there, I was happy' (Horace, *Epistles*, 1.10.50).

288 **pronounced his Latin in the new-old way**: a new reformed pronunciation of classical Latin was formulated around 1870 by Oxford and Cambridge scholars. See W. Sidney Allen, *Vox Latina* (1965), pp. 102–10. Gissing commented on the charge in a letter to his sister Ellen of 2 May 1897 (held by the Boston Public Library; printed in *More Books*, 1947).

288 **Nullifidian**, etc.: a 'nullifidian' is one of no faith or religion; 'morbific' – causing disease; 'psychogenesis' – the genesis or origin of the soul or mind (the meaning 'psychic origin of mental illness' is a twentieth-century usage).

288 *Gott ist eine Träne,* etc.: God is a tear of love, shed in deepest secrecy, over human misery. From *Das Wesen des Christentums* (*The Essence of Christianity*), 1841, chap. 13, by Ludwig Feuerbach (1804–72). In Gissing's manuscript and previous editions *Träne* is given in its obsolete form *Thräne*. The use of the quotation is discussed in *George Gissing at Work,* pp. 86–7.

289 *sens dessus-dessous:* topsy-turvy, in confusion.

336 Bordighera: Italian Riviera winter resort.

366 things work together for such obvious good: 'All things work together for good to them that love God' (Romans, VIII, 28).

366 the world is the best possible: *Dans ce meilleur des mondes possibles* (In this best of all possible worlds) – recurrent phrase put into the mouth of Dr Pangloss in Voltaire's *Candide*; a jibe at Leibniz's philosophy of optimism.

370 Royat: a spa in Auvergne, near Clermont-Ferrand.

375 'sunless gulfs of doubt': 'In seas of Death and sunless gulfs of Doubt' (Tennyson, 'Prefatory Sonnet to the "Nineteenth Century" ').

377 If to labour is to pray: *'Laborare est orare'* – the ancient motto of the Benedictine monks.

378 'There sinks the nebulous star': 'There sinks the nebulous star we call the sun,/If that hypothesis of theirs be sound' (Tennyson, *The Princess,* IV, 1).

379 Francis Newman's book on *The Soul: The Soul: her Sorrows and her Aspirations* (1849) by Francis William Newman (1805–97).

381 That's the the bald statement of the cause: the manuscript reading, 'cause', may be a slip for 'case'.

387 that 'conversion' on the mattress-grave: Heinrich Heine (1797–1856) was ill for the last eight years of his life, probably with venereal disease of the spinal cord; he called his sick-bed *'die Matratzengruft'.* In his suffering he acknowledged a personal God, partly to quarrel with His governance of the world. See Jeffrey L. Sammons, *Heinrich Heine: a Modern Biography* (1979), pp. 295, 305–10. Gissing reverted to the subject of death-bed 'conversions' in *The Private Papers of Henry Ryecroft,* Autumn, XII. Ironically, he himself was reported to have been converted on his death-bed, a fact which his friends contested: see Roberts, *The Private Life of Henry Maitland,* chap. XII; and Jacob Korg, *George Gissing: A Critical Biography* (1965), pp. 252–4.

416 *Geehrter Herr* – Respected Sir; *gestorben* – died.

416 circular notes: letters of credit from a banker (e.g. in London) to bankers in other countries, in favour of a named person, usually someone on tour.

GISSING AND HIS CRITICS

Contemporary critical responses to Gissing's fiction can be found in *Gissing: The Critical Heritage*, ed. Pierre Coustillas and Colin Partridge (1972). The following unsigned review from *The Times* (1 July 1892) is included in that volume (pp. 203–4). Though more perceptive than the average notice, it typifies Victorian responses to *Born in Exile* in finding Godwin Peak's psychology bewildering.

> *Born in Exile* is, like all Mr George Gissing's recent works, a suggestive novel, full of close thought and carefully-drawn character. To skim it is impossible. Read attentively, as it deserves to be, it must leave the impression of a power and penetration not possessed by many modern novelists. On the other hand, in lighter and far commoner qualifications, such as humour, pathos, picturesqueness, or stirring narrative, Mr Gissing is deficient. His novels appeal neither to the heart, nor the senses, nor the imagination, but almost exclusively to the head; and they, moreover, are pervaded by a certain provincialism of tone and topic. The principal characters belong to a group of rather clever young men educated at the institute of a big Midland town; and the odour of this institute and its classes tends to cling to the story from beginning to end. Of the young men, Godwin Peak is the most conspicuous figure. Described flatteringly, he is a natural aristocrat clogged by plebeian connexions and plebeian breeding. Described unflatteringly, he is a snob. We should be doing an injustice, however, to Mr Gissing's subtlety of treatment if we adopted this latter description. Peak goes forth into the world a fierce, if undeclared, Radical and atheist. But blended with his Radicalism and atheism is an intellectual disdain of the populace,

which ripens first into a feeling of social repugnance, and finally into a yearning to move in the circles with which his mental and social affinities ally him. So far, Godwin Peak is an interesting and genuine study in human nature, and we cannot lightly dismiss him as a snob. But we cannot find the same plausibility in the false step which he is led to take by his overmastering desire to scale the social heights above him. Having been seized with admiration for a young lady of some social station, it suddenly strikes him that he might recommend himself to her and to her father by entering the Church – the Church which, as his intimates know, he derides in private, and has even derided in print. On the spur of the moment he calmly announces his intention to take Holy Orders. Forthwith he casts science to the winds, and settles down in the neighbourhood of his friends the Warricombes, reading divinity and preparing defences of the faith in order to improve his position with Warricombe *père*. For a while all is well. Then his falsity is detected and he is humiliated in the eyes of the woman whom he loves and who has begun to return his love. It does not seem to us that there is any adequate motive for Peak's unpremeditated treachery to himself. To a strong, self-contained, and proud character – and Peak's had been so presented – such a sudden and violent deflection from ordinary straightforwardness appears well-nigh impossible. However, it could hardly have failed to occur to Peak that in the nineteenth century he was far more likely to attain the social position he coveted by persevering in his own work than by masquerading as a clergyman. Nor does society receive every clergyman with open arms. It may be said that this is human nature, to go hopelessly astray just when one would have least expected it. Perhaps; but, if novelists are to avail themselves freely of human fallibility as a spring of action, where will consistency of characterisation – heretofore considered the prime merit of the novel writer – come in? The minor characters are all cleverly drawn. The Rev. Bruno Chilvers, in particular, is an excellent satire upon the broad, complaisant clergyman who is so tolerant that he would smile benignantly upon Apollyon, and welcome him as a disguised supporter of the Christian religion. The author of the *Pseudodoxia Epidemica*, we might add, was Sir Thomas Browne, not Sir Thomas Brown. But here, no doubt, it is the reviser who is at fault.

A new phase in criticism of the novel was inaugurated by Jacob Korg's essay of 1959, 'The Spiritual Theme of *Born in Exile*', reprinted in *Collected Articles on George Gissing*, ed. Pierre Coustillas (1968). The following extracts (pp. 135–9, *passim*) show how Korg places the novel in a European perspective.

The disturbing paradox of *Born in Exile* lies in the fact that Peak's hypocritical deception is due, not to lack of moral responsibility, but to uncompromising intellectual honesty. Man's life, seen from a scientific point of view, seems to him to be trivial and futile . . . Having learned from his scientific studies the impossibility of ultimate knowledge, he feels that advocating any philosophy of life, even agnosticism, is to claim knowledge inaccessible to man. The only true honesty, Peak feels, is to act according to one's desires, for that is being true to such knowledge as man can have. Thus, his deception, undertaken to gain as much of life's good as possible, is really a moral imperative . . .

'Peak,' wrote Gissing to his German friend, Eduard Bertz, 'is myself – one phase of myself.' The novel is indeed a remarkably candid confession. The details of Peak's sophistical reasoning must have been drawn from his own thoughts at the time of the Owens College episode and from speculations that ran through his mind when he visited the wealthy homes of his pupils, a poor tutor deeply envious of the luxury and refinement he saw. But Gissing does not seem to have been aware of the ideological dimension of his experience, or of the fact that others shared it with him, until he encountered it again and again in European novels. In works by the Russians, Turgenev and Dostoevsky; the Frenchman, Paul Bourget; and the Dane, Jens Peter Jacobsen, he found young heroes intoxicated by the moral freedom offered by materialism, as he himself had once been. He wrote to his sister Ellen that Turgenev's character 'Bazaroff' exemplified 'the purely *negative* mind, common enough now-a-days in men of thought'. The resemblances of these fictional characters to each other and to himself were unmistakable, suggesting that the nihilism of Russia, the Positivism of France, and the agnosticism of England were all forms of the same historical impulse. Through these novels Gissing learned that the moral sophistry of his youth was representative of a general crisis of the European spirit . . .

Thus, *Born in Exile* emerges as one of a widely-scattered group of novels devoted to a spiritual problem characteristic of the nineteenth century. Such characters as Peak, Raskolnikov, and Bazarov may be regarded as striking anticipatory personifications of Nietzsche's doctrine that man is free to make his own morality, and that prevailing Christian beliefs, which favour the weak and humble, are 'bedwarfing'. Certainly, the voice of Zarathustra is clearly heard in these novels. The nature of man's heroic destiny, left vague by Nietzsche, was given a definite form in the minds of many people by the philosophy which arose from the general progress of science in the nineteenth century . . . This attack of science on metaphysical tradition, which Comte termed the central intellectual conflict of the nineteenth century, is the real theme of *Born in Exile*.

Korg's reading of *Born in Exile* was contested in *Gissing in Context* (1975), by Adrian Poole, who saw the novel primarily as an anatomy of the psychology of exile. This extract is from pp. 173–4.

Jacob Korg has argued the case for its relation to a number of European novels of spiritual crisis, Turgenev's *Fathers and Sons*, Jacobsen's *Niels Lyhne* and Dostoevsky's *Crime and Punishment*. Gissing was certainly a great admirer of these three novels, and had re-read the first two the spring previous to the writing of *Born in Exile*. One cannot help feeling however, that it is misleading to yoke these novels together as forcefully as Korg does, and then to extrapolate a 'real theme' in the following way:

This attack of science on metaphysical tradition, which Comte termed the central intellectual conflict of the nineteenth century, is the real theme of *Born in Exile*.

Gissing certainly *uses* this 'intellectual conflict', but it is hard to accept that this is the novel's 'real theme', since it so conspicuously fails to explore the 'ideological dimension' in the way in which Dostoevsky does (and to a lesser extent the other two also). For Peak's conflicts are not primarily 'intellectual'. The 'ideological dimension' that Korg singles out may align Peak with other 'young heroes intoxicated by the moral freedom offered by materialism, as he [Gissing] himself had once been', but this cannot surely be claimed as the *centre* of the novel. And 'intoxicated'? Surely an inappropriate word for Peak or Niels Lyhne, or even Bazarov. Peak's 'enlightened scientific views' are in themselves rationalisations of his antagonism to society. His deception is not undertaken out of 'uncompromising intellectual honesty'. He finds himself swept into the deception before he has time to think – 'without premeditation, almost without consciousness'. It is 'under the marvelling regard of his conscious self' that he displays his new-found piety.

In his introduction (pp. xi–xii) to the Harvester edition of the novel in 1978 Pierre Coustillas included a discussion of its biographical basis.

Born in Exile derives much of its strength from Gissing's personal predicament, the early phase of which had come to an end in 1888, when his first wife, Marianne Helen Harrison, died in a Lambeth slum. A new leaf of the drab book of his life had been turned when on 25 February 1891 he had married Edith Underwood, a second partner as unsuitable as the first. By the time he settled in Exeter he felt he was no more than a close relative of his former self, a man who could view his past with detachment, yet could recreate it with feeling. The short-lived serenity of his domestic life in the spring of 1891 enabled him to look back upon his past from a middle distance and to convert it dispassionately into material for the life of Godwin Peak. Many biographical elements have transparent counterparts in the book. Whitelaw College, Kingsmill, is Owens College, Manchester. Twybridge stands in the same relation to Peak as Wakefield did to Gissing. Peak's experience and attitudes at college, his ambiguous social position are recognisably borrowed from the novelist's Manchester days. The resemblances extend to the two families, actual and fictional. Nicholas Peak shares various opinions of Thomas Waller Gissing; Mrs Peak and her surroundings remind one of the writer's mother after she became a widow. The narrative contains innumerable echoes from actual life: a detailed analysis of them would amount to a study of Gissing's creative methods, of the mental alchemy through which the data supplied by memory, observation and imagination were fused into the fully realised people and events of the story. In Part 1 we are constantly on the verge of autobiography, but Gissing is never content to transcribe reality. The fictional Sir Job Whitelaw is a combination of John Owens, whose legacy made possible the foundation of the college named after him, and of Sir Joseph Whitworth, the pioneer of standardisation, a self-made man who did much to promote technical education and who gave substantial sums for the creation of scholarships and exhibitions at Owens College. In a typically masochistic manner, Gissing denied Peak successes that he himself had scored; he did not miss the first place for the Manchester district at the Oxford Local Examination, as Peak actually does in the Kingsmill district at the Cambridge Local Examination. The Poem Prize which Gissing won with 'Ravenna' goes to Earwaker for his poem on Alaric. It is also characteristic that Peak is made poorer than young Gissing was: more retiring, too. In actual life, Gissing *could* afford to subscribe to the students' union: he was even for a short time editor of the *Owens College Magazine*.

The class and ideological implications of *Born in Exile* were analysed in 1978 by John Goode in *George Gissing: Ideology and Fiction*. The following extracts are from pp. 60 and 69.

. . . the novel [is] strictly comparable with *Jude the Obscure* with this difference – that *Born in Exile* is *Jude* in reverse. For Jude too is born in exile and aspires towards an integration through culture. But Jude's journey is through and beyond theology towards knowledge as it is, through and beyond marriage towards the 'free' family that he creates with Sue. In other words it is a dislocating war upon the hegemony. Whereas Peak's is a journey back from science to theology, back from the freedom of Bohemian opposition towards the family and his death in exile, [and] is not like Jude's a protest against an oppressive system but simply a record of the failure to achieve integration. Both Jude and Peak fight their intellectual battles as a class war, but they fight it in different directions . . .

[Peak] rejects the absolute of integrity: 'he was essentially a negativist guided by the mere relations of phenomena'. Relativism, which is at the core of the critical ideology of the anti-bourgeois intelligentsia at the end of the nineteenth century, may seem to have found a strange manifestation here, but it is what constitutes the ideological definition of Gissing's uniqueness. For in the relativism of hypocrisy, the 'erotic madness' and the life of the mind find a strange reconciliation: the traditional intellectual organises himself. Ideologically Peak observes with 'the sensibility of the proletarian' (II, ii) but he can reconcile himself to the Church to some extent because it offers a cause to 'combat the proletarian challenges' (III, ii). It is a class war Peak is fighting, both a war on his exclusion from Olympia, and a war to keep Olympia as a place to aspire to. And this is firmly linked to the erotic madness. Earwaker has decided to do without women, Moxey and Malkin cultivate socially conditioned ideals which are mystified into literary types. Peak's ideal is embodied in a class type: he loves Sidwell because she is representative, the ultimate Olympian prize.

In his study *George Gissing* (1983) Robert L. Selig drew a parallel (on pp. 67–8) between the predicament of Godwin Peak and that of twentieth-century scholarship boys as described in Richard Hoggart's *The Uses of Literacy* (1957).

Richard Hoggart has provided a detailed account of twentieth-century scholarship boys in England, and his analysis of this sociological type corresponds quite closely to *Born in Exile*'s hero, although it does not, of course, match the intense evocation of Peak's lonely arrogance. In essence, Hoggart sees the scholarly son of the poor as lost between two worlds: he can no longer respect his own family's culture, but neither can he win the respect that he desires from cultivated middle-class people. His bookish learning and his test-taking skills have carried him into a social void. He resents the cheap clothing, the inelegant speech, and the unrefined manners of his parents, but he still feels uneasy about his own clothes, pronunciation, and manners. He tends to blame his lack of poise upon the group that bore him instead of blaming himself and his own rootlessness. He usually leads a gloomy and isolated life and finds it hard to make friends 'even with others in his condition'.

Worst of all, he feels anguished at 'the discrepancy between his lofty pretensions and his lowly acts'. Hoggart's description fits Godwin Peak well, except for the minor divergence that Peak's unpretentious mother does have country relations in at least 'decent circumstances' (I, ii). Of a slightly higher status than a lower-class scholarship boy, Peak can more readily identify with the values of the landed rich: 'men and women who represented the best in English society' (II, iii).

Charles Swann's essay, 'Sincerity and Authenticity: the Problem of Identity in *Born in Exile*', *Literature and History*, 10:2; (Autumn 1984), pp. 165–86, took its title from a book by Lionel Trilling, but argued that *Born in Exile* shared perceptions with Nietzsche, especially in its questioning of the concept of identity and its challenge to traditional moral discourse. The extracts are from pp. 169 and 175–6.

It is my contention that *Born in Exile* may be better understood in the light of the clash, the gap, the conflict implied by Trilling's title – and that Gissing's novel should be seen as a work torn between the older values defined or evoked by such terms as 'sincerity' and the newer definitions of the self which give rise to the concept of 'authenticity'. Gissing, in his attempts to locate and define Peak's character (if that is the right word), lacks a word or words to evaluate his creation, and thus is forced to employ an inadequate moral vocabulary even though it is clear that those categories do not allow an adequate judgment of Godwin Peak to be made. He runs through the repertory of terms culturally available for describing and judging his fictive creation, and, in doing so, 'shows' their inadequacy, leaving a gap that the narrative must fill. The narrative resists or subverts the moral categories it contains: it is the lack, the historical and cultural absence of a word which *generates* the narrative, in the novelist's attempt to capture a concept under the net of narrative . . .

Particular attention must be paid to how, why, and *when* Peak makes his move into impersonation. The actual move when Peak articulates his 'decision' to be a clergyman is in private conversation with his old friend from college days, Buckland Warricombe. But that follows some time after the crucial psychological (unconscious?) moment of commitment. That comes at lunch with the Warricombes, when, though he overcomes his 'ignoble self-consciousness', he is still 'introspective', but hopes 'by the force of his personality' to 'make good his claim to be deemed a gentleman'. He is asked what he thought of a sermon. He suffers 'a confused doubtfulness', but his nervousness 'did not prevent him replying with a natural air of deliberation'. He claims to have been struck by a passage about the barren fig-tree:

The words might have expressed a truth, but in that case a tone of sarcasm must have winged them. As it was, they involved either hypocrisy or ungenerous irony at the expense of his questioner. Buckland could not but understand them in the latter sense: his face darkened. At that moment, Peak met his eye, and encountered its steady, searching gaze with a perfectly calm smile. Half-a-dozen pulsings of his heart – violent, painful, and the fatal hour of his life had struck.

That linking of hypocrisy and irony is acute: both involve the abandonment of an open declaration of one's beliefs. Irony can be defined as saying one thing and believing another, and as such it exists in an uneasy cousinship with hypocrisy. This is, however, Buckland's formulation of alternatives which come from his old knowledge of the unbeliever Peak, who responds as much to Buckland's 'look' as to the question. The 'truth' may be more complex. Peak's 'effort of exegesis' does not of itself, after all, involve any overt statement about Peak's beliefs, though it may allow certain inferences.

What did Peak intend (if that word is allowable)?

Peak's reply was one of those remarkable efforts of mind – one might say of *character* – which are sometimes called forth, without *premeditation*, almost without *consciousness*, by a profound *moral* crisis ... Now, under the marvelling regard of his *conscious self*, he poured forth an admirable rendering of the Canon's views, fuller than the original (my emphases).

My emphases are tiresome, but they are a convenient way of indicating something of the complexity of the situation. This reply is more-or-less spontaneous – it certainly cannot be said to be willed. It follows after and contrasts with a scene in which Godwin has been notably self-conscious and introspective. After his mini-sermon, 'No longer did he calculate his phrases.

A spontaneous aptness marked his dialogue'. Yet if his 'conscious self' watched, just how is the reader to identify who it was that retold the episode of the barren fig-tree? It is indeed 'the oddest of intellectual processes', in its gratuitousness, in its discontinuity.

Gissing cannot name what happens in Peak's divided self. He can only narrate the movements of Peak's 'mind' – when even the will has become problematic.

In *George Gissing: the Cultural Challenge* (1989) John Sloan noted that the novel refuses to place its hero's paradoxical ambitions in a limiting perspective of irony. The extracts are from pp. 106–7 and 108–9.

Peak's perspective remains unequivocally modern. Driven by the social aspirations and financial insecurities of his class to 'fight the world with his brains', educated among the sons of 'the robust employers of labour' who 'were for the most part avowed Radicals, in theory scornful of privilege', Peak's outlook on life is one of scientific rationalism and the survival of the fittest. The novel registers in effect a fundamental disjunction in English life; for while the social system remains actively aristocratic, in an ideological sense at least, the prevailing conditions of existence are directed by economic individualism which emphasises 'careerism' as a means of validating worth. It is this opposition which gives birth to the novel's complex and interrelated levels of discourse; one involves Peak's intellectual challenge to moral and meta-physical presuppositions; the other, the imperatives of social mobility as a means of personal validation. It also produces the central paradox or contradiction inherent in Peak's attempt to infiltrate the sanctity of the upper middle-class household by exploiting Warricombe's belated hope of reconciling rational-ism and religion . . .

Peak's violation of the Warricombe house is accompanied by feelings of deference as well as of scorn, exhibiting all the 'emotional ambivalence' which Freud was to associate with the active social stricture of 'taboo', and in particular with that conflict between solicitude and hostility characteristic of people's attitude to rulers and 'privileged persons':

alongside of the veneration, and indeed idealisation, felt towards them, there is in the unconscious an opposing current of intense hostility . . . in fact . . . we are faced with a situation of emotional ambivalence.

It is clear in this connection that we are not meant to see Peak simply as someone who has sacrificed his moral and intellectual integrity for the sake of social advancement. Peak is caught in a double-bind. He is committed not only to the demands of rationalism and self-validation, with their necessary refusal of the sacred institutions of rank and privilege, but also to a still-active veneration for those very institutions.

John Carey's polemical study *The Intellectuals and the Masses* (1992) argued that modernist writing is dominated by contemptuous attitudes to 'mass' culture. He saw Gissing as a precursor of these attitudes and Godwin Peak as, partly, an embodiment of Gissing. The extract is from p. 113.

Godwin Peak in *Born in Exile* is another deluded superman. He believes himself 'an aristocrat of nature's own making – one of the few highly favoured beings who, in despite of circumstance, are pinnacled above mankind'. The uneducated revolt him: 'I hate them worse than the filthiest vermin. They ought to be swept off the face of the earth.' But Godwin is a pathetic case. His whole life is a fraud. A working-class scholarship boy, he worms his way into the confidence of a rich family, hoping to marry their daughter. Union with a 'perfectly refined' woman of high birth has always been his dream. There is a revealing scene when he stands in a crowd in Hyde Park, watching two aristocratic women drive by in their carriage. He feels, in himself, their fineness and their scorn for the herd.

They were his equals, those ladies; merely his equals. With such as they he should by right of nature associate . . . In his rebellion, he could not hate them. He hated the malodorous rabble who stared insolently at them and who envied their immeasurable remoteness.

These feelings – uncannily prefiguring D.H. Lawrence's attitude towards the high-born – were Gissing's as well as Peak's. 'Peak is myself – one phase of myself,' he admitted. The qualification is significant. It is as if Gissing stands both inside and outside Peak, feeding into him his own opinions, but exposing him to disgrace and failure. For the rich family find out about Godwin's deceit, and he dies shamed. His fate can perhaps be read as masochistic self-criticism on Gissing's part. But much of what Godwin believes in, Gissing himself never renounced or outgrew. Godwin's fulminations against the debasement of art and literature by popular taste, and against the kind of people whose spiritual guide is the Sunday newspaper – 'only a consuming fire could purify the places where they dwell' – are eminently Gissingite. So is Godwin's weakness for peasants and rural artisans – the only species of uneducated people he can tolerate. In creating the character of Godwin, Gissing performed some unsparing self-analysis, and the result is a base, deluded character. Yet Godwin never quite forfeits our sympathy, and Gissing seemingly felt ambivalent too.

SUGGESTIONS FOR FURTHER READING

(Extracts from items marked with an asterisk are included in the section Gissing and his Critics.)

On Gissing's life the best book is still Jacob Korg, *George Gissing: A Critical Biography* (1963). A primary, but not wholly reliable source is Morley Roberts, *The Private Life of Henry Maitland* (1912).

For the social and literary historical context of late nineteenth-century British fiction, see Peter Keating, *The Haunted Study: A Social History of the English Novel 1875–1914* (1989).

For an accessible introduction to evolutionary thought and its effect on the emotional life of the nineteenth century, see D.F. Bratchell, *The Impact of Darwinism* (1986). For a more detailed account, consult James R. Moore, *The Post-Darwinian Controversies* (1979). An overview of the topic is offered in John Hedley Brooke, *Science and Religion: Some Historical Perspectives* (1991).

The following critical studies of Gissing contain sections on *Born in Exile*:

   Gillian Tindall, *The Born Exile: George Gissing* (1974).

*Adrian Poole, *Gissing in Context* (1975).

*John Goode, *George Gissing: Ideology and Fiction* (1978).

*Robert L. Selig, *George Gissing* (1983).

   David Grylls, *The Paradox of Gissing* (1986).

*John Sloan, *George Gissing: the Cultural Challenge* (1989).

   The following articles or essays are also useful:

*Jacob Korg, 'The Spiritual Theme of *Born in Exile*', in *Collected Articles on George Gissing*, ed. Pierre Coustillas (1968).

*Pierre Coustillas, 'Introduction', *Born in Exile* (Harvester edition, 1978).

*Charles Swann, 'Sincerity and Authenticity: the Problem of Identity in *Born in Exile*', *Literature and History*, 10:2 (Autumn 1984), pp. 165–86.

CLASSIC FICTION
IN EVERYMAN

A SELECTION

Frankenstein

MARY SHELLEY
A masterpiece of Gothic terror in its
original 1818 version **£3.99**

Dracula

BRAM STOKER
One of the best known horror stories
in the world **£3.99**

The Diary of A Nobody

GEORGE AND WEEDON
GROSSMITH
A hilarious account of suburban life
in Edwardian London **£4.99**

Some Experiences
and Further Experiences
of an Irish R. M.

SOMERVILLE AND ROSS
Gems of comic exuberance and
improvisation **£4.50**

Three Men in a Boat

JEROME K. JEROME
English humour at its best **£2.99**

Twenty Thousand Leagues
under the Sea

JULES VERNE
Scientific fact combines with
fantasy in this prophetic tale of
underwater adventure **£4.99**

The Best of Father Brown

G. K. CHESTERTON
An irresistible selection of crime
stories – unique to Everyman **£3.99**

The Collected Raffles

E. W. HORNUNG
Dashing exploits from the most glam-
orous figure in crime fiction **£4.99**

£2.99

£5.99

£5.99

AVAILABILITY

All books are available from your local bookshop or direct from
**Littlehampton Book Services Cash Sales, 14 Eldon Way, LinesideEstate,
Littlehampton, West Sussex BN17 7HE.** PRICES ARE SUBJECT TO CHANGE.

To order any of the books, please enclose a cheque (in £ sterling) made payable to
Littlehampton Book Services, or phone your order through with credit card details (Access,
Visa or Mastercard) on 0903 721596 (24 hour answering service) stating card number and
expiry date. Please add £1.25 for package and postage to the total value of your order.

CLASSIC NOVELS IN EVERYMAN

A SELECTION

The Way of All Flesh
SAMUEL BUTLER
A savagely funny odyssey from joyless duty to unbridled liberalism **£4.99**

Born in Exile
GEORGE GISSING
A rationalist's progress towards love and compromise in class-ridden Victorian England **£4.99**

David Copperfield
CHARLES DICKENS
One of Dickens' best-loved novels, brimming with humour **£3.99**

The Last Chronicle of Barset
ANTHONY TROLLOPE
Trollope's magnificent conclusion to his Barsetshire novels **£4.99**

He Knew He Was Right
ANTHONY TROLLOPE
Sexual jealousy, money and women's rights within marriage – a novel ahead of its time **£6.99**

Tess of the D'Urbervilles
THOMAS HARDY
The powerful, poetic classic of wronged innocence **£3.99**

Wuthering Heights and Poems
EMILY BRONTE
A powerful work of genius – one of the great masterpieces of literature **£3.50**

Tom Jones
HENRY FIELDING
The wayward adventures of one of literatures most likable heroes **£5.99**

The Master of Ballantrae and Weir of Hermiston
R. L. STEVENSON
Together in one volume, two great novels of high adventure and family conflict **£4.99**

£3.99

£2.99

£3.99
